SCOTLAND TO THE MAX

GRACE BURROWES

D1598171

SCOTLAND TO THE MAX

By Grace Burrowes

Book Three in the
Trouble Wears Tartan series

To those who have a special needs loved one

Scotland to the Max is Published by Grace Burrowes Publishing

21 Summit Avenue Hagerstown, MD 21740

graceburrowes.com

Print ISBN: 978-1941419656

Ebook ISBN: 978-19414

❀ Created with Vellum

CHAPTER ONE

The luggage carousel went around twenty times before Max Maitland permitted himself to swear. "The damned things aren't here."

"Beg pardon, sir?"

Max almost couldn't understand the guy, so thick was his burr,
but the Edinburgh Airport Security uniform spoke clearly enough, as
did the way he'd hovered at Max's elbow for the last five rotations of
the baggage conveyor.

"My luggage has apparently not come up from London with me,"
Max said.

"Did ye cam tru Heat-row, then?"

Fatigue, the mother of all headaches, and towering frustration
made translating difficult. "I beg your pardon?"

"This way," the man said. "We'll fill out a wee lost-bag ticket and
have ye on yerr way in no time a-t'all."

Max's suitcases were far from wee, because he was all but moving
to Scotland, or that was the plan. He dealt with waiting in line—his
favorite thing to do—to get the form to fill out.

He dealt with explaining the obvious to an uninterested public
servant—his very most favorite thing to do.

And to add a splash of kirschwasser to his I Hate To Travel sundae, the person assigned to meet him had apparently bailed.

"Yer heid painin' ye, laddie?" the lady at the coffee counter asked. She looked to be about eighty years old, maybe five foot one in her orthotic shoes, and Max would not have tangled with her on a bet.

Your head paining you, laddie?

"Something awful. I don't enjoy flying, and thunderstorms at Dulles meant a three-hour delay before we took off."

"Isn't that always the way? Now you listen to me. Go through those doors and make a wee stop at the apothecary. We have much better over-the-counter remedies than you do in the States. You tell the man Annie MacDuie sent you, and you need something for your head. Go on now, and the luggage folks will send your bags along as soon as may be."

Clucking and fussing was a universal dialect, particularly when done by blue-haired ladies.

"Thank you, Annie. I appreciate it." Not everyone would have been as kind to a stranger, but then, Scotland was reputed to be one big tourist trap, a postcard outside every window, a quaint whisky distillery in every glen.

Every wee glen.

Whatever a glen was. Max was counting on Scotland's tourist appeal, and on its recession-resistant economy. His faith in its over-the-counter pain meds was another matter. He picked up his backpack and wandered off in the assigned direction, letting the hum and bustle of foot traffic pass around him.

Though the hour was nearly noon in Scotland, the sun had barely risen in Maryland, and Max felt every second of the circadian dislocation. He couldn't call Maura at this hour, he didn't feel like breakfast, and how in the hell did a guy get a hotel room at eleven in the morning?

"Mr. Maitland?"

He got out his cell phone, that's how.

"Mr. Maxwell Maitland?"

The voice was soft, female, and accented. Max beheld a petite blonde whose eyes were the same blue as... the little flowers that grew next to sidewalks. Began with a p.

"I'm Maitland."

"Jeannie Cromarty." She stuck out her hand. "Sorry I'm late. Uncle Donald was supposed to be here, but the flight delay meant some shuffling about on our end. Did your bags not arrive?"

Her voice had a lilt to go with the burr, a musicality not entirely a product of the accent. To a man deprived of sleep and dislocated by five long time zones, that voice was soothing.

Max had to shift his knapsack to shake hands. "My suitcases are supposed to be catching up to me. I wasn't sure where I'd be staying tonight, so all the lost-luggage people have is my cell."

"They'll find you," Jeannie said. "I've never known them to fail, though sometimes they take a day or two. How was your flight?"

He made chitchat the best he could, which was not very well. Jeannie had a graciousness about her, though, an ease that had Max relaxing despite exhaustion and travel nerves. She spoke more slowly than Max was used to. Didn't fire off sentences like a lawyer being paid by the syllable.

"Is that the drugstore?" he asked as they passed one of the airport shops.

"The pharmacy, we call it. Did you need something?"

Max needed about three solid days of sleep—after he called Maura—and a protein shake. "Something for a headache. One of the ladies at the coffee shop said you have good over-the-counter meds here—better than in the States."

"That, we do. I'll show you."

Jeannie explained the situation to the guy at the register, and Max soon had a bottle of water, a banana, and some pills. He waited until he was sitting on the wrong side of Jeannie's compact car to eat the banana and take the pills.

"Have you been to Scotland before?" Jeannie asked as she maneuvered the vehicle through the airport traffic.

"Never, but I'm looking forward to renovating Brodie Castle, and if that means spending a year in Scotland, then I'll spend a year in Scotland." Hopefully, no more than that, and Max would make many, many trips home during that year. "Have you ever been to the States?"

"Oh, aye. Back in college. Went for some sunshine. Winters here can be so very dark."

Max had figured the shorter hours of daylight into the project schedule, though floodlights could turn night into day, for a price.

"Are we driving up to Aberdeen today?"

The whole business of driving on the wrong side of the road, sitting on the wrong side of the car, and road signs not being the same was disorienting. Jeannie handled the car with easy confidence, but part of Max wanted to close his eyes—and wake up in western Maryland.

"That was the plan, but that plan assumed you and your luggage would arrive together. How about if you stay in our holiday cottage in Perthshire tonight, and we'll travel on to the castle tomorrow?"

Max had purposely arrived on a Friday morning, so he'd have a weekend to shake the jet lag.

Hanging out in a quiet cottage would be a fine way to go about that.

"Sounds like a plan. Tell me about Brodie Castle." If she was a Cromarty, then she was a cousin of some sort to the Scottish earl— Elias Brodie—who owned the castle. His lordship was at present kicking his handsome heels on one of the finest patches of farmland Maryland had to offer and enjoying wedded bliss with one of Maryland's finest farmers.

Lucky bastard.

"The castle is lovely," Jeannie said. "We've had many a wedding there. It's been in the family for at least a thousand years, though of course, the earliest structure was a mere round tower. Elias was mostly raised in the baron's lodge, which sits at the foot of the castle hill, and any family member who's at loose ends has been welcome to bide with him there. You can rattle around that old place for a week and not find the front door. Uncle Donald calls it the Plaid Purgatory, though he was born there."

She prattled on, about Queen Victoria, the local council, and the Pipe Band, while Max struggled to keep his eyes open. The last thing he saw before falling asleep was a pair of great silver horse heads rearing up from the river immediately beside the highway.

Elias Brodie had warned him that Scotland would make him daft but happy. Apparently, the daft part came first.

COUSIN ELIAS'S scheme became clear the instant Jeannie laid eyes on Max Maitland.

The American was gorgeous, and not in a pretty, manscaped, gym-rat way. Maitland was tall, broad-shouldered, and trim, a perfect wedge of manhood topped with dark hair, sky-blue eyes, and a voice that was made for issuing commands to underlings and whispering naughty suggestions in bed.

He'd reached that stage of maturity where his looks wouldn't change much for decades. His features were weathered around the edges—crow's feet at the corners of his eyes, a complexion that had spent whole summers in the sun. The slight wear only made him more attractive, a man in whom all traces of the boy had been swallowed up by hard work and ambition.

Perhaps Uncle Donald had taken a notion to find Jeannie her rebound romp, in which case, Jeannie would be disowning her uncle—again. She'd purposely stepped away from the castle project, for any numbers of reasons. Max Maitland's fine broad shoulders would be reason number 376.

Jeannie had driven past the Falkirk horses before she realized Mr. Maitland had fallen asleep. He hadn't put the seat back, hadn't snored, hadn't done anything other than go silent and close his eyes. She had recently made the acquaintance of bone-deep, relentless exhaustion herself, so she let him rest.

Little more than an hour after leaving the airport, she navigated the fern-bordered driveway to the cottage and shut off the car's engine.

"Mr. Maitland?"

Nothing.

Jeannie got out of the car, came around, and opened the door on his side. She shook his shoulder, which was like trying to shake a four-hundred-year-old oak.

"Mr. Maitland, we've arrived at the cottage."

His eyes opened, just that. "Apologies for napping. Where exactly is this cottage?"

Jeannie stepped away so he could unfold himself from her car. "The property sits on the banks of the River Tay in rural Perthshire. We've a lot of big trees, great fishing, and gorgeous views of the Highland Line. Also proper beds to sleep in. Come, I'll show you."

He fetched his knapsack from the back of the car and followed Jeannie into the cottage. The family art history professor—Liam Cromarty—had designed the place as a sort of earthbound tree house. The windows were large and many, the footprint simple. Downstairs consisted of an open area that was half kitchen, half living room, and a back room mostly used as a craft and pottery studio with a half bath under the stairs. Upstairs was a master bedroom, two full baths, and a bedroom-cum-office. Both bedrooms had skylights, balconies, and views of the river.

Mr. Maitland opened and closed the front door twice and fiddled with the latch mechanism. Jeannie's Welcome to Scotland speech hadn't riveted his attention, but a doorknob did.

Engineers. Jeannie had fallen in love with one and realized her mistake too late to prevent substantial damage. The sooner she could turn Mr. Maitland over to Uncle Donald, Cousin Liam, or the river fairies, the better.

"The cottage is my little project to manage." Also Jeannie's only reliable source of income at present. "We had a cancellation this weekend, else I'd be putting you up in a hotel."

"It's..." He set his backpack down and peered around. His gaze traveled over the paneled ceiling, picture windows, hardwood floor, fieldstone fireplace, and shiny kitchen appliances. "Solid. Quality first, the only way to design."

Not pretty, not inviting, not cozy or cheerful. *Solid.* Jeannie had rushed to make time to put the bouquets of variegated tulips about the place—one on the coffee table, a bud vase in each bathroom, another bouquet in the master bedroom—and Mr. Maitland pronounced the cottage *solid.*

"The castle is very solid," she said. "You'll have a grand time renovating it. May I fix you some lunch?"

He left off admiring the fireplace, his gaze suggesting the hint of irony she'd tossed at him had hit its target. "You don't need to wait on me, Jeannie."

Harry would have been telling her exactly what he wanted on his sandwich and how to make it—mustard on one piece of bread, mayonnaise on the other.

"I'm hungry. Making two sandwiches instead of one is no bother. Have a look upstairs, and I'll see to lunch."

"I have some protein bars."

"Which will doubtless keep until Christmas and taste just as awful when you do choke them down. Upstairs, Mr. Maitland. Grab a shower if you like. The towels are laid out."

He picked up his knapsack. "Are all Scottish women so bossy?"

"We have to be. We share the country with Scottish men and their offspring."

Jeannie opened the fridge, expecting she'd had the last word—for now—but Mr. Maitland plucked a pink and white tulip from the bowl on the table.

"Thank you, Jeannie Cromarty. I'm hungry, tired, and far from home, and your hospitality is much appreciated." He disappeared down the hall, knapsack over his shoulder, tulip in hand, but first he fired off a slight, weary smile.

That smile hinted of sweetness, humor, and even—as it reached his eyes—shyness. Jeannie stared after his retreating figure—jeans covering long legs, coattails covering what was doubtless a muscular backside.

He turned and pointed with the tulip. "You will please not allow me to nod off again. I'll never get sorted out by Monday if I take another nap."

"Away with you," Jeannie said, waving the bread knife. "I've sandwiches to make, and I do not take well to men telling me what to do, Mr. Maitland."

The smile came again in a faint echo. "Call me... You can call me Max, if that suits." Then he disappeared up the steps.

Under her breath, Jeannie called him several different things, but not Max.

THE COTTAGE HINTED of fairy tales and honeymoons, which Max appreciated in a professional sense, though he had no personal use for either. The forest beyond the picture windows was dotted with spectacular conifers, ancient hardwoods, and all manner of soft, leafy undergrowth.

The lot would be a nightmare to clear. The tree-save plan alone would go on forever, though the views from the balconies and porches were just a few gnomes short of postcard-perfect. Somebody had done a good job of designing a dwelling that suited the land and finding land that suited the purpose of the dwelling.

Max glanced at his phone, but it was still too early to call Maura. She wasn't merely a creature of habit, she was its devoted acolyte.

He used the bathroom to freshen up—he'd shower later—and

inspected the choice of bedrooms. Like the rest of the cottage, the master bedroom was simply furnished—king-size bed, dresser, two reading chairs—and the outdoors was invited in by virtue of big windows, a balcony, and a skylight.

He took the smaller bedroom because it boasted that loveliest of all interior design features, an ergonomic workstation with a flat-screen monitor, complete with a modem/router flashing its blue light in welcome to the rhythm of Max's heartbeat. He'd set down his knapsack, taken the oh-so-comfy office chair, and put his fingers on the curved, illuminated keyboard when Jeannie called up from downstairs.

"Lunch is ready!"

Damn. "On my way."

He brushed his hand over the top of the sleek monitor—*I'll be back, sweetheart*—and prepared to make small talk over sandwiches.

Jeannie had made four sandwiches, not two, and opened a bag of chips. The table was set with coordinated place mats, dishes, and mugs all in the same cheerful pink, purple, white, and yellow colors as the tulips. A bowl of apples, clementines, and bananas sat beside a plate of brownies, and abruptly, Max felt famished.

Also homesick, which made no sense. "You didn't have to go to all this trouble."

Jeannie set a carton of half-skim milk on the table and regarded him with a quizzical smile. "You are my guest, Mr. Maitland, and you are in Scotland to develop one of the finest hospitality venues in the Highlands, if your press release is to be believed. Why wouldn't I show you the same welcome I show every visitor at this cottage?"

Max could look at a set of plans and see the finished site. He could scan a spreadsheet and spot the error without having to consciously do the math. When it came to people... He'd erred with Jeannie, not badly, but the same way somebody who wasn't a native speaker would occasionally square-peg an idiom into a conversation.

"If I eat lunch, I'm usually sitting at my desk, swilling coffee and gnawing—"

"A protein bar," Jeannie said, taking a seat. "Tell me about your plans for the castle."

What Max had developed for Brodie Castle was more than a plan. He had a dream, fueled by necessity and determination.

"Brodie Castle will take advantage of the follow-on potential generated by the Scottish tourist industry," Max said, laying his napkin across his lap. "People will see Scotland when they're vacationing and go back to the office ready to attend any conference, any industry workshop, any off-site gathering held here. I'll give them the venue that combines professional association and recreation, with first-rate conference facilities and endless interesting activities, all in a genuine Scottish castle."

Jeannie pushed the plate of sandwiches at him. "If you announce that plan to Uncle Donald, he'll sabotage the whole project, and don't think he can't do it."

Max bit into a sandwich made on actual saw-off-one-slice-at-a-time bread. The meat was lightly smoked and also appeared to have been carved rather than processed beyond all recognition.

"Uncle Donald is my mandatory family board member?"

"I declined the post myself. Uncle Donald is a ferocious advocate for family history," Jeannie said, picking up her sandwich. "As stubborn as they come, knows all the castle history, though he's a Cromarty rather than a Brodie, and he's been keeping an eye on the project since the late earl signed the first contracts. He'll have some questions for you and a few suggestions, or he'll declare the whole business a crashing bore and you won't hear from him until the fish stop biting."

The emphasis she put on the word *suggestions* was a bit too cheerful. "Is this the condemned man's last meal, Jeannie?"

"Of course not. We've supper and breakfast to get through." She took a bite—not a nibble—of her sandwich.

Elias Brodie had warned Max that Scottish humor was different. "Every development project meets with resistance because change can be scary. That goes with the territory."

"Change involves destruction," Jeannie replied. "When change destroys a place I've known and loved since infancy, Mr. Maitland, I'm not afraid, I'm furious. Go carefully or go home—a friendly warning."

He'd finished his first sandwich. She offered him the plate that held seconds.

"Fruit for me," he said, choosing a clementine. "Though the sandwich was very good."

The brownies sat not a foot from Max's elbow, looking gooey and delicious. He knew better than to indulge, because a hit of sugar on top of jet lag was just plain stupid. Then too, taste seldom matched appearance with pretty desserts.

"I'll show you the paths before I leave," Jeannie said, "and give you the number for my mobile." She used a long "i" for mobile.

"I'll need directions to this place, if the luggage guy is ever to find me."

"Good point. I can leave those too, though it's simple enough. Two miles past the village shinty pitch, you look for the fairy mound in the cow pasture on your left. Take the second right beyond that and turn off at the first lane. The sign is in Gaelic and nailed to the redwood stump."

Her description was as casual as it was incomprehensible. "I deal well with maps," Max said. "Diagrams, drawings, charts."

"Right." Jeannie picked up a small square of brownie. "Engineers love their schematics."

True, but somehow not a compliment.

She gave the brownie her full attention. When she bit off a portion, she closed her eyes and chewed slowly, a woman in transports. For some reason, this reminded Max that once upon a long time ago, he'd enjoyed sketching. If the project went well, maybe he'd find time to send Maura some landscapes.

Or he could attempt to sketch a few portraits. Jeannie Cromarty enjoying a brownie would make an interesting study. For the time it took to consume one brownie, she was a sybarite in jeans, flannel shirt, and battered running shoes. She gave off an air of tidiness, otherwise. A competence that included graciousness warmed just enough to count as genuine rather than professional. Max liked competent women if they pulled their share of the workload and didn't play games.

He was fairly certain Jeannie did not like him, or didn't like the notion of developing the castle, which amounted to the same thing. She was pretty—Viking-blue eyes, golden hair that brushed her shoulders, and a light, friendly voice.

Not a hint of flirtation, though, for all she was romancing that damned brownie.

"What will you do with yourself this afternoon?" she asked.

"Dump email and voice mail, do some more research on the financial ecosystem surrounding the castle, review the status reports that are supposed to come in every Friday at close of business."

In Maryland, that had been easier, because close of business in Scotland was five hours ahead of close of business on the East Coast. Then Max had had plenty of time to take Maura out for dinner and, for a short time, put aside the whole week's frustrations and challenges.

Maura would miss him—she had assured him of this repeatedly, which made calling her soon imperative.

"You've likely had one hour's sleep in the past twenty-four," Jeanie said. "Can't that email nonsense wait?"

That nonsense was Max's livelihood. "If I nap again, I won't acclimate as quickly."

"Right." Jeannie patted his hand. "You have a year at least to acclimate, but why put off until Monday what you can accomplish by overtaxing yourself today?"

She rose and took her plate to the sink. Her comment hadn't been judgmental so much as... a lament. For him, for all the fools who failed to have a life beyond the next project deadline. If the castle renovation went well, Max might acquire the luxury of sharing her perspective.

Perhaps she'd also been lamenting her own circumstances? This cottage, modest though it was, occupied a corner of the hospitality industry in a country that thrived on tourism. For the high season at least, Jeannie was likely kept busy.

"A hike by the river sounds like a good idea," Max said. "I need to move, and the natural light will help get my circadian rhythm synced to local time."

Jeannie ran water over her plate while Max ate his clementine and longed for a brownie that tasted as good as it looked.

"We can hike, or we can go for a daunder," Jeannie said, "because it's a beautiful day to stroll by a lovely river, and all those emails, voice mails, and reports will be there when the sun has set."

Max brought his plate to the sink. "Along with a hundred new ones."

"If a hundred people feel entitled to intrude on your peace in the space of an afternoon, Mr. Maitland, you need an assistant."

She was... right.

She also smelled good up close, woodsy with a hint of mint. A scent to pipe into a designer hotel's conservatory. Max passed her his plate and used his phone to make that note.

They tidied up in companionable silence, the brownies going into the bread box. Jeannie washed the dishes by hand rather than using the dishwasher, and Max got the job of shaking the place mats out on the deck.

"So the birds can enjoy the crumbs," Jeannie said, tearing off a pinch of bread and crumbling it onto the place mat Max held.

Maybe wasting bread on birds was a Scottish good-luck custom. Max did scroll through his email and voice mail while on the back terrace and found nothing marked urgent. He'd cleared the decks in every possible regard to prepare for traveling, but to manage the development of a property was to live in a minefield, especially on Fridays.

Jeannie came out onto the terrace and folded the place mats Max had draped over the rail. "Letting the folks back home know you're safe and sound?"

"Making sure I have reception."

"Let's make sure you have a little fresh air." She marched off down the steps and into the lovely, leafy forest.

Max jammed his phone into his pocket and followed her.

CHAPTER TWO

Scotland had been awarded the honor of Most Beautiful Country in the World, and Max Maitland was too busy checking his email to notice. Jeannie didn't begrudge him a nap on the way from the airport, but to stand amid the lush greenery of Perthshire without even looking up...

She would not attribute such blasphemy to all Americans—some were nature hounds—but perhaps it was a failing of many engineers. Alas for Mr. Maitland, Jeannie was determined to steal some time out of doors, even if she had to drag him kicking and scrolling to the riverbank.

"Nobody knows how old these trails are," she said. "They probably date back thousands of years, as long as the river has run in its present course."

The Tayside forest was lovely in all seasons, but Jeannie hadn't been on this path since last autumn. The summer version of the woods was busy with birds, squirrels, breezes, and the sound of the river. The scent was as beautiful as the greenery—verdant, fresh, earthy.

"That's Liam's property," she said, gesturing to a rooftop peeking from the trees to the right. "Designed and built it himself. You and he could probably share a wee dram while sketching ideas on napkins and comparing the calculator apps on your phones."

Mr. Maitland kept up easily. "Does your family include an engineer?"

Not anymore. "I've run across a few. Watch your step. We had a good rain on Wednesday. The ground can be boggy."

"Are we in a hurry, Ms. Cromarty?"

Jeannie slowed her pace. "I haven't come this way in too long, and I miss it desperately. The cottage is usually booked straight through the high season, and I never have time to enjoy the property lately."

Never had time to enjoy much of anything, other than an hour or so of reading before bed, until she fell asleep with the book still in her hands. Everybody said life after a divorce grew easier with time, but everybody had also said that Jeannie and Harry had been perfect for each other.

The quiet of the forest gradually overtook the breathless, never-on-time anxiety that had dogged Jeannie for months. Mr. Maitland did her the courtesy of remaining silent, meaning the whisper of the river going by and the occasional birdcall could sink into her weary soul and soothe the tumult.

The past year had been hard. The next year loomed as another bleak slog. Finances were an issue, exhaustion was an issue, as was the sheer boredom that came with—

Mr. Maitland halted. "Osprey."

Jeannie shaded her eyes, but couldn't make out any large raptors in the trees ahead. Mature ospreys were white across the breast and head and banded brown elsewhere. Among the shoreline trees, they were nearly impossible to detect when still.

"Where?"

Mr. Maitland turned her gently by the shoulders. "The notch of that big oak, about thirty feet up." He pointed over Jeannie's shoulder, standing close behind her. "Mama's serving lunch."

What mamas did best.

"They stopped breeding in Scotland for more than a hundred years," Jeannie said, getting out her phone. "But they came back, and the population is gradually increasing."

She adjusted the zoom and snapped a picture. Not that the nest would be easy to spot even in a photograph. Still, an osprey family was a hopeful image, and she needed those. She put the phone away and stood watching the mundane miracle of lunchtime at the Osprey household. Mr. Maitland remained motionless at her back, and that was...

Nice, in an odd way. Jeannie wasn't keen on his plans for the castle, she wasn't keen on men generally, and she wasn't keen on people who lived glued to their jobs. That Mr. Maitland would notice the birds, point them out to Jeannie, and *appreciate* them let her like him a little, nonetheless.

No harm in a little liking.

"Shall we go back?" Jeannie asked. "I could spend all afternoon tramping these trails, but I'm sure your email is calling you."

And Jeannie was overdue to check in with Millicent.

"If you'd like to hike farther, I can find my way back on my own."

She was tempted, tempted to simply sit and watch the river go by, something she hadn't done in far too long.

"I've places to go, people to see," she said, turning. "My time is not my—"

Never hike wearing trainers. Jeannie formed that thought as one foot slipped, her arms flailed, and she nearly went down amid the bracken.

Mr. Maitland caught her and drew her back against his chest. "Careful. The ground can be a bit boggy, I'm told."

He was strong and utterly steady—*solid*, to use his word. For an instant, Jeannie nearly let herself lean against him, let herself feel again the security of a male embrace. By virtue of shoving and cursing, she got herself righted.

"My apologies. Shall we be on our way?"

She gestured up the path, and though she was blushing, and Mr.

Maitland was smiling, he was gallant enough not to remark on her mortification.

So much for daydreaming. They returned to the cottage without further incident—Jeannie was very careful of her footing. She passed him the set of keys she kept for guests and emailed him the link to the directions on the cottage website.

"I'll be along tomorrow morning about eight," she said. "That will get you up to the castle well before noon. We can stop along the way for provisions, though Aldi's delivers to the Baron's Hall."

"I have an international driver's license," Mr. Maitland said, accompanying Jeannie to the driveway. "Give me your phone."

Was he daft or simply rude? "Why should I give you my phone?"

"So I can call myself, and then we'll have each other's numbers."

Jeannie passed over her phone.

"What's the plan if my luggage hasn't caught up with me by tomorrow?"

"Explain to the nice people how to get to the castle. I'll see you tomorrow, Mr. Maitland. Help yourself to anything in the kitchen and call me if you need anything."

Jeannie's phone chimed to the opening bars of Parcel o' Rogues. That would be Millicent, with a reminder that Jeannie had half an hour of liberty left.

"You need something," Mr. Maitland said, frowning at Jeannie's car.

"I beg your pardon? The black shows the dirt, I know, but— shite." Shite, hell, and bloody damnation. This was the price of stealing forty-five minutes to walk by the river, the price for paying more attention to tulips than tires. Again.

Why couldn't one day—just one, single day—go right anymore?

"Looks like a puncture," Mr. Maitland said, hunkering at the driver's side front tire. "Slow leak. Probably picked up a nail days ago and haven't noticed the loss of pressure. I can have the spare on in ten minutes."

"No," Jeannie said around the lump in her throat. "No, you can't, because the bloody spare needs a bloody patch, and I haven't had the bloody money to fix it."

CHANGING a tire was one of the last, best bastions of male competence in a changing world, and Max relished the opportunity to solve a problem on his first day in Scotland. Tires were tires, and he had changed dozens.

He wouldn't be changing this one.

"Can you have it towed?"

"Not soon enough." Jeannie looked at the car as if a favorite pet had just flatlined. Despair, betrayal, and more upset than a bad tire deserved.

"The afternoon's only half gone. Does Scotland close down at two p.m. on Fridays?"

She gazed at the surrounding trees with a far different expression than she'd turned on the ospreys. The woods were clearly no longer lovely, dark, and deep.

"The man who drives the tow truck, Abner MacShane, is the fiddler in the ceilidh band. They play every Friday night at the community center, so they rehearse on Friday afternoons at the pub. I won't get Abner behind the wheel until noon tomorrow."

Max needed to be at the castle by noon tomorrow. "No car rental in the village?"

"The nearest car rental is in Perth."

"What about the architect over at Falling Waters—Lester?"

"Liam." Jeannie brightened and got out her phone, then her expression dimmed. "Not home. He and his wife are forever going off to take in art shows."

"Architects are different."

Jeannie smiled at him, not in the sharing-a-joke way, but in the sharing-a-life-moment way. "That they are."

"How far is the village?"

"Two miles, give or take."

"Then I'll just jog into town, pick up a spare, and bring it back out here. Shouldn't take more than an hour." Max geolocated himself on his phone, enlarged the map, and prepared to enjoy another couple miles of fresh air.

"You'd carry a spare all the way out here?"

"They'll probably give me a donut. Do they know your car?"

Jeannie described the make, model, and year. "The man who owns the garage is Abner's uncle, Dairmid MacShane. If you tell him I'm stranded here, he'll likely give you a ride back. I'd call him, but if he's busy, he'll ignore the phone until Monday."

"You might need these." Max passed her the keys to the cottage. "See you in an hour or so."

"I shouldn't let you do this. I could call somebody."

"And they might come pick you up, but will they fix your car?" Max understood and admired a self-reliant impulse. Jeannie's reluctance to accept help was something more substantial.

"I might be able to get a truck out from Perth."

"Which will cost you next week's groceries. Whoever he was, Jeannie, I'm not him and I won't leave you stranded here. My computer is in that cottage along with my only two pairs of clean undies and my personal stash of protein bars. If that doesn't prove I'll come back, nothing will."

Ah, a smile. A small, but genuine smile. "Next month's groceries," she said. "Be off with you, then, and mind the traffic along the road."

"Save me one brownie."

Her smile blossomed into a grin, and Max took off up the drive at an easy jog. He was at the garage in less than half an hour, much of that time spent on the phone with Maura. Despite his "Yank accent," he made the situation plain enough and was soon back at the cottage, trading tools with Ewan MacShane—a gangly teenage motorhead— and putting on not a donut, but an honest-to-*Braveheart* spare.

"This one's on me," Max said, getting out his AmEx.

Ewan was about six foot three, reed-thin, freckled, and red-haired. "Keep your money, Yank." He sounded like the wrath of the Highlands, when five minutes earlier he'd been merrily cursing the damned Germans who overengineer "every feckin' ting."

"Have I just committed a typical American blunder?"

Ewan wiped his hands on a rag. "Nah. Feckin' Harry MacDonald blundered. Left a good woman with a crap set of tires. What sort of rat-turd molly-balls weasel fart does that?"

Jeannie's tires were far from new, though they'd probably pass inspection. Harry MacDonald was apparently flunking on all counts. This pleased Max, for reasons he didn't examine.

"Thanks for the help, then. Let's get the spare and the tools put up."

"Jeannie would rather owe us than a stranger," Ewan said. "The Cromartys have their pride."

"But if she owes you, then she'll eventually find a way to repay you."

Ewan scratched his nose while he considered this, getting a streak of grease on his cheek. "Jeannie's a first-rate cook. Has a way with sweets."

The way to an almost-grown-man's heart...

"Wait here." Max went into the kitchen, found the brownies, set one aside, and brought the plate out to Ewan. "Payment in full."

Ewan took the cellophane-covered plate, turned it upside down, and used the cellophane to wrap up the batch. "With interest. You're all right, Yank."

Not a single brownie would survive the two-mile journey back to the garage, which Max considered chocolate well spent. When Ewan's Land Rover went bouncing back up the lane, Jeannie not only had four functional tires, she had an inflated spare as well.

Max at first thought she might have gone for another ramble along the river, but he spotted her phone on the coffee table.

Three missed calls from somebody named Millicent.

He found Jeannie in the office, fast asleep, a quilt pulled over her,

her worn running shoes beside the bed, socks draped over them. She'd doubtless assumed he'd prefer the master bedroom. The heel of one sock was going thin, the toe of the other had a hole.

In sleep, she wasn't as formidable—and she was deeply, entirely asleep. A novel with a cowboy on the cover—*Luckiest Cowboy of All* —was open faceup beside her pillow. This was not a catnap, but rather, much-needed slumber.

Harry MacDonald had apparently worn out more than Jeannie's tires.

Max decided to give her another thirty minutes. He set the cowboy aside, took the ergonomic office chair, and brought the computer purring and glowing to life.

JEANNIE WAS WARM AND RELAXED, which made her aware of how little true relaxation she'd had lately. On some level beneath conscious thought, she knew that this version of "I must get up" was less urgent than the usual varieties. She'd been dreaming of a cowboy named Jace who had looked suspiciously like Max Maitland.

And that dream had been the farthest thing from a nightmare, but this was not the Prairie Rose Ranch.

Mr. Maitland sat at the computer, the wire-rimmed spectacles on his nose making him look sexy, dammit. Smart and slightly rumpled, a man who spotted nesting ospreys and could solve a flat tire with common sense and a little effort.

That effort had been beyond Jeannie. She'd longed to put in a good five miles along the river, but knew she hadn't the energy. Instead, she'd left a message for Millicent—slight delay, see you before supper—and resigned herself to being humble and grateful for help when help was needed.

She'd managed half a chapter of Jace and Carlene's second chance romance and then awoken to find a man near her bed for the first time in months. Mr. Maitland was utterly, entirely focused on his work, tapping the keys with deft efficiency, moving a fancy mouse that he must have brought along in his carry-on.

Jeannie inventoried her emotions for any hint of attraction to Max Maitland and found... some. A hint, a mere pilot light of interest, which was more than she'd felt for any male in the past year. Maitland was in Scotland to wreck the castle, in Uncle Donald's words, which meant Jeannie's path might cross his from time to time.

She decided to be encouraged by that pilot light—not that she'd act on it—because surely, noticing that a man was attractive was a sign of returning normalcy? Though here she was, dozing away the afternoon ten feet from the computer, and Mr. Maitland seemed oblivious to her presence.

Which was... fine.

He glanced at his watch—who wore a watch these days?—and swiveled his chair to face the bed.

"You're awake."

"Barely. What time is it?" And where was her phone?

"Going on four."

Jeannie was sitting on the edge of the bed, reaching for her socks in the next instant. "Is the car fixed?"

"It cost you a batch of brownies, but yes, the car is fixed, and you have a trustworthy spare as well, compliments of Clan MacShane."

Jeannie yanked on a sock and heard a ripping sound. "Thank you, more than I can say." She was gentler with the second sock, which already had a hole in the toe. "Have you seen my phone?"

He tossed her the phone, but she wasn't quick enough to catch it. "Somebody named Millicent is trying to get hold of you. I figured she could wait another thirty minutes."

Three messages was *not* good. "I left her a message telling her I'd be late. She hates it when I'm late."

"I suspect you're late about twice a year. Tell her sorry, it won't happen again, and chill the hell out. Tires go flat." His tone was so, so... pragmatic.

So ignorant. "You don't understand. Millicent doesn't understand." Jeannie got her shoes on, folded up the quilt, and began rehearsing her groveling.

A slow leak, could happen to anybody...

The garage was busy...

Band rehearsal...

Millicent would have sympathy for none of it.

Mr. Maitland trailed Jeannie down the steps and to the front door. "You'll be back tomorrow at eight?"

"I absolutely will," Jeannie said. "I am charged by no less person than the Earl of Strathdee with getting you up to the castle, where you can start to wreak your havoc on the ancestral home."

"My magic." He came out to the terrace with her, and it occurred to Jeannie he was *walking her to her car*. Harry had done that, for the first few dates. She suspected Max Maitland would do it for his wife even after thirty-five years of marriage.

There were good men in the world. Jeannie knew this—her family included many good men—but beyond them, she hadn't seen firsthand evidence of much masculine virtue. Perhaps she'd been too upset with Harry to allow herself to see it, because Harry had also seemed a fine fellow at first.

"I'm sorry to dash off," Jeannie said, "but I really must go. Thank you." She went up on her toes and kissed Mr. Maitland's cheek. Two years ago, anybody would have described her as affectionate. She offered him a quick buss as a gesture of hope that someday she might again be described that way.

His smile was a little puzzled. "You're welcome. See you tomorrow." He opened the car door and stepped back.

In her rearview mirror, Jeannie saw him as she drove off, a tall, good-looking man amid the lovely forest, making sure his hostess was safely on her way. She held off until she'd driven through the village, but then she reached for the ever-present box of tissues and let a few tears fall.

∽

MAX HAD ALREADY ENJOYED his third cup of coffee on the front terrace when Jeannie's black Audi puttered up the drive. The birds left their perches overhead, an enormous rabbit lolloped into the ferny undergrowth, and a squirrel that had been chittering nineteen to the dozen went silent.

The Audi could use a tune-up, something Max had been too tired to notice the day before.

Jeannie stepped out of the car and arranged her sunglasses as a sort of hairband. "Mr. Maitland, good morning."

"Morning." Max's body wasn't sure it was morning, but the sun was up, therefore, morning it must be.

"Has your luggage arrived?"

"Not yet. Last night, I was told the suitcases had made it as far as London, and I'll be contacted today regarding further attempts to deliver them. Shall we be on our way?"

"Too much peace and quiet here for you?" Jeannie asked.

Too much Beatrix Potter. "I'm anxious to see the castle." Anxious to get to work turning it into a profitable venture.

She opened the front door to the cottage, poked her head inside—Max had washed every dish he'd used *and* put it away—then pulled the door shut and locked it.

"Did you sleep well?" she asked.

"I was comatose." Max pulled open the passenger's side door, though in his American brain he'd been prepared to find the driver's seat on that side of the car. A tiny waving fist stopped him.

"Who is *that*?"

In the Audi's back seat, an infant occupied one of those impossible-to-get-your-kid-out-of, designed-by-NASA devices. Cute little guy with perfect baby mini-Chiclet teeth, a drooly smile, and big blue eyes.

"That is wee Henry."

Four little words could convey love, pride, protectiveness... and resignation. "Your son."

"My pride and joy. Shall we be off?"

Max set his backpack on the seat beside the baby and gave the kid a finger to grab. "Morning, Henry. Pleased to meet you."

"Buh." Said with much kicking and bouncing.

"Buh to you too. You're the reason your mom had to abandon me here in the forest primeval yesterday, so behave yourself."

"Buh-buh-buh!"

"It's a guy thing," Max said, taking the front seat and buckling in. "He who makes the manliest grunt wins. Will he fall asleep?"

Jeannie started the car, then paused with her wrist draped over the wheel. She made a nice picture, sunglasses back on her nose, ready to take charge of the day.

"He will nap, then he'll be up all afternoon, and there's no telling whether that means he'll be up all night, or he'll sleep for twelve straight hours. Henry is not a predictable child. Have you children of your own?"

Ouch. "I have not been so blessed."

She gave him an odd, pensive look, then turned the car around and navigated the lane.

The baby explained a few things—Jeannie's fatigue, her lack of funds, that subtle sense of an organized woman coming slightly unraveled.

"So where in the hell is Harry MacDonald, if that's his only begotten son in the back seat too?"

Henry blew a raspberry.

"Please watch your language around Henry. If his first word is something vile, my cousins will never let me live it down."

Max thought that's what cousins were for, not that he had any. "My apologies. Where in the Sam Hill is the kid's father?"

They turned onto the two-lane road, then passed the odd hump of earth in the pasture that was probably the fairy mound.

"I will kill whichever gossiping MacShane made you privy to my business," Jeannie said. "Henry's father and I encountered an irretrievable breakdown of our marriage."

The breakdown had doubtless started right about the time Henry had become more than a gleam in his daddy's eye. Jeannie's carefully matter-of-fact tone suggested the breakdown was extending into the parenting phase of the festivities.

"Henry's father is an idiot."

They tooled through the village, then had to slow to a crawl as a herd of noisy sheep poured across the road. An old guy in wellies, complete with a deerstalker hat, a shepherd's crook, and a pair of border collies, manned the gates.

"You call Harry an idiot," Jeannie said, picking up speed again. "What about the woman who married him, tried to start a family with him, and then didn't contest the divorce when he took off?"

"That woman is smart enough to give up on a doomed project. Tell me about the castle."

Max had already read everything written about the Brodie family seat. He'd seen more pictures, drawings, graphs, and charts regarding the castle than he'd seen online advertisements offering to cure erectile dysfunction, but he wanted to change the subject. Jeannie's situation was her business, and he should not have been asking nosy questions.

Lest she start asking nosy questions that could lead nowhere.

She rattled off dates relevant to the castle's history—mostly battles—and names all starting with "Mac," unless the name was Brodie or Logan. The land they traveled through rolled with agricultural confidence right up to a line of high, craggy hills to the northwest.

"That's the Highland Line?" Max said.

"The very one."

Max liked geology, and Scotland was the birthplace of the modern science of geology. Appropriate, because some of the oldest rocks on earth had been found in Scotland. Rocks were still very much in evidence. Every village and widening in the cow path they drove through consisted of stone houses of one sort or another. Stone walls separated pastures, stone bridges crossed the numerous rivers and streams. No wonder the Romans had been tantalized by this place.

"Henry's asleep," Max said after Jeannie had spent twenty minutes regaling him with the castle legends in which the first earl, "Auld Michael," and his lady, Brenna, figured prominently.

"And I've nearly put you to sleep again. Aren't you interested in love stories from long ago, Mr. Maitland?"

"Seems to me, a guy coming home from ten years at war, raising seven children with the woman who waited for him, and turning his castle into the center of a livestock-exporting business is more family history than a fairy tale."

Though happy family history, if the ten years of war and separation were conveniently ignored.

"If you're to make a go of your venture, you'd better be able to present that story as something more than simple history. The old people say Michael and Brenna can still be seen on soft nights, kissing and canoodling on the parapets."

Oh, fer the love of baby bunnies. "You think that sort of horse... horsepucky will bring people to the castle?"

"The castle has been a wedding destination throughout its history. I was married there."

And look how that turned out. "Business conferences are a lot less hassle than weddings. All the businesspeople want is good coffee, reliable internet, and functional tech. None of this bride's retiring room, rose petals on the dance floor, or Uncle Bob getting tipsy."

Jeannie gave him a look that Maura sometimes turned on him: *Men.* Or perhaps that look was unique to *Max*, but it apparently translated internationally.

The terrain shifted, becoming mountainous, and the road narrowed and twisted accordingly. Henry woke up and began to fuss.

"He'll settle in a minute," Jeannie said.

He did not settle. His fussing became crying, then wailing.

"That contraption he's sitting in might be pinching him," Max said.

"I paid a fortune for that contraption. It's not pinching him. He'll settle."

He did not settle. His little face turned bright red, tears coursed down his cheeks, and Max went nuts.

"Pull over," he said. "Please."

"And then he won't settle," Jeannie retorted.

"He's not settling. If he's half as stubborn as his mother, he won't settle until he's conquered Scotland for the he—sheer cussedness of it."

The nearly raised voices inspired Henry to howling. Jeannie found a lay-by to pull into—Scottish roads were too damned quaint by half—and Max got out and opened the back door.

"What in tarnation is all this noise about?"

The baby paused, his expression putting Max in mind of a disgruntled cat.

"Your poor mama needs to concentrate on her driving, and I need to form a positive first impression of Scotland. You are not helping."

Henry wiggled and fussed. Max knew that wiggle, knew that fuss. He'd seen it too many times not to recall what it meant.

"You have a diaper bag?" he asked Jeannie.

"Just because I drove around with a flat spare for a few days... Of course I have a diaper bag."

From the back of the car, Jeannie retrieved a voluminous robin's-egg blue shoulder bag sewn in some sort of nonstick fabric that would likely still be the same color a million years after its internment in a dump.

"You intend to change my son's diaper?"

"I intend to arrive at Brodie Castle with my hearing intact. You think I can't change a diaper?"

She passed over the diaper bag. "Best of luck. He kicks."

Max fished out the necessities, used his jacket to protect Henry from the car hood, changed the wet diaper, and handed Jeannie her kid.

"Make sure I didn't tape his loincloth on too tight."

"You didn't," she said, kissing the now smiling baby's cheek. "I changed him right before I picked you up."

Max shrugged into his jacket and stuffed the supplies back into the bag. Jeannie had even packed resealable plastic bags for dirty baby wipes.

"I'm told he's not predictable."

"Neither are you." Jeannie gave the baby another kiss, and Max's insides did a funny hitch.

He put the diaper bag away and closed the back hatch. "He probably didn't mind his wet diaper so much as he knows that Mom doesn't typically drive around with strange guys. He was putting me through my paces."

Jeannie's smile was sweet and genuine, not the professionally gracious smile she'd turned on Max before, not the slightly ironic version she'd served him with lunch.

"Another guy thing, Mr. Maitland?"

Max thought back to 911 calls, social workers, and mornings at the bus stop hoping, hoping, hoping somebody had dropped a quarter that Max could pick up without being noticed.

"A kid thing. We're protective of our parents."

A car went by, and still Jeannie regarded Max with that Mona Lisa mom-smile. "I think you will turn the castle into one of the most sought-after international wedding destinations in Europe. Shall we be on our way?"

God, yes. Max climbed into the car while Jeannie dealt with Henry and his baby seat. By the time she pulled back onto the road, Henry was slurping contentedly on his fist, and Max was desperate to avoid the inevitable questions.

Where did you learn to change a diaper?

How did you know that was a change-me cry?

Who told you a diaper shouldn't be too tight about the baby's middle?

He got out his phone and pretended to scroll through email, but they'd apparently hit a patch of Scotland with no cell reception.

"Tell me some more about the family legends," Max said. "And not the ones that involved international weddings or royal honeymoons."

Henry blew another raspberry, while Jeannie obliged with tales of Queen Victoria and Prince Albert—nine royal offspring, for the luvva kilted laddies—Aberdeen-Angus bulls, royal tartans, and Max knew not what the Sam Hill else.

He should not have changed that kid's diaper, and the castle could not come into view too soon.

CHAPTER THREE

"I want to go to Scotland." Maura used her inside voice and looked at the person she was talking to, because those were the rules. The rules were often dumb—people could hear you whether you looked at them or not—but Max said looking at people that way was polite.

Looking at people at other times was staring, and that was not polite. Even Max hadn't explained the difference very well.

"We've had this discussion, Maura." Miss Fran was about to count to five, which Maura *hated*.

"You cannot go to Scotland. You'd have to fly across the ocean in a big plane for hours and hours. Max will visit you in a few weeks, but he needs to focus on his new project."

They were having this talk in the living room. Pammie was in her bedroom playing solitaire, and Joan was having breakfast with her aunt, because Joan always had breakfast with her aunt on Saturdays.

While Max always had a new project and he always worked. "If Max can fly across the ocean, why can't I? We could have dinner. We have dinner on Fridays, but he went to Scotland instead."

Maura hated Scotland, because Max would rather be there than have dinner with her.

Miss Fran brushed Maura's bangs aside, which made Maura want to bat her hand away. "Please don't touch me."

"Maura..."

"I said please. We keep our hands to ourselves." Another rule that not everybody followed.

Miss Fran's smile was tired. "You're right, we do. Would you like to write Max an email?"

"I could text him."

Miss Fran's smile faded to that *what should I tell her?* look Maura saw all too often. Miss Fran was a very nice cottage manager, but if she was really, truly nice, she would help Maura get to Scotland.

"Because the ocean is so big," Miss Fran said, "Max's phone can't get texts from us here until he gets his plan updated. He can read emails, though."

Max had told Maura the same thing over and over, but it still made Maura want to cry. "I miss Max."

"You saw him Thursday, Maura, just the day before yesterday. You had a long talk with him yesterday morning and he promised he'd call you before you ate dinner today."

"I miss *Max*, and I want to go to *Scotland*."

Miss Fran straightened the pillows on the couch, though Pammie would just mess them up again.

"Inside voice, Maura. Let's write Max an email and tell him how much you miss him. We could also make a calendar, to count the days until Max's next visit."

"Can I use the markers?"

"Yes, you may use the markers, and the ruler, and we'll start our morning with some hot chocolate to inspire our creativity."

"I like hot chocolate. I want whip cream and sprinkles on mine."

"Don't we all?"

"And I want to go to Scotland." Maura had waited until Miss Fran had left for the kitchen to mutter that. She wanted to go to Scotland, and she missed Max, and a few weeks was forever, and she was not going to wait that long to see him again.

MOMMY GUILT FOLLOWED JEANNIE EVERYWHERE. She should be more attentive to her son. She should set firmer limits. She should get a full-time job. She should work from home... Maybe talk the family into buying more cottages, so she could buy more tulips and bake more brownies, while eking out a living on the manager's percentage of the income and waiting for Henry to grow past infancy.

She should never have trusted Harry to be a father.

She should never have trusted herself to be a mother.

She should have anticipated becoming a mother and handled her finances differently.

And she should most assuredly have said no when Uncle Donald claimed a schedule conflict prevented him from dealing with Mr. Maitland's delayed flight.

"This is the castle village," she said. "The old people still call it that. On the maps, it's Strathdee. In theory, the earl owns this village, and everybody pays him annual rent."

"In cash on the barrelhead?"

"Elias arranges a ceilidh at the pub every December, puts out a tip jar, and the proceeds go to the Anglers Charitable Society or the Kilts and Quilts."

Mr. Maitland was watching the village go by, just another collection of low, gray stone cottages, a general store, an pharmacy, a few shops... and the pub, of course.

"Kilts and Quilts sounds like some romance-reading group."

"They took the name from a romance series written by a lovely American author. The group makes quilts for newborns. Henry has one. Bunnies, teddy bears, robins, and butterflies backed with flannel."

Jeannie had tried to be gracious about the gift—the quilt was wonderful—but the ladies and gentlemen making those quilts distributed them "to the less fortunate," and how that had stung.

When had Jeannie Cromarty become less fortunate? How had that happened?

Harry MacDonald was how, and her own stupidity.

"What is it with Scotland and flowers?" Mr. Maitland asked, for every stoop and window box was abloom with pansies, geraniums, and all manner of floral color.

"The days are very long this time of year. The flowers like that."

"The castle's construction crew is liking it too. Overtime out the... ears."

Maxwell Maitland was focused. He'd never let his life get tossed into the ditch by what should have been a passing fancy. Jeannie resented him a little for that—and admired him too.

"Have you hired a landscaper yet?"

"It's on the list."

"We've an in-law, Declan MacPherson, with a landscape and gardening business. You might know his wife, Megan. She used to own a flower shop in Damson Valley, and I believe you hail from there."

"I was not a frequenter of flower shops. Holy... Ned, that's a castle."

High up on the hill behind the village, the castle rose like a benevolent guardian. The curtain wall had stood for centuries and would likely stand for many more, an undulating granite façade against blue sky and green hills. The castle itself rose from the bailey, thrusting up fanciful turrets and towers from crenellated parapets. Mature trees marched up the slope—great oaks, stately pine, a smattering of lesser citizens—giving the castle a postcard-perfect setting.

"The first three earls did a wonderful job of taking a genuine medieval castle and blending it with baronial additions," Jeannie said. "Liam brings his architecture students around every year to study a thousand years of Scottish building practices in one location."

The castle winked out of view behind the trees as the car began to climb the hillside.

Mr. Maitland was tapping a note into his phone. "Bet this hill is a bear when it snows."

"We have plows, Mr. Maitland. Weather forecasts, even, and salt trucks."

Henry, with the timing known only to infants, was stirring awake in the back seat.

"Plows cost money, and road salt is bad for the environment and most road surfaces. Costs money too."

The enormous wooden doors to the bailey stood wide open, so Jeannie drove through into the inner court. The car bumped over the cobbles as she eased it around the building supplies stacked and sitting under tarps.

Even on a Saturday, the castle was bustling. A fine baritone from inside was bellowing through "Green Grow the Rashes, O." Somebody else was pounding away with a hammer on the upper floors. A power saw whined intermittently, which should have set Henry to screaming when she extracted him from his car seat.

Instead, Henry gazed raptly all around, much as Mr. Maitland did. "Your castle, sir."

"My project, not my castle," he said, turning in a slow circle. "The pictures don't do it justice."

A small tension eased inside Jeannie. She had wanted Mr. Maitland to like the place, to see the possibilities and the history here, not the problems, of which there were many. That was another reason she'd passed the project reins into other hands.

"I'll take you to meet your foreman," she said. "Fergus can give you a tour of the facility while I get Henry his lunch."

Mr. Maitland left off visually scaling the parapets. "You're abandoning me?"

I have a life, she wanted to retort. *Employment adverts to pore over, a mountain of laundry to do, flower boxes to fill because they're the only thing keeping me going.*

Besides Henry, of course. The truth was, she no longer had much of a life beyond two a.m. feedings, Henry's irregular nap schedule, and bills that piled up no matter how hard she tried to minimize them.

"The drive back to Perth is long," she said. "You'll be in good hands here. Fergus can show you the path down to the Baron's Hall, and you can order any groceries you need from the local supermarket. I wish you the best, Mr. Maitland."

Fergus MacFarland, the project foreman, strode from the castle's main doors, which stood open to the morning sun.

"Miss Jeannie Cromarty, big as life with the wee man himself. How's our Henry?" Fergus was a dark-haired, blue-eyed man who stood several inches over six well-muscled feet, all of him exuding energy and good cheer. He plucked Henry from Jeannie's arms, which earned him a gummy smile.

Henry liked men. Once upon a time, Jeannie had too.

"Fergus, this is Mr. Maxwell Maitland, and he'll need a tour of the premises such as only you can give. Mr. Maitland, your project foreman and the Scottish caber-tossing champion from the year—"

"Enough of that ancient history." Fergus shifted Henry to one hip and stuck out a callused hand. "I'm also your head pain in the arse, most days. Pleased to meet you."

"A thankless job," Mr. Maitland replied, "but somebody has to do it. Thanks for coming in on a Saturday."

A subtle shift in Fergus's gaze suggested that had been a shrewd place to start.

"Come on, then," Fergus said. "I'll drag you around the castle while you're still too jet-lagged to comprehend all the horrors you face."

Now that the moment to part had come, Jeannie wished she'd found an excuse to tarry. Max Maitland was an adult, somebody other than family, and he took Henry in stride, wet diapers and all. Around him, Jeannie had had something to talk about besides teething, crawling, playdates, and whether Henry was loving or hating applesauce this week.

"You have something that belongs to Miss Jeannie," Mr. Maitland said.

"This wee parcel of trouble?" Fergus held Henry high above his head on arms roped with muscle, and Jeannie's stomach dropped as Henry's expression shifted to terror.

"Heights don't agree with Henry," Mr. Maitland said, appropriating the child from Fergus's grasp. "And when Henry is displeased, he could bellow down even these walls."

He passed Jeannie her child and smoothed a hand over Henry's red hair.

Fergus widened his stance and put his hands on his hips. "You can't coddle 'em when they're that young. I have three younger brothers, Mr. Maitland, and I hope you're God's gift to castle renovation—for nothing less than God's gift will bring this old pile right—but if you're appointing yourself an expert on baby boys, we'll have a few words."

Fergus dealt the livelong day with stone and the men who crafted their livelihoods from it. He'd learned to be forceful and relentless, which was a fine thing in a mason. Jeannie had little use for that approach to raising children.

"I am no expert on baby boys," Mr. Maitland said, "but I do know that Jeannie is Henry's mom, and until she gives me permission to take Henry aloft, buy him a round, or talk with him about girls, I'd best respect her wishes."

"Henry's getting over a wee cold," Jeannie said before anybody started pawing the cobblestones, though, really, Mr. Maitland's display of respect was... endearing. "I'll get him out of this breeze, and you two can be about your business. Mr. Maitland's luggage has yet to find him, Fergus, and he'll need somebody to show him the path down to the Baron's Hall. The pass code is 1314."

"The year Robert the Bruce kicked the English in the cods at Bannockburn," Fergus said. "Easy to remember. Don't suppose you brought the lads one of your signature batches of shortbread, Jeannie Cromarty?"

"She made brownies," Mr. Maitland said. "The guys at the garage near the cottage got them."

"Reived our brownies?" Fergus said. "And you let those lackwit MacShanes get away with this?"

"Lulling them into a false sense of security," Mr. Maitland replied. "Jeannie, if you can spare a minute, I'd like a word."

"I'll be in the solar," Fergus said. "Just keep going up and up from the great hall until you can't go up any higher." He strode back into the castle, work kilt swinging about his knees.

"He'll be a problem," Mr. Maitland said.

"He's among the best in the world at what he does," Jeannie replied. "At least in his own opinion. Our head mason, Nick Aiken, can usually make him see reason if nobody else can."

"The best in the world is no use to me if he's not also willing to compromise, listen, and take direction from the other experts on the work site. I think I need a nap."

"I need to get home." Back to a council flat in a not-very-pretty part of town. Back to endless laundry.

Mr. Maitland left off frowning at the open castle doors and turned blue eyes on Jeannie and Henry. "Don't be a stranger, Jeannie Cromarty. Come around to see how we're doing, and you don't have to bring brownies or shortbread. You do have to bring your little buddy, though."

Mr. Maitland smiled at Henry, who was all grins now that he was clinging to Jeannie.

"Don't let the crews push you around, Mr. Maitland. They need to know you are the authority on this project. Make them document their work on time, and inspect everything regularly and irregularly."

Mr. Maitland walked with her to the car. "I need to thank you for that too. Elias Brodie said you straightened out the paperwork mess left behind by the previous earl, kept the crews in paychecks, and prevented the project from dying on the vine. We'll name the bridal suite after you if you like."

That was meant as a compliment. It only felt like a dagger to the heart. "I needed a project, Mr. Maitland. I can't be buying tulips and baking treats all the time. Best of luck." For abruptly, it had become imperative to get this parting over with, which was silly.

"One last thing: I need directions to the Baron's Hall if my luggage is to find me."

"I'll text them to you, or email them. Call me if you need anything." That last offer was said automatically to any cottage guest Jeannie encountered. She'd used to say the same to family, before... Henry. And they had called her, which was how she'd become entangled in the castle paperwork and the cottage.

They didn't call her now.

"Good-bye, then," Mr. Maitland said, touching a finger to Henry's cheek. "You made my arrival in Scotland not only bearable but gracious. I saved this for you."

He withdrew a small square wrapped in cellophane. A brownie. Jeannie's mouth watered at the sight. She ought not to take it. He was the guest, the newcomer, the one deserving of hospitality.

She took it. "Thank you."

She kissed him again, intending a brush to his cheek, but his arms came around her gently—not the half-self-conscious squeeze she endured from cousins or uncles, but an *embrace*. Henry was included in that gesture, carefully, lest he realize he was in the midst of an opportunity to fuss.

For little more than an instant, Jeannie let herself be held, let herself be close to a man she'd likely never see again, outside of a possible Christmas gathering. Max Maitland was tall, fit, male, and warm. His scent was lovely and light—woods and spice.

Jeannie barely had time to wonder if he'd left somebody at home in the States, a female somebody. Then Mr. Maitland was stepping back, and Henry got his fist entangled in Jeannie's hair.

"Safe journey home," Mr. Maitland said. "Wish me luck with the castle."

"Good luck." Jeannie extricated her hair from Henry's little fingers. "Call if you need anything."

Mr. Maitland retreated to the foot of the castle steps, and Jeannie loaded Henry into the car seat. She bumped over the cobbles through the open gates and mentally wished Mr. Maitland all the luck in the world.

He'd need it.

CHAPTER FOUR

Max had taken on two other renovation projects in his twenty years in the development business. They had both been disasters, going egregiously over budget while they limped along months behind schedule. Both times, he'd promised himself *never again*.

Brodie Castle was larger, older, more complicated, and more expensive than either of the previous projects, and it was in Scotland. What Max knew about Scottish building regulations would barely make a credible doorstop. What he knew about Maryland's building and land-use regulations would have made a long, hard undergraduate curriculum, with summers spent doing backbreaking construction labor. He'd added a master's program that had included practicums in accounting, project management, and human resources, and picked up law school at night.

The PhD could be conferred only by experience holding the actual reins and taking the risks.

Fergus seemed to delight in showing Max every crack, subsidence, uneven floor, and irregular window on the site. Max had seen most of them before in videos, drone footage, and photographs, but the granite reality was altogether more depressing.

Likely more expensive too.

"The old castles are all like this," Fergus said. "The floorplans are ridiculous, the modernizations a hundred years old, the challenges bad to start with and worse once you roll up your sleeves. I love 'em."

Because those sorts of projects lasted forever and became so idiosyncratic that bringing on new crew meant an endless learning curve. The managers who were in on the ground floor had years of job security at good wages.

"Who's your assistant?" Max asked as they ambled through the great hall. His steps echoed off of the enormous vaulted ceiling, the stone beneath his feet covered with that grit known to every active construction site.

"I don't need an assistant, Mr. Maitland. We have a dozen masons hard at it. They know their jobs, and I know mine. Assistants clutter the place up, countermand orders, cost money, and agitate."

Here we go. "You've yet to show me the project office. Perhaps we'd best have this discussion there."

Fergus smiled, a prizefighter ready to enjoy thrashing somebody. "Haven't one of those either. We keep the paperwork in the porter's nook, so everybody knows where to get the forms for the time sheets and progress reports. All you'll need is a safe and a desk, and you'll be good to go."

Max ambled for the door, and Fergus strode along beside him.

"Let's finish touring the outbuildings," Max said, "and then you can point me to the Baron's Hall."

"Jet lag is the very devil."

Said with *such* sympathy. "The Baron's Hall is part of the work site, an important part, and I can't keep the housekeeper waiting forever on a Saturday. Elias Brodie asked her to come in this afternoon as a favor to him, and she's in the best position to tour that facility with me. I enjoyed a fine night's sleep at the cottage, and I have tomorrow to catch up if that wasn't enough."

"Cranky," Fergus said. "That's always the way when I'm knackered."

This needling in the form of commiserating was a variety of Scottish humor. Max recognized the tactic because Elias Brodie, the earl who'd granted Max's investors a ninety-nine-year lease on the castle, was a gifted needler.

Also a hellaciously skilled negotiator.

"This would be the laundry," Fergus said as they approached a building made entirely of pale granite. "The drains give it away, as do the light and ventilation. You noticed the lavender growing along the walk, that's another possible indicator of a laundry. The laundresses would spread the linens on the bushes to dry, or string a clothesline downwind of the border so everything caught the scent."

"Lavender is a good smell." Neither masculine nor feminine, and while it would fade, it didn't decay over time as some fragrances did into less-than-elegant finishes. Aromatics were now part of high-end property management, just as floral arrangements and noise abatement were.

"Lavender keeps the vermin down," Fergus said. "The Victorians conquered half the known world because their womenfolk first sharpened their swords on the challenges of bugs, dirt, and illness."

Always, the history lessons.

The laundry was airy and high-ceilinged. Oriel windows near the eaves let in light and had probably been intended to let out heat and humidity. The design was simple—three rooms in shotgun layout, the two rooms on the ends smaller, while the central chamber was a good twenty by thirty feet.

A perfect conference-cum-war room, in fact. "Original glass?" Max asked.

"Victorian, possibly Georgian. I haven't sent the glaziers around to have a look because this building is in relatively good shape."

Good shape—for a place without running water, electricity, or heat—except it did have two enormous fireplaces in the central room.

"Where do the drains lead?"

"Right down the hillside, I assume."

Not a good enough answer. When an edifice sat at the top of a high, steep hill, storm-water management was a significant issue. Max tapped yet another note into his phone.

Fergus waited while Max peered around at odd rings stuck into the walls, window casements that—thanks be—did not leak, and floors that were solid, for all they'd been designed with a slight grade toward a shallow central gutter.

"This will be the project office," Max said. "We can move a generator over here Monday, and I'll make a list of supplies to get it set up. The purchasing agent can have the back end, the project will use the middle, and we'll put the break room out front."

Fergus took up a lean against stone walls three feet thick at the base. "Will we, now?"

"State your objections, Fergus, and I'll listen. Neither one of us has time to waste."

"A break room means the lads will be waltzing out of the castle to wander over here, by way of the bushes, their cars, a smoke break, and a wee chat with the missus four times a day. A project office over here means that you—the grand high manager of us all—aren't where the work's being done, keeping an eye on things as they happen, rather than as they're relayed to you by various interested parties."

Max kept his expression neutral, though the conversation was taking a predictable turn, which was a relief.

"Don't hold back on my account, Fergus. Give me the benefit of your thinking."

"Again, if you set up shop here, you set yourself apart from the people doing the work, making you harder to reach. If a man wants to report a safety concern, he's seen making an appointment with you—probably through another flunky—and then all know who went tattling to the head Yank. You aren't on hand to be consulted, so nobody consults you—too much bother to fetch you when you might not even be at your desk."

"Anything else?"

"Expense. Why do you need to use up a whole building, get it

wired and lit and heated, when money is always tight, and we don't
have enough laborers for the work ahead of us?"

"Good points. Let me address them. First, I carry a phone at all
times. Nobody has to hit pause on a critical decision and waste
twenty minutes scaring me up. Second, I want my crews to have the
option of bringing me into a decision or leaving me out of it.

"I am not a mason," Max went on, "or a glazier, plumber, electri-
cian, carpenter, or landscaper. I don't want the trades coming to me
to make decisions that are better off made by the trades. If I'm underfoot, or eavesdropping on every conversation, that's exactly what
they'll do. Third, we have a safety officer—or we soon will have—and
safety concerns ought to be brought to his or her attention before
anybody comes to me with them."

Fergus studied the oriel window as if seeking divine guidance
from the sunlight beaming down. "I take it you are not finished."

He was listening, or had sense enough to pretend he was.

"I am not finished," Max said. "If this was a private renovation, just
another wealthy earl moving the staircase or dropping in a light well, then
we'd have much more latitude. This effort will soon become a commercial
job, and different rules apply. We need a project office off premises for
visitors to report to, so they can be equipped with escorts and hard hats."

"Oh, for the love of—"

"Competitors will try to spy on us, children are always curious,
and spouses drop by with forgotten cell phones. Safety matters, and
so do liability and confidentiality. The crews need to know that everybody not employed on the site reports first to the project office, which
will soon be one of the few non-hard-hat areas on the grounds."

"I forget you Yanks are always suing each other, and your government lets your accidents and illnesses become a source of somebody
else's profit."

You Yanks... Except, Fergus wasn't wrong. He also wasn't making
a relevant observation.

"Businesses sue each other too, even here, Fergus. Breach of contract and tortious interference with an advantageous business relationship are not American inventions. They arrived on the Mayflower along with religious intolerance."

Fergus pushed away from the wall. "Go on."

"A project office adds a layer of security, putting financial matters behind another set of locks and keys and making sure critical plans aren't all kept on the work site. A fire, a flood, a crime—"

"Now you're murdering my crews?"

"If a serious crime occurs on a job site, the authorities can turn that job site into a crime scene, and we lose our right to ingress and egress until that crime-scene tape comes down. I damned near lost a project once over an accusation of theft. Do you know how long it takes to dust a building site for fingerprints? How long it takes a forensic detective to investigate one hard drive?"

"I take the point, but my lads and lasses don't steal."

"I never said they did. Add up all the factors—privacy, management efficiency, safety, security, and risk management—and having a project office makes sense. I'll set it up myself within a day."

Fergus looked at his phone. "A long day. I'm supposed to have a wee chat with the glaziers about the solar in ten minutes."

Max snagged his backpack and headed for the door. "That's another reason I want a break room. I want a place for the trades to mingle, to catch up with each other and swap gossip without having to call it a meeting, complete with managers and foremen foghorning at them."

Fergus fell in step behind Max as they crossed the bailey. "Do you not have pubs in America?"

America had bars, which were usually not the same thing. "Only some of the people we have working here can stop for a pint at the end of the day, and the pub is... public. Some things are better aired on the job."

"Like all those murders and thefts we'll be having. I see."

"We'll have a tidier work site if the employees have a place to stash their coats, their lunch boxes, their whatever. Personal items left all over the castle will invariably get in the way or go missing."

Fergus took the castle steps two at a time. "Is this obsession with crime unique to you or something all Americans lug about?"

"People lose things, Fergus. They pick up the mallet they're sure is theirs when it isn't. Their stuff gets moved because the carpenters decided to tear out an extra set of cabinets. A break room means nobody's personal effects are sitting where they shouldn't be. A break room is also a place to take a load off, hydrate, sit down over some as-builts. It's not a meeting if the discussion is in the break room."

"Hydrate. Is that like drinking water regularly? My English—"

"You don't have the temperatures here we do in the US. I doubt your winters get as severe as they do on the northern Great Plains, and I guarantee you've never had to run a jackhammer for eight straight hours under a one-hundred-and-ten-degree sun. So yes, I'm aware of the need to hydrate. A break room is also a central location for all medical supplies and a place to post job openings, schedules, assignments, and safety notices."

Fergus started up the spiral stairs leading from the great hall. "My objection is not to a break room in itself. I was an apprentice once too. My objection is to putting that break room across the bailey, in the front parlor of your royal presence chamber."

Max remained at the foot of the steps, because no way was he making that hike again if he didn't have to.

"So where would you put the break room?"

"There's a parlor near the solar—the countess's parlor—with a magnificent view of the hills. The lads seem to gravitate toward it when they're eating lunch. It's one floor up, on the east side of the old castle, which is fairly central. The carpenters knocked us together some benches, but it could do with a proper table and such."

"I'd rather have the break room in the laundry."

"Then why ask me for my opinion, Mr. Maitland?" Fergus stood several steps up, the curve of the stairway casting him in shadow. He doubtless knew what a menacing picture he made. Put a broadsword in his hand and he could have held off an army.

"You say the men have already chosen this parlor, more or less?"

"That I did."

"Then we'll put the break room there. Will they be offended to have lockers assigned?"

"Put the lockers in the corridor outside the break room, leave it to the men whether to put locks on them."

"Done."

Fergus turned to finish ascending the stairs, then shot a look at Max over his shoulder. "Why do I have the sense you went through that whole discussion—the murders and spies and whatnot—just to put the break room exactly where I wanted it?"

Because I did. "Your concerns matter to me, but I'm the guy who has to keep the investors happy. Without their backing, none of us have jobs, Fergus, and you don't know what it takes to keep them happy."

"So you play them the way you just played me?"

"I negotiated with you."

Fergus smiled, showing a lot of big, white teeth. "I suppose our negotiations will continue on Monday, then. Welcome to Brodie Castle."

"Before you dodge off after having the last word, how do I get to the Baron's Hall?"

"Easy," Fergus said. "Out the gates, take the path to the right descending the hill. Can't miss it. At the fork in the woods, go left, and you'll be there in no time. It's a pretty walk, and there's a bench about halfway down that the young people like to use for smoking pot and canoodling on long summer evenings."

What was it about this castle and canoodling? "Thanks, Fergus. See you Monday."

Max took the path Fergus had indicated and made his way through another lush, mature forest. No river whispered by, but the canopy was full of birds, and a red deer looked Max over before leaping away through the undergrowth.

At the fork in the path, Max took the left option, as directed. He was preoccupied with mentally drafting a purchase order for the furniture and supplies needed to fit out the project office and break room, and thus it took him another fifteen minutes to realize Fergus had sent him not to the Baron's Hall, but to the village. Another hundred yards on across a field and the path would end up on the main street, a few doors up from the pub.

"I've been negotiated," he informed a shaggy red cow chewing its cud on the far side of a stone wall. He switched his backpack to the other shoulders, and continued on toward the village, checking his phone to see if Jeannie had sent him directions for the lost-luggage delivery.

That would be a nope, which resulted in a small disappointment. He'd liked her, she'd kissed his cheek twice, and the small hug in parting had felt... comforting. The only person to hug Max Maitland in recent years had been Maura, and she was happily ensconced in her Saturday routine thousands of miles away.

"DAMN UNCLE DONALD for a lazy old disgrace." Elias Brodie, Earl of Strathdee, re-read Jeannie's email, but the words didn't change. The family member assigned to sit on the board of the Brodie Castle Corporation had preferred a day of fishing—genteelly termed resting up with a bout of bursitis—rather than guarding the family interests or making a good first impression on Max Maitland.

"Something wrong?" Violet asked.

Elias's wife was on her side of their office/sunroom, drafting a blog post about window-box herb gardens. She and Elias were living at her farmhouse, while his larger dwelling across the road was undergoing some maintenance... a lot of maintenance. The plan was to eventually use her house for staff quarters, because a thousand acres of Maryland farmland, plus a farm store, greenhouses, and a mail-order business, would be more than one newlywed couple could manage.

Assuming all went well and enough skilled help could be hired.

Elias passed Violet his tablet. "Jeannie had to not only fetch Maitland from the airport, but also put him up in the cottage overnight, then drive him out to the castle."

Violet closed her document. "Is Donald all right?"

"He's doubtless fine as five pence, hip-deep in the River Tay, reciting poetry to the fishes. He's off to Germany next week. Some kind soul has arranged guest passes for him at a trout fishing operation in Bavaria. Donald loves to meddle, but keeping his hand in for the long haul is another matter."

"Your burr gets thicker when you're worried."

"I'm no' worried, I'm angry. The only tether I have on Maitland is a family member sitting on the board of his development corporation. If Donald intends to be this cavalier about his duties, then I've chosen the wrong family member."

Though for all the effort and sacrifice Elias had gone through to find a way to save the castle from ruin, *any* family member should have been happy to step up, particularly one retired and without many other obligations.

Violet set aside the tablet and settled into Elias's lap. She was a fifth-generation farmer, sturdily built and wonderfully curved. Elias's arms came around her and some of his worry—his anger, rather—slid away.

"Who are your other choices?" she asked.

"Liam is an architect married to a potter. They'd bring an educated eye to the job of overseeing renovations."

"Newly married," Violet said. "And very busy collecting art to rent to corporations and billionaires who lack the time or taste to find their own. Liam also has classes to teach. Who else?"

"Niall could look in on the project. A former pro golfer has rubbed shoulders with big money and bigger egos."

Violet kissed Elias's ear, which tickled. "Niall's in the middle of high season for golf tourism and busy expanding his golf course, and also his family."

Another newlywed Cromarty, blast the luck. "He's married to an attorney. Perhaps Julie wouldn't mind riding into battle in the boardroom."

"See 'expanding family' above," Violet said. "And I don't think contract law is her area of expertise. What about Magnus?"

"Already spending much of his time in airplanes trying to juggle businesses in Scotland and Montana."

"You could appoint yourself, Elias."

Elias and Violet were waiting to start a family until their farm-store business was better established. Violet had a thriving farm life blog, two hundred and fifty acres under cultivation and a world of practical knowledge. Elias had added his eight hundred acres, a PhD in economics, and an imagination that delighted in hard work and big dreams.

"Myself is the most newlywed of all. Are you really so anxious to get rid of me, Violet?"

She scooted around so she straddled his lap and looked him directly in the eye. "I'd go with you. That's how marriage works." She punctuated her lecture with a tight hug, and Elias admitted to himself that this was at the bottom of his vexation with Uncle Donald.

Too many years cleaning up after the late earl, too many years trying to show not-for-profit corporations how to turn one dollar into three, or how to clean house so their boards of directors would be more than expensive ornaments. Too many years feeling like every problem on every hand could be solved only by Elias Brodie stating the obvious while wearing a bespoke suit, and sipping exotic spring water from a crystal glass despite his arse aching after too many hours in a supposedly ergonomic boardroom chair.

"I hate to fly," Elias said. "I hate to drag you away from the farm when we've finally reached the summer lull."

The summer lull was a few precious weeks between the second cutting of hay and the harvest. The weeding slowed down, the crops matured, the animals were neither breeding nor giving birth, and severe weather didn't relentlessly threaten fences, crops, or buildings.

Elias and Violet had no lull, because expanding a business required every available hour. If they weren't shopping for new equipment, they were laying out next spring's community gardens; fitting out Elias's fieldstone barn to convert into a farm store; handling the chores that went with keeping up Violet's sheep, chickens, and crops; haggling with the bank; twiddling with the website; or meeting with Elias's lawyer relatives, Jane DeLuca and Dunstan Cromarty.

Violet smoothed Elias's hair back, one of the most soothing of her many gestures of casual affection. "Dunstan might enjoy a chance to strut around and intimidate Maitland."

Max Maitland respected Dunstan—*and Jane.* "Jane's on the nest. We can't ask it of them."

"That leaves Declan MacPherson, if you consider in-laws of in-laws family."

In Scotland, that counted as a family connection. "It's high season for landscapers, and Declan has his own farm. I'd hoped Maitland would hire Declan for the landscape work at the castle."

"So you'd have a spy on the grounds," Violet said, repeating the caress. "But isn't landscaping one of the last aspects of property development to happen?"

Elias dropped his forehead to Violet's shoulder. "I can't think when you do that. Don't stop." She was right, though. Declan MacPherson might sit in on some planning meetings or submit a few estimates, but his real work wouldn't begin until next summer, or next spring at the earliest—if Maitland even chose MacPherson for the landscape work.

"What about Jeannie?" Violet asked. "She's familiar with the project, knows the crews on-site, has a good head for figures, already has a toe in the door of the hospitality industry, and does not suffer fools."

Elias raised his head to peer at Violet. "I asked her first. She turned me down, plead motherhood and a need for regular hours. Jeannie among us all has too much on her plate, and I should never have asked her to look into Uncle Zebedee's renovation plans." Though thank heavens she had. Jeannie had found fully executed contracts, invoices, bills of lading... a renovation ready to launch, but for the necessary coin.

In exchange for a ninety-nine-year lease, Maitland, a Damson Valley lawyer-turned-property-developer, had taken on the challenge of bringing the castle into the twenty-first century, and—may God have mercy on his soul—turning it into a profitable venture.

"Jeannie strikes me as one of those people who can get an amazing amount done," Violet said, "all without appearing ruffled, and still have time to read."

"Romance novels," Elias said, rising with Violet wrapped around him. "I'd think she's had enough of romance with that damned Harry MacDon—"

Violet kissed her husband as he settled with her on the couch. "This is romance. This right here. Talk of problems to solve, family matters, and what we'll have for dinner tonight. This."

Violet scooted closer, and Elias forgot all about romance novels in favor of the real thing.

"We'll come back to the problems at the castle," Violet said, leading Elias to the stairs fifteen minutes later. "In an hour or so."

"Two hours," Elias said. "Or possibly tomorrow."

CHAPTER FIVE

Jeannie was paying her bill at the Strathdee pub when she realized she hadn't yet sent Max Maitland directions to the Baron's Hall.

"You distracted me," she informed Henry, who was flirting with Fern Logan, the tavern owner.

"Don't they all?" Fern passed over Jeannie's change. "He seems like a good little lad."

"At this age, they can only be good, or so my aunts insist."

"Do you see much of his father?"

Fern had finished graduate school and taken over the tavern from her parents, who'd taken over from their parents, on back as far as anybody could recall. There had been Logans in the valley as long as there had been Brodies, which was far back indeed. Fern thus wasn't being nosy, exactly, to raise that question.

More sisterly, or cousinly. "Harry is a rigger. He goes where there's work."

"Harry is an idiot, but a good-looking idiot." Fern's abrupt need to polish the bar's spotless surface suggested Harry had turned her head on some occasion. Or turned up her skirts. He'd professed a weakness for redheads, the rotter.

"He's in the Eastern Mediterranean," Jeannie said. "Lots of natural-gas exploration going on there." Harry liked the risk, liked the excitement, the sense that his industry hovered close to major political and economic power. He also liked the money, though that money hadn't been much in evidence during their marriage.

"Hard road, being married to a rigger." Fern flipped a thick, coppery braid over her shoulder. "He might have done you a favor, taking off like that."

Jeannie set Henry on the bar and kept a hand on his belly to steady him. He was growing heavy, which was good.

"When I met Harry, he swore he was done with being a rigger, ready to become a weaver in the Outer Hebrides."

Fern took a sip of water from a beer glass. She had pretty hands, freckled along the backs, and a lovely jade thumb ring on her right hand.

No ring on her left hand, though she was a very attractive woman. "They all say that. Three weeks later, they're back on the rig, and so few of them manage to save anything."

She and Jeannie shared a moment of purely female exasperation, while Henry tried to wiggle away down the bar.

Fern set about refilling the garnish tray with maraschino cherries, colored toothpicks, lime wedges, and drink umbrellas. "All the activity up at the castle has been great for business."

"But you worry," Jeannie said, "about when the castle opens for business. Will anybody want to come for a meal at the Earl's Pint when they can do the fancy up the hill?'"

"Incomers of any kind are a mixed blessing. The whole project is financed with American money, and you know—"

The door swung open behind Jeannie, and Henry started bouncing on his diapered bum and waving his arms. "Buh! Duh-duh-duh-buh!"

"That's an American walk, I bet you a bridie," Fern murmured before pasting on her signature bartending smile. "Good day, sir. Can I pull you a pint?"

Max Maitland stepped up beside Jeannie. His fragrance hit her first—lush greenery and spices—followed by the warmth he gave off.

"That depends," he said. "What's Henry having?"

The time of his busy little life. "Henry just dined on chips," Jeannie said, "with a few nibbles of haddock and watered-down apple juice."

"Fish and chips it is. To go, please. I'll pass on the nectar of the gods."

"Won't take but a moment," Fern said, disappearing into the kitchen.

Henry continued to coo, kick, and wave until Max lifted him from the bar into his arms. "The bouncer will toss you out on your handsome ear, Henry. Settle down."

Henry was glad to see Max, which was troubling. Jeannie was glad to see him too, though, which was silly when they'd parted less than two hours ago.

"I take it you stopped in for lunch on your way home," Max said as Henry took a swipe at his nose.

"Henry hadn't eaten. A preemptory lunch break was in order. We ran into Darrell MacPherson—he's head of the local council—and nothing would do but I catch him up on what every member of the family has been up to. Darrell's's kin to Declan, who owns the landscape business."

Max gently unwrapped Henry's fingers from his nose. "I'm glad you're still here. Can I talk you into touring the Baron's Hall with me?"

Jeannie loved the Hall. She wasn't all that particular about how renovations at the castle proceeded—if marching armies, religious violence, a thousand winters, and a few earthquakes couldn't bring down the castle, neither would renovations, not if Max was in charge.

But the Hall was gracious, personable, filled with family memorabilia, and the closest thing Elias had had to a home when his parents had passed on. The Hall mattered.

Jeannie chose a purple drink umbrella and twirled it for Henry's amusement. "I should be getting back to Perth." Because dirty laundry was so often stolen by the fairies.

"If you must go, I won't keep you, but I'd like the company, and the ally."

Oh dear. "Trouble already?"

Before Max answered, Fern set a white paper bag on the counter, redolent of fried potatoes and lightly battered haddock. Max passed the baby to Jeannie, got out his wallet, and paid for the meal.

"I take it you're here to work on the castle?" Fern wore her friendly smile, but Jeannie heard the challenge in the question. Strangers were always cause for caution, especially strangers clearly not of Scottish extraction.

"Fergus MacFarland has dubbed me the Yank with the Bank," Max said. "Not exactly flattering, but yes, I'm here to work on the castle. I'll be staying at the Baron's Hall for the duration, and I'd like to talk to you about delivering a load of sandwiches with all the trimmings over to the Hall on Monday."

"What constitutes a load of sandwiches, and who are you?"

Max stuck out his hand. "Max Maitland, and you would be?"

"Your new best friend, Fern Logan." She withdrew a pencil from behind her ear. "Will you want some desserts with those sandwiches?"

Max shot Jeannie a look.

"Of course he wants desserts. Shortbread, tablet, brownies, the works. Fruit salad and some sliced veggies with dip, plenty of paper plates and napkins."

"Can we have a bowl of fruit instead of salad?" Max asked, setting his backpack at his feet. "The hungries can ambush a laborer midafternoon, and an orange or a banana can hit the spot."

Fern kept scribbling. "What sort of bevvies?"

"Beverages," Jeannie translated.

Fern looked from Max to Jeannie. "Fizzy juice? We have them all."

"Soft drinks," Jeannie said. "That will do, along with some water."

"For how many?"

Max took up twirling the umbrella Henry was trying to swipe from the bar. "The full crew should be on-site Monday, which is about sixty people, so let's say... ninety, because they're working construction."

Fern was quiet for a moment, her pencil moving on the paper. "Guess who won't be at Sunday services tomorrow?" She passed Max the paper with a figure at the bottom underlined. He passed over a credit card.

"You can keep that card on file," he said. "If you have a private dining room, I'd like to use it for corporate functions occasionally."

"For a price," Fern replied, "you can use all my worldly goods except my fiddle and my mountain bike."

Five minutes later, Jeannie had stashed Henry in the back seat of the Audi and was driving Mr. Maitland to the Baron's Hall.

"So was that a smart move or a dumb move?" he asked.

"Both," Jeannie replied. "Americans are always throwing their money around, but Fern needs the business, and her opinion of any incomer matters significantly. What are all the crews supposed to do with their bag lunches on Monday?"

"Before I left the States, I told Fergus I'd provide lunch at an all-hands meeting Monday. My other option was to have the grocery store deli cater, but Fern is the more significant potential ally. I don't suppose you can be here Monday to introduce me?"

"Why me?"

"Because your dear old uncle Donald shows no sign of being around to perform that courtesy, and I'll meet with less resistance if even one of the earl's relations is on hand when I show up."

Jeannie turned down the lane that led to the Hall, stone walls fencing off cows on one side, sheep on the other.

"You expect to meet with resistance?"

He opened the white bag, inhaled, and withdrew a fat wedge of fried potato. "Want a fry?"

Jeannie leaned over and took a bite. "We call them chips."

Max ate the other half. "I call them delicious."

The moment was unremarkable, but also intimate in a friendly sense. Normal between two people who both liked chips—fries—and might even like each other.

"Mrs. Hamilton will be horrified that you settled for fish and chips when she was here to make you a proper meal."

"I will explain I was currying favor with the local publican. Good God, does this ever call for a cold beer." He held up another fry, and Jeannie took another bite. She'd eaten most of her lunch but skipped breakfast. She'd only had time to feed Henry before leaving the house, and her appetite for damp toast and infant banana pudding seldom exceeded one bite of each.

An aroma wafted forward from the back seat.

"Henry's digestion is healthy," Max said, rolling the takeout bag closed and cracking his window.

Jeannie turned down the alley of lime trees that led to the Hall proper. "Elias likes cars and engines. At moments like this, he usually makes a remark about intake and exhaust. The stink wasn't half so bad before Henry started on solid food."

Henry made a remark that sounded like a baby getting ready to fuss loudly.

"Henry, my boy," Max muttered, "we could use you to fumigate the castle dungeons."

"More guy talk, Mr. Matiland?" Max's comment made Jeannie smile. The chance meeting with Max Maitland made her smile. The shared snitches of chips—fries—made her smile, but under no circumstances could she tarry here until Monday. She didn't have a change... well, she did have clothes stashed at the Hall. A few. And some baby supplies.

But she also had a job hunt to pursue and Millicent to placate. Yesterday's flat tire had strained the scant goodwill Jeannie had with her former mother-in-law, and the weekend's racketing about had disturbed what little routine Henry followed.

Jeannie pulled around the Hall's circular driveway and stopped at the foot of the front steps, though family usually used the lot behind the kitchen.

"I want you to get the full Scottish baronial effect," she said. "The entrance hall is impressive."

She extricated her stinky, fussy son from the car seat, and Max shouldered his backpack. He also retrieved the bright blue diaper bag. He should have looked ridiculous lugging a diaper bag, but to Jeannie, he looked... entirely relaxed, a little tired, and oddly dear.

She let him open the enormous arched wooden door and stood silently while Max did a slow pirouette in the entrance hall.

"That is a *lot* of weaponry."

"A lot of history, Mr. Maitland."

Targes, halberds, blunderbusses, and dirks were arranged in fan patterns. Fowling pieces, great swords... The walls on three sides of the entrance hall were festooned with the tools of war and hunting. Two stag heads peered down on the front door with regal impassivity, and a stuffed hare was poised to leap the steps into the atrium.

The Duke of Atholl had a more impressive display, but only just.

Max got out his phone and tapped for a moment. "This will all have to go."

"I beg your pardon?"

"This," he said, waving a hand to indicate centuries of family history. "Maybe we can find a museum to take it, but you don't welcome business leaders from all over the world to an elite hospitality venue by flashing your *Braveheart* set pieces at them."

"*Braveheart set pieces?*" Jeannie had allowed a small pathetic wish to sprout—a wish to get to know Max Maitland better, certainly nothing more—but she mentally yanked it out by the roots and tossed it into the diaper pail.

"If any of it's authentic," Max said, taking the stairs into the atrium, "then we'll find a place for it, but Brodie Castle isn't a Disney theme park."

"Maxwell Maitland, how dare you? Every single item on these walls is authentic and has historical significance to my family. It stays."

From the back of the house, Jeannie heard a door close. Mrs. Hamilton had doubtless seen the car, and soon they were to have an audience.

"Let's change the baby," Max said. "If we're going to have an argument, then it's unfair to expect me to battle chemical weapons at the same time."

"We're going to have an argument," Jeannie assured him. "And you will lose."

"Then I'll lose, but while you tend to Henry, I have a phone call to make to somebody in Maryland, and I promised I would make that call right about now."

"SO WHAT'S HE LIKE?" Hugh Morven asked around a mouthful of meat pasty. "The Yank?"

Fergus left off trying to total the column on his time sheet—his time sheet from three weeks ago. The sun had changed angles, so the countess's parlor wasn't as well lit as in the mornings.

"Maitland's like a Yank. He talks funny."

Hugh—six foot three of bonnie wee carpenter in his handsome prime—smacked Fergus a love tap on the back of the head that had Fergus's ears ringing. "You talk funny."

Hugh was an Aberdonian on his father's side, and if anybody talked funny, it was the folk from rural Aberdeenshire. "Maitland will be underfoot for the next year at least. You can make up your own mind about him."

Hugh balled up the paper wrapped around his bridie and tossed it over his shoulder to join the discarded sandpaper, sawdust, and stray nails casually swept into a corner.

The countess would have had a fit if she could have seen her parlor now. She and her earl were said to haunt the castle.

"In other words," Hugh said, situating himself on an empty barrel turned on its side, "you might like Maitland, but you don't want to admit it in case he turns out to be a horse's arse. I'm not sure if that's a good sign or a bad sign, considering your taste in football teams."

Fergus got up from the carpenter's workbench—the only level surface in the room—retrieved Hugh's trash, and pitched it at his face. "Bin it, ya eejit. Maitland will make some changes, most of which I applaud. Can't have the work site looking like the Glasgow city dump when the bankers might come sniffing about without warning."

Hugh, whose mum was a Glaswegian, lifted the balled-up paper into the air with the tip of his steel-toed boot, then caught it in his hand. "I don't care for bankers."

"But we all care for their money, and Brodie Castle is a good old pile of rock. The earl had to do something with it when the National Trust has castles to burn. A couple hundred years fancied up to take money from Yanks, oil sheikhs, and Germans isn't a bad plan."

Hugh tossed the trash back at Fergus's crotch and unwrapped a second meat pasty. "Does Maitland know what he's doing? I don't mind working for an arrogant sod as long as he knows what he's doing —witness, present company."

Hugh was the same age as Fergus. They played on the same football teams, occasionally faced each other on a shinty pitch, and had downed many a wee dram together. No finer carpenter ever wielded a hammer, and the men liked working for him.

But God, Hugh could do with a proper thrashin'.

"In the space of less than two hours," Fergus said, "I did not form an opinion of Maitland's technical expertise. He's smart, and he'll gather information before he makes up his mind, but he's a lawyer and admits freely that the trades have knowledge he lacks."

Hugh gestured with the uneaten half of his bridie. "Which he oughtn't have done the first time he met you. Showing you his cards. Or was he showing you only the cards he wanted you to see?"

"Or was he showing me the cards that would make me tip my hand?" Or—interesting notion—simply being honest?

"Poker's a stupid game. Dinty Dundee says he saw the earl and the countess up on the parapets last night."

Last night had been Friday, Dinty's traditional drinking day. "Tell him to take his drinking down to the pub. Fern will let him sleep it off in the common."

"It's the waxing quarter moon, Fergus. You know what that means."

"It means our great-great-great-granddas would have been out stealing each other's cattle."

Hugh balled up his second bit of trash, righted the barrel he'd been sitting on, and lobbed the paper over his shoulder lay-up fashion into the bin.

"When the earl and lady walk under a reiver's moon, somebody's courtship is about to commence." He tossed the rest of his litter into the barrel and glanced around the room. "Somebody should clean this place up. Doesn't do to let the American think we're a pack of lazy slobs."

He sauntered on his way, leaving Fergus to sweep the litter in the corner into the barrel.

"YOU WILL REMOVE these precious items of Scottish history from these walls over my dead body," Jeannie said, stepping nose to nose with Max.

Max resisted the urge to pinch his own nose shut. Henry's exhaust fumes packed a wallop.

"We'll talk," Max said. "After I've made one phone call and seen the rest of the premises. We might be able to find another use for all of this... this..." Junk. Clutter. Nonsense. "Memorabilia, but it's hardly a welcoming prospect."

The dead animals in particular just didn't...

"The purpose is to *impress*," Jeannie said. "To announce the might and history of the family to any who come within these walls. To inspire a traveler granted hospitality to pause for a moment and consider their host's stature and power. To make relations taking shelter at the family seat recall the might we have when we stand together."

"The power Bonnie Prince Henry is wielding right now is about knocking me off my feet."

Though Henry was apparently impressed by his mother's ferocious lecture, as was Max. He'd seen Jeannie Cromarty's personal fire as a cheerful glow, practical and gracious, if a bit buffeted by the winds of motherhood. The torch brandished in her words now had the power to singe, if not incinerate.

Jeannie laid the baby on a twelve-foot-long glass-fronted case that held more implements of murder and mayhem to go along with the collection on the walls. Max dug in the diaper bag and fished out wipes, a clean diaper, and a sealable plastic bag.

Also a stuffed bear with a lopsided grin.

Jeannie dealt with the dirty dipe, passing it tightly taped and rolled to Max, who sealed it up in the plastic bag along with the used wipes. Some things never changed. Jeannie faced at least two more years of this, which fact Max did not feel compelled to state out loud.

"Consider this," he said, tossing the bear in the air and catching it. "Corporations with diverse boards and diverse workplaces have been shown to be more profitable. Those are precisely the successful, well-informed organizations that I hope will be booking their management off-sites, yearly retreats, and even holiday parties here. As many women as men will be walking through that door, making those arrangements, and deciding where to bring the family next summer. Do you really think dead animals and weaponry will impress that demographic with our hospitality?"

Jeannie tucked Henry against her shoulder. "Those are precisely the women who ought to understand an impressive display of power and familial fortitude."

Max wasn't going to win this debate in one round, and a short, white-haired woman who bore a striking resemblance to Queen Elizabeth II stood smiling at the top of the steps.

"We'll finish this discussion later," Max said, hefting the diaper bag. "I understand that family history and a glorious past are part of the ambience unique to this property."

"And you'd sell the lot of it on the internet." Jeannie swept past him, trailing streams of affronted Scottish dignity. "Mrs. Hamilton, hello. How have you been?"

Jeannie had a gracious smile for the housekeeper, and much fussing and cooing over the baby ensued while Max took the phone back outside to place his call to Maura.

She didn't answer her cell, so Max phoned the cottage. The manager on duty told him Maura was in the shower, and he promised Max he'd have her call when she got out. Very likely, she was angry with Max, which the counselors had told him to expect. They'd also warned him that keeping to a set routine of phone calls and regular emails would require effort, but that Maura needed the structure and would adjust eventually.

Nobody had seemed concerned about Max making the same adjustment, but he would dearly, dearly liked to have heard Maura's voice, even if only to endure her grumbling. Once the phone calls and emails were going well, Max would add video chats, again on a fixed schedule.

After rejoining the ladies, he was led from one high-ceilinged, plaid-covered room to another. The hall was enormous, the basements equally vast, the attics blessedly empty on one side of the house, horrifically full on the other. Everywhere, Max was assaulted by wool and plaid, plaid and wool, and more history than he'd been exposed to in his entire upbringing.

And the housekeeper spoke with obvious affection about the

earl's collection of whisky. The whisky hoard was the pride of several generations of earls, and Elias Brodie had exempted the transfer of any rights to his whisky from Max's leasehold. The whisky could be displayed, but not consumed or sold, nor could it be removed from the premises without Elias's permission.

"The larder is full," Mrs. Hamilton said when Max had hiked the equivalent of the West Highland Way in stairs and corridors. "I made up both the earl's apartment and the blue guest room, because I wasn't sure if you preferred a view or proximity to the kitchen. I'll be back on Wednesday to tidy up, and you can leave a list on the fridge of any groceries you'd like me to order. Please do recall to wipe your feet when you come in, Mr. Maitland. My nephew Dinty is among your crew up at the castle, and I know construction can be very dirty work."

Verra *dairty wairk.*

She went on her way after giving Jeannie a hug and Henry a smile. Max felt as if he'd been given a warning.

"You never did eat your fish and chips," Jeannie said. "Shall I heat them up for you?"

To tour the house, Max had mustered false energy, keeping up with a woman old enough to be his granny, rather than admitting that jet lag was landing on him like a load of wet cement.

Or possibly, jet lag, low blood sugar, *and* a growing sense of having bitten off more than he could chew. *Again.*

"I want to sit and make a map of this place while ideas are fresh in my mind, but you don't have to cook for me. I'm a bachelor, and I know how to fend off starvation. I have some protein—"

Jeannie pushed past him. "Spare me your protein bars. Mrs. Hamilton would be mortified by such disrespect for her full larders."

Jeannie led the way to the kitchen, which Max might not have been able to find on his own. The Baron's Hall presented an impressive façade to the front drive, but the place felt to Max like two or three country houses connected by glassed-in walkways, galleries, and hidden stairways. The result was several enclosed courtyards, which would, of course, need serious landscaping before they'd become the charming semi-open green spaces the castle guests should adore.

The kitchen was a metaphor for what Max hoped the Hall would become—the past respectfully in evidence, the latest conveniences right at hand. Exposed beams, a brick hearth, bay windows at ground level, a porcelain sink full of house plants—herbs, perhaps?—and plaid towels, runners, and a hearth rug all pointed to the past.

The enormous, gleaming appliances faced toward the future, thank God, and the barstools at the end of the counter were blessedly padded—with plaid cushions, of course.

"Will you throw a pot of boiling water on me if I say some of the plaid has to go?"

Jeannie passed him Henry and opened the fridge. "Of course not. Wool is durable. As a result, virtually any article of tartan cloth to cross the threshold in the past two centuries is still on the premises. There's a lasagna in here. I hope you like pepperonis. Mrs. Hamilton made you a salad, and there's a sticky toffee pudding cooling on the range."

Henry was watching his mom, as was Max. Jeannie knew her way around this kitchen, had hauled the kid all over Hogwarts's plaid annex, and had been prepared to swing her verbal claymore at any Yank presuming to dishonor the family baubles.

Max said nothing as Jeannie excavated a backhoe-bucket-sized piece of lasagna from the dish, stole a pepperoni from the top, and set the lasagna on a plate. He should be doing that himself, he could be doing more than finger-wrestling Henry, he should be scaring up a pencil and sketch pad, he should—Instinct, or something close to it, dropped an insight into Max's tired, daunted mind. *I need Jeannie Cromarty.*

"Will you stay for the all-hands meeting on Monday?" Max asked.

She stared into the gleaming bowels of the fridge. "I'd rather not.

Your plans for this place and my notions about it will put us in conflict."

"Exactly. When I'm in conflict with you, you will get in my face, explain my error, set me straight, and not miss a beat. If I'd asked a crew of Fergus's laborers to pack up the entrance hall, they'd have done it, then punctured my tires some dark and stormy night."

Jeannie thunked a carton of half-skim milk onto the counter. "They'd alert Elias to your daft scheme and then invite you to play shinty. Don't accept. It's a glorified brawl followed by a drinking competition among the fallen. Where's the—?" She extracted a long, serrated knife from the butcher block knife holder on the counter and sliced off two hunks of what looked like homemade bread. Onto each, she troweled a wheelbarrow's worth of organic butter.

"You will educate me without drawing blood," Max said. "You will stop me before I've ripped out too much plaid, but agree that some of it needs to go."

She paused, knife in hand. "Is that a metaphor?"

"It's a fact. You can save me a lot of time and hassle, probably a lot of money too. This is why Elias wanted a family member's hand on the tiller."

"Elias wanted to be able to stick his nose into your business. He's good at that, and he always has the best intentions."

She bit off a corner of bread and got a smear of butter on her cheek.

Max wanted to lick it off, a troglodyte impulse he was too tired and hungry to keep trapped in his lizard brain.

"So you'll stay for the meeting?"

"I'll think about it. Henry's falling asleep."

Makes two of us. "I can eat with one hand." And had on many occasions. "Take a load off, Jeannie, and tell me what the guidelines are for renovating the Baron's Hall."

Because he did need her— or to be precise, his project did—and Max was determined that what his project needed, his project would get.

CHAPTER SIX

Jeannie Cromarty was more passionate than she looked.

Max's conclusion wasn't sexual, but rather, the result of several hours of arguing, discussing, brainstorming, wandering the Hall, poking around in the closets and corners, and passing Henry back and forth.

The baby was a solid little guy, which made Max happy in an entirely irrelevant way. No heart surgeries for Henry, no apnea monitors starting with the first night home from the hospital, no dreading every appointment with the pediatrician and endless rotation of specialists. A new parent shouldn't have to deal with those heartaches, much less a new single parent.

"Are you ready for some sticky toffee pudding?" Jeannie asked when she and Max had returned to the kitchen.

"I'm ready for bed." Max had showered and borrowed a pair of Elias Brodie's sweats, along with a worn T-shirt that felt like the greatest comfort known to weary man. "But the sun isn't cooperating."

"This is the gloaming." Jeannie turned the kettle on and removed a plaid towel from a square glass pan that looked like it held gingerbread. "This time of year, we don't get pitch dark most nights. We get a summer sky. If the moon's neither full nor new, the countess and her earl are sometimes seen walking the parapets."

Max gently extracted the salt shaker from Henry's fist, though not soon enough to protect Max's knees from being dusted. "Have you seen them?"

"I have not, but then, I'm only here for weddings, family gatherings, or lately, to collect paperwork from Fergus. Elias saw them fairly often as a boy and said they are the most cheerful, besotted ghosts in all of Scotland. He saw them again before he left for Maryland this spring and joked about the legend being a lot of nonsense."

This was normal for her, to talk of ghosts at the family castle.

Henry went after the pepper grinder next, which Max let him have. "What's the legend?"

She set a glass measuring cup of some dark syrup in the microwave. "If the earl and his countess walk under a reiver's moon, somebody's courtship is about to begin."

In two seconds flat, Henry figured out how to twist the pepper grinder and add to the mess. "That's the whole legend? No foretelling of deaths, misfortune, or calamity?"

"We get the ghosts we get, Mr. Maitland, though there are many family stories. Elias has a desk in his study upon which Auld Michael is said to have first kissed his Brenna when he came home from ten years of war. Earl Michael left a history of the Napoleonic Wars as seen by a Brit from the French side. He was a spy rather than a traitor, though nobody would use that term at the time to speak of a man with a title."

The microwave dinged, which distraction allowed Max to rescue the pepper grinder from Henry's grasp. An aroma of caramel heaven filled the kitchen as Jeannie cut two pieces of gingerbread and set them in the microwave next.

"Is there a marketing angle to having besotted ghosts?" Max asked.

She passed a glance over Henry, who was gumming Max's forearm. Not exactly gumming—Henry had a few teeth.

"Who knows?" Jeannie said. "Perhaps at Valentine's Day. Michael and Brenna had seven children. One doesn't accomplish that after a ten-year separation without a significant level of marital accord."

Max was tempted to pull out his phone and make a note: *Talk of the first earl's wedded bliss makes Jeannie sad.* "That stuff smells terrific."

"Whisky sauce, though most of the spirits have been cooked off." She set the warmed gingerbread on the counter and retrieved a tub of vanilla ice cream from the freezer. "I could eat sticky toffee pudding for three meals a day."

"Mrs. Hamilton made enough to last you at least until Tuesday."

The cold ice cream went over the warm gingerbread, and the hot whisky sauce went over the ice cream. Jeannie brought both servings to the bar end of the counter and pulled up a stool.

"Here," Max said, sliding the larger piece in front of Jeannie. "Motherhood has its privileges."

She looked pleased, surprised, and willing. "Thank you. For what we are about to receive, we are grateful."

Henry was content to munch on a teething cracker, while Max embarked on an experience of gustatory bliss.

"I want Mrs. Hamilton's recipe." The whisky was subtle, more an aroma than a flavor, while the sauce was sweet, the ice cream rich, and the pudding itself the perfect intermediary to blend the two. The textures melded while the temperatures contrasted, and ye gods... to enjoy this with a good single malt...

Max reached for his phone, though he'd left it in his room.

"Just eat the pudding, Mr. Maitland. I'll ask Mrs. Hamilton if she'll part with the recipe, though I suspect I know which one she uses. The whisky sauce is where most of the secrets are."

"First, ghosts, now secret sauce?"

She dipped her spoon into a swirl of melting ice cream and

whisky sauce. "Not *secret* secrets, just little cooking secrets. A dash of pepper, a hint of cinnamon, those sorts of secrets. God, I love this."

For the first time in more than a day, Jeannie Cromarty wasn't managing, explaining, cajoling Henry, cajoling Max, lecturing Max, reciting history, dealing with a baby's endless needs, or keeping either Max or Henry from starving. She was purely, happily in the moment, and again, Max realized...

She was a lovely woman. He'd liked her voice the first time he'd heard it, and now he liked how the rest of her went with that voice. Light, warm, sturdy. Not a pushover, which from Max was high praise. She'd badger Fergus for his progress reports and make it sound like teasing, but those reports would happen on time, nonetheless.

She'd badger Max too, and be the reason he avoided eighteen different disasters in the first week.

"You look sad," she said. "Is the homesickness catching up with you?"

He'd tried calling Maura again and left a message that he'd try tomorrow before dinner. Then he'd replied to her earlier email, attaching a picture of the view from the countess's solar. Lush green fields, a silver ribbon of river running down from high hills to the west... Damson Valley's geological older sister, though beautiful in much the same way.

"It's the time of day," Max said. "Darkness approaches, though as you say, it's the darkness of a summer night. When I'm far from home and facing a project that's still mostly a dream, this time of day—the transition from afternoon to evening—can leave me feeling..." *Melancholy* was the word, but Max refused to say it. "Reflective."

"The Germans probably have a word for it," Jeannie said, considering a spoonful of half-melted ice cream. "Time-of-aching-thoughtful-evening-heart or something. Whoever she is, I hope she waits for you, Mr. Maitland."

The comment punched an empty place in Max's heart. "I don't expect any woman to wait for me. Property development means travel, long hours, stress, work-site drama, and frequent moves." And only a very special woman would understand the role Maura played in Max's life.

"Your life sounds like that of an oil rigger," she said, tipping up her bowl to scrape the last of the sauce onto her spoon. "I agree—that's not a formula for a successful relationship. Somebody has eaten all of my pudding."

Max passed her the last of his. "Stuff is rocket fuel. I'll go into a hypoglycemic coma in forty-five minutes."

Henry began to fuss. If Max had to guess, he'd suspect another wet diaper. He used the worktable to effect the requisite change and began a slow circuit of the kitchen with Henry on his shoulder while Jeannie tidied up the dishes.

"You'll put him to sleep before he's had his bath," she said when she'd hung the towel over the oven handle.

"One night without a bath won't lead to a life of crime. Thank you for staying."

She gently peeled Henry from Max's arms. "Somebody has to defend the castle from your heathen notions."

Her smile was impish, and Max endured an odd impulse to kiss her. She'd kissed him—on the cheek—but he'd written that off as Scottish hospitality. This urge was different, personal to her, to somebody who'd take him to task for his own good, and to somebody who was turning her life inside out on behalf of a fatherless kid.

Dangerous ground. Mixing business with pleasure even for a casual encounter was invariably stupid. Jeannie was family to the castle's owner and thus firmly in the business column.

"Have you plans for tomorrow?" she asked.

"Catch up on emails and reports, sketch the floor plan of the castle, poke around up there when nobody else is on the premises. Site security is seriously deficient, the project needs a safety officer, and I need to figure out where sixty workers can assemble comfortably and eat lunch without leaving a mess when the castle doesn't have a dozen chairs to its name."

"Have the meeting in the ballroom here," Jeannie said. "We have the chairs, the washrooms, the tables. Won't be much bother to set up for a few dozen men."

The project needed her. "First-rate idea, which we'll discuss at greater length in the morning. Thank you again for sticking around."

"I'll wish you good night, then." She wafted from the kitchen with Henry cradled in her arms. Max had insisted she have the earl's apartment because it had a kitchenette and a second bed where Henry could be banked in with pillows.

Max's bedroom—the blue bedroom—was across the corridor from the earl's apartment and about four doors down. He poured himself a glass of water and made his way there, intent on firing up his laptop and drafting a job description for a safety officer.

He'd fallen asleep in the middle of that very task when the insistent ring of his phone—*Scotland the Brave*—woke him the hell up.

HENRY WAS SETTLING in for a Bad Night. He'd perfected that dark art before the age of three weeks. First, he collected catnaps all day long. Second, he pretended to crave sleep at bedtime with the endearing conviction of a tired baby. Third, he pretended to drop off so sweetly, drifting away to the land of baby dreams just long enough for Jeannie to dodge into the shower—door open, of course, one ear cocked at all times—tend to her evening routine, and curl up with a book.

When Henry was in top form, he'd time his first cries for the very moment when Jeannie was deciding that she ought not to read even one more scene. She'd reach to turn out the light, ready to sleep the sleep of the single mom, and Henry would whimper softly.

That whimper had been twenty minutes ago, and any hope that Henry would give up had been dashed when he'd shifted into full-fledged wailing.

He never "cried himself to sleep." Not after thirty minutes, not after forty-five, not after an hour, which was the limit of Jeannie's patience, particularly when her neighbors at the apartment took to pounding on the bedroom wall.

So helpful, that.

Mr. and Mrs. Abercrombie were an older couple, no children, but plenty to say on the matter of irresponsible young people and single mothers mooching off the dole. The Abercrombies might well call the authorities if Jeannie tested Millicent's "let him cry it out" theory once too often.

Instead, she resorted to the advice of her pediatrician, which was to offer a colicky baby a rotation of distractions—walking, singing, rocking, touring a different room, listening to music, going outside to admire the stars, trying a bottle, trying a snack, playing with Henry's stuffed Bear-Bear, then Bun-Bun, then Duck... At one point, Jeannie had taken to sitting on the washing machine with Henry while running a load, and for a few weeks, that approach had soothed him.

Nothing soothed him now.

"I haven't a washing machine," Jeannie said over Henry's cries. "Haven't your stroller or bouncy seat, haven't—"

A knock sounded on the door of the apartment.

"Jeannie?" Max Maitland, here to tell her that Henry was awake, no doubt.

"Coming." She opened the door. "He's not wet. He's just... fussy."

Max stood before her in nothing but sweats, the phone in his hand. "The luggage guy is about five miles away and wants to know how to get here."

Henry's screeching paused.

"Give me the phone," Jeannie said. "You take the limb of Satan." They managed-the exchange, and Jeannie went into the hallway, shoving Max into the apartment and closing the door.

Ye gods... Max Maitland without a shirt, sweats riding low on trim hips... Muscle and man, in lovely, tousled quantity. And his bare feet... Why did the sight of a man's bare feet have to be so personal?

Jeannie stared at the phone for a moment, trying to recall what she was to do with—ah, yes. Luggage. "Hello?"

The delivery guy had a strong Glaswegian accent and sounded affronted by life in general. Jeannie explained the landmarks twice, slowly, and then made her way to the front door to put on the porch light and wait for the delivery.

By the time two enormous suitcases had been set in the entrance hall and the delivery man had gone on his way, grumbling about the bloody bedamned coos, and the feckin' hour of the nicht, and the infernal country lanes, fifteen minutes had passed. Jeannie returned to the earl's apartment and paused outside the door, fortifying herself against another encounter with Max Maitland half dressed.

He was gloriously fit and had clearly spent time shirtless under a summer sun. He had the perfect dusting of dark chest hair that arrowed down a flat stomach to disappear south of where Jeannie should never have been looking. She'd recognized that he was good-looking, in a distracted, where-did-I-put-Henry's-Bun-Bun? sense.

But Max Maitland was also *attractive*. He'd given her the larger piece of sticky toffee pudding. He'd twice changed Henry's diaper without being asked. He'd asked for her help.

Nobody asked Jeannie for her help anymore, though Henry made ceaseless demands on her.

She opened the door and beheld Max Maitland stretched out on the sofa—a sofa long enough to accommodate even him—with Henry on his bare chest.

"Little bugger wore himself out. I've been taken hostage by the Lilliputians, and I don't dare move."

Jeannie couldn't move either, felled by a sense of... dread? Tenderness? Amusement? The tiny boy was indeed fast asleep, his cheeks working on an invisible thumb, his sighs fanning over an adult male chest slabbed with muscle and probably the perfect tempera-ture to soothe a fussy baby. Then too, Henry would be listening to the steady heartbeat of an adult who held him protectively, and what more could a child want than such palpable reassurance that all was well?

Max's eyes held that hopeful, anxious look shared by caretakers of upset babies the world over.

"Your luggage is here. I'll help you carry it up in the morning. You can't sleep with Henry on your chest. It isn't safe."

Max cradled Henry's head against a large palm. "Why do I feel as if it isn't safe to move?"

His smile was self-conscious but happy, and Jeannie's heart ached. "Let him drift for a while longer, then I might be able to sneak him into his bed." She passed Max Henry's favorite blanket, the one edged in satin binding that Henry liked to scratch as he fell asleep. Max wrapped the blanket around the baby and rubbed Henry's back in a slow, soothing rhythm.

"How old is he?"

"Ten months. He tried to creep the other day. Pulled himself up on the edge of a coffee table and looked more pleased with himself than if he'd climbed K2. He got a couple of sidewise steps in before he went down on his butt, but he'll be back at it."

"Be glad he's on track," Mr. Maitland said. "Nothing is more heartbreaking than a baby in precarious health." He kissed the top of Henry's head.

Was a great grief behind Mr. Maitland's peripatetic, rootless life-style? Had he learned his competence with a baby at the cost of some private sorrow?

"You know what the milestones are," Jeannie said. "I didn't. I had to learn them from a book and from new-mommy websites. I haven't any younger siblings, never did much babysitting when I was growing up. Babies are... a new challenge for me."

"Babies are a challenge for everybody," Max said. "That's good. I think this baby is down for the count."

"Another five minutes," Jeannie said, sinking into a wing chair. "He's fooled me before."

"I gather his father fooled you too."

Jeannie considered the question, propping her feet on a hassock. "I simply lack good judgment where men are concerned, and every few years I seem to need a reminder of that. Harry caught me at the end of a long drought, and though I'd met his like once or twice at uni, I'd forgotten what a public menace a charming man can be."

Henry kicked at the blanket. Max tucked it back up around the baby's shoulders. "We all make wrong turns, Jeannie Cromarty."

"Even you?"

"I thought I'd found the one. Shayla was smart, ambitious, charming, told me I was the bee's knees, and liked the development business. But she and I did not see eye to eye when it came to some significant issues, and when she had an opportunity to take on a major project on the Canadian plains, we could not find a way to resolve those issues."

Jeannie tried looking at Max's feet to distract her from the picture he made cradling the baby to his chest, but even his feet interested her—big, high arches, second toe longer than the first, a scar on his left ankle... What had he been saying?

"She expected you to leave your responsibilities so she could pursue her ambitions?"

Max sent Jeannie a disgruntled look. "I want you to resume the job you were doing for Elias, being the project administrator. You connect dots and prevent disaster, and that is the position description in a nutshell."

He was offering her a job? Just like that? "We don't all get what we want, Mr. Maitland, though I think it's safe now to try putting the wee demon to bed."

Sitting in the dim living room spinning fancies about a half-naked Max Maitland was not safe. He'd be gone from Scotland as soon as the castle was open for business, if not long before. Harry had been the restless sort, always ready to drop one dream to chase another, larger dream. That was not the sort of role model for a tiny boy, no sort of partner to throw in with.

Maybe for a fling... but no. Harry had started off as a fling. Every romantic disaster in Jeannie's life had started off with a maybe.

She rose and crossed the rug, intent on scooping Henry off Max's chest. That maneuver necessitated bending over the man lying on the sofa, insinuating her hands between his naked chest and the sleeping baby, and trying to ignore all the heat, longing, and curiosity that intimate contact inspired.

Henry's blanket was wedged between Max's hip and the sofa back, so Jeannie had to pause, holding the baby a few inches from the man, while Max lifted his hips and freed the blanket.

Jeannie wasn't embarrassed by this intimacy, she was frustrated. Why did her body have to choose now to recall a life outside motherhood? Why did her heart have to select Max Maitland as a reminder that the world was full of good men, and some of them were even good-looking too?

He remained on his back, entirely unself-conscious. "Good night, Jeannie. See you in the morning, and thanks again for staying."

Do not look at Max Maitland's mouth, or his chest, or his shoulders, or—most especially—his hands.

She eased Henry to her shoulder, and thank the angelic choirs, he was truly, absolutely asleep. Jeannie let a thought form: *I could tuck Henry in and share a cup of hot chocolate with an adult male, let matters progress as they will, and indulge in a little harmless pleasure.*

Stupid, pointless thought. "After we get you introduced on Monday, I'll return to Perth, though you can always call me if you need anything."

"Thanks, from the bottom of my jet-lagged heart." He rose from the sofa in one lithe move and prowled for the door, closing it behind him with a soft click.

Max Maitland thanked Jeannie frequently, and his expressions of gratitude were more than platitudes tossed off between family members. Jeannie liked him, she respected him, she was attracted to him...

And just as she'd said, she'd leave him to his castle and return to Perth by sunset on Monday.

~

"HERE'S THE THING," Pete Sutherland said. "My wife is Scottish —my current wife. I know that terrain, and you do too."

Marty Ebersole's rhythm remained steady as he sawed at his steak. "Played the Old Course at St. Andrews many times, so has Dwayne. I suspect Frank and Hal and most of the guys have too. Owning a property an hour away will come in handy."

The point of the discussion was not where to conveniently park a damned golf cart. "Right, you know the neighborhood, while Max Maitland is a jumped-up lawyer who managed to snag a Professional Engineer's license when he should have been doing wills and divorces. What does he know about Scotland, and why should he literally hold the keys to the castle?"

Marty was the primary investor in Brodie Castle—he liked hotels and condos—while Pete preferred residential developments. Each had its risks and rewards. When Max Maitland had pitched his Brodie Castle project, Marty had left off banging his bimbo long enough to take an interest.

"Max closed the deal," Marty said. "He found the deal, he researched Elias Brodie with a high-resolution proctoscope, and he convinced Brodie to part with a thousand-year-old castle. Max knew what to say and when to say it. I'm not in favor of switching horses early in the race, and Max has only just arrived in Scotland."

Pete took a bite of Fourchu lobster supposedly flown in from Cape Breton Island that morning—gotta love New York restaurants.

"So we give him a few weeks to put his signature organizational stamp on the project, then send him an assistant. When she has the lay of the land, we buy Max out and promote the assistant at a savings to us."

Marty chewed, knife and fork held in each hand. "You're up to something. Maitland negotiated a hefty buyout, which we signed because we know he never walks on a project. Now you want to boot him before he's unpacked his skivvies. What are you up to, Pete?"

This was the problem with co-investors. Pete chose people he had enough in common with that he could trust them and communicate with them. Those same people tended to be a little too presuming, a little too familiar when a guy needed room to maneuver.

"I'm not up to anything," Pete said. "I'm developing options. You would never have heard of the Brodie deal without me."

Marty sawed off another bite of beef. "You would never have heard of the Brodie deal without Max, and you would never have closed the deal without me. Pass the salt."

Pete passed the salt after he'd sprinkled some on his lobster. "And as usual, this deal will make you a nice pot of money, the same as all our deals do."

"Not Poplar Cove, Petey-boy. You doubted Maitland's handling of the locals, went up to the town meeting, and got your ass handed to you by none other than Elias Brodie's current wife—or maybe she's his duchess? I know squat about medieval titles. In any case, the last time you doubted Maitland, we all lost money. Leave him alone to do his job. If and when he screws up, then you'll have a reason to put your current fling in charge, though she'd better know what the hell she's doing. The Scots do not mess around."

And that was the problem. Mrs. Sutherland—the fourth and present Mrs. Sutherland—had been made some promises on the occasion of her marriage to Pete. Those promises had included at least six months of the year spent in her homeland, stepping and fetching for her aging parents. Pete had liked the concept in theory—a woman loyal to her parents wouldn't abandon a husband who was no longer young—but the practice had eluded him.

Scotland was cold, the people talked funny, and whisky wasn't Pete's drink of choice. If he had to move to Scotland, he'd at least take a few comforts with him, and one of his current comforts was Shayla Walters. Oddly enough, Pete had met Shayla through Max

Maitland, who might have at one time had something casual with Shayla.

Shayla was a woman who knew how to catch the bigger fish, and Pete had no intention of wiggling off her line.

Why did life have to be so complicated?

"All I'm asking you to do is think about hiring an assistant project manager for Maitland," Pete said. "He's the lone American on the job site, our only eyes and ears there, and he's the new kid on the Scottish block. He's the first one to champion redundant systems, backups, and safeguards for corporate memory. A number two on a project this complex only makes sense."

Marty crossed his knife and fork over a mostly empty plate. He was aging well and gave off an enviable sense of energy. Working out compulsively to hang on to fading youth was a phase. He'd get through it and soon realize the ladies didn't mind a little paunch or thinning hair as long as a guy could still show 'em a good time.

"I agree that a number two makes sense, but that is Maitland's call. As project manager, he has final say on hiring and firing, because undermining his authority would be stupid. We're not engineers, and you're not a lawyer. We're the money guys."

Marty was a lawyer. Had a degree from George Washington University's National Law Center, summa cum laude, and all but whacking Pete over the head with his bar association creds was a game with him.

"And the money guys, as we all know, have the final say regardless of what's in the contract. How was the steak?"

Pete changed the subject to trivialities because the conversation had advanced his objectives. He'd have dinner with Dwayne at the end of the week and tell him that Marty had mentioned the lack of a number two on the Brodie Castle project, and did Dwayne have anybody in mind?

Dwayne seldom had more in mind than his next eighteen holes, leaving Pete free to "come up with a few names." He'd mention that Shayla Walters was rumored to be finishing up her projects in

Canada and would be an excellent second-in-command. She had worked with Maitland before and was willing to travel for the sake of professional advancement...

Then would come lunch with Joe and Arnie, and soon, Shayla would be on her way to Scotland, so that when Pete capitulated to the missus's grumbling, all the comforts of home would already be waiting for him in rural Aberdeenshire.

It didn't take an engineer with a law degree to solve the important problems, just a smart guy with some means and motivation.

CHAPTER SEVEN

The Hall's ballroom was an interesting space. A minstrel's gallery had been built along the longest interior wall, so musicians could be on hand without being underfoot. The eastern end of the vast room had been raised slightly, making it an ideal space for the kind of meeting Max hoped to start in about ten minutes. The washroom facilities nearest the ballroom were spacious if quaint. A terrace flanked the outside wall, opening to a lovely view of the valley, with the church steeple peeking above trees and fields in the distance.

The place had enormous potential and endless problems.

"I am getting rid of those damned antlers," Max said, referring to the tiered display of antlers arranged on the wall opposite the stage.

Jeannie passed him a plate laden with a thick roast beef sandwich, sliced veggies and dip, and chips. "You can sell them, I'm sure, but you should save a few for the lodge."

The property had a hunting lodge on some little lake—loch, rather—a few miles up the valley. "Can you take me out there after the meeting?"

Max hadn't pushed the idea that Jeannie should sign on as the project administrator, mostly because the timing wasn't right. Henry had apparently kept her up half the night for two nights in a row—possibly for ten months in a row—Millicent had left a couple of messages that Jeannie hadn't been pleased to listen to, and Uncle Donald wasn't answering Max's emails or Jeannie's phone calls.

In the bright light of day, Max was backpedaling from the idea of hiring Jeannie.

He liked her forthright nature, liked how she jollied Henry through the day, liked that she kept her smarts and her fire mostly out of sight, then came out, both barrels blazing, at the times of her choosing.

But Saturday night, he'd felt her hands sliding across his bare chest. He'd stoutly ignored the compulsion to touch his fingers to her lips when she'd hung over him to scoop up Henry. Then he'd scampered out of her apartment and stood in the chilly hallway for a long five minutes, arguing his idiot male parts into submission. He'd walked back to his bedroom rather than make an excuse to turn around and say something stupid to a woman who wanted only a good night's sleep.

The journey down the hall to his own bed had been long and lonely, and that was why hiring Jeannie was a dangerous idea.

Max was lonely. He'd been aware of the empty feeling inside for a few years, ever since Shayla had dumped him for the oil fields of Edmonton, but as long as he'd had Maura to focus on, and could see for himself that she thrived, the loneliness had been subdued by busyness and job stress. Nothing and nobody could come between Max and the security he was determined to provide his sister.

Jeannie was lonely too, Max was almost sure of it, the special kind of lonely that came around when a woman had no privacy from her offspring and no intimacy beyond maternal demands.

Work sites became microcultures, developing dialects, taboos, rituals, and relationships all their own. A single mom and a project manager who liked each other, who shared quarters—albeit in a hall with 127 rooms—and who worked in the same pressure cooker of a project office could too easily become entangled.

Max had no room in his future for entanglement.

"How's your sandwich?" Jeannie asked.

Henry was in a makeshift playpen of pillows in a corner of the stage. He'd been entertained by the racket of setting up chairs and a buffet table, but Max wondered if the floor wasn't drafty.

"The sandwich is terrific."

"Brodie beef," Jeannie said, taking the ponytail holder from her hair. She shook her head, sending blond locks cascading about her shoulders. The movement was unconsciously feminine, as was the competence in her hands when she gathered up her hair and refastened the band around it.

"Get yourself a plate while Henry is distracted," Max said. "Fergus and his merry band will soon be here, and there won't be a sandwich left."

Fern Logan was going down the table, counting off items against a list. Jeannie took up a paper plate and moved toward the veggie dips, while Fern approached Max with her list.

"All present and accounted for. I set aside some extra and put it in the kitchen. You're going to leave Henry up on the stage, lord of all he drools upon?"

Max finished crunching a stalk of celery, though he'd save the last piece of carrot to distract Henry with in case the kid started fussing.

"Henry's happy in his blanket and pillow fort. If Henry's happy, Jeannie's happy."

"And that," Fern said, "makes you happy. Break Jeannie's heart and I'll poison your sticky toffee pudding, Mr. Maitland." She was smiling, beaming at him, in fact.

"What if she breaks my heart?"

Fern patted his arm. "You're on your own, Yank. I'll be down in the kitchen until you're ready for seconds, though please make the lads dump their trash. Tell 'em Fern said so, or nobody gets any complimentary pints until Christmas."

"Yes, ma'am."

She disappeared through the doors that led to the kitchen, and

Fergus sidled up to Max. "Scotland is run by fierce women. They feed their menfolk into submission, and we're docile as lambs." He was chomping on a brownie, and the look on his face suggested Fern's sweets had him thoroughly conquered.

"So how do you subdue the ladies?" Max asked.

"We don't. We love 'em as they are." Fergus took his plate and sat on the lip of the stage as men in steel-toed boots, work kilts, jeans, and work belts filed into the ballroom. The noise level rose accordingly because the ballroom was a temple to hard surfaces.

When everybody had a plate, Max took the place beside Fergus. "You about ready to call this meeting to order?"

"Are there any desserts left?"

Max took a gander at the previously full table. "Not many."

"Then we'd best be about it." Fergus stood and passed Max his plate.

"Listen up, lads, the Yank wants to say something." He sat back down. "Your meetin's called to order. If you don't want those chips, I'll be happy to see that they don't go to waste."

Max handed Fergus the plate, but before he could get to his feet, Jeannie had taken the steps to the stage.

"Ladies and gentlemen—and you too, Dinty—if you'd take your seats please and put your phasers on stun, I'd appreciate it." Dinty, a skinny guy with flaming-red hair, saluted Jeannie with a pickle. "A couple of announcements first." She paused while chairs scraped, cell phones were set to mute, and the room quieted.

"Thank you. I'll be brief, because I know you are ready to brawl over the last few bites of Fern's shortbread. If you get blood on this ballroom floor, Lady Brenna will curse you with ingrown toenails and you won't be able to dance at Friday's ceilidh. First order of business is thanks to Fern for coming up with the spread on short notice. Bin your trash, or you'll answer to her. Second order of business is that some of you have doubtless fallen behind on submitting time sheets. Catch yourself up quick, or no paycheck."

She sent Max a smile. "I'm allowed to say that, aren't I, Mr. Maitland?"

Fergus answered around a mouthful of chips. "You're a cruel woman, Jeannie Cromarty. See what we've put up with, Maitland?"

Jeannie blew Fergus a kiss. "Love you too, Fergus."

Catcalls and hoots followed, while Max tried to figure out what, exactly, Jeannie was doing—besides charming sixty people at once—and how she was doing it. This was how a project meeting should be done—part pep rally, part briefing, part family reunion.

"The second announcement is that the man who conceived the Brodie Castle renovation project and convinced Elias Brodie to commit to it has arrived in our midst. Max Maitland is prepared to take up the thankless job of making sure you lot transform our favorite pile of rock into an international hospitality venue we can all be proud of. Give a warm welcome to Mr. Maitland, friends, or I'll toss you all from the parapets."

She led the applause, which qualified as polite—barely—and Max took the podium.

"Thank you," Max said, though what he saw on the faces before him was not gracious welcome, but rather, thinly veiled skepticism. "Fern will bring up more desserts when I'm finished speaking, and I promise I'll only take up about ten minutes of your time—for now."

This merited a few cheers from the back.

"I'm both an attorney and an engineer, which ought to give almost everybody in the room reason to distrust me." That wasn't a joke, but somebody laughed. "I know that, and so I make it a point to prioritize honesty. You don't like me, that's fine, but say so to my face rather than spreading rumors in the break room. We're setting up a break room, by the way. If I have a problem with your work, you'll hear about it from me. You'll have a chance to speak on your own behalf and correct mistakes. I'll make mistakes, I'm sure, and I expect you to call me on them.

"I'm not skilled in any of the trades, so I will rely on you, who are very skilled, to keep this project moving forward. My job is to prevent trouble, solve problems, and keep us on schedule and within budget. Mostly, I keep the money guys from interfering with the people who actually do the work. Give me the information I need to do my job, and you'll have work on this site for a long, lucrative time."

Henry, who'd been watching the proceedings from his pillow fort, tried to climb over a couch bolster pressed into service as an infant bumper. Jeannie was busy downing her sandwich while Fergus whispered in her ear.

"Any questions?" Max asked as Henry made another attempt to scale the pillows.

"Any chance the money guys will be underfoot any time soon?" somebody asked. "Don't fancy a lot of suits telling me how to do m' job."

"Neither do I," Max said, "which is why we'll implement site safety protocols, effective today. Nobody except project employees gets into the castle without an escort and hard hat provided by the project office, and certain areas will be declared off-limits to visitors in the interests of minimizing our liability for injuries. Say the word liability to the money guys, and they get real cooperative real fast. If they do visit, they'll snoop around according to our rules when they're on our turf. Next question?"

Henry was determined to escape and had his front end up on the bolster, while his legs pushed and churned in an effort to gain him the purchase he needed to clear the obstacle. One more good shove, and he'd...

Go right over the round bolster and do a face-plant on the cold, hard stage floor, his legs hung up on the bolster and kicking madly.

The little guy started whimpering, then howling, and before Jeannie could set down her plate, Max scooped Henry up.

"I think you all know Henry. Next question?"

Henry knew how to work a room. He grinned at the audience, waved at Jeannie, and grabbed for Max's nose.

"Is wee Henry on the payroll, then?" somebody asked.

Another voice answered from the back, "Wee Henry could swing a hammer better than you do, MacTaggert."

A third voice joined in. "My auld grannie could swing a hammer better than MacTaggert does. He's more interested in swingin' his wee, shriveled—"

"No bad language in front of the boy," Max said, "by order of his mom."

Jeannie waved. Nobody commented.

"Any more questions?"

Fergus spoke up. "When's Fern coming back with seconds?"

Fern called from the doorway, "I'm waiting for you lot to leave off setting a bad example for the youth of Scotland."

Max shifted Henry to his hip. "Then I'll conclude my remarks with thanks for all your hard work and a standing invitation to discuss any issue at any time."

As a polite stampede in the direction of the buffet commenced, Jeannie took Henry from Max. "That went well. They like you."

"They like Henry, and they love their chow."

"Saving a castle is hard work, I'm told. You really will need to ride Fergus for timely paperwork. He's a good supervisor, knows the job inside out, and gets on well with the crews, but documentation is his least-favorite duty."

"Then Fergus and I will have to come to an understanding, because documentation is how the investors know their money is being spent responsibly. Did you get to finish your sandwich?"

"I did," Jeannie said. "Shall I run you out to the hunting lodge? It's very pretty. Queen Victoria and Prince Albert borrowed it more than once when they wanted a respite from construction at Balmoral."

Max led Jeannie out onto the terrace, which overlooked the front drive. Her little Audi sat at the foot of the steps. Max had stashed the diaper bag in the back seat after breakfast, his emotions a blend of relief that Jeannie hadn't mentioned his job offer again and regret that she was heading back to Perth.

"Will a royal couple trysting at the hunting lodge help sell honey-moon bookings?" Max asked.

"I can't imagine anything more effective for marketing to newly-weds. Victoria and Albert are well regarded in Deeside, and they did have nine children."

Ye gods. "Can you imagine eight more just like Henry?"

Jeannie straightened from buckling Henry into his car seat. "One of their children was a hemophiliac. He lived to be thirty and had a child, but still... to be taken so young, despite all his parents' efforts to protect him... I cannot fathom how Victoria coped or how deeply she grieved for him."

Jeannie's words were a bucket of cold water dumped over Max's silly quibbling over a nascent attraction. Sure, he'd like to get to know Jeannie better, and for certain, he and Jeannie could have a great time in the sack.

But that wasn't meant to be.

Max knew all too well how low genetic cards could give some-body a bad hand in the longevity sweepstakes. Family and loved ones might do everything possible to argue with fate, all to no avail. He kept those thoughts to himself and let Jeannie navigate the track to the hunting lodge in silence.

ONE OF MAX MAITLAND'S many fine qualities was that he didn't chatter, but this silence was different. Something about the meeting had started him brooding, staring out the window at the woods going past, while worrying some problem Jeannie could only guess at. The day was lovely, the river a sparkling ribbon beneath a brilliant blue summer sky.

"The river's low this time of year," Jeannie said, "but don't trust it. If there's a cloudburst in the hills to the north, the level can rise at a dangerous rate."

"Flash flooding," he said. "Like when the bank, the occupational safety inspector, the environmental protection task force, and the attorneys all show up unannounced on a Friday morning. The site's usually a mess, everybody's tired, and nobody wants to stand around making small talk with a passel of greedy fools."

He occasionally sounded cynical, but that comment had been bitter. "Are you having second thoughts about the project?"

"No. I'll turn that pile of rock into a conference destination. I'll bring the job in on time and within budget and then turn it over to the management crew and collect my percentage of the first five years' proceeds. I gave my word, and I do not go back on a promise."

He wanted to. His litany hinted of doubts, regrets, unspoken wishes.

Jeannie turned down the track that led to the lodge. "Do you like your job?"

Henry was awake, thank heavens, and fascinated with the flicker of sunlight through the trees.

"I like ensuring a job goes smoothly, but development is a jealous mistress. The business pays well, and that's why I persist with it. I can make much more turning straw into gold for a lot of rich guys than I can hanging out a lawyer's shingle in a small town or slaving away as a project engineer."

"That's too bad." Though how odd to think she could pity Maxwell Maitland. "I honestly enjoy managing the cottage. I like contributing to a holiday or a honeymoon. I like making people feel welcome and appreciated."

Max rubbed a hand across his forehead. "Is any of this lumber ever harvested?"

"Over on Skye there's some forestry, but the deerstalkers have the prior claim here."

The road ran along the shore of a crystal-blue lochan. The water would be cold as hell, also clear as heaven. Jeannie hadn't been this way for ages, though the memories here were good.

"As teenagers, the cousins would assemble at the lodge in summer, have bonfires and all-night card games while nipping whisky and feeling wickedly sophisticated. Winter was for skating parties and ice hockey."

"You have family. You have good association with that family."

Didn't everybody have family? "I'm not too fond of Uncle Donald right now—he's bound for Germany to do some fishing—and several of the cousins weren't very pleased with Elias's decision to develop the castle."

Max left off studying the landscape. "You talked them around."

"I'm the first among my generation to have a child, much to my surprise. If Henry had ended up with that castle hung around his neck, I'd want him to be free to do with it as he pleases. It's a fine old place, but if we refuse to let it evolve as the present earl sees fit, we pass a worse problem on to our children."

"A commendable perspective. The project wasn't my idea, by the way. Elias Brodie pitched it to me when what I wanted was to buy his farm out from under him."

Jeannie had known that. "A bit of embellishing for the sake of your reception made sense to me. I suppose you'll want to return to Maryland when the project is done?"

She'd managed a casual tone, but her stupid, lonely heart was interested in the answer. Maybe now wasn't the time to fancy Maxwell Maitland, but Henry wouldn't be an infant forever, and a lot could happen in the months and years it would take to get the castle up and running.

"What family I have is in Maryland."

And that seemed to decide the matter for him. Well... crap.

The lodge came into view a few minutes later, a two-story stone structure with a wood and glass A-frame addition on the lakeside.

"Zebedee, the previous earl, added the A-frame during his last flush period, about twenty years ago," Jeannie said, putting the car in park. "I think old and new blended well here, and the trout fishing is outstanding."

"Isn't salmon fishing more prestigious?"

"More lucrative, you mean? Do you think only of money?"

She knew he did not. He thought of Henry's wet diaper, Fern's good opinion of him, the safety and well-being of the crews on the site, and apparently of his family in Maryland.

"I have to think of money, Jeannie. I have to think of it seriously and often." He retrieved the diaper bag. Jeannie freed Henry from his car seat and led the way to the front door by way of stone steps that rose to a spacious covered porch.

"The benches need a good sweeping," Jeannie said. "The place also wants flowers, of course. Pansies, because the shade is fairly deep on this side of the house. Petunias and geraniums would do well on the lakeside."

"Is the code the same as for the lodge?"

"Aye." She rotated the tumblers in the lockbox and passed Max the key.

He opened the door and stepped back, allowing Jeannie to precede him into the front hallway. The lodge made a lovely first impression, with a stairway rising on a curve to the right and a high-ceilinged great room opening straight ahead. The back deck and the loch were visible through two-story picture windows, and a stone fireplace occupied the corner beneath the stairway.

"I see heating bills," Max muttered. "Great big, expensive heating bills."

"You've solar panels on the lakeside of the roof," Jeannie said. "Elias modernized to at least that extent. The woodstove in the dining room sends out a terrific amount of heat."

Jeannie expected Max to get out his phone and make a note, but he wandered to the fireplace and ran a hand over the rocks.

"Native stone and handsomely done," he said. "Somebody cared for craftsmanship."

Jeannie let him meander from room to room, until they'd made their way from a gleaming kitchen to the spacious deck, past various comfy bedrooms to the master suite.

The balcony looked out on the lake. The bathroom sported stained-glass windows and a claw-foot monstrosity of a tub. Jeannie set Henry in the tub along with Bear-Bear and some soft-textured ducks that rattled and chimed when moved.

"He's dry?" Max asked.

"He is dry. What do you think of the place?"

He gazed up at the exposed-beam ceiling, then out at the lake shimmering azure in a bowl of high green hills.

"This is my dream home," he said. "Plenty of room to work, domesticate, socialize, and rest. Great workmanship, smart design, excellent location, and first-rate build-out and finish. It's a house that can accommodate multiple generations without losing the sense of being a home rather than an expensive dormitory. I'm impressed."

"You're also sad." Happy baby sounds came from the bathroom, which only made Jeannie more certain of her conclusion.

Max took Jeannie's hand, his grip warm. "May I kiss you?"

Of all the—? Jeannie would drop him off in the village and then head back to Perth. She might not see him again until the ribbon-cutting ceremony months from now. She might never see him again.

So why not enjoy a kiss?

"Yes, you may kiss me." She slid her arms around his neck. He settled his hands on her waist. The fit was lovely, the mood too sad for a pair of people indulging in a very small, ill-advised pleasure.

"Now would be good," Jeannie said. "Henry is a fiend for interrupting at all the worst times."

Max smiled, then brushed his lips over Jeannie's mouth. She at first thought that was to be the extent of the festivities—a mere tease —but then he drew her closer and did it again.

He stole into the kiss by inches and degrees, letting Jeannie get used to the intimate feel of him. Then came his taste—slightly sweet and cinnamon around the edges from Fern's shortbread. He was a patient kisser, giving Jeannie time to relax and run her hands over his chest and shoulders, then sink her fingers into his hair.

She pushed the diaper bag to the floor and got a knee between his legs, twining herself into his embrace and into the kiss.

All hell broke loose inside her as longing, glee, desire, and joy welled. *I am not dead to all pleasure. I am not simply an exhausted single mum with money woes and a compulsive reading habit.*

Max was growing aroused, which made Jeannie want to haul him to the bed on a trail of discarded clothing and abandoned reservations.

"This has to stop." He cradled the back of her head, pressing her cheek to his shoulder. "We can't. I didn't mean for this to become that sort of kiss, but I'm not sorry it did."

If there was one rule Jeannie would drill into Henry's head when he approached adolescence, it was that no meant no. Boundaries were for respecting, not heedlessly ignoring.

"We have to stop?" she asked.

"I don't want to, but... yes. We have to stop."

Still, she remained in his embrace. "Why? I'm not employed on the project, we're consenting adults, I like you, and I believe you like me."

She sounded like a very young woman, one who needn't think beyond a moment's pleasure, when that wasn't who she was. Not anymore.

"I like and respect you tremendously, which is why..." He stepped back and took her hand, leading her not to the bed, but to the sofa that looked out on the lake. "I have family." He reached into his back pocket, and if he produced his phone, Jeannie would open the sliding doors and pitch it into the water.

He got out a worn leather billfold and opened it. "That's Maura. She's my sister, my only living family. Dad died of a heart attack at fifty-one. Mom died of ovarian cancer two years later."

Maura was a sweet-faced brunette with a sunny smile. She looked out on the world with an innocent joy that Jeannie associated with young children, though clearly, she was well into adolescence, if not early adulthood.

Max put his wallet away. "Maura has mosaic Down syndrome. Took some time to figure that out because we didn't have the money for a lot of fancy testing. Maura is smart, but vulnerable, and I'm all she has."

Jeannie put an arm around his shoulders, for in a few words, he'd sketched a reality as inescapable and compelling as being a single parent—or more so, because nobody grew out of Down syndrome.

"Tell me about her."

Max rose, and Jeannie let him go. "She's stubborn, good God, is she stubborn, but she's also compassionate, tenacious, determined... She can look after herself to some extent. Hygiene, laundry, microwaving—she has all of that knocked, but she has no sense of what shirt will go with what skirt, and she can be easily distracted. She really has to watch what she eats, which frustrates her, and she has health problems."

The words came out all in a rush, followed by a self-conscious silence.

"She sounds very high-functioning." And very much beloved by her brother.

"Mosaic Down is unpredictable. Maura doesn't have the classic Down features at first glance, but she got some of the cardiac issues, the thyroid problems, mildly delayed speech and language, and she's not exactly graceful."

Jeannie rose and took the place beside Max at the sliding glass doors. "You love her." This explained how Max knew his way around a diaper bag, why he never entirely lost awareness of Henry, why Henry instinctively trusted him.

"I took one look at her in that hospital incubator—she was so tiny and so fierce—and I promised her she'd never have a reason to doubt me. I was thirteen, and I've kept every promise I've made to her."

Jeannie rested her head on Max's shoulder and put an arm around his waist. "You promised her you'd come home from Scotland."

"Every three weeks, I'll pop back to Maryland, if it kills me. I will finish the project on time, if it kills me, and I will return to Maryland, if it kills me."

His father had died at fifty-one. His mother might not have made it even that far. "The money is about Maura, isn't it? Your government won't provide for her if anything happens to you."

"Eventually, adult protective services might get involved, but Maura's IQ is substantially higher than a typical Down IQ, even though it's still too low for her to be in any way self-supporting. She can read and write, slowly, and she has jobs at the facility where she lives. This time of year, she's in their gardens and greenhouse most of the day, but she can also answer phones, and run copier or scanner because somebody took the time to show her—over and over—how they work. That work history also counts against her if she ever needs to qualify for disability."

"That is stupid."

"I've used much worse language to describe the disability support system back home."

Henry's rattling and tinkling went on unabated, though much had changed in Jeannie's view of Max Maitland. "You are concerned that you'll die as young as your parents did, and Maura will be left with nothing and nobody."

"I look after myself, but you can't argue with your genes. Mom and Dad both smoked, they became parents later in life, and they neither exercised nor watched what they ate. Then Maura came along, and life was one operation after another, one specialist after another, one crisis after another. Down syndrome can mean the immune system under-functions, and Maura caught every cold and virus going around and as often as not turned it into pneumonia."

A wet diaper would be nothing to a guy who'd gone through that with a baby sister. A crumbling castle would simply be business as usual to him.

And a relationship of any significance would be asking too much of him.

"Why are you telling me this?" Jeannie asked, because she was stubborn too.

Max wrapped his arms around her and kissed her forehead.

"Because you are somebody special, and you tempt me. I hope I tempt you too, but I'm not the guy who can step in as Henry's male role model, not the guy who can take you to Majorca for a two-week holiday, even. I'm the guy who will get all the inconvenient phone calls from Maura's cottage staff, the guy who will spend every spare minute flying back and forth to Maryland to see his sister, the guy who will leave Scotland for good when Brodie Castle opens its doors."

He was being honest, unlike Harry, and yet, Jeannie didn't like this honesty any better than she'd liked Harry's charming duplicity. "And are you the guy who provides for his sister's every need?"

Max stepped back. "Nobody else is going to do that, and if I drop dead of a heart attack, or Fergus drops a load of concrete on me by accident, then I'm the guy who has been slowly building up Maura's special-needs trust fund, so she'll lack for nothing even if I'm not around to look after her."

Jeannie sank to the bed, a king-sized expanse of fluffy comforters, soft pillows, and crisp sheets. She'd never dive under these covers with Max Maitland, and that was... damned unfair, like most adult realities. Unfair to him, most of all.

"Your plan has a flaw, Max."

He picked up the diaper bag and slung it over his shoulder. "I like when you call me Max, but then, I liked when you called me Mr. Maitland too."

"You can pile up all the money in the world for Maura, but unless you can find somebody to manage those funds for her, somebody whose integrity you can trust, then she might still end up penniless and alone if anything happens to you."

Jeannie had made a will within a week of Harry asking for a divorce. Henry had family, by God, and they'd look after him no matter what.

"That thought has crossed my mind," Max said. "A few million times. I'm working on it. It's a legal problem, and I'm a lawyer, and for now, Maura and I are in good health."

The problem was not legal, but Jeannie let Max's reply suffice. He had done so much more for his sister than many parents did for their own offspring. She collected a happy Henry from his bathtub playpen, stashed his toys in the diaper bag, and took a last look around the lovely bedroom.

"This will be the scene of more than a few happy wedding nights," she said. And it has been the scene of one sweet, doomed kiss.

Max led the way back to the car. Thirty minutes later, outside the Earl's Pint, he kissed Jeannie's cheek and climbed from the car. She drove off and did not glance in the rearview mirror until she was sure the bend in the road had taken Max from her sight.

CHAPTER EIGHT

"Maitland seems all right, for an American," Hugh said. "Can't imagine what would compel a man to get schooled in both law and engineering, though. That would take a permanent toll on a body's sanity."

Fergus and Hugh were among the last onto the path up to the castle, having graciously assisted Fern with the cleanup of the ballroom and repacking her catering van.

"Maitland's got no woman, no children," Fergus said. "He's had time for too much schooling."

"Pitiful thing, when a man's got nobody, but then, you'd know all about that."

Fergus gave him a shove, and Hugh took half a step into the ferns beside the path. "Pitiful thing, when you can wield every tool in your toolbox, but haven't any opportunity to wield the one God equipped you with at birth."

"Now, that's your blood sugar plummeting," Hugh said. "Makes a lad cranky. You should not have had that second brownie."

"I think it's the fourth one causing problems."

They rounded the next turn in the trail, the castle parapets peeking through the trees.

"Maitland will eventually get into those files, Fergus. Why you didn't spend the weekend tidying up the reports and bringing the time sheets up to date, I do not know. He won't appreciate a nasty surprise."

Fergus had done summaries, as required, and sent them along at the end of each week—and he had spent the weekend trying to bring order to the chaos, but thoughts of unrequited longing had interfered at every turn.

Ridiculous, that. "I'm not lying to the man."

"You're guessing at how many hours the lads are putting in, estimating what's owed to the subcontractors on the next progress payment, and seat-of-your-pantsing the material orders. I haven't said a word, but we don't employ fools on this project."

"There's Dinty."

"A hard worker and one of the best masons this valley will ever see, drunk or sober."

"He actually does better when he's been at the Speysides." Fergus had tried having a wee nip between searches for missing invoices, and the whisky hadn't helped.

The path angled upward in a series of switchbacks, until it emerged outside the castle gates. Fergus would have cheerfully wandered in the woods until Hogmanay, rather than face the crapstorm of forms, spreadsheets, and schedules waiting for him in the solar.

"I don't suppose you'd let me help you sort this out?" Hugh asked.

Hugh was a handsome charmer when he was bantering and teasing, a fine specimen when wielding his hammer and saw. When he turned a serious gaze on Fergus, he was a god of the forest, offering understanding when Fergus deserved a sound beating.

"I've made one hell of a muddle since Jeannie stopped coming around, Hugh. Another set of hands moving things about, another set of eyes trying to decipher my notes won't make the process go any faster."

Above Hugh's shoulder, a peacock butterfly fluttered by on wings of orange, black, yellow, and violet. A crossbill *chirp-chirp-tweeeeeted* from the canopy, and a prettier summer's day had probably never graced Deeside.

So why did Fergus battle a compulsion to drive into Aberdeen, get drunk, and never lay eyes on Brodie Castle again?

Hugh slung an arm around Fergus's middle and thumped him a wee tap between the shoulders. "I have faith in you, Fergus, me lad. You'll subdue the powers of darkness, and your estimates and guesses are doubtless more accurate than all of Jeannie Cromarty's careful figures. When Maitland has you taken up by the queen's man for embezzling, I'll even smuggle you a nip from time to time and speak of you fondly on holidays."

"Mind you bring me a decent Speyside, none of that Campbel-town crap you rot your innards with."

"A blasphemer and an embezzler," Hugh said, putting Fergus in a headlock and scrubbing a set of hard knuckles over his crown. "I do fancy a man who can multitask." He let Fergus go with a friendly shove, though by the time they emerged from the trees, Hugh was once again striding along, not a care in the world.

Fergus took what comfort he could from Hugh's affection and parted from him at the castle gates. A smart site foreman would have gone straight up to the solar, sat down with the orange crate full of paperwork that was his worst nightmare, and faced his demons.

Fergus instead took the path to the laundry and set the lads to scrubbing every surface within an inch of their lives.

MAX WAS NOT SORRY he'd kissed Jeannie Cromarty. He was

very sorry he'd never have that privilege again. This regret dogged him through the week as activity picked up both in the castle and at the Hall.

"I don't understand something," Fern said, sliding next to Max on a bench at the Earl's Pint. "Who would want to attend a conference where you have to tramp through the woods to get from your hotel room to your classroom? Only so many bird watchers and hill walkers are devoted to Deeside, and most of them prefer the holiday cottages."

Holiday cottages were a threat to the castle's success, and one of Scotland's most ubiquitous features. Every unused garage, English basement, and spare lot sported a tidy little dwelling with a lockbox discreetly tucked near a side door. The cottages tended to be well built, well maintained, and well managed, damn the luck.

"Only the largest conferences will need to move traffic between the Hall and the castle," Max said, "and most people who regularly attend these gatherings learn the value of some outdoor time throughout the day. Sitting in meetings and workshops for hours dulls the mind, particularly when sitting in the bar or the restaurant is all the break you get."

Fern set a basket of silverware and a pile of green and white plaid napkins on the table. "I've been to a few. Pub owners love to get together and bemoan the challenges of their trade. Have you heard from Jeannie?"

Max took a sip of very fine beer. "I have not, nor do I expect to. She bailed me out when I needed bailing out, and I wish her the best."

Fern set a knife, fork, and spoon on a napkin and rolled the linen around the silverware. "You miss her, then."

Fern's good opinion of Max mattered. He'd taken to stopping by for a beer once work at the castle had wound down for the day and grabbing some takeout to bring home to the Hall.

Though the Hall wasn't home, and takeout wasn't a home-cooked dinner. Mrs. Hamilton's lasagna and salad, chased with sticky toffee pudding and shared with Jeannie Cromarty, were but a fond memory.

"I can't miss somebody I hardly know, Fern. I met Jeannie less than a week ago."

"That Henry's quite the handful." She set a pile of napkins in front of Max. "Harry MacDonald was a rascal."

Max had waited tables, because in Maryland, construction all but stopped during cold weather, and what few jobs were available in winter went to the old hands and union members. He positioned a knife, fork, and spoon on the napkin and rolled up the cutlery.

"Into each life," he said, "some rascals must fall."

Dinty shuffled in, waved to Fern and Max, and kept right on shuffling until he was behind the bar, building himself a perfect pint. Over in the corner, two old women were playing a ferocious hand of some card game, and three geezers by the fireplace where arguing over a game of cribbage.

This wasn't home either, though the Earl's Pint was a consolation for homesickness.

"Harry MacDonald was worse than a mere garden-variety rascal," Fern said. "We had a casual friendship before he married Jeannie, and he was more than happy to keep that friendship up even after he'd taken a wife and Henry was on the way. I'm not in the business of judging others, but Jeannie's a friend. Harry MacDonald is no longer welcome in my establishment."

All the while she spoke, she worked, efficiently rolling silverware.

"Are you warning me?" Max asked. "I all but offered Jeannie a job, and she didn't even sniff at it long enough to ask about salary and job duties." Which was for the best. Max had reached that conclusion before he'd kissed her, and he was reassuring himself of its truth nearly hourly now.

"You've met Elias," Fern said as two laborers and a mason wandered in. Dinty set the pint he'd pulled for himself on the bar and began on another.

"I have had that pleasure, and I'm acquainted with his wife." Violet Hughes—Violet Brodie now—was a formidable, relentless woman. Max admired her from the safest distance he could keep.

"Elias has that fancy PhD in economics. He sits on the boards of a dozen charities, owns property all over the UK, and is on cheek-kissing terms with princes and princesses."

"He's learning how to raise chickens, last I heard." Even the hens loved the Earl of Strathdee, but then, chickens were not noted for their brains.

"When he deigned to join his Cromarty cousins for a family gathering, do you know who would brace Elias on economic theory and the latest banking news? Not Uncle Donald, who's a devoted amateur investor; not Liam, who buys and sells art all over the world; not Niall, who did the international golf-pro bit for years, complete with groupies and sponsors."

"Does that leave Jeannie?"

"That leaves Jeannie, who had the foresight to turn a fishing cottage into a source of revenue, when the family has an architect among its numbers and plenty of strong backs to handle the build-out. She could have done that all over Deeside and Tayside, but instead she got tangled up with that wretched Harry MacDonald."

The pile of silverware was dwindling, and having something to do with his hands soothed a restlessness Max tried to ignore.

"Jeannie's smart. This is not news."

"She is smart, you need help up at the castle, and she needs a job."

Jeannie did not need a casual fling with a guy who'd be spending every third weekend on an airplane.

"I have responsibilities in Maryland, Fern. Family responsibilities."

"Are you married, then?"

"I am not. I have a younger sibling with special needs and no other family to help out." He should probably not have said that. "My personal situation is not for publication, and yes, I did tell Jeannie."

"I'll overlook that insult, Mr. Maitland. The trust placed in a
tavern owner is more sacred than the confidentiality of the confes-
sional." She collected Max's pile of rolled cutlery and arranged it in
the basket. "Dinty, stop nickin' my cherries."

The guys at the bar hooted, and Dinty nicked another cherry,
dangling it by the stem over his open mouth.

"The man does brilliant work with stone," Fern said, "but if he
doesn't stop snacking on my garnishes, I'll grant his death wish."

"Not until my castle is put to rights," Max said.

"I still don't see how you'll accomplish that when anybody who
wants to travel between the castle and Hall has to pretty much hike
through the trees to do it. Put a few inches of snow on that hillside, or
a fresh winter breeze, and a mere covered walkway won't serve."

"My job is to solve the problems nobody else is working on, and
that's at the top of the list."

Not quite the top. The top of the list was occupied by the challenge of forgetting Jeannie Cromarty's kisses.

Fern stacked the last of the wrapped silverware. "Will you take a
break from your problem-solving long enough to join us for the
ceilidh tomorrow night?"

"That's a dance of some sort?"

She used her wrist to draw a wisp of red hair from her brow. The
gesture was graceful and a little weary.

"A ceilidh is mostly a social gathering, but quantities of drink and
food are consumed, so the dancing becomes necessary, and then the
dancing inspires more drinking and eating. All quite jolly and loud.
Everybody comes, including the children, and if the old ladies ask
you to dance, you'll learn the true meaning of stamina."

"I'd better pass. I need the weekend to rest and catch up, and the
guys won't want me gate-crashing their fun."

Fern hefted the basket onto her lap. "You'd better not pass. In
case you haven't noticed, you employ both women and men on your
work site, and if they're to learn to trust you, you will have to give
them a chance to look you over."

Max expected her to move off—Dinty was working on the olives now—but she scooted to the edge of the bench and remained there.

"I would never speak ill of a friend," she said.

"My discretion rivals that of a Scottish pub owner."

"Fergus will never ask you for help, Mr. Maitland, but I sent him an invoice nearly two months ago for a spread like the one I did for you on Monday. The crews were celebrating Elias's decision to lease out the castle. I've yet to be paid. Fergus knows the name of every person on your job site, whether they have aged parents in Peeblesshire or a spouse on temporary duty in Budapest. He can fill in for any trade and keep up with an architect arguing with a lawyer and an accountant. He cleans up amazingly well, if you ever need to put him in a suit, but he's allergic to paper."

Max thought back to weeks of terse emails and summary reports. "That's not good."

"You mustn't let on I told you. Fergus has his pride."

"Fergus has a job too, and part of that job is handling a blizzard of documentation. I'm glad you spoke up. I'll see that your check is cut tomorrow."

She ran a hand over Max's hair, the gesture maternal or sororal. Not flirtatious. "My thanks."

Fern crossed the common, stopping to chat with the ladies, then peeking over the shoulder of one of the duffers at the cribbage board. She was a natural-born pub owner, and if Fergus thought he could hide or fudge lousy paperwork, Fergus was a natural-born fool.

"HE'S BEEN FURLOUGHED," Millicent said. "My Harry's a good, hardworking man who knows everything there is to know about an oil rig, and they furloughed him."

Jeannie coaxed Henry's arm into the sleeve of his jacket, for the week's weather was ending on a brisk note, and Millicent had decided to serve lunch on her back deck. Her home overlooked the

River Tay, though more than an acre of manicured yard lay between the house and the water.

"I'm sorry to hear Harry's had some bad luck," Jeannie said, "but he's resilient, and his skills are in demand. I'm sure he'll be called back shortly." She was equally sure he wouldn't use his free time to visit his son, not when he could be larking about the Greek Isles or bicycling in Croatia.

Harry did not pay child support, something he'd promised to work out with Jeannie when he was next in Scotland, but he had paid six months' rent on the apartment before announcing his decision to resume a bachelor's life. Jeannie anticipated having to pay rent out of her as-yet-nonexistent paychecks in four week's time.

"Henry's outgrown that jacket already," Millicent said, gathering up plates.

The jacket was new and far from snug. "He is growing quickly. He'll soon be a year old." And Harry was missing all of it.

Millicent left off scraping plates to spear Jeannie with a look. Harry's mum was a tall, athletic blonde who'd passed on both her height and her Nordic coloring to her son. She poured the remaining half of Jeannie's glass of water into the potted salvia at the center of the table.

"If you can't afford decent clothes for the boy, Jeannie Cromarty, then it's time you got back to work. I mean that kindly, one mother to another. I'm more than happy to look after Henry so that you can be about paying the bills. I know you weren't entirely to blame for Harry's decision to move on, but if you think you'll get him back by keeping a hand in his pocket, think again."

Henry was not interested in putting on his jacket. He was having a grand time playing Frustrate My Mum, which was fortunate. Without Henry to distract her, Jeannie might have burst out laughing.

"I know Harry's decision to leave is final. He told me so himself, and I consider his honesty a kindness." At the time, Jeannie had considered his piking off rank immaturity. She still did, but at least

Harry hadn't tried to blame her for his decision. "I am looking for work, though I appreciate your very generous offer. You've been more than kind, and I'm sure Harry appreciates all the time you spend with Henry too."

Not that Harry had ever said as much to Jeannie, and not that Millicent spent much time with Henry. On weekdays, if Jeannie dropped Henry off for an hour or two with his grandmother, Millicent's housekeeper, Mrs. Nairn, looked after Henry. She was a kindly soul and a grandmother herself. Leaving Henry with Millicent for most of Friday the previous week had been an experiment, and a desperate one.

Henry had been tired, cranky, and hungry when Jeannie had retrieved him, and his diaper had been soaked.

"Harry is that boy's father," Millicent said quite firmly. "If Harry can't be here, then the least I can do is step in to fill that void."

Harry had *chosen* not to be present for his son. Jeannie turned back the cuffs on the sleeves of Henry's jacket and reminded herself —for the thousandth time—that she had *chosen* to marry Harry and had chosen *with* Harry to bring a child into the world.

"I'm sure there will be times when Harry will work closer to home," Jeannie said. "When that happens, he can spend more time with Henry." Harry-fashion, those times might not arrive for another seventeen years.

Millicent took Jeannie's plate, though Jeannie had had plans for the rest of her raspberry cheesecake.

"I'm glad you don't intend to go dangling after the next handsome rascal who comes along," Millicent said. "I'd take a dim view of any attempt to replace Harry with some daddy-come-lately. Blood is thicker than water."

Neither blood nor water kept Henry warm and dry, so to speak, and as a father, Harry's involvement was less than come-lately.

"Might you wrap that piece up for me? Your raspberry cheese-cake is not to be missed."

Henry made a grab for a spoon, which Millicent snatched out of baby range. "Hands to yourself, my lad."

"Fuh."

Millicent started a game of keep-away with the spoon, which amused Henry not at all. Before he erupted into full-throated indignation, Jeannie retrieved her barely touched piece of cheesecake and maneuvered it onto a paper plate.

"I should give you the recipe." Millicent had been not-giving Jeannie the recipe since before Henry had arrived. Jeannie took that to mean the recipe was actually Mrs. Nairn's.

"I'd love to have it, and your recipe for sweet rolls too."

Millicent gave up tormenting Henry with the spoon. "Harry loves my sweet rolls."

Harry loved his mother, which Jeannie had initially considered one of his strengths. Over time, she'd seen that his regard for Millicent was laced with both guilt and greed. Millicent was a wealthy widow, and Harry was a shrewd, lazy charmer. He flattered his mum with attention, and she lent him her credit card. When she became too controlling, Harry found another rig in need of an engineer.

"Thank you for lunch," Jeannie said, though she'd had little chance to eat, between feeding Henry and dodging Millicent's sermons. "Next time, I'll have you over to the apartment."

Millicent rose while Jeannie packed away toys, a cloth diaper for burping, a bottle of watered-down apple juice, wipes, Bear-Bear, and Henry's favorite blanket.

"Do you have a will, Jeannie?" Millicent asked. "A mother can't be too careful, and with Harry out of the country, you ought to have Henry's situation properly documented."

"His situation?"

"If anything happens to you, I'll become Henry's guardian. You don't have to thank me, because I know that's what Harry would want."

So that's what this three-fork display of graciousness had been about. "Have you seen Henry's spoon?"

"He's old enough that he can use regular utensils, Jeannie."

Jeannie fished the spoon out of the pile of silverware on the stack of plates. The baby spoon was small enough to be comfortable for a tiny mouth, and the bowl was covered with some soft white plastic material that would be easier on teething gums.

She stuffed the spoon in a pocket of the diaper bag. "You gave him that spoon, didn't you? It's his favorite, and he'd miss it. Thanks again for lunch." Jeannie looped the diaper bag over her shoulder and extricated Henry from his high chair—Harry's high chair, in fact.

Millicent followed her around the side of the house to the driveway. "I'd be happy to make an appointment for you with Vernon MacEnroe. Every *responsible* parent should have a will. Vernon's a very good solicitor and has been handling the MacDonald family affairs since before Harry was born."

No wonder Harry had fled to the Mediterranean Sea. "I do have a will, Millicent. Elias was most insistent that I tend to it. He considers himself the head of my family, and I respect his advice in legal arenas. Please thank Mrs. Nairn for a lovely meal, and we'll see you again soon. Wave bye-bye, Henry."

Mentioning Elias had been cowardly, though effective. He was an earl, wealthy, very well connected, and the equal of any attorney. Also the equal of any meddling granny.

Jeannie made her escape feeling as if she'd been ambushed by a press gang. Millicent would not rest until she'd badgered Jeannie into naming her as Henry's potential guardian. She'd badger Harry as well, and then Harry would badger Jeannie—from a safe distance of several thousand miles—and another wrong turn would happen out of sheer maternal exhaustion.

Elias would become Henry's guardian if anything happened to Jeannie. A man orphaned in childhood was well suited to look out for a grieving little boy.

Though Elias was in America to stay, and Millicent would fight tooth and claw—sparkling white teeth and manicured, painted claws, rather—to keep Henry in Scotland.

"I need a job," Jeannie muttered when she'd buckled Henry into his car seat. She climbed in behind the wheel and started the Audi. "I need a good job, one that lets me work from home or pays enough that I can afford decent child care."

Jeannie negotiated the driveway, which wound through half a mile of towering rhododendrons and ancient lime trees. If Harry had been furloughed, she could not rely on him to provide any more rent money. He had money—she was almost sure of it—but they'd not commingled their finances, so she'd never glimpsed the extent of his reserves.

"I don't want to go to court."

"Buh."

In fact, she could *not* take Harry to court. "If I go to court, Millicent will unleash her pet barristers and make me look like an unfit, lazy, mooching gold digger. Harry will feel terrible about it, but never cross his mum, and that will be that."

Jeannie took the road back to the highway slowly, thinking and worrying, worrying and thinking. Should she email Harry? Call him? Let Niall and the cousins know what was afoot? Liam and Niall had both married attorneys, though the ladies were Americans and wouldn't know Scottish family law.

"Perhaps I should have accepted Max Maitland's offer."

But, no. That way lay heartache, and his offer had been a mere thought in passing.

Jeannie was hungry, thirsty, worried, and not a little angry. She nonetheless pulled into the parking lot of the first fast-food place she came to and tossed Millicent's raspberry cheesecake into the dumpster.

"I MISS MAX." Maura had told Max she missed him when they had finally talked on the phone Wednesday night. She would tell him again when they talked on Saturday, but Max was in Scotland.

And Scotland was very, very, *very* far away.

"I'm sure he misses you too," Alex said. He was the cottage manager on Friday evenings, and Maura hadn't decided whether she liked him. He'd had the job for only eight months, though he sometimes substituted during the week or on weekends for the other managers.

Alex liked his computer *a lot*. He was handsome, in a skinny, restless way, with thick dark hair and watchful brown eyes. He didn't talk much, but he had a nice smile.

"When is Max coming home?" Maura asked, though she knew the answer. She also knew Alex was paying more attention to the laptop he'd set beside the milk jug on the kitchen table than he was to her.

"Soon," Alex said, tapping away at the keyboard.

Two weeks was not soon, and that would be for only a visit. "The milk will go bad if you leave it out." Pammie was always leaving the milk out, and Miss Fran was always scolding her. Maura had learned to sniff the milk before pouring it. Maybe Pammie wasn't the only person ignoring the rules.

Alex moved his mouse, hopping from screen to screen. "Maura, shoulder surfing is rude, and I'm on break right now."

No, he wasn't. Staff didn't take breaks without first telling each other, so they didn't both go on break at the same time. "Are you chatting with your girlfriend?"

"She's my fiancée."

"What's that?"

"Maura..." Alex turned the screen a little, so Maura couldn't see it. "My fiancée is the person I'm planning to marry."

"If I had a fiancée, would I have to live here, or could I live in Scotland?"

Alex scooted his chair a few inches around the table, so he faced his screen. "Scotland is very, very, very far away, Maura. Your friends are all here, and Max didn't want you to have to leave your friends. This is where you live, and we'd miss you if you left us."

"Can you show me Scotland on the computer?"

Maura had tried searching, but the computer in the living room had a lot of filters and no privacy. Everybody could see from across the room what was on the screen.

"You can see Scotland on your phone," Alex said, holding out his hand. "I'll show you."

He took Maura's phone and tapped the colorful G to get the search bar. "See that?" Then he tapped the search bar itself to make a tiny keyboard pop up.

"I know the rest." In fact, Maura had had a vague idea that she could search on her phone, but she'd forgotten how. "You should put the milk away. It goes bad, and then Miss Fran blames Pammie, but if you are the person who leaves it out, then the milk going bad is not Pammie's fault."

Alex put the milk away. "Why would she blame Pammie?"

Because Pammie was sweet and easy to blame. "Because Pammie forgets. I'm going to my room."

Alex glanced at his screen. "You can't call Max, Maura. We've discussed this. You can talk to him again on Saturday. Right now, it's past bedtime where he is."

Maura didn't understand that. Miss Fran had tried to show her, with a globe and a flashlight, how the sun lit up different places at different times, but the explanation had been complicated.

"Max's phone doesn't work the same in Scotland," Maura said. "He has to call me, and he called on Wednesday. He'll call me again this weekend."

Though when she'd been helping in the office yesterday, she'd overheard Miss Fran talking to Max on the phone, suggesting *some-body's* phone was able to reach Max, or *somebody* wasn't being honest about how phones worked in Scotland. Miss Fran had said several times, "Maura is fine," and "Maura understands why you had to go," but Maura was not fine, and she didn't understand.

"I'm going to my room now," she said again, because Alex sometimes needed reminders. Maura would close her bedroom door to let everybody know she wanted privacy, then she'd search for Scotland, and figure out a way to go there.

CHAPTER NINE

Max had ignored his usual Friday end-of-day email scroll until it was time to put in an appearance at the Pint. In addition to an email, Elias Brodie had graced him with a text: *Quit ignoring my emails and call me.*

"Tomorrow, your lordship," Max said, stuffing his phone in his pocket. Even standing outside the Pint, the noise was considerable. A fiddle and a concertina could be heard through the open windows, and patrons, most holding beer glasses, were grouped on the walkway and on the front terrace. A small boy who looked to be contemplating scrambling from the window to the bench below it was whisked out of sight by an older woman.

"Mr. Maitland," Hugh Morven called. "Come to enjoy a spot of dancing?"

"He'll enjoy a spot of falling on his arse if you're on the dance floor, wee Hughie," somebody replied.

"I've come to see what a ceilidh is," Max said, "and to enjoy a cold beer at the end of a long week."

"You Yanks and your cold beer," Dinty scoffed. "Sacrilegious, the lot of you."

You Yanks was becoming one of Max's least-favorite phrases. "Seen any ghosts lately, Dinty?"

"Saw the ghost of Fergus the Weary in the solar, up to his armpits in invoices and time—"

"The musicians are tuning up for the Dashing White Sergeant," Hugh said. "It's an easy dance, Mr. Maitland, and you get to hold the hands of two ladies at once. Let's go on in, and I'll walk you through it."

"Hope you're wearing steel-toed boots, Mr. Maitland," Dinty muttered.

Many of the men had turned up in kilts, most of the ladies wore dresses. Babies, elders, and everybody in between ranged around the walls of the Earl's Pint, while the tables had been pushed away from the center of the common. The musicians had set up near a window, and Max spotted a buffet table through the open door of a private dining room.

"Is there a cover charge?" he asked, having nearly to shout over the noise.

"Tip jar on the bar. Pay what you can and order at least two drinks."

"Come on, then. I'm buying."

Max had settled on Tennent's as his preferred brew among the Pint's offerings. Hugh was drinking Deuchars. Behind the bar, a smiling, harried Fern presided at the taps, and an older woman who resembled her was mixing drinks.

"The Dashing White Sergeant has about six moves," Hugh said with every sign of seriousness. "Circle this way, then circle that. That part's easy because you're holding hands so you can't muck it up. Then you circle with your partners, which you also can't muck up because they'll grab you and throw you about where you ought to go. Watch out for that Morgan. She's a vigorous dancer after about the third drink."

Max was already lost, though the beer was good.

"Then you do the left shoulder figure of three," Hugh said. "Just wander around smiling and try not to step on anybody. Bumping into your partners is all part of the fun, though knocking people over is frowned upon. You form up in threes again, raise your arms, and start over with a new set. Nothing simpler."

Max barely had time to set his drink on the mantel before Hugh grabbed him by the hand—*by the hand*—and dragged him into a line.

"Maitland is a ceilidh virgin," Hugh bellowed, now holding Max by the wrist, like a referee in a prizefight. "Reward his courage with hospitality, or I'll partner you right oot ta windae. Morgana May Malcolm, I'm looking at you."

This announcement occasioned a cheer and some applause. Morgan was a fine specimen of tall, red-haired womanhood, and she soon had Max by one hand and Hugh by the other.

The fiddler, a white-haired bantam with snapping blue eyes, stood up. "We'll walk through the pattern once," he said. "Think of it as a test. If you can't remain upright for the walk-through, you'd best yield your place while you take some air." He tucked his fiddle under his chin and flourished his bow. "Form lines and greet your partners."

Max had been forced to take square dancing in college, a scheduling quirk resulting from the vagaries of the third-year engineering curriculum. Phys ed had been mandatory, but the only courses available that hadn't interfered with core requirements had been bowling, square dancing, and fencing. Square dancing was an easy A and thus the favorite of any major where grades determined life expectancy in the profession.

The Dashing White Sergeant wasn't a square dance, but it was easy enough, except for the figure of three. Max muddled through, nearly being plowed over by a granny, bouncing off Hugh twice, and getting bumped into by Morgan on nearly every figure.

When the dance ended, Max found his beer, and damned if the taste hadn't gone from good to ambrosial.

"Morgan's friendly," Hugh said. "That's your only warning." Morgan blew him a kiss. Hugh saluted with his beer and then marched off, kilt swishing.

"You're wondering what it's like to wear a kilt," Morgan said. "But then, Hugh more than does justice to his native attire. A pity that. Shall we take some air?"

Max wasn't given a choice, because Morgan took him by the hand and led him outside, where the sky still wasn't quite dark.

"So what is it like to wear a kilt?" Max asked.

"Comfortable," Morgan replied, leading him to a bench beyond the light pouring from the open windows. "Classy and bold. If you want to see it done properly, wait until somebody gets down the swords and then watch Hugh on the dance floor. He grew up in a dancing family, did the competitions, and taught the lads for a while."

The moment should have been friendly and superficial, but the feeling was homesickness. Men back home did not, by and large, wear kilts, compete in sword dancing, or spend Friday evening dancing with everybody from grannies to girlfriends to each other.

The degree of casual affection going on inside, the noise, the community reminded Max that he was the stranger and far, far from home. Though even at home, he also was usually the stranger.

"Does Fergus frequent these gatherings?" Max asked.

"Aye, and he's a fine dancer as well. Knows his way around the tin whistle and the bodhran and can be brilliantly funny once he's had a wee dram or two."

Morgan spoke as if rendering a professional opinion, reciting the dating-app keywords she'd choose for Fergus. Max was abruptly conscious of where the evening might end and why Hugh had partnered him with this particular lady.

As the evening progressed, the dance unfolded in moves Max knew all too well.

In conversation, Morgan found reasons to press momentarily closer. When Fern got out her fiddle to play a slow triple-meter duet, Morgan was in Max's arms. When the grandmas began to pack up the children and the teenagers had drifted off to the shadows on clouds of pot-scented smoke, Morgan's fingers were laced with Max's.

"You could walk me home," she said. "Have a wee dram to finish off the evening. I live at the foot of the lane that turns off past the garage."

The mating game hadn't been overt throughout the evening. Established couples had danced with each other, but also partnered others. People sat outside in small groups, though a pair wasn't unusual either. To the locals, though, Morgan's plans for Max would have been easy to decipher.

A slight headache had started up at the base of Max's skull, probably from the noise. "I'm happy to walk you home."

Thus did he find himself outside in what passed for summer darkness, an attractive single woman keeping him company.

"In winter, the cold sobers you up before you've staggered to the corner," Morgan said, falling in step beside him. "And the cold arrives well before we're ready for it. Winter will slow you down, won't it? Up at the castle?"

"We have an ambitious schedule of interior work to do at the Hall. We'll keep nearly a full crew straight through for the next year."

"That's good, then." She slipped her hand into Max's. "Elias likely knew your project would result in jobs."

God bless Saint Elias—tomorrow. Weariness landed on Max along with curiosity. Had Jeannie met her Harry at one of these dances? How would Henry take to a noisy, friendly Friday evening at the Pint?

"Is there somebody waiting for you back home?" Morgan asked as they turned onto a gravel lane.

"Not in the sense you mean, but Maryland is home. I'm admitted to the bar there and nowhere else. I'll be going back once the castle is open for business."

She dropped his hand, and that was a relief. "Seems like foolishness to leave as soon as things get interesting. You work for months to spin straw into gold, and then you ride into the sunset, never having a chance to see the results of all your efforts. How much job satisfaction is that?"

Did Harry MacDonald ever wish he hadn't ridden into the

sunset when things had become interesting? What sort of man turned his back on Jeannie Cromarty and his own newborn child? But Max knew the answer to that, because he'd been raised by such a man.

"I'm good at what I do," Max said, "and like every person on my crews, I have to go where the work is."

Morgan led him to a stone dwelling that sat apart from the other homes on the lane. The porch light was on, illuminating riotous baskets of petunias and pansies and a black cat sitting on the windowsill.

"You'll put me out of business," Morgan said. "You and your fancy castle."

The castle still belonged to Elias Brodie. "What is your business?" For a moment, Max wondered if she was in the oldest profession. In the UK, that wasn't illegal—not quite.

"I own the shop between the bus stop and the grocery store. Some months, I sell more bug repellant than anything else, and I do a good trade in fishing gear and hiking supplies, but I also feature the work of local craftsmen and artists. By trade, I'm a weaver, but if an item is locally handmade, I'll find a place for it in my shop. Pottery of all kinds, sachets, iron trivets, farrier's puzzles, jigsaw puzzles. Almost every household creates something that's both artistic and useful."

Sleeping with the enemy was an age-old means of gaining a tactical advantage, though informing a man he was the enemy didn't usually figure into the negotiations.

"The castle and the Hall will each have a gift shop," Max said.

"I thought so."

Morgan's features by the porch light were merely stoic, as if the decimation of a business she'd likely spent years developing was merely another overdue bill.

"And those gift shops will need inventory," Max went on. "If we stock the usual trite, predictable tchotchkes found in every tourist trap from here to London, we aren't likely to move much merchandise. If we instead stock locally sourced goods, supplemented with a few tasteful items of general interest, we'll have sales to show for it and save on shipping. We'll also be in a position to direct people into the village, where more choices and perhaps even better prices are to be found."

The cat hopped off the windowsill and sniffed delicately at Max's jeans.

"That's your plan?"

Max sat on the porch steps, because Morgan had apparently reached the part of the evening to which the previous flirtation and flattery had been leading. The cat appropriated Max's lap and commenced purring.

"What I have to sell are fine accommodations in a beautiful setting," Max said. "For conferences, family reunions, weddings... I want any group that needs a comfortable and gracious place to gather to look at Brodie Castle before they look elsewhere. I am not in the business of selling crafts. I am not interested in putting Fern's pub out of business. I took on this project in part because I am tired of feuding —with zoning boards, farmers, local newspaper reporters, school boards that can't be bothered to move a single bus stop for safety's sake if it will add two minutes to a driver's route..."

His thoughts were coming together as the words left his mouth, and they were the truth. He was tired of having to fight the community while finessing the site politics with his crews and cajoling the investors into honoring their obligations.

Tired of the usual development job, in other words.

"So you'll leave on good terms," Morgan said, coming down beside him. "But then you'll be gone, and some wet-behind-the-ears MBA will get the bright idea to let an Edinburgh management service buy for your gift shops, and there won't be anything you can do about it."

"If that happens, that will be a year or two from now. You'll have time to build your cyber footprint, establish relations with the castle management team, and tailor your inventory to the castle's guest demographic."

Though the dreaded tadpole-MBA might indeed become a reality. The money guys, increasingly, were money guys and little else. They wanted return on investment yesterday-if-not-sooner and didn't see a symbiotic relationship with the local economy as a priority. Win-win was a cliché, usually trotted out when win-lose was all but obviously in the offing. The money guys never thought long-term, never realized that investing was *supposed* to take time to yield a return.

"What grand words you have, Max Maitland, but the boot's on the other foot. You are betting the future of the castle on the ability of Deeside and its surrounds to attract a clientele that will keep you in business. Deeside was here long before Elias got the bright idea to bring in a developer, and Deeside will be here when your castle has crumbled into the loch." She paused to scratch beneath the cat's chin. "Shall I take you to bed?"

"Are you talking to me or the cat?"

"Both, I suppose, or whoever feels so inclined."

Max liked sex, liked the physical pleasure, the affection, the sense of putting aside everything else to enjoy being a healthy, consenting adult.

He liked Morgan. Liked how direct she was, how philosophical, how bold.

He did not like that bedding him might figure in some instinctive calculation Morgan had made about the best way to preserve her livelihood, and he truly abhorred the notion that he might join her in bed and wish she was Jeannie.

After which, he'd feel predictably stupid in the morning.

"I'm flattered," he said, passing her the cat, which had to weigh a good twenty pounds, "and I'm tempted."

She remained sitting on the steps, the cat in her lap, a pretty, determined woman who didn't look too disappointed to have been spared a night in Max's company.

"What's the but?"

"But I'm new around here, still figuring out when yes means yes, and soon means next week. I don't have my bearings, and I need to go carefully." He was talking a lot and not saying much, but then, Morgan wasn't entitled to an explanation. She'd offered, he'd declined.

"Maybe a rain check," she said, rising and cuddling the cat to her middle. "But probably not. You said there isn't anybody back in Maryland, but I wish for your sake there was. Thanks for walking me home."

She disappeared inside the cottage, though Max had the sense she was thanking him for declining her offer of "a wee dram." On any other project, he'd have happily joined her, which was how he and Shayla had taken an interest in each other.

And look how that had turned out.

He ambled back the way he'd come and, by the light of a rising half-moon, made his way through the woods to the Baron's Hall, which was cavernous, and full of potential, and also not his home.

"I DON'T KNOW where Bear-Bear has gone," Jeannie crooned. "He's hibernating."

Henry went on howling against her shoulder, a child in misery on a lovely Saturday morning. Bun-Bun had somehow got raspberry jam on his ears and had been taken to the dry cleaner along with two of Jeannie's silk blouses—job interviews required professional attire, not that Jeannie had any interviews lined up.

When Bun-Bun had to be surrendered to the cleaners, Jeannie's usual strategy was to press Bear-Bear into service and distract Henry with walks about the tot lot or an outing to the park. Henry loved the ducks, though right now, Jeannie doubted even the ducks could console him.

"Please, child," she muttered. "Please settle down before—"

The neighbor thumped the wall, which inspired Henry to unprecedented decibels of despair. Jeannie went into the bathroom with him and shut the door, though that only seemed to make his wailing reverberate against her last nerve.

"Henry, I love you from the bottom of my heart, but if you can't cease this—"

Her phone buzzed, doubtless Millicent calling to tell her about a job opening in some janitorial firm halfway to John O'Groats...

She switched Henry to her other shoulder and swiped into the call. "Jeannie here."

"Sounds more like Jeannie and a pack of screaming zombies."

Max. Why was he calling now? "Henry is upset."

"Henry is contemplating the end of life on the planet, from what I can hear. Is he cutting more teeth?"

"Probably." Henry was also taking an intermission to grab for the phone. "I think he can hear your voice. Say hello."

"Henry, are you trying to destroy your mama's hearing? Bad strategy, fella. He who bellows down the rafters doesn't get many smooches."

Henry's little brows knit. "Mub!"

"He might be trying to say Max." Jeannie held the phone slightly away so Henry could hear the conversation. "You haven't perhaps come across a brown stuffed bear?" The longer she thought about it, the more certain she was that Bear-Bear was crammed among the couch cushions in Elias's apartment.

"Brown fur, brown eyes, doesn't say much?" Max asked. "I was calling to ask if he'd escaped from the diaper bag while you were here. Want me to put him in the mail?"

Today was Saturday, though by the time Max got to a post office, the mail would likely have gone, meaning the soonest the package might arrive was... Tuesday.

Henry whimpered and got a hold of Jeannie's ear. "I'll come get the bear," Jeannie said. "I was supposed to spend my day drafting one résumé for event coordination and another for property management, but if Henry doesn't get his bear, I'll spend the rest of my weekend courting eviction."

Again. When Henry had begun cutting teeth, he'd gone on a three-night crying jag that taught Jeannie about a whole new level of maternal worry.

"Jeannie, are you okay?"

No, I am not. She sank to the cold, closed lid of the potty. "It's been a lively morning. If I leave now, I should be up there by about one p.m. Don't feel you have to wait around for me. Just leave the bear in the kitchen, and I'll find him."

"I have homemade pizza sitting in the fridge, tempting me to overindulge. While you're here, I'd like to discuss a situation pertaining to the castle."

For homemade pizza, Jeannie would have trudged through drifted snow, uphill, with a—Henry had got a hank of Jeannie's hair in his mouth and tugged sharply.

"What sort of situation, Max?"

"Nothing serious, but I don't want it to become serious. Drive carefully and tell Henry his bear will be waiting for him."

The call ended, and Jeannie stared at the phone. "I wasn't going to see him again, wasn't going to speculate about him, wasn't going to miss him, or wonder how he's getting on."

Which pretty much described her past week. Fern had sent Jeannie an email earlier in the day, kindly attaching a photo of Max on the dance floor with Morgan smiling up at him. Morgan was a fine dancer and a lovely person, but did she have to look so damned pretty and charming and curvaceous when she danced?

"So single and free?" Jeannie asked, tucking the phone out of Henry range. "Not that I'd trade you for anything, Henry Charles Bascomb MacDonald Cromarty."

Henry gave her a gummy smile, and of course, her heart melted. She wrestled him into his jacket, stuffed some extra baby clothes into the diaper bag, along with baby food and a couple of fresh bottles, and was on the road within fifteen minutes.

Not, of course, that she was in a hurry to see Max again.

MAX WAS STILL GRINNING at his phone when Elias's number showed on the screen.

"Maitland here."

"You've got trouble," Elias growled, "and if you have trouble, I have trouble, and my castle has trouble. And if my castle has trouble, then half of Deeside will soon be up in arms, blaming me for their every misfortune."

Max wandered across the kitchen, taking Bear-Bear with him. Jeannie was on her way up from Perth, and nothing would ruin Max's good mood.

"A Scottish burr can make even a struggling chicken farmer sound formidable. Have you had breakfast yet, Brodie? My crew chiefs are firm believers in managing blood-sugar levels. They discuss this at length when they should be doing some honest work. Morgan says hello, by the way. She's pissed that you'd bring a viper like me into her Highland paradise."

"I am not a chicken farmer. We own an egg operation, a very different proposition."

Could anybody sound as affronted as a Scotsman? "My apologies, to you and the chickens. What has you in a swivet on this fine summer's day?"

Max tossed Bear-Bear in the air and caught him, pleased beyond telling that Henry and his familiar would soon be reunited.

"Maitland, have you been at the whisky?"

"Your whisky? I wouldn't go near it. Your pet ghosts would haunt me all the way back to Maryland."

"They don't look like ghosts, Maitland. The lord and his lady look like a handsome couple very much in love. Disrespect them at your peril."

Elias Brodie was the kind of guy tailors probably loved to dress— tall and broad-shouldered, well portioned, great smile, sky-blue eyes.

Then he opened his mouth, and that Scottish burr turned handsome into swoon-worthy, according to Max's former admin.

The word *peril*, for example, came out sounding like a portent of doom: pairrrr-ill.

"I might get myself a kilt," Max said. "I'll practice strutting around, talking Scottish. 'Hand me that wee hammer, Hughie me lad.' And, 'Cease yer bluidy natterin', Fair-gus. Can ye no' see I'm tryna wairk here?'"

"God save me, I've created a monster." Elias sounded more amused than impressed. "Fortunately for you, Uncle Donald has decided to extend his fishing trip, or you'd find out what happens to a Yank who mocks our kilted laddies."

"I'm managing," Max said. "Thanks for asking. The crews seem willing to give me a chance, the Hall and the castle have good bones, and the locals are friendly. The paperwork has me a little worried, but when does paperwork do anything but cause worry?"

"Forget the paperwork, Maitland, there's treason afoot. Pay attention, because Violet will soon be done visiting with her quilting group, and then I'm to go tomato shopping."

"Oh, how the mighty have fallen. From murdering Englishmen in their beds to picking out heirloom toe-mah-toes." Max set Bear-Bear on the windowsill, the better to watch for Jeannie's arrival.

"Your boy Pete Sutherland is planning a sneak attack," Elias said. "I'm friends with the spice heiress who once owned the farm I inherited here in Damson Valley. She's a lovely older lady who's been presiding over some garden club in Baltimore since Adam and Eve were chased out of Eden.

"Sutherland's wife is a Scotswoman," Elias went on, "with an interest in gardening, and she mentioned to Adelaide that Pete was planning to drop in at 'his' castle, oust the present project manager, and set himself up as director. He's recruited some Canadian to do the actual work. Mrs. Sutherland is delighted, because Pete promised her a home in Scotland when they married, and that was several years ago. I am *not* delighted."

Well, crap. "I'm not too happy myself. Pete Sutherland couldn't manage his way out of a paper bag with a flashlight and a guide dog."

Which, of course, was not Pete's own assessment of his abilities.

Elias spoke more softly. "My contract with the investment consortium says that I'll be consulted on all substitutions of key personnel, but I can't stop Sutherland from changing out his staff. What the hell is he up to, Max? I assumed you had better control of your investors than this."

So had Max. "He's being Pete, meddling at the worst possible times in the worst possible ways. Any idea who my successor is supposed to be?"

"A woman. Has never managed a renovation, apparently, but can manage Sutherland."

All of Max's joy in the day, all of his delight at finding one small brown stuffed bear, wafted away on a summer breeze.

"With Pete, it's frequently a woman. This is not good." Pete was not the brightest guy to begin with, and when it came to the ladies.... "Sutherland in love—or his version of love—cannot be reasoned with. I could be Leonardo da Vinci, and he'd find fault with my engineering abilities. Whoever she is, she has chosen her mark well."

"You've only been there a week. How can Sutherland find cause to toss you over?"

Dinty's comment about Fergus being up to his armpits in time sheets came to mind. "Don't you have to go tomato shopping, Elias?"

"Soon."

"I have a few reports to look over. When will I hear from your uncle Donald?"

"When you least expect it. He'll come nosing around, flirting with the ladies, and telling everybody how to do their jobs. You're safe for the next week or two, because he's scored a Guest Past to fish in Bavaria."

"Isn't telling everybody how to do the jobs you've never attempted your role?"

Elias muttered something Max didn't catch, then, "Violet says hello."

"Give her my regards, and don't be too concerned about Pete's penchant for drama. He has too much money and not enough to do."

"Keep me posted," Elias said. "I mean that. Don't think you can manage the renovation, spend days each month traveling, get the lay of the land in a foreign culture, and keep tabs on your idiot banker friends without support."

Support was good, documentation was better. "You have my back?"

"I have to go tomato shopping. Don't muck this up, Maitland. Violet will never forgive me if that castle falls into the wrong hands."

The line went dead.

Max turned Bear-Bear around to face the kitchen. "Houston, we have a problem." Several problems, if some woman had set her sights on Pete Sutherland's deep pockets.

Part of Max wanted to jog up to the castle and start pawing through Fergus's files, though the files weren't going anywhere. If Pete Sutherland was planning a raid, then Max had better his ducks in a tidy, damned row.

He got out his sketch pad and began experimenting with possible layouts for a covered walkway, something not too architecturally awful, expensive, or unsightly that would connect the Hall and the castle without offending the historic preservation buffs, creating schedule delays, or generating cost overruns.

How hard could that be?

CHAPTER TEN

"Thought I'd find you here." Hugh turned over a bucket and sat, knees splayed despite the fact that he wore a kilt. "We missed you last night."

Fergus tossed down the pencil he'd been using to total figures that refused to add up. "A man can't seek a little peace and quiet to tend to his work on a fine Saturday morning?"

Stupid comment. With walls twelve meters thick in places, the castle was quiet. Close the door—an arched monstrosity carved of two matching oak panels—and the solar was as silent as an abandoned chapel.

Hugh picked up the pile of papers that was all the vendor invoices Fergus could find. Fergus smacked Hugh's hand.

"Fern has an unusual accounting system," Hugh said, leaning back against the wall and folding his hands over a flat belly. "She stashes the bills owed to her in a shoe box by the cash register. Dinty was behind the bar a lot last night because nothing would do but Pete and Fern play a duet every other set."

At least Fern had a system. Jeannie Cromarty had had a system too, and she'd shown it to Fergus and emailed him her lovely spreadsheet and then sat with him and whipped through all manner of cleverness. Fergus had nodded and murmured appreciatively and told himself he'd figure it all out later. Maybe buy a spreadsheet course or do a tutorial or something.

Hugh moved the bucket around to Fergus's side of the table, the plastic rim scraping on the slate floor. "You aren't listening to a word I say."

Hard to listen when a man smelled like the first day of spring. "If you'd leave me in peace, I might stand a prayer of catching up on the few reports that aren't exactly complete. Maitland's a reasonable man, and he's always going on about data security and corporate memory. Perhaps he'll hire me a pretty little admin, and then you can pester her."

Hugh grabbed Fergus by the scruff of the neck, and—have mercy upon a poor kilted laddie—his grip felt wonderful.

"If you lose your job over this, Maitland will bring in some fancy Yank who won't be content to sit over in his project office making notes on his phone for most of the day. The lads like working for you, Fergus, and you've never had a problem keeping the tallies before. What the hell is afoot?"

Why did Hugh have to have such beautiful eyes, such long lashes? "I've been distracted." For the past six years, ever since Hugh had slung an arm around Fergus's shoulders after a particularly brutal shinty match and kissed him on his sweaty temple.

Working on the same project had escalated the preoccupation into an affliction, though that was really no excuse.

"The auld earl, Zebedee, he left you a mess, didn't he?" Hugh sat back. "Then Jeannie came prancing along and set everything up her way—like she was managing some holiday cottage—and you were lost even before all the new hires came on board. You jotted everything down on your damned yellow pads, and Maitland hasn't a clue what a mare's nest you're dealing with."

"I'm planning to tell him."

"Fergus, my dear, this cannot end well."

Truer words.... "So leave me to it, and I'll do what I can before Maitland and I have a wee chat."

"Dinty says you haven't paid Fern for that spread she put out nearly two months ago. Fern will have a wee chat with Maitland, assuming she hasn't already. If there's one way to piss in the well with a Scot in trade, it's to pay late or short, and Maitland has been very careful to stay on good terms with the locals."

Fern was a dear, darling woman, but not to be trifled with when it came to her family's business.

Hugh grabbed the invoices before Fergus could stop him. "I'm guessing we have until Monday to get this sorted out, or it will have been very nice knowing you."

"The payroll taxes should be up to date," Fergus said. "Those weren't a part of Jeannie's meddling, though I have no notion how she tracked them as part of the larger project budget."

"So you've been signing checks and keeping a list?"

"Lists," Fergus said, feeling heat rise from his neck. "I never throw anything away, so I know they're here somewhere."

Hugh slugged him on the arm. "I'll visit you wherever they keep the embezzlers. Probably some posh campground for wayward bankers. You can teach them all to play the tin whistle while you compare the size of your regrets."

Was that a joke? A scold? A *line*? Just because a man was on good terms with the womenfolk didn't mean he wasn't also...

"Read off the names of the vendors, the dates of the invoices, and the amounts owed, and I'll compare them to my list," Fergus said. "Don't sit so close. You're in my light."

Hugh scooted closer. "Now I'm not in your light. You owe Fern a goodly sum, which surely foretells a period of teetotaling misery for you, if not outright banishment from the pub..."

He read from the stack. Fergus checked his list and suffered torments of unrequited love far worse than any misery he'd experience if Fern locked him out of the Pint.

JEANNIE WAS PATHETICALLY glad to see Max, who stood at the kitchen counter in worn jeans, a plain black T-shirt, with a tea towel of Scottish wildflowers tucked into his belt like a makeshift apron.

The kitchen was perfumed with oregano and basil, and a tossed salad sat in parts on a cutting board—shredded baby spinach on a towel, chopped hard-boiled egg, black olives, tomatoes, sliced red peppers.

Good, fresh food, not the heat-and-eat poison Jeannie had been subsisting on.

"You can cook," she said as Max lifted Henry from her arms.

"If a man can't put together a salad, he's a sorry excuse for a man." He nuzzled Henry's cheek, provoking an enormous smile from the baby. "You're assigned to quality assurance, Henry. I've set aside product samples to keep you out of trouble."

Slices of red pepper, carrot, and celery were laid out on a paper towel, along with an eighth of a peeled apple.

The contrast with the hospitality Millicent had offered yesterday —nothing prepared for Henry, not for his nourishment or for his entertainment—fortified Jeannie's pleasure in Max's company.

"I brought his booster seat. I'll fetch it from the car."

Max left off nose-tickling Henry's ear. "We'll get it. You can check on the pizza. I grated extra cheese, in case you're as fond of a little pizza with your cheese as I am."

He and Henry disappeared out the back door, and Jeannie was left to marvel at the pleasure of not having to lug every blessed thing —one-handed—from car to house to car to house and everywhere in between.

By the time she'd snitched some cheese and added the rest to the baking pizza, Max and Henry were back with the booster seat. The meal was soon on the table—amazing how much more efficient Jeannie could be when Henry had somebody else to focus on—and Max was pouring a round of ginger ale for the adults.

"Your ginger ale tastes more like ginger than what's typically served in the States," he said. "I prefer it. For what we are about to receive, we are grateful."

He passed Henry the sliced veggies while Jeannie helped herself to a wedge of pizza that was nearly as deep as it was wide.

This meal should have been nothing—casual food consumed with a friend at the kitchen table—but Jeannie was unaccountably upset by it.

"You do not look like a woman who is contemplating gustatory bliss," Max said. "Mrs. Hamilton made bread pudding if you'd rather go straight to the treats."

"I'm trying to recall if Henry's father ever fixed me a meal—or a peanut butter and jelly sandwich, for that matter."

Max passed her the salad. "Do you miss him?" The question was merely curious, but not one anybody had asked Jeannie.

Not one she'd asked herself for months. "I thought I would, though a rigger is gone for weeks and then home for weeks. I dreaded the days when Harry would leave, because what if the baby came early? What if I fell and something awful happened? Harry told me I was being silly, that some pregnant women send their menfolk off to war..."

"I don't think I'd respect Harry very much, though I'm sure he's likable as hell."

Jeannie scooped out some salad, aiming for the black olives. "You've put your finger on something. I'm struggling for a reason to respect Henry's father and finding it honestly difficult."

"Henry's young. Some people do better parenting older children. Some people shine with babies. Some are better parents for one gender as opposed to the other. How's the pizza?"

Max might have made a comment about finding something to respect about a man before marrying him and conceiving a child with him. Jeannie sliced off the tip of her piece of pizza, wound the melted cheese around her fork, and took a bite of heaven.

"The pizza is delectable."

"Duh!"

"The official taster has weighed in," Max said as Henry resumed gnawing on a portion of crust Max had cut for him. "Tell me about your job hunt."

"I'll spoil your appetite."

"When I was job hunting, I figured for every hundred résumés I sent out, I'd get five interviews and one offer. For every ten offers I got, one of them would be acceptable. For every ten acceptable offers I got, one of them would be worth taking. Hunting for a job is a job."

"Now you're spoiling my appetite."

He set down his knife and fork. "You could come back to work at the castle."

Not exactly an effusive offer. "I've thought about it," she said, "because I liked keeping everything organized and liked the idea that Elias asked me to help, but I'd have to move up here. Harry's mum would disapprove. She lives outside Perth and takes an interest in Henry."

Was Max relieved by that answer? Disappointed? Neither? Did Max assume that even a casual relationship could go nowhere if Jeannie went back to wrangling time sheets, invoices, bank statements, and bills of lading?

"May I discuss something with you that's work related?" he asked.

"Of course."

Max cut off a fresh section of crust, dabbed butter on it, and passed it to Henry. "How conscientious is Fergus about his book-keeping?"

Oh dear. "If you're asking, then he hasn't printed you out the incurred-expense report, has he?"

"I've only been on-site a week. He said it's usually a monthly report, which struck me as odd. A lot can go wrong in a month when dozens of people are clocking in every morning and deliveries are showing up several times a day."

Jeannie debated having another slice of pizza. Max picked up the knife, cut a slice, then cut it in half and put the larger share on Jeannie's plate.

"You don't dare suggest an actual time clock be installed," Jeannie said. "The crews would be insulted."

"They're easily insulted. I got away with requiring hard hats only because it will help keep the bankers from wandering at will. Damn, I make a good pizza."

"Fergus is known to be a first-rate project manager, and he's done a number of castle renovations. Zebedee wasn't as keen on modern management tools as Elias is, but I made sure to show Fergus my system and to walk him through it."

Max paused with his slice of pizza halfway to his mouth. "I'm only now realizing I've never seen Fergus with a computer actually on, much less seen him with his fingers touching a keyboard."

"If he's a slow typist, he'll save the data entry for when nobody's on hand to watch. The guys are brutal to each other when they're in a certain humor."

"But let me criticize Fergus while one of the masons is within earshot, and I'll find a hammer accidentally dropping on my head the next day."

Henry pitched a carrot stick across the table, and Max put a hand on Jeannie's wrist before she could get up.

Oh, she had missed his touch. Missed the sound of his voice, his steadiness, his ability to treat Henry as something other than a cute nuisance.

"Give it a minute," Max said, "or he'll think he has you trained to step and fetch. In fact, if I were made of steely reserve, like I'm supposed to be, I'd ignore the little guy when he pulls that stuff."

"You're sure he's pulling crap, rather than simply enjoying himself?"

Max dusted his hands over his plate. "Not sure, but where's the harm in letting the carrot sit there until we're ready to clean up?"

The exchange was like the meal—pedestrian, nothing remarkable— but it was a discussion Jeannie could not have had with Harry, Millicent, or even a friend like Fern. Parenting Henry was a moment-by-moment experiment in love, behavior modification, resource allocation, and luck. Max had the knack of being supportive and making no-big-deal conversation out of issues Jeannie would have worried over by the hour.

"I suspect tossing food is a way to signal that he's through," Jeannie said. "Then I wonder if Henry throws food when I'm frustrated and his infant radar has picked up on my mood."

"Are you frustrated now?"

Yes—though not in the sense Max meant. "I'm full of very good pizza. Shall we go for a ramble before getting into the bread pudding?" She'd liked watching Max eat. Liked watching him run the tip of his finger around the edge of his glass. Liked imagining his hands on her, God help her.

"Let's clean up first, or I'll fall into bachelor habits, letting the dishes pile up in the sink, scandalizing Mrs. Hamilton."

Tidying up the kitchen took only a moment, and Henry spent that moment getting reacquainted with Bear-Bear. Jeannie spent it stealing glances at Max—ye gods, he did justice to a pair of worn jeans—and not allowing herself to touch his hand when he passed her a washed glass.

When the last plate had been rinsed and dried, and Max had wrung out the washrag and draped it over the faucet, he reached for Jeannie's dishtowel. She wasn't expecting him to grab for it, and kept hold, and was thus tugged a step closer than was sensible.

Max gave the dishcloth another little tug. Jeannie held on, watching his gaze shift from surprised to interested to... pleased.

"I asked the first time I kissed you, Jeannie Cromarty. When you look at me like that, I want to ask again."

Jeannie kissed him, pressing him against the sink and going full frontal on him without any preliminaries.

"I thought of you all week," she managed.

"Dreamed of you," he replied before resuming the kiss. He wrapped her close, then hoisted her up to sit on the counter, all without taking his mouth from hers. The angle let Jeannie get her legs around him, and her hands in his hair, and her—

A three-inch-long slice of celery hit Jeannie's arm. Henry grinned from his booster seat and bounced on his butt.

"Unless you want to get beaned with a stuffed bear," she said, "we'd better continue this discussion when Henry's gone down for a nap." Still, she kept her legs around Max's waist and her arms around his neck.

He rested his forehead against her shoulder. "I wasn't going to let this happen." He sounded bewildered rather than resentful. "I can't offer you much, Jeannie, so it will be a short discussion. I didn't call you to lure you to my kitchen, but I've missed you."

That he wasn't particularly pleased to have missed her was fine with Jeannie. "I can't offer you much either, and I know your plans take you back to the States, but right now, I can't see beyond sunset, Max Maitland."

He glanced at the wall clock. "Sunset is hours and hours away."

"I'm overdue for a friendly fling." Jeannie eased down from the counter. "I suspect you are too." A friendly fling sounded credible— getting back on the horse, rebounding from a starter marriage gone awry, taking a break from being all mom, all the time. A fling with Max Maitland sounded lovely, in fact.

And if it was a mistake, then it would be a small mistake, and one fondly remembered. Surely Jeannie was entitled to at least one of those?

MAX HAD AWOKEN in a *state* every day for the past week, with Jeannie Cromarty on his mind. A few minutes of self-indulgence during his morning shower hadn't evicted her from his imagination. Neither had hard work, a near miss with Morgan, or a five-mile jog through the Scottish countryside earlier in the day.

He was half aroused merely from one kiss, though a few months of sexual drought wasn't helping his self-restraint either.

"You went to the ceilidh last night," Jeannie said. "Did you enjoy yourself?"

For their post-pizza ramble, they were taking another path around the hill, the right fork rather than left. The way was steep, but the views magnificent.

"Who tattled?" Max asked.

"Fern sent me a picture of you on the dance floor with Morgan."

Max held back a branch so Jeannie could pass in front of him. Henry was strapped into a contraption on Max's back. The baby was a warm, wiggly little bundle of preciousness that put Max in mind of Maura's infancy.

Jeannie's expression was as carefully neutral as her tone, suggesting Max truly wasn't the only camper suffering a case of inconvenient attraction.

Better that way, if nobody expected a fling to turn into something more.

Despite stupid hope to the contrary.

"Hugh introduced me to Morgan," Max said. "She was mostly interested in figuring out how fast the castle would put her shop out of business."

"She loves that shop."

"With any luck, her grandchildren will be loving that shop, but those grandchildren won't be related to me."

Jeannie stopped at a widening in the path. "I didn't mean to imply that anything..." She glanced around at the surrounding trees, as if fairies might be eavesdropping. "Morgan would sleep with a handsome Yank to protect her shop. If I owned that shop, I'd likely do the same."

Henry left off pulling Max's hair to grab his ear. "She offered, I declined. I don't think she judges me for that and is, in fact, mostly relieved. But can we get one thing straight, Jeannie?"

She moved off a few yards, to the edge of the clearing. "A fling is a fling. I know that, Max. I have enough on my plate without trying to make... without romantic complications. One doesn't want to make a fool of oneself, though."

The angle of her chin was determined, the set of her shoulders resolute. Everything about her posture radiated independence, which only made her more... dear.

Max walked up to her and wrapped his arms around her from behind. "I am in trouble, okay? I went for years without being tempted, then ran into a woman I thought was everything I'd ever wanted in a partner. She was smart, funny, ambitious, attractive in ways beyond the physical, and she said she was equally gone on me. Better still, she knew my line of work and talked shop with me by the hour. It didn't work out, so I went for a few more years without being tempted."

As Max spoke, an insight emerged: He'd been devastated when Shayla had turned him down and walked away. The greater blow had been not to his heart, but to his pride. He'd been conned, thoroughly, and like most well-chosen marks, he hadn't had a clue he was being played until the damage had been done.

Shayla had dumped him only after meeting Maura, only after realizing that Max paid for every cent of Maura's expenses and was even building a trust fund for her.

Jeannie turned and wrapped her arms around him. "You're in trouble?"

Over her shoulder, the castle wall rose against the blue summer sky. A pennant flapped in the breeze, not the flag of the Earl of Strathdee, because the owner of the castle was far away, enjoying wedded bliss and building a different sort of castle.

"I want to go tomato shopping with you," Max said. "I want the pillow fights and parenting discussions, the stupid arguments that teach us how to make up and move on. I want the long nights and the... I want treasures I have no business wanting, Jeannie. I'll settle for a sunset, maybe even a sunset every so often for the next few months, but that's all I can offer."

God, she felt good in his arms. Warm and lovely, fresh and feminine.

Henry whacked Max on the ear. Jeannie smiled.

"Let's get back to the Hall," she said, "and get a certain unruly young man ready for his nap." She kissed Max on the cheek and strode off down the path.

~

"I CAN PUT her off for another week or two," Pete said, "though Mrs. Sutherland is a determined woman. We'll call it a house-hunting trip, while I'll be focused mostly on the status of the Brodie Castle project."

The venue was quiet, as only an establishment run by Brits could be quiet. Pete hadn't chosen the location—he wasn't a member of the Hibernian Club, or whatever it was called—but Boston was an okay place to spend a summer evening.

Connor Maguire was the last of the investors Pete had to meet with. The discussion among the others was moving forward nicely, with consensus forming around the idea that Max Maitland needed a second-in-command, at least, and that a guy who'd never handled a job outside the Lower Forty-Eight might not be the most cost-effective resource for the position.

Marty Ebersole had made a few more noises about Max's buyout clause, which Pete would get around to reading—or having his lawyers read—soon.

Maybe on the plane to Scotland.

"You're planning an ambush," Maguire said. "Less than thirty days after your handpicked project manager puts down his suitcase, you're sniffing around, letting everybody on the job site know you lack confidence in him. Why?"

This was the problem with outsiders—Maguire was an Irishman, a friend of Marty's. They'd met at a polo tournament a few years back, and Marty had been mad for hotels ever since.

"Maguire, you wound me." Pete signaled the waiter for another round. "I'm making a show of support, letting the locals look over one of the investors in person. My objective is to build trust, to get everything off on the right foot—and to keep peace with my wife, who will not appreciate my meddling with her real estate adventures."

Maguire was the youngest of the investors and the twitchiest. New money tended to be twitchy, but Pete didn't know if Maguire was new money. Marty had vouched for him when one of the regulars had dropped out of the project on the advice of a divorce lawyer. Marty claimed Maguire had turned a bunch of old British country houses into high-end venues and then sold them to the Germans, Russians, and Chinese.

"I've met your wife," Maguire said, lifting a glass of some unpronounceable single malt. "Lovely woman who takes animal welfare seriously."

Mrs. Sutherland's animal-welfare interests were expensive, though they added a nice veneer of public spiritedness to Pete's portfolio.

"She hasn't mentioned meeting you, but then, she and I have our separate interests, and you and I haven't done business together before—not directly."

"So humor a new business acquaintance and explain what exactly you intend to do on this goodwill mission."

A business acquaintance, not an associate, not a friend, not a partner.

Maguire's hair was dark red—there was a name for hair that color —while his eyes were a curiously light green. The combination was disconcerting, as if the eyes of a large, feline predator looked out of a human face.

"I've never seen the castle, for one thing," Pete said. "Did the drone videos, looked over all the topo and boundary maps, the virtual tours, the room-to-room footage and elevations, but I like to get a feel for where my money's going."

Maguire drank his whisky neat, and before he took a sip, he held the glass beneath his nose—more predatory behavior, sniffing his drink. As if they'd serve anything but the best in a place like this? The steak had been superb, the fancy French vegetables interesting, the raspberry mousse—they called it fool—both rich and light.

Maguire cradled the tasting glass in a large hand that bore a white scar across the back. "I can't criticize a man for taking a personal interest in a project that could cost him a great deal of money. The castle has tremendous potential, but I see some significant challenges as well."

Pete remained silent until the waiter had left a second Bloody Mary—or a third?—and ghosted off with the empty.

"You mean the road situation? That was one of my first concerns." Arnie had pointed out the lack of major highways in the area, but then, his family had been in oil and gas for at least four generations. Arnie liked big roads and lots of 'em.

"The roads are fine, for Scotland, and you won't be asked to do any off-site road improvement. I expect significant cost overruns with the build-out—castles being what they are—but I'm curious as to how the two buildings will be connected. The front of the Hall sits nearly two hundred feet lower than the castle, though you could throw a stone from the castle's postern gate and easily hit the roof of the Hall. Nonetheless, I have yet to meet the tourist who wants to face an uphill hike at the end of a long journey."

"Two hundred—?" Too late, Pete realized those celadon eyes were watching him, collecting information Pete shouldn't have given away. "I thought it was closer to one hundred fifty feet, but you do have a point. That's exactly the sort of concern I can raise with Maitland in private, where a stray email or a pair of big ears won't be a problem. You having another?"

Maguire smiled, though his expression wasn't friendly. "This is sipping whisky, Mr. Sutherland."

"Call me Pete."

Maguire glanced in the direction of the maître d', and the guy was scurrying over, a pen and leather-bound folder in hand. He set them on the table, bowed—honest to God bowed—and took a step back before turning away.

Maguire set aside his drink and picked up the pen, which had a wooden barrel and had probably been handcrafted by one-hundred-twenty-year-old elves toiling away in the bowels of a medieval Irish mead hall.

"I signed on with the Brodie Castle project because the investment is modest," Maguire said, "relative to some renovations I've seen. The Hall at least has been in continuous use since it was built, and I knew the previous earl from his interest in polo. The present earl also seems like a decent sort, though I'll be honest with you, Mr. Sutherland. If your merry band of trust-fund golf buddies can't make a go of the place, I might approach Elias Brodie about buying it outright."

Vodka and tomato juice roiled in Pete's belly, and a few choice curses begged to be muttered in Marty Ebersole's direction. Maguire was taking the first step in positioning himself for a hostile takeover: buying enough of the target's stock to see all the shareholder disclosures, sit in on the meetings, and chat up the opposition.

"We have a ninety-nine-year-lease on that castle, Maguire. Brodie can't sell a single cobblestone unless the subsequent owner honors the terms of our lease." If the lease agreement didn't provide at least that much security, Max Maitland was one unemployed liability.

Maguire checked his watch, which might have been a newer Patek Philippe.

"I honestly hope our little gang of rogues can make a success of this project." Maguire used the fancy pen to scribble his initials on the bill, then set the leather folder and pen aside. "We have obligations under that lease agreement, schedules to keep, revenue projections to meet. In the sad event that we default on our obligations, we'll have made Brodie Castle a costly ruin. Not fit for habitation, not historically preserved. Brodie will have to do something with it."

Son of a bitch. "In which case, you intend to be there, cash in hand, ready to solve all of his woes?"

Maguire took a last, leisurely sip of his whisky, not a care in the damned world. "I intend to do whatever is required of me to make our renovation project a success, because I have an obligation of good faith and fair dealing to all parties involved in that lease agreement. Should the lease agreement become void by virtue of a default by the investors, then my obligations to them end as well."

Maguire set down his glass. He moved languidly, like a wealthy scholar of some arcane literary genre, and he never raised his voice. Pete hadn't heard him laugh, hadn't seen a genuine smile from him.

A cold bastard, though Pete could be as ruthless as any upstart Paddy. "We won't default. The castle will become the destination venue Maitland has promised us, or homelessness will be the least of his worries. This is exactly why I'm going to see for myself how things are getting off the ground and exactly why the other guys support hiring additional management staff for the project."

Maguire's gaze swept the room, and the toady in tweed was at the table, collecting the leather folder and salaaming again.

"Another excellent meal," Maguire said. "My compliments to Esme."

"Thank you, Mr. Maguire. I'll be sure to pass that along to the kitchen."

"Tell your mother-in-law to bet on Graham's Knight to win in the Lavelle Stakes out at the Downs next weekend. The bookies aren't paying attention."

"Graham's Knight?" Gone was the professional deference of the maître d' and, in its place, the enthusiasm of a betting Irishman.

"Meggie says the colt's in top form, stronger by the day, and ready to take the world by storm."

"Thank you, Mr. Maguire." The toady bounced away from the table, and rather than return to his post behind the lectern at the door, he disappeared into the kitchen.

"You follow horse racing?" Pete asked.

"My sister is a steeplechase jockey who morphed into a trainer. Never met a horse she didn't like." He rose and stuck out a hand. No jewelry, no shine on his fingernails. "Been a pleasure, Mr. Suther-land. I'll look forward to hearing how your jaunt to the Highlands goes. Please give my regards to your lovely wife."

"Will do," Pete said, remaining seated because all the life coaches said that was the power position. "Can I tell the guys that you're in favor of expanding the project staff too?"

"Of course not. You haven't made your goodwill tour. See what you find, and when you've reported back, we can make a decision based on more than speculation and gossip. Safe journey."

Maguire left the table, pausing to exchange a few words with an older woman sharing a drink with a guy half her age. Pete downed the rest of his Bloody Mary—good vodka should never go to waste, and even for a connoisseur, the vodka was first-rate.

Maguire strode off after kissing the older woman's cheek, which was just too goddamned Old World for words. Pete's wife liked that crap, though. The cheek kissing and door holding. Maguire probably sent his mother flowers for no reason.

Pete stashed the pretty pen in his pocket, then approached the gal behind the bar. "I'll need a cab to the airport. Down front in ten."

"Of course, sir. The bell staff will take care of that for you." She had an Irish accent and a smile that was close enough to real that Pete considered another drink.

But, nah. He had a plane to catch—flights out to Edmonton weren't all that frequent—and what the hell, he had flowers to order for his wife.

CHAPTER ELEVEN

Jeannie had had flings before—not many, but enough that another should follow a predictable pattern: interest, anticipation, opening moves, the highlights reel, the smile and wave farewell. Sometimes, the progression took a few weeks to run its course, sometimes a few hours. Harmless pleasure, a little comfort, and heigh-ho, life goes on.

Max Maitland was different. A fling didn't look shy and adorable while admitting he was "in trouble."

A fling didn't have that talk about expectations. A lack of expectations was obvious when flinging.

A fling didn't schedule everything—food, hikes, sex, conversations —at the convenience of pint-sized tyrant, not that Jeannie had had any flings since Henry had been born.

"Having second thoughts?" Max asked as they trooped into the kitchen.

"The thoughts I'm having do not fit that description, Mr. Maitland."

Max sat at the table so Jeannie could wrest Henry from his infant pack, a tiny consideration for Henry's safety that Jeannie might not have thought of herself.

"He's sinking fast," Max said, brushing a finger over Henry's cheek. "Let's do the dido-check and get him snuggled up."

Henry yawned his way through the rest of the routine—diaper check, quiet walk to the spare bedroom in the earl's apartment, a few soft sighs with Bear-Bear's ear clutched in one tiny fist, the blanket binding between the fingers of the other.

And then he was asleep.

"I want to hurry," Jeannie said as she and Max beheld that greatest gift to any child-minder, a peacefully sleeping baby. "But if we hurry, he'll know, and then he'll wake up at the worst possible moment."

"I want to hurry too." Max tucked the blanket up around Henry's shoulders. "My eagerness has nothing to do with His Highness's mommy-management radar."

He took Jeannie by the hand, led her from the room, and closed the door save for a few inches. They hadn't even made it three steps down the hallway—three quick steps—before Max had her up against the wall, his mouth on hers.

Free climbers probably had a word for what Jeannie did next. She got one leg around Max's hip, braced herself with her back to the wall, secured the second leg, wrapped her arms around his shoulders, and *ascended* into his kiss.

And oh heavens, to devour Max was lovely. To be simply a woman awash in desire and anticipation, her hands free to roam broad shoulders, a strong back, trim hips, and a muscular butt...

He eased her away from the wall and carried her, still wrapped around him, to the master bedroom. Jeannie rested her head on his shoulder and remained in his arms even when they'd arrived beside the bed.

"I don't want to let you go." Foolish words, also the truth.

"Be a challenge undressing, which does seem to be a necessary part of the proceedings."

Engineers. She let her legs slide down his flanks. "I'm out of practice."

"Thank God," Max said, stepping away and pulling his T-shirt over his head. "If this is you out of practice, then Jeannie Cromarty at the top of her game would be my last, best memory. I'm out of practice too, but it all comes back to me when you look at me like that."

She was looking at his bare chest, a landscape of male muscle dusted with dark hair. He let her look, though his smile said the paybacks would be lovely hell.

"I'm not in shape." Jeannie sat on the bed and yanked at a shoelace. "Not like I used to be."

Jeannie wasn't sure what she'd just announced. She resented that pregnancy and motherhood had taken control of her body, resented that she was too tired to work out, even assuming she could find a gym she could afford with a day care service she could trust.

She hadn't gone completely to pot. Not yet. God knew she and Henry went for walks, stroller rides, and hikes by the mile.

"When I worked construction back in high school and college," Max said, taking the place beside her and brushing her hair back over her shoulder, "I could bench-press the world, run a half marathon for fun, and routinely skip a night of sleep. Now I'm more into durability than stupid displays of masculine prowess. You're a physically attractive woman, Jeannie, but that's only part of why I look forward to being intimate with you."

This was true for Jeannie too. The chemistry was there, but so was a purely adult liking and appreciation. Jeannie was sitting on the bed with the man who liked her son, who worked hard but not too hard, who would do right by the castle not only because that was his job, but also because that's who Max was.

She toed off her shoes and stood to shuck her jeans. Max did likewise, which meant...

He was naked.

Jeannie abruptly could not find the snap on her waistband.

"Would you like to use the bathroom first?" Max asked, draping his clothes over the back of a reading chair. "There's a stash of guest toothbrushes in the second drawer on the left."

"You go ahead."

She watched, a little embarrassed to gawk, but unwilling to deprive herself of the sight of Max strolling naked into the bathroom. He didn't close the door all the way, but left it open a few inches—for conversation, apparently.

"Do we need to have any awkward discussions about birth control?" he called.

"Not awkward. You'll use condoms even though I'm on the pill."

"Works for me."

And actually, that *hadn't* been awkward. The water ran, followed by the sound of teeth being brushed. Max had very likely raised the topic of contraception when out of sight as a courtesy to Jeannie's newfound self-consciousness. She undressed the rest of the way, but appropriated Max's T-shirt and sat on the bed until he emerged from the bathroom.

"I will never wash that T-shirt again. It looks much better on you, by the way. Bathroom's all yours."

He was so relaxed, so casual. He propped a shoulder on the bathroom doorjamb and crossed his arms over his chest. He was somewhat aroused, well endowed, and apparently at ease with both realities.

"I expect Henry to wake at any moment," Jeannie said. "Somehow, motherhood equates to not deserving any pleasure."

"Is it motherhood, or the post-divorce self-shaming syndrome? Once bit, twice shy, with a side helping of why bother when I always screw it up?" He pushed away from the door, ambled over to the bed, and turned down the covers. How could even a naked man in great shape look sexy doing something so pedestrian?

"You speak from experience?" Jeannie asked.

"How 'bout you use the facilities, and then you can tromp around in my head all you please, Jeannie Cromarty. That boy won't nap forever."

"No," Jeannie said, rising from the bed. "But he does nap daily, sometimes twice." She brushed a hand over Max's lean flank and crossed to the bathroom.

He was in the bed when she emerged, sitting up against the headboard and looking entirely at home. The bedroom was a compromise between respect for the past, which would have covered every surface in tartan wool if the Victorian "mad for plaid" craze hadn't been contained, and sensible comfort. The bed was a huge four-poster covered with a simple brown cotton and velour duvet, while the extra blanket was a brown, red, cream, and black plaid.

The walls were half-paneled oak, the rugs forest green on oak parquet flooring, while the wing chairs continued the plaid motif. The fireplace and mantel were a pinkish marble, the drapes brown.

A masculine room, putting Jeannie in mind of the trees that surrounded her holiday cottage. Max Maitland fit in here. Physically, the high ceilings, substantial furniture, and floor-to-ceiling windows were on the right scale for him.

Emotionally, the emphasis on comfort and practicality suited him too, which sent a pang of sadness through Jeannie as she climbed under the covers. If she wasn't careful, she could fall hard for Max Maitland—harder than she already had, and for all the right reasons. She'd fallen for Harry MacDonald for the wrong reasons—loneliness, boredom, the creeping fear of never finding a true partner.

"Come here," Max said, holding out his arms. "I am considering strategy, and I'm sure I'll do that better while I hold you and you hold me."

Oh yes. Jeannie snuggled up to his side, wrapped an arm around his middle, and rested a thigh across his legs.

"You smell good, Max Maitland. Up close,"—she sniffed his chest—"you smell clean and... manly." An old-fashioned word, much ridiculed, but appropriate for him and the open forest scent he wore. "Will you tell me of your bout with post-divorce self-shaming sour grapes?"

His hand traced a slow pattern on Jeannie's back, and for a moment, she thought he might not answer. Why in blazes had she put on his T-shirt when she might instead have been skin to skin with him?

"I haven't gone through a divorce, but my parents split up. Mom never dated. I don't think Dad did either."

"This has to do with your sister."

"Any kid with a special-needs sibling is handed an impossible riddle. You have to be a normal kid, because your parents and your siblings desperately need you to be normal. Get good grades, have friends, go out for sports. You have to be the normal kid, but you also have to never need anything. Clearly, your sibling deserves all the help and support there is to give. You can't be jealous, you can't be resentful, you can't lose your temper or let anybody down."

Jeannie shifted over him, so she straddled his hips. "But it's normal to be jealous, and resentful, to occasionally get mad, or drop the ball. That's part of growing up in a family."

His gaze was bleak. "I had no older siblings, no close cousins. Somebody forgot to send me the memo about flaws being normal, though Maura's counselors at some point hauled me in for a few family sessions and put some of the pieces together for me. Maura, who has more on the ball than most of her cottage mates and friends, gets a dose of the same dynamic. She's high-functioning enough that she's the one who can't take up precious resources needed by other members of the household. I connected my own dots belatedly."

Jeannie kissed him and slid down onto his chest. "Family is such a challenge." Though at the moment, she was overwhelmingly grateful for the family she had and for the child sleeping down the hall. Henry was stubborn and demanding, but he'd never spent a night in hospital. He was developmentally on track and so easy to love.

She waited, hoping Max might say more, but instead he threaded his hand through her hair and tipped her chin within kissing range.

If he was in a hurry, it was a luxuriously steady, luscious hurry. He moseyed his tongue into her mouth, teasing, exploring, and waking up parts of her far distant from her lips. His previous kisses

had been enthusiastic, skilled, and interesting. This kiss was... relentlessly intimate.

Jeannie wanted it to go on forever, and she wished some magic,
extra set of hands might ditch the T-shirt she was wearing, because
she was too busy touching—

Max eased the hem of the T-shirt up, inch by inch. Jeannie
paused the kissing long enough that he could slip the shirt over her
head and toss it to the foot of the bed.

"Where were we?" he asked.

"We were fetching your jimmy hat, because I'm this close to
losing my self-restraint."

"Already?"

He looked far too pleased with himself. Jeannie got a hand
around his arousal and stroked the smugness right off his face.

"I haven't your reserves of restraint, apparently," she said, easing
her hand up and down his shaft. "I'm weak like that. I get naked, I
start kissing, the next thing you know—"

Max arched into her grip. "I'm as hard as Scottish granite and
trying to recite the Greek alphabet backward because you have
exactly the right touch, exactly the right rhythm, exactly the right—
condoms are in the nightstand."

Jeannie dealt with the condom—no frills—and shifted down to
her back. "Up you go."

"I love a woman who knows who and what she wants."

The word *love* pricked a growing balloon of desire. Max Maitland did not love her, had all but promised he never would, and that
was fine... just fine. Henry already had one male role model dodging
on and off stage, he didn't need—

Max settled over her. "Where did you go, Jeannie?" His gaze held
concern and tenderness. His touch as he brushed his fingers over her
brow was devastatingly gentle.

"I'm here," Jeannie said. "Right now, I'm here and so are you."
She tried for a smile and suspected she wasn't fooling Max. The
mood had acquired an edge of wishes unspoken and dreams ignored.

They could still have pleasure, though, so as Max eased into her body and the lovely physical sensations of intimate joining pushed aside regret, Jeannie gave herself up to that indulgence. She held nothing back, saved nothing for next time or later or any of the impossible wishes. She gave and received pleasure until the room spun and her heart spun with it, until everything else fell away, even regret, even dreams that could not come true.

HENRY SCOWLED at Max with all the disapproval of a child who well knew that his age entitled him to break into a loud bout of stranger anxiety.

"We're buds," Max said, scooping the baby from amid his blankets. "Buds hang out together while your mom catches up on her sleep. She'll be happier for getting some rest, and we both like when she's happy. Got it?"

Henry slapped him on the cheek.

"We'll work on that rabbit punch some fine day when your mom isn't likely to interrupt us." No, actually they wouldn't, and Max had the sense Henry knew BS when he heard it. "You hungry?"

Henry yawned.

"Time for a wardrobe change," Max said when Henry's diaper proved to be damp. "That apple juice must be quicker than beer. The magic dido bag is in the kitchen, where another piece of pizza might be in order."

Jeannie was a fierce and tender lover, as Max had suspected she'd be. Even in sleep, she'd kept hold of his hand, wrapped an arm around his waist, or otherwise maintained a physical connection. None of that wham-bam-get-lost-Sam stuff. She cuddled with as much conviction as she kissed.

Max dealt with Henry's diaper, but knew better than to put the baby back in the high chair. That would signal time to eat, which it might not be. The baby carrier would mean time for a walk, which was also not going to happen.

"So I'll do the one-armed-bandit thing," Max said when he'd washed his hands. "I'll introduce you to the arcane science of decoding the weekly project report. Boring as hell—don't tell your mom I said hell. Boring as... chopping veggies? You'd probably like chopping veggies, terrifying your mom by playing with a sharp object. All those pretty colors, and all that food can go into your mouth, which according to infants is the natural order decreed by God."

Max had talked to Maura the same way when she'd been a baby, because a language delay had been one of her predictable afflictions.

"A slight delay, thank heavens, though it's both receptive and expressive language, meaning she has feelings she can't talk about, and she doesn't grasp what's said to her as easily as it might appear."

Other times, Maura comprehended more on sheer intuition than Max could figure out with reason, two professional degrees, and a fair amount of logic.

Henry grabbed the collar of Max's T-shirt—a clean T-shirt, because Jeannie might want to wear the other one again—and pulled.

"Right. Time to get to work."

Though it took time, Max got himself, Henry, and the laptop arranged at the table with the mouse out of Henry range, and assorted toys—an hourglass egg timer, napkin rings in primary colors, Bear-Bear—within snatch-and-grab distance.

The work went slowly, in part because Max's mind kept drifting back to Jeannie, snuggled up in that big bed, exhausted on a level probably only another single parent could grasp. He should not have become intimate with her, because...

"Because I didn't listen to my own public service announce-ment," Max muttered. "No long-term potential here. Nothing to see, nobody to fall in love with. Just keep moving, until..."

Until when? Maura was twenty-two and had transitioned through the gap years of eighteen to twenty-one, when the child-protection safety net and the adult-services safety net each pretended the other organization "had more to offer the client."

Max had never been so grateful to have a legal degree as when he'd been begging and browbeating Maura's various service agencies into doing their part for her.

"How did you get that?" He gently pried the mouse from Henry's fingers and turned the egg timer upside down. "You're not helping me with these reports, micro-dude."

Though holding Henry felt wonderful. He was a happy little guy, ready to take on the world, provided his mama loved him, his diaper bag never went empty, and his belly was occasionally full. With luck, boy could grow up happy even without a father on the scene, though Max did not envy Jeannie and Henry the challenge they faced.

"Though you have first-rate fine motor skills too."

"Muh."

"Give it a month or two, you'll be ordering everybody around. You can tell your mom you love her too." Something Max would not say, no matter that it was probably already true. "Maybe Fergus will listen to you better than he listens to me."

That was the other factor making the weekly review go more slowly. Max was double-checking the spreadsheets, manually veri-fying totals, and coming up with discrepancies. Spreadsheets were tricky—a mistake could ripple on for pages, and mistakes were easy to make when rushing through a job.

He was still muttering over his figures, entertaining Henry, and occasionally swearing, when Jeannie padded into the kitchen wrapped in a Black Watch plaid bathrobe, and a pair of Max's hiking socks on her feet.

"I slept like the dead," she said, going straight to the fridge. "I don't know whether to thank you, or be horrified that you left the bed to stare at that computer. Is that my son making free with Mrs. Hamilton's napkin rings?"

Her hair was disheveled, her cheek still bore a crease from the pillow, and her bathrobe and socks—Elias's bathrobe and Max's socks —were Not Sexy At All. Max had never seen a lovelier sight.

"I've found a few discrepancies on Fergus's spreadsheets. He needs to do more cross-checking, because problems like this can snowball."

Jeannie set the leftover pizza on the counter. "I'm famished. Shall I heat some up for you?"

The domesticity of the offer yanked on a heartstring Max needed to ignore. "Please, and I think my boss will be getting hungry again soon too. He woke up wet, though he was bearing up manfully."

While Max was barely coping with some confluence of emotions —desire, of course, but also affection, longing, regret, resentment, protectiveness... A damned mess that he wouldn't trade for all the spreadsheets in Maryland.

Jeannie turned the oven on and stood with her back to Max. "You heard the baby and I didn't?"

Max rose and set Henry in the high chair. "Don't do that. Don't do the mommy guilt because you found all of two hours to enjoy yourself and rest. I did not hear Henry. He was barely stirring, and you started scooting around in bed. You woke me up, then I decided to check on Henry. He might well have gone back to sleep, but I had to stick my big nose into his room, and then he decided to wake up after all. I suspect you heard him, and in another two minutes, you would have been trudging across the hall to step and fetch for him."

She'd turned to regard Max as he'd delivered that tirade, her expression wary. Now she crossed the kitchen and hugged him.

"I slept very well, thank you. I feel like a new woman, and I'm grateful for the rest. Shall we get into the bread pudding too? Dinnertime is nearly upon us. If we eat early, I can be back in Perth before dark."

He should tell Jeannie that sounded like a fine plan, but instead he wanted to put a hand gently over her mouth. To stop the soft flow of words, the pragmatic good cheer. She remained wrapped around him, suggesting that pragmatic good cheer had cost her—some consolation.

"Why not stay the night?" Max said. "If you have plans, then don't let me interfere with them, but my weekend will be mostly paperwork and scheduling. I've been warned that one of my investors might drop by, and I only have one more weekend before I'm supposed to do my first hop back to the States."

Don't beg.

Jeannie nuzzled his neck. "This is when I'm supposed to say, that's a lovely offer, but I really must be going. Thanks for... everything."

Don't say it. Please don't say it. "You have to do what's right for you, Jeannie—for you and Henry. I'd love to have the company." He stopped short of utter folly: *Maybe you could come up again some other weekend, or I could see you in Perth. No reason you should have to do all the driving in this non-relationship that isn't going anywhere, ever.*

"I think the change of scene is good for Henry," she said. "He's beginning to notice a world beyond himself and his mother, and he's taken to you more readily than to most of my family members. Then too,"—Jeannie kissed Max's cheek—"you let me get some sleep. We'll stay until tomorrow morning."

Over Jeannie's shoulder, Max winked at Henry. Henry grinned back, and for a moment, life was sweet.

"Let's put the hurt to that pizza," Max said, "and then I'd like to show you some of Fergus's reporting. I'm not worried yet, but my site foreman and I need to have a talk."

"Eat first," Jeannie said, easing away. "Business later."

"What time does Henry go to bed?"

She set the pizza in the oven and fiddled with the timer. "Not soon enough, but if you want him to go to bed, that means he'll be awake until at least midnight."

"No way I can stare at Fergus's reports until midnight." Particularly not if Jeannie was in the same room.

EVEN BEFORE HER WEDDING, Jeannie had reconciled herself to the notion that Harry MacDonald was full of charm, but not exactly affectionate. If he hugged his wife, he'd soon be kissing his wife, and from there, insinuating his hands beneath her clothes was— in his mind—the expected progression.

Harry had been a restless sleeper, thrashing about rather than settling into a cozy, dreamy embrace. Then Jeannie had conceived, and nocturnal trips to the loo had become more frequent. Harry had decamped to the sofa, claiming he didn't want to inadvertently add to Jeannie's sleep deprivation.

Matters had deteriorated further when Henry had arrived, with Jeannie more often stealing night naps beside Henry's crib, Harry on the sofa, and nobody at all in the bedroom.

Max, by contrast, was a team sleeper. He'd spooned himself around Jeannie, a warm, friendly companion who knew how to remain comfortably close without octopus-ing his bed partner out of real rest. She'd woken in the middle of the night only once to find Max's side of the bed empty.

In the apartment's barely lit living room, she'd spied Max giving Henry the three a.m. bottle, the two of them rocking slowly in a chair by the empty hearth.

She'd sneaked back to bed, tears threatening. A few minutes later, a lullaby had drifted from Henry's bedroom, and Jeannie had pulled a pillow over her head. When she was an old, old woman, she'd still recall the sound of Max Maitland singing her son to sleep.

She shrugged the memory aside and refocused on the task at hand. Henry was in his backpack, wreaking havoc with Max's hair, while Jeannie clicked from screen to screen on the laptop Fergus kept in the solar. Breakfast down at the Hall had been cheerful, nutritious, and full of post-coital smiles, because the third condom had met its fate as the sun had risen.

Up in the castle's solar, the agenda was business and all business.

"Fergus has combined categories, possibly," Jeannie said, "but I don't see anywhere that he's tracking some of the consumables—trash bags, signage, orange mesh barrier fencing—and that stuff adds up."

Max was across the room, rifling through an orange crate full of manila folders. "I can't find a time sheet for Fergus. You'd think that would be the one document he'd keep track of. He puts in long hours, or he has in the past week. Where in flippin' heck is his time sheet?"

Gone was the lover of infinite patience and diabolical tenderness. Exasperation and annoyance laced Max's voice.

"I see spreadsheets saved at six a.m. and eleven p.m. Friday, Max. Fergus was here when the rest of the shire was out dancing and drinking. We can't fault him for shirking."

Henry was gnawing on a bright blue plastic dispenser that had held white correction tape, though somebody had used the entire roll. On what?

"This isn't good," Max said, cramming a file back into the orange crate. "Some of the time sheets aren't signed. Some skip a week."

Jeannie closed yet another incomplete spreadsheet. "Maybe that's a week of holiday?"

"Then we should be tracking the hours as vacation, personal leave, or leave without pay. You don't just ignore a yawning gap in the data, which any auditor will seize upon as proof of a faulty system, or worse."

Henry pitched the plastic dispenser against the wall. Max ignored him.

"You only just got here," Jeannie said. "You can't be held accountable for Fergus's mucked-up recordkeeping from last month."

Max rose and hoisted the crate back onto the empty cable reel where he'd found it. "I am the project manager. Therefore, the systems established to control the project are my responsibility. Fergus started sending me information weeks ago, shortly after we signed the deal with Elias. I was so busy preparing to relocate that I gave the weekly reports a glance and patted myself on the back for doing even that much."

That was rank overreaching. "Fergus has been at this castle since spring, nosing about, talking to Zebedee, then getting the work under way before any mention had been made of turning this place into a hotel. He's had months to get organized and failed to so do."

Max brought a file over to the computer, pulled up a smaller empty cable spool to use as a stool, and came down beside Jeannie.

"Let's do a little experiment, shall we? Do you have the time log for three weeks ago?"

Jeannie fished around—Fergus had no file-naming protocol—and found it. "This looks complete. The trades are here, in order— masons, electricians, carpenters, glaziers—plus admin, consultants, civil engineering... the usual lot."

Henry was peering over Max's shoulder at the computer screen, though any minute the baby would demand to get down and move around.

"Let's try this," Max said. "I'll read off a few time sheets, you tell me if the document matches the data entered. Can you find Dinty?"

"He's a mason." Jeannie found his row on the spreadsheet. "If we go back three weeks, this says he put in forty-eight hours."

"His time sheet says forty-six. Look up Hugh Morven."

Jeannie paged over to the carpenters. "Also forty-eight hours."

"His time sheet says fifty."

They went through a dozen time sheets, pulling from all of the trades. Some matched, but most were off by a few hours. The net difference was likely a wash, or close to it, but the perception would be inaccurate records.

And that perception would be right.

"My site manager is either computer illiterate or he's losing his eyesight."

"Fergus can use a computer. He might be slow, but he's not backward."

Max waved the file as he got to his feet. "Then what the holy frabjous heck is going on, Jeannie? He's here at all hours. He's sent me one report after another. Was he trying to sabotage the project a month before I even took over?"

"Pah!" Henry bounced in his backpack, his intonation in even a single syllable matching Max's ire.

A footstep sounded on the stone stairs leading up to the solar.

"If that's you, Dinty," Max called, "I tossed your stash when I found it on Thursday. You shouldn't be drinking that rotgut, much less having it on the project site."

Fergus loomed in the arched doorway. "Dinty doesn't drink rotgut. The young Pole working with MacKinnon's glaziers leaves his spare bottle here so he can have a drink before he hikes down the hill of an evening. I see you've been poking your nose where it doesn't belong, Maitland."

CHAPTER TWELVE

Scotland, Scotland, Scotland.

Maura's phone had told her a lot about Scotland. The population was 1,395 people, which didn't strike Maura as enough for a whole country, but Max had said it was a small country.

"Are you texting somebody?" Miss Fran asked from across the kitchen.

"Reading."

The lovely scent of bacon and toast distracted Maura, though she kept scrolling. Some creek with a very long name formed one of Scotland's borders, but they also had a Potomac River somewhere near Scotland, which was odd.

"Are you going to put jam on your toast, Maura?"

"Yes. Is there more than one Potomac River?" Max had taken her hiking along the Chesapeake & Ohio Canal towpath, which had been pretty, but also buggy. The towpath ran between the Potomac and the canal, though the canal was now mostly a long ditch in the woods.

The microwave dinged, sounding like a great big phone.

"I think there's a North Branch and a South Branch to the

Potomac," Miss Fran said. "The name is pretty, and smaller rivers might be named after it."

"Then how do you know which river is which, if they have the same name?"

"I guess by the rest of the conversation. If you're not having any jam, Maura, then please put it away."

What if Scotland was near the same Potomac River that ran next to Maryland? Why would Max make up all that nonsense about a wide, wide ocean, and the time being different, and airplanes?

"Maura, it's rude to sit at the table glued to your phone when you're in the middle of a conversation with somebody."

"I'm not glued to my phone. Somebody is in a bad mood."

"Maura!"

Maura rose. "That is exactly what you say to me. 'Somebody is in a bad mood.' I'm trying to use my phone to find stuff out, which you say I should do before I pester you with questions. Nobody else is at the table with me, and I didn't put the jam on the table, you did. Besides, you lied to me. You said my phone wouldn't call Max in Scotland, but I heard you talking to him on the phone this week. If anybody is entitled to be in a bad mood, it's me."

Maura had not yelled, but inside, she was yelling loudly enough to be heard in Scotland... wherever Scotland was. She left her toast on the table and marched out to the back porch. If Scotland was not across the ocean, and Max could call her, then Maura was determined to figure out why he'd lied, and to make him stop.

MAX CAUGHT JEANNIE'S EYE. She rose and extracted Henry from the backpack, then helped Max peel off the contraption.

"What's going on here, Fergus?" Max asked. "We have a relatively straightforward project less than sixty days out from its official launch, and the bookkeeping is a sh—a shambles."

"A shitstorm, ye mean."

"Not in front of the baby." Max and Jeannie spoke at the same time, which had Henry grinning.

"Beg pardon," Fergus said, "but the term applies. Shall we sit?"

Fergus took a bench. Jeannie returned to the chair, Henry roosted in her lap. Max leaned against the granite wall, arms crossed.

"Tell me what's up, Fergus, and don't dodge the truth, because you will not get a second chance to explain."

Fergus scrubbed a hand over his face, gazed out the long row of east-facing windows, and then stared at his boots.

"Zebedee was not one for details. That's not an excuse, it's context. He'd get an inspiration and act on it. I suspect he knew his health was precarious, because he took off in about eight directions at once. With a project like this, you get the architects crawling about the place, draw up the plans, then assess how to get from the present reality to the architect's pipe dream. This process should take months, with consultations, second opinions, revisions of plans, and reconsiderations. You bring the locals into the discussion because they know details of the site you don't, and they have to live with the final result."

He stretched out his legs and leaned back against the wall. "The neighbors might have no official say in what's planned, but if they aren't supportive of your aims, their children will move the surveyor's stakes and use them for toy swords. Their dogs will knock over the trash barrels. The ghost stories they've been telling with such fond affection for the past century will take a sinister bend, and expensive tools will start disappearing or dropping over the parapets."

Max pushed away from the wall. "Ghosts do not falsify time sheets, Fergus."

"Watch your word choice, Maitland. I don't falsify documents."

Henry had become determined to grab the mouse, which would invariably result in the mouse flying into a stone wall in the next three minutes. Jeannie tried shifting the chair away from the table, which inspired Henry to fussing.

Max scooped him from Jeannie's lap and went to the window.

"When the quarterly auditor looks at the disaster you call your project accounting, he or she won't be half so polite, Fergus. If you want to keep your job, then spare me the Highland temper. You got yourself into this."

Max's tone was mild, his expression was thunderous. He paced along the windows, giving Henry something to see other than stone walls and unhappy adults.

Jeannie waged a silent war with herself: to offer to help, or to take Henry and return to Perth. She wasn't being asked to help, the job would be temporary, and there was Max... looking remote, and impossibly attractive with Henry in his arms.

"That, I did," Fergus said. "I got myself into this, and I apologize for the lack of consistency between the time sheets and whatever is on the spreadsheets. I can straighten it out, and I was whittling away at it, but this project..."

He was staring at his boots again, the big, scuffed boots of a working man, not an accountant.

"This is the most ambitious job you've managed," Jeannie said. "Is that it?"

"Aye. If I'd had my arms around it from the start, if Zebedee hadn't been flying hither and yon and then dropping dead. If Elias had taken a hand. If you hadn't left, lass... I know I should have rung you up, asked what category the blasted trash pickup goes under and where to code a holiday or a day off... but you focused on the contracts, the receivables, the invoices. The labor side of this job has become enormous."

"Time and materials," Max muttered. "I gather you were writing paychecks based on the time sheets, but estimating hours worked for data-entry purposes. How much progress have you made correcting your spreadsheets?"

Henry was making put-me-down wiggles, which on this cold stone floor would never do. Jeannie had half risen when Fergus crossed the room and plucked Henry from Max's arms.

"The wee lad is bored with all this talk. Aren't you, Henry, my man?"

Henry smiled enormously and smacked Fergus's chin. "Bah!"

"He likes you," Max said. "Right now, I can't say the same. Is there a place to start, Fergus? A single week you know is accurate? The first week maybe?"

Fergus set Henry on his feet, keeping hold of Henry's hands. This game had only begun for Henry a few weeks ago, and it still had the power to absorb his attention.

"I had the first three weeks worked out, and then I overwrote the damned spreadsheet. Hours and hours of work. Damned Hugh came in here with his cork-brained questions and some joke about a parrot in a freezer and I saved the wrong bloo—blooming thing under the wrong blooming name. Henry will enter the next Highland Games as a sprinter."

Henry was tottering from foot to foot, swaying precariously, but holding fast to Fergus's callused fingers.

Max wore an odd half-smile as he watched Fergus with the baby. "Do you like children, Fergus?"

"I'm the oldest of eight, with three younger brothers. I either learned to like the weans, or I'd have run away from home before my twelfth birthday. But who wouldn't take to such a fine, bonnie laddie as our Henry?"

He lifted the baby to his chest and tickled Henry's belly. A lively little chortle filled the solar, and Jeannie hoped that whatever ghosts walked the castle halls heard that happy sound and rejoiced.

I should take Henry and go. The words were on the tip of her tongue when Max spoke up.

"Who among the men do you trust?"

Fergus left off tickling Henry to scowl at Max ferociously. "I trust every one of them, or I wouldn't have them on my job site. Goes for the ladies too." Henry got Fergus on the ear this time.

"Sorry, lad, didn't mean to sound cheesed off, but the yon Yank asks foolish questions."

"I mean, trust to keep his or her mouth shut," Max said, "because the pile of sh—doo-doo we have to shovel through will take more than one person's effort."

There it was, the opportunity to speak up.

"The crews love to gossip," Jeannie said, which bore no resemblance at all to *Let me have a look at the spreadsheets.* "Makes the day go more quickly. Then they head down to Fern's and sit around swilling their poison of choice and gossip some more."

"She's right." Fergus picked up the blue correction tape dispenser Henry had pitched against the wall. "The lads and ladies love a good natter."

"Jeannie?" Max asked. "Anybody on this work site that you'd trust to keep his or her mouth shut about bookkeeping that's been hosed up by Tropical Storm Fergus?"

Me—though that wasn't what Max was asking. "Hugh. He's a flirt and a tease and never seems to be in a hurry, but Hugh's sharp and can be surprisingly discreet."

"Not Hugh," Fergus said, pitching the blue plastic into the trash with considerable force. "I just need a wee bit more time."

"Fergus, you've had time," Max said. "You've had weeks, and you're only digging yourself a bigger hole."

Fergus, with the baby cuddled against his chest, marched up to Max. "I've made some headway, but there's this meddling Yank always peering over my shoulder, hurlin' thunderbolts about safety officers, hard hats, all-hands meetings, and Fern's dam—dratted invoices. If he'd leave me in peace for a few days, I might get a bit of proper work—"

Max's phone rang. He glowered at the screen. "The Earl of Mischief, whose ears were doubtless twitching." He swiped into the call, hit a few buttons, and put the phone on the table.

Which left Jeannie wondering: Why not call Elias back? Why not finish this difficult discussion and let Elias wait for fifteen minutes?

"You're on speaker," Max said. "Jeannie and Fergus and I are having a meeting. Henry's in charge and you're up early."

"Married life agrees with me," Elias replied. "Do you know a man named Connor Maguire?"

Max's posture changed, his body going still, his gaze unreadable. "He's one of my investors. Never met him, but flipping country estates into hospitality venues is what he knows best. He was always conferenced in for the investor meetings. Why?"

"I know him," Elias said. "The polo community is small, and Zebedee dragged me around to enough matches that Maguire's path and mine crossed. He's on his way to Scotland."

"Now?"

"He'll catch a red-eye to London tonight. What the hell is going on, Maitland? I leave my castle in your hands, and a lot of trust-fund buffoons start playing stupid games before you've even sighted your first ghost."

Max propped a hip on the table. "I've never met Maguire, and you expect me to explain his actions to you? He might be jaunting over this way for some polo, for all I know. How did you learn he was coming?"

"He dropped me an email."

"Why?"

"That, I don't know. Don't underestimate him, Maitland. He's not one of your overfed, overbred, self-impressed rich dunces. He knows castles like Violet knows chickens."

"Was that supposed to be a brilliant analogy?"

"That was a warning. If your project isn't running like a well-oiled top, Maguire will know, and what he'll do with that knowledge is anybody's guess."

"I've been here a week. No project this size gets organized in a week flat, and a little warning about the doo-doo storm your uncle left in the bookkeeping department would have been appreciated."

Fergus had taken the seat behind the desk, Henry in his lap.

Henry was again diving and grabbing for the mouse, which had a lovely green light softly pulsing on one side.

"Doo-doo storm? Have you been nipping from Dinty's flask, Maitland?"

"Not yet, but the idea has increasing appeal. I'll keep you posted."

"See that you do."

The call ended, and Jeannie stared at the phone, angry with Elias, though she knew he hadn't meant to sound so... so... impossible. Angry with herself for wanting impossible things. Angry with Max for being Max.

"So, Fergus," Max said, tucking the phone away. "It's not just your backside in a sling if we don't straighten out the books, it's mine and potentially that of every person employed on this site. Still think we ought not to enlist Hugh's aid?"

At the moment when Jeannie would have spoken up—*I'll help. I'm here, I'm willing, I need a job, and you need me*—Henry pitched the mouse against the wall. Batteries, bits of technology, and purple plastic went in all directions, while Henry beamed at all three adults.

MAX LEFT Fergus with a simple task: take the information on the time sheets and, using a pencil, correct the printout of the spreadsheet from three weeks ago. Keeping Fergus away from data entry seemed prudent, lest he overwrite another document and create an even bigger mess.

Henry had been left to supervise Fergus, another reason to keep the proceedings well away from the project laptop.

"The view up here is beautiful," Jeannie said, leading the way along the parapets. "I can see why the ghosts like this perspective."

Brenna, the first Countess of Brodie, had walked these heights while waiting for her Michael to come home from years at war. The third countess, also named Brenna, had been the first to mention seeing ancestral shades embracing on a lovely summer evening.

Max had read that bit of Brodie family lore one night the previous week, when he should have been tearing up Fergus's so-called reports. Birds strutted around on the rooftops and towers below the parapets, and one gargoyle sported an enormous nest on its head.

All of which had nothing to do with anything. "Jeannie, Fergus hasn't even made backups of his mess. Not a thumb drive, not a backup cloud service, not hard copy..." The enormity of the disaster had grown as Fergus had walked Max and Jeannie through his version of a recovery plan.

Nothing—not the labor-hour documentation, receivables, sched-ules, receipts, bills of lading, or contracts—was unscathed.

"I kept backups," Jeannie said. "Until three weeks ago, the mate-rials side of the project was in good order."

The chaos swirling inside Max receded behind a breeze of incredulity. "You kept backups?"

"Aye. Elias hadn't anybody else minding the till, so I took it upon myself to put the information in his online files. I can download it all if you like."

She hadn't offered to come on board, hadn't suggested Max could hire her even temporarily, and he didn't want to. He wanted—twenty-twenty hindsight—to be her lover, her friend, her *whatever*, for as long as circumstances allowed.

She wasn't offering much encouragement in that regard either, but then, what fool had been handing out public service announce-ments by the dozen only yesterday?

Max joined her at the parapets. "I'd appreciate..." The pennant luffing in the breeze caught his attention, as if somebody had towel-snapped him in the face. An eagle was lazing through the sky on ther-mals rising from the valley floor, not a care in the world. The day was beautiful, the view was beautiful, and Jeannie was lovelier than the weather and the scenery combined.

Damn the luck.

"Did you enjoy yourself last night?" Max asked.

Her smile was puzzled, as if she'd expected a different question. "I've enjoyed myself since I got Henry unbuckled from his car seat yesterday, Max. You?"

He rested his elbows on the stone wall. The sun had warmed the granite, the tree canopy made a green quilt right down to the village, and the River Dee wound placidly through fields and pastures. The Baron's Hall rose partway down the hill to the east, much closer than the winding paths suggested.

What a marvelous place this would be to propose marriage. The thought whispered through Max's mind, useless, but nonetheless true.

"Where can I buy more condoms without half the village knowing what size and flavor I purchased?"

Jeannie's smile was snatched away with the freshening breeze. "You brought me up here to ask about your supply of jimmy hats?"

"I wasn't going to ask in front of Henry—or Fergus—and you started to get that, 'I'll just be going now' look in your eye. I want to see you again, Jeannie."

Ah, the smile was making another hesitant appearance. "But you said... and I said. *We* said we hadn't any designs on each other."

"I have it on good authority that I talk a lot."

"Your sister?"

"Maura is honest, sometimes to a fault, and she's the reason I meant what I said yesterday, Jeannie. I might learn to love it here—part of me already does—but in Maryland, Maura has everything from heart specialists, to speech and language therapists, occupational therapists, friends... Finding friends who are at a comparable developmental level is almost impossible for her. Her world is in Maryland."

"And you are the guardian of that world. I would no more ask you to abandon your sister than you'd ask me to leave Henry with Harry's mum."

At least Jeannie sounded sad to make that declaration. "Would Henry's grandmother want custody of him?"

"I suspect she would. She recently warned me that my love life will be subject to her approval for the rest of Henry's life."

Max slid an arm around Jeannie's waist, which was stupid of him. Anybody could glance through the trees and spy them up here.

"I hope you told her to go to hell?"

"I haven't that luxury, Max, though it's tempting."

The feel of Jeannie next to him, the warm sunshine beaming down, the valley stretching out below to green hills against a perfect blue sky... This was a moment to savor, and yet, a part of Max didn't dare. Savoring could lead to kissing, and kissing could lead to distractions, and Fergus was likely to appear with a wet, squalling Henry at any moment.

"On the site maps, the Baron's Hall looks much closer to the castle than it seems when you have to hike between the buildings."

Jeannie brushed a twig away from the wall, sending it cascading down to the forest below. "You are thinking about site maps?"

"Trying to. The architects proposed a number of ways to connect the buildings, all of them expensive. Parking will have to be down at the level of the Baron's Hall, but the most impressive entrance to the facilities is right through the castle's main gates. I don't mind that the options are expensive—my guys have money—but I mind that they all destroy the castle's profile. The solutions proposed aren't aesthetically acceptable. Sooner or later, my brilliant investors need to have an answer to the riddle of the site plan."

Jeannie turned in his embrace, and Max's arms came around her. "I can help you with your project, Max. I can get the materials straightened out, check inventory against bills of lading—I suspect nobody has—do the data entry to correct the labor-hour reports, and otherwise get the recordkeeping on solid ground."

I can help you... How often had anybody said those words to Max? How often had they said the words and meant them?

Max wallowed in the pleasure of holding Jeannie for the length of three heartbeats. "If you save this project, then you get paid for your efforts." He stroked a hand over her hair, hating his job, hating Scotland, and resenting his homeland. The wealthiest nation in the history of nations didn't think Maura—the sweetest, most loving, stubborn, miraculous, delightful person ever to beat all the odds—was worth providing for.

"I need the money," Jeannie said. "I'm too Scottish not to make you pay for hard work, because it will be hard work."

Which she, being Jeannie, sounded downright cheery about.

Max stepped back, because his next words might result in an attempt to pitch him over the parapets.

"I don't sleep with my co-workers, Jeannie. I tried it once, and that ended badly. I'd offer to spot you some cash while you keep job-hunting, but I suspect you're too proud to take it, and neither one of us likes the implications of money changing hands after intimacies."

The breeze whipped a strand of her hair across her mouth. Max jammed his hands in his pockets rather than tuck that lock of hair behind her ear. Far down the hill, a pair of masons were tidying up the drystone wall that ran between the village and the river. They looked like an industrious, happy pair, while Max felt as if he'd just found his own personal rain cloud to drag with him everywhere.

Jeannie shaded her eyes to watch the eagle frolicking. "You're saying I have to choose between having you for a boss and having you for a lover?"

At least she wasn't ranting. "I have a fiduciary duty to this project, Jeannie. I owe the damned castle my loyalty, in other words, and if there's a relationship between us, somebody could claim I have a conflict of interest—I put you in charge of the books for my own convenience, not because you are the only person who can possibly rescue me from Fergus's mess."

She folded her arms school-marm fashion. "I see. Now you're withholding your favors as a kindness to me? Preserving me from nasty talk?"

Max knew better than to say that. "Preserving us both from the kind of gossip that can get me booted from the project. I need this job, Jeannie. I need the revenue it will generate for years to come."

She again faced the wide green valley below. "Because you are the sole support of a woman who will never be able to look out for herself. You're a good brother, Max Maitland."

The eagle enjoying the summer winds caught an updraft and flew straight at the castle. Its shadow passed over Max as the bird alighted upon the only tower to stand higher than the crenellations.

Big bastard, and the look he gave Max suggested fricassee of project manager might be on the dinner menu—or maybe that was a she-eagle.

"I may or may not be a good brother," Max said. "I suspect right now, Maura doesn't think I'm much of a brother at all, but I'm all she has. If anything happens to me, she could well end up homeless, or worse."

"We understand taking care of our own in Scotland, Max."

He'd never had any claim on Jeannie—they'd had the proverbial hookup, nothing more—and yet, Max felt as if something precious and irreplaceable was being sacrificed to a castle he didn't even own.

"You'll take the job?"

"What does it pay?"

They dickered for a few minutes, finally settling at a decent wage —to Max's relief, Jeannie knew damned well what she was worth—as well as accommodations in the earl's apartment for the duration of the effort. Jeannie fussed about that, but Max reminded her that Elias would kill him for charging her anything like rent, and she backed down.

"What do we tell Elias?" Jeannie asked.

"I'll tell him the truth. The project documentation is a mess, and you have kindly offered to take over the thankless task of keeping the books, at least until the chaos has been spun into order. We keep Fergus's name out of that discussion, because he tried his best and was stranded in a quagmire by the last earl's death."

"Why not fire Fergus and replace him with an American?" Jeannie asked.

"The investors would likely try to do just that, but I would have rebellion on my hands before sundown the same day."

Jeannie pushed away from the wall, and Max's guts twisted. She was the loveliest woman he'd crossed paths with, she was rescuing his project, and he'd just parted with the privilege of holding her, much less sleeping with her, for the foreseeable future.

Because he needed the money, to be blunt.

"I'll take the job," Jeannie said. "I commend you for being such a good brother, but Max?"

She was being gracious, and that cut Max to the bone. "Yes?"

Jeannie cupped his jaw against her palm. "You are a loyal, hardworking, commendable brother and a highly conscientious and skilled project manager."

"And now for the but?"

"There is an and. And you are a sumptuous lover." She kissed him on the cheek, then disappeared down the winding stairs that led to the solar.

Max remained by the wall, wondering if he'd just lost the best thing that had ever almost-happened to him, made the only prudent choice, or both.

On the tower roof above, the eagle was strutting around, glowering at Max like the Wrath of Deeside.

"I'm leaving," Max said. "I'm leaving right now, and sooner or later, I'll be leaving Scotland."

The eagle squawked and flapped—its wingspan had to be six feet across—and pecked at the roof, sending some pebbles cascading down the slate shingles.

Max took one last look at the gorgeous view—a view that would bring in a lot of money, if all went well—and headed for the steps. Before he ducked into the winding stairway, a pebble rolling down the roof beaned him on the top of his head. The weight was nothing, but the impact stung like he—like heck.

CHAPTER THIRTEEN

Jeannie loved the work. Loved the detail, the sheer volume of numbers, the relevance. When bricks were delivered, she calculated the number on each pallet and checked the total against what had been ordered. She verified that any mortar sent to the site contained the type of cement specified by the head mason and then counted the sacks as they were off-loaded.

The job required as much moving around as sitting, which appealed to Henry. He peered at the world over Jeannie's shoulder when she had to track down Fergus or one of the crew chiefs for a signature, and he kept her company at the project office as she chipped away at the labor-hours records.

Fergus, Hugh, Dinty—everybody—made an excuse to stop by the project office, and half of them played with Henry. The welders made Henry a tiny hard hat, though it certainly wouldn't meet any safety standards, and Hugh's carpenters carved Henry an entire barn-yard full of animals.

"How's the boss?" Max asked, filling a paper cup with water from the cooler.

"He's having the time of his life," Jeannie said. "These past two weeks have been Henry's idea of how life ought to go on, with every-body paying him some attention."

Max set the cup on Jeannie's desk. "I meant, how are you?"

Ah, different question. Jeannie didn't dare answer honestly. "Catching up. Another two weeks, and we should be out of the woods. Any word from your investors?"

"Suspiciously quiet—all of them—which means they're doubtless plotting among themselves. Maguire is somewhere in the British Isles, but then, he's Irish so he's allowed to be here. You really think it will take two weeks to finish with those spreadsheets?"

This was how Max did much of his project management. He wandered through the castle, poked around in the Hall. Chatted up the apprentices, asked a few questions. The question Jeannie heard him ask most often was, "Do you need anything to stay on schedule?"

Before he wandered away to the next group, she often heard, "Keep up the good work. We're off to a great start."

Small, perfunctory words, but as far as renovation of the castle was concerned, the project truly was off to a great start.

And now, Max was managing her. "If you would kindly stop all project activity, I could have the records straightened out in a week, provided Henry doesn't recommence teething, or give up his remaining daily nap. Because the project is ongoing, I have to keep up with the new time sheets, the new deliveries, the outgoing purchase orders, and so forth, or we'll always be behind."

"Sensible," Max said, taking the guest chair opposite Jeannie's desk. "Elias forwarded me an email he got from Maguire last week."

And for at least five days, Max had been roosting on whatever problem that email contained. He was pleasant to everybody, but Jeannie detected a distracted quality in his replies and in his gaze.

"You've been brooding. Are you in a general brown study or pondering a specific problem?"

Max might as well have been a ghost in the Hall, he was so careful to leave Jeannie her privacy. She'd run into him once near midnight in the main kitchen, and the urge to hug him—simply to hug him—had nearly overwhelmed her. He was up at the castle shortly after dawn and often the last one down the hill at the end of the day.

Who thanked Max for his good work? Who reassured him that the project was off to a great start?

"Maguire raised the issue of how to link the two buildings, and if he spotted that problem, I can't expect the other investors not to eventually stumble upon it."

"This worries you." Perhaps it was a metaphor for bringing the whole project team together, from the apprentices, to the crew chiefs, to the local merchants, and the American investors.

Max rose and picked up Henry, who'd been sitting in a playpen batting at the fish mobile strung across the middle.

"When I presented the project to the investors, I made it plain we have a problem to solve in terms of connecting the Hall and the castle. I did not include a budget for that solution in my project estimates."

He raised Henry slowly over his head, and the baby grinned and waved his arms and legs. Henry was a more confident child than he'd been even two weeks ago, and that was wonderful.

"How could you budget for a solution that hadn't been chosen yet?"

Max brought Henry against his chest and dipped a discreet finger down Henry's diaper. "Time for a wardrobe change." He grabbed the diaper bag from beside Jeannie's desk and laid Henry on the cloth diaper spread on one end of the credenza.

"I can do that, Max."

"Henry and I haven't had our guy time lately, and this won't take but a minute." After he'd untaped the damp diaper, he held it curled loosely over Henry's belly, while Henry peed again, one of his more recent games.

"Next, you'll be writing your name in the snow," Max muttered. "Try to have some dignity, little dude. There's a lady present."

"Bah!"

The clean diaper went on smoothly, despite much waving and kicking on Henry's part. Jeannie powered down the laptop, just for something to do instead of watching Max tickle Henry's belly.

They liked each other. Not such a profound thing, for a man and a baby to get on well, but because Max took Henry in stride, everybody on the work site did as well, and Jeannie could make a good wage without having to pay for child care.

"What will you do about the puzzle of connecting the castle and Hall?" she asked.

"I'll keep puzzling. My estimates clearly state that additional expense will be incurred to create a unified venue out of the two buildings. Pete Sutherland is not one for reading fine print, though, and when he ought to be nagging me every seventy-two hours for a status report, he's gone to ground. I do believe this boy has grown just in the short time I've known him."

Max nose-rubbed with Henry, who chortled and blew raspberries.

"He slept through the night last night."

"Well done, young Henry. See that you make a habit of it."

"I woke in a panic and at first thought I was dreaming the sun had risen, because I hadn't given Henry his three a.m. bottle."

Max gently lowered Henry to the playpen. "You are a good mom, Jeannie Cromarty. Henry is lucky to be your son."

Those words, so quietly offered, landed with the force of a blow to the heart. "Not everybody thinks so."

Max gave the fish mobile a push. "Millicent thinks if she gets her mitts on Henry, then Harry might come around more often. Harry ought to be ashamed of himself twice over for neglecting both his mother and his son, but that is not your problem. If I haven't said it before, I'm saying it now: You are rescuing this project and me, Jeannie. Thank you."

He brushed a hand over Henry's head, then sauntered out the door.

"I'm going to cry," Jeannie said to nobody in particular. She was rummaging in her desk drawers—no organizational skills evident there—for a tissue when Hugh came in.

"Wee Henry, how's life at the throbbing heart of all meaningful progress toward Scotland's glorious future?" Hugh twirled a sprig of lavender under the baby's nose, and a game of grab-and-snatch ensued. "Are you looking down in the mouth over our fearless project manager, Jeannie love?"

"Max is not fearless." But he was honorable. Too honorable. "Have you ever lost your heart to somebody impossible, Hugh?"

His smile was crooked, his gaze bleak. "Every other week or so."

"Henry likes Max."

Hugh offered her a one-armed hug. "We all like Max, despite our best efforts to the contrary. For a Yank, he's all right. Henry, you're not to tell him I said so."

Hugh helped himself to a handful of fish-shaped crackers from the box on Jeannie's desk and was out the door, his black work kilt swinging around his knees.

Hugh was sweet, drop-dead gorgeous, a fine dancer, and charming, but he wasn't Max.

"You know what the worst part is?" Jeannie asked as Henry tried to pull himself up on the playpen's netting. "Max would make a good dad. He'd make a wonderful dad, and when I'm around him, I feel like a good mom."

Also lonely, hopeless, and sexually frustrated, but a good mom.

"HAS JEANNIE STOLEN YOUR LAPTOP?" Hugh asked.

Did he have to look so damned delectable lounging in the doorway to the solar? Hugh used his toolbelt as a sporran, the leather riding low on his hips. The result was so casually sexy that Fergus wanted to punch something—or someone.

"Jeannie and I keep redundant records. Maitland's orders."

Hugh sidled into the room. He never moved quickly, and yet, his hands were seldom idle. He picked up a wad of paper Fergus had tossed in the direction of the trash barrel and lobbed it over his shoulder.

Fergus took a folder to the filing cabinet rather than remain at his desk.

"Now that you've been freed from the tyranny of your spreadsheets," Hugh asked, "why don't you join us on the shinty pitch of a Saturday?"

"Because I don't have a death wish." Or a wish to spend hours pretending all that physical contact was in the name of one of the stupidest sports ever devised by frustrated man.

"You're not that slow," Hugh said. "And you're fairly accurate, considering you're getting on in years. Will you at least come to the ceilidh this Friday?"

"You're in my light."

"I'll take that for a no. When is the ordination?" Another wadded-up piece of paper went into the trash. "For surely I'm in the presence of a man contemplating holy orders. You don't drink with the men anymore. You don't bash heads on the shinty pitch. I haven't seen you stand up for a dance in weeks. You must be composing sermons or praying for the souls of the damned."

"I'm the site manager," Fergus said, shoving the file into the front of the drawer, "which means I'm kept busy. Maitland likes a safe, tidy, well-organized workplace, and the lot of slobs and layabouts we have on the payroll wouldn't know a safety regulation if it pissed in their beer."

The Brodie Castle project had one of the finest rosters of talent Fergus had ever had the pleasure to supervise. The crews thrived on challenges, cooperated with the natural genius of talented professionals, and took pride in their work without being arrogant.

"That Tina has us all prancing around in hard hats," Hugh said, "taking our breaks, putting up our tools. I feel like I'm back at summer camp, though we at least don't have to sing smarmy songs for our new safety officer."

Instead, Fergus was baying at the moon. He resumed his seat at
the desk for the sake of his dignity, because Hugh in a serious mood
was that irresistible.

"When you are done handling every object on my desk, wasting
your entire break, and otherwise entertaining yourself at my expense,
do you suppose you might be on your merry way?"

Hugh set down the stapler. "You're in a foul humor, Fergus. Is
your nose out of joint because Jeannie is having to sort out the shitstorm you made of the paperwork?"

What the hell? "What would you know about it?"

"I know she has the time sheets sitting on her desk, plain as day. I
know she's comparing purchase orders and deliveries. I know you
finally have the time to get off your arse and see how the work's
coming for the glaziers, welders, masons, and electricians, but you
never bother to chat up the carpenters. Why is that, Fergus?"

Because the sight of you makes my hands itch. "Get out of my
office, Hugh. You have work to do."

"If you have a problem with me, Fergus, then tell me. I consider
you a friend, not simply the horse's arse that struts around this site
looking for slackers and lost hammers."

Hugh was leaning over the desk, his blue eyes glaring daggers at
Fergus. Good God, the man was in a bro-pout, while Fergus had
reached the limit of his self-restraint.

"I said get out." Fergus rose and got a hand around the back of
Hugh's neck, intent on shaking sense into him—or starting a proper
brawl. Anything to avoid the questions in Hugh's eyes.

Hugh, though, simply stood still, eyes closed, neck arched into
Fergus's touch. His posture was that of a man in pain, though Fergus
hadn't grabbed him hard.

"Did I hurt you?" Fergus asked.

Hugh opened his eyes and heaved out a breath. "A delicate flower
such as yourself would have to try much harder than that to put a
mark on me, Fergus MacFarland." He glanced around the room, at

the door, and then at Fergus before stepping back. "But I ache, man. You touch me, and I ache."

The words were so unexpected, had they not been matched with a miserable, searching gaze, Fergus would have doubted his ears.

Hugh propped his hip on the desk and took out his tape measure. "Say something. Drop me over the parapets. Laugh. Give me an awkward pat, tell me we'll always be friends, and then never look me in the eye again. I know how it's done, Fergus."

He drew out the metal tape, then squeezed the release so it snapped back into the case. Did it again, while Fergus's world acquired new and brighter dimensions.

He came around the desk so he stood in Hugh's line of sight. "You ache... *for me?*"

"No accounting for taste, is there?"

The bravado in Hugh's smile was heartrending. Fergus closed the door and stood before it. "Clearly, there is no accounting for taste, because I ache for you too."

The tape measure hit the floor. Hugh stared at it. "Say that again, please."

"I ache for you too, Hugh. Have for years." Fergus kept his distance, because the moment was too lovely to be rushed.

"So why are you standing clear over there by the door? Am I to sweep you off your wee feet?"

His smile said he was contemplating exactly that.

"Hugh, me lad, once I get my hands on you, it will be some time before I turn you loose."

Hugh pushed away from the desk and swaggered—that was the word—across the room. "Feeling's mutual. What are you going to do about it?"

God, he smelled good. Sawdust, sweat, soap, and hope. "I'm going to lock the door."

≈

AVOIDING Jeannie in the Hall had resulted in a sort of torture for Max. He'd observed her closely enough to learn her routine—hers and Henry's—and kept sufficient distance that their paths seldom crossed.

His present strategy for avoiding her was to lurk in the portrait gallery, a room more than a hundred feet long. Max told anybody who asked that he was learning Brodie family history to incorporate into the final decoration scheme, but in fact, he was allowing Jeannie the run of the main kitchens.

For two weeks, Max had impersonated a project manager for whom all was going well, and in fact, the work was gaining momentum. He'd neglected to take the long Scottish summer days into account when scheduling, and the men often arrived early and left late without recording every hour on their time sheets.

They well knew that what summer gave with one hand, winter took with the other, as Dinty had said.

Max wandered down the row of smiling, attractive Brodies. The family had had some rotten luck—one earl had died young as a result of a bad fall while hillwalking. Another had been killed in the trenches of World War I. For the most part, though, the Brodie family had thrived.

"Good genes," Max said to the third earl. He was a red-haired Victorian gent who'd shipped high-grade Aberdeen bulls all over the world and enhanced the fortunes of the next three generations of Brodies.

"If this project goes well, then I can at least achieve security for Maura."

The earl seemed to smile upon that aspiration, but smiling was easy for him. He hadn't had to put up with a pack of squirrelly investors whom Max suspected were up to no good. Pete Sutherland in particular had an unerring instinct for sticking his oar in at the worst moment, and Connor Maguire was a troubling unknown.

Max's phone chimed, a reminder that the kitchen was likely free of all lovely, tempting, off-limits Scottish women and their adorable offspring. He bid the various earls, countesses, barons, and their progeny farewell, took the stairs down to the ballroom, and made his way to the kitchen.

"Timing is everything," he muttered, for there sat Jeannie at the table, Henry parked in his booster seat with something fruity smeared around his mouth.

"Hello, Max. We're sporting our blueberry buckle facial mask tonight. The turkey compote was a great favorite, with only half the jar ending up in Henry's hair."

Henry waved a sticky fist and brought it down on the table, like a Viking at his mead.

"What did you have for dinner, Jeannie? I don't see any turkey compote in your hair."

Beautiful hair, so soft and shiny Max had dreams about freeing it from whatever ponytail or braid Jeannie trussed it up in.

"I hadn't got that far yet. Henry took a late nap, and now our schedule is all at sixes and sevens."

"Is the project office too busy for him? We can set you up a space down here." *Please say yes. Please say you'd prefer to be where I can't make fifty excuses a day to be in the same room with you.*

"Don't be silly." She did that thing parents did, running the spoon around the baby's mouth to collect another load of food. "If I were down here all day, I'd spend most of my time running up the hill to check a delivery, grab a signature, or heckle one of the crew for a time sheet."

Henry opened his mouth, a hungry little Viking, and the blueberry whatever disappeared down his maw.

"God made cell phones," Max said, opening the fridge. "How about a burger and side salad? We don't have buns, but there's plenty of bread."

I did not just invite Jeannie Cromarty to share the evening meal with me. Henry was on hand to chaperone, some comfort.

"You'd cook for me?"

"Yes. You are turning the Brodie Castle project around so it faces in the right direction. If we'd tried to use those damned cinder blocks in place of quarried granite, the ghost of Auld Michael would have haunted me for the rest of my days."

"Supposedly, it's Countess Brenna who has the slight temper. A burger sounds fortifying." She used a damp cloth to clean the food off Henry's face, an ordeal he protested with a squawk and a glower.

"Am I working you too hard, Jeannie? I can hire you an assistant, but sometimes, teaching the understudy the job is just another inefficiency. How do you like your meat?"

"Medium-well done. Mrs. Hamilton made a chocolate mousse. If you hadn't happened along, that might have sufficed for my meal."

Mrs. Hamilton's mother was one of the card-playing regulars down at the Earl's Pint. Max had been introduced, but Dinty had warned him not to sit with the ladies. They regarded every pair of fresh ears as desperately in need of a complete recitation of Brodie family history.

Max had learned to cook because Maura's diet mattered. Not only did she need to watch her weight, she also needed regular good food to keep mood swings, headaches, junk-food binges, and acne from plaguing her.

Because what plagued Maura very soon plagued everybody around her.

Jeannie approached the sink where Max was running cold water over leaves of romaine. "You get a particular look in your eye when you're thinking of home. Is your sister managing?"

Max shut off the water. "No, actually. She's being difficult. I've assured her every time we talk that I'll be home this weekend, that she'll have a whole day with me, at least, and I will tell her all about Scotland. She has become argumentative, secretive, and difficult. The staff warned me we'd face a difficult transition until Maura trusts that I haven't abandoned her."

Jeannie took the lettuce and gave it a good shake. She stood close enough that Max could detect the lemongrass scent of her shampoo, which inspired him to breathe through his nose like a fool in love.

"Some problems simply take time." Jeannie laid the wet lettuce on a towel and folded the cloth over it. "You're also worrying about your investors, aren't you?"

Max wasn't going to do this. Wasn't going to turn shared use of an enormous country house into an excuse to domesticate with Jeannie. But having made the offer to share dinner—where was the harm in that?—reason didn't seem to be reasserting itself now.

Couples chatted about their day, so did people who worked together.

"I'm not worried about the investors, per se. They signed an employment contract with me that I more or less wrote. The trap-doors are closed, the cover-your-ass—assets—language on my side is in place. I wrote in safeguards that will stop any one investor from rail-roading me off the project. Where's the—?"

He found a bowl large enough to accommodate a pound of ground beef. Henry sat in his booster seat, playing with Bear-Bear, a teething cracker, and some dry cereal.

"What sort of safeguards?"

"Only the full board can let me go, by a proper vote, at a meeting on the record. If I'm let go for anything other than a proven cause, I get a sizable buyout. The usual." He sprinkled salt, pepper, and seasoning over the meat, tossed in a raw egg, and mixed the result with both hands.

Jeannie watched him, while Max tried not to watch her.

"You do that with your hands?"

"Faster. My hands are clean. Why?"

"No reason." She took to staring at the contents of the fridge, which she'd doubtless seen many times before. "Shall I toast the bread?"

The toaster was on the opposite counter. "Sure, why not?" He started the meat cooking and laid a couple of place settings on the table, anything to keep moving someplace Jeannie was not.

"Wine?" she asked, peering into the pantry, another landscape with which she was familiar.

"Wah," Henry replied, his cadence so conversational both adults stared at him.

"He'll be yammering away any day now," Max said. *I hope I get to hear him.*

"He hears men's voices all day long up at the castle. I think he likes that. I can't drink a whole bottle by myself, so I'll pass on the wine if you're not interested."

Max could have guzzled a bottle of wine easily. "No wine for me."

Jeannie hummed as she made the salad, Henry tossed cereal in various directions, the meat sizzled, and Max's heart broke. The only element of domestic bliss missing was the part where Max hugged Jeannie hello, Jeannie gave his butt a soft pat, and Max returned the gesture when she was busy tossing the salad.

A future, in other words. A tacit expectation that they'd snuggle together when Henry went to sleep.

"Are you making any progress with your site plan?" Jeannie set the bowl of salad on the table.

"No, I am not, unless discarding options counts. I can link the Hall and castle with a tram or a covered escalator, but both are unsightly and expensive."

"What about an elevator? The castle sits higher than the Hall, and an elevator would seem to be the easiest solution. The Hall is all but built into the side of the hill, while the castle has cellars and dungeons that drop several floors below the inner bailey."

The burgers were done. Max got down plates and served up the meat, adding a sliced tomato for eye appeal—also because lycopene was good nutrition.

"Dropping a pair of elevator shafts would mean blasting, and given the age of the castle, blasting beneath its foundation is taking an enormous risk."

"Have you found the siege well?" Jeannie asked, putting a little more cereal in front of Henry.

"What's a siege well?"

"Back in the day, if you couldn't storm a castle, catapult boulders through its walls, or sneak a sleeping potion into the well, then you laid a siege. Parked your whole army outside the walls and waited for the castle inhabitants to run out of food. Somewhere in the bottom-most dungeon, there will be a well that never ran dry, because a castle can go without food for weeks, but a lack of water would break the siege in a matter of days. What are you drinking?"

Max felt besieged, but no well of self-restraint was fortifying his dungeons, so to speak. "Water is fine for me."

She filled a glass for him. For herself, cold milk, and for Henry, watered-down berry juice in a sippy cup.

Max got through the meal because he was hungry, and he was determined. Determined to avoid brushing Jeannie's hand when reaching for the salt, determined to keep his gaze above the level of her chin, determined not to cancel his trip to Maryland for the simple pleasure of rattling around under the same roof as Jeannie for two straight days.

"Are you packed?" She set half a romaine leaf in front of Henry, who used it to make a hat for Bear-Bear.

"I'll only need my backpack. I can pack in five minutes. Ready for mousse?"

Jeannie gave him a look that said she heard the forced joviality in his question. "I've missed you, Max."

"Mah, mah, mah, mah."

Max resumed his seat at the table. "We see each other dozens of times every day."

She rose and took the plates. "That's not what I mean. You might as well be in Maryland, for all the effort you put into avoiding me. In another two weeks, your recordkeeping will be up to date, and you can hire Mrs. Hamilton's granny to do my job."

Henry gave Max a curious look. *Why does Mum sound unhappy?*

"Is that what you want? To bail me out and then go back to Perth?"

She set the mousse on the counter rather firmly. "Has it occurred to you that it's my castle you're mucking about in? I was married in that castle, as were most of my cousins. My parents were married there. Queen Victoria paid calls there. If I'm repairing a few spreadsheets and making sure we have enough trash bags, that's in part because that castle means something to me and my family."

Max hated that she was upset, but he loved what happened to her accent when she was emphatic about her words.

"That castle means a lot to a lot of people, I get that. Dinty and his canoodling ghosts, the lavender border along the countess's walk that dates back to the first earl, Hugh's unwillingness to open the postern gate after sunset because that invites the fairies in... It's important."

Max kept a list of these features in his phone, because they all had something to contribute to the eventual presentation of Brodie Castle to the public. Maura would love these fanciful aspects of the castle, though she'd never have a chance to enjoy them.

Jeannie jammed a spoon into the mousse. "At least assure me that keeping your hands off me is as hard for you as keeping my hands off you has become for me."

Henry was merrily flinging cereal all over the kitchen. Max's heart was similarly aloft, heading for a hard crash on the kitchen floor. He knew that leaving intimate dealings with Jeannie behind was the wise, sensible, professional thing to do. He also knew he'd hurt her, and she did not deserve the pain.

He took the spoon from her and set it aside. "I can give you that assurance, because if you're having half the trouble I am, then... Jeannie, I'm sorry."

Standing this close to her was a mistake. Having this meal with her was a mistake. Leaning close enough to catch her fragrance was the worst mistake of all, because Jeannie leaned up at the same time, as if she'd rest her weight against him and take a momentary respite from sense. Instead, her mouth brushed his. The kiss caught, held, and burst into flames.

CHAPTER FOURTEEN

"Baby, I know. I was supposed to be up at the project site last week, but the realtors..." Pete paused, because mentioning his wife's house-hunting agenda to Shayla Walters was a bad idea. Making this call while the missus was in the shower was a really bad idea, but Shayla was not a patient woman.

"What realtors, Pete? And don't call me 'baby'. That's egregiously inappropriate during business hours."

Shayla was not using her kitten voice. That was her *I am a Professional Engineer used to kicking stupid male butt, and you're next* voice.

"I'm trying to get a feel for comparable venues," Pete said. "Newsflash: Americans don't have country houses or castles, not like they do here. Every one of those venues will compete with the Brodie project, which Max Maitland failed to take into account when he got all lathered up about this job."

Hearing Maitland insulted should settle Shayla's feathers, though Max had included plenty of comps in his project presentations. No two castles were alike, though, and none of them had been built to modern engineering standards.

"That's what I can't figure out," Shayla said. "Why did Max Maitland, who is notably slow to lather, get so enthusiastic about this job? Max isn't flashy, but he's thorough and shrewd, and I thought he had one foot nailed to the Maryland State Bar Association."

That unsolved riddle bothered her, clearly. Shayla was flashy. Nearly six feet of smart and sexy in her heels, equal parts ambition, curves, charm, and brains. Pete had taken one look at her and started rearranging his schedule. The next step had been to suggest Mrs. Sutherland might enjoy a little shopping in Paris or Singapore.

"Max is bored with housing developments," Pete said. "So were some of the guys looking to invest, and the project has potential to make bank, even for Max."

A slight hesitation ensued on the other end of the line. "He negotiated a percentage? That's in the project manager's contract now? Max gets a percentage of initial revenue?"

Shit, shit, shit. The cost of bringing Shayla onto the Brodie Castle team had just quintupled. "He gets a token amount, but we also threw in a few treats if he finishes the build-out ahead of schedule and under budget, which I assure you, he will not do."

"Because he screwed up the site plan. Some guys are better off sticking to HVAC schematics or tree-save plans. So when will you show me around the site?"

The water stopped running in the bathroom. The current Mrs. Sutherland didn't wear a lot of makeup, didn't take forty-five minutes to choose which pair of designer jeans went with which scarf. She had a natural flair for looking good, and once upon a time, Pete had loved how easily she got herself together.

She didn't keep a guy waiting, didn't mind if he mussed up her hair in the course of exchanging a little marital affection.

"Peter, I asked you a question."

"We'll be in Scotland by the end of the week."

"We?"

"I'm hoping some of the other investors can join me. Explaining the situation to Max will be easier if he realizes he faces a united front."

The bathroom door opened. "Peter! Can you bring me my hairbrush? It's in my purse."

Good God. "Gimme a minute. I'm on the phone."

"I want a copy of Max's contract, Pete. You offered him something that pried him loose from Outer Cowplop, Maryland. Did you know he has a sister?"

As if one more nagging female made a difference in a man's life? "I don't know if I can disclose his contract. In fact, I think that might qualify as egregiously inappropriate, to use your phrase. I'm pretty sure there's a gag clause, and Maitland's a lawyer. If he finds out I've been bending the rules, he'll make it hurt."

Would this phone call never end?

"You own enough shysters to make him regret his mistake. Send me the contract, Peter."

Another waft of humid air crossed the hotel suite, bringing with it the scent of roses. "Petey dear, my purse is in the closet, and I need that hairbrush if I don't want my hair to dry all frizzly."

"I'll see what I can do, Shay. I'm off to meet another realtor."

"You're in the UK?"

"I'm in London."

"That's lovely, Peter. So am I. I'll expect a copy of Max's contract by close of business tomorrow, and I'll be ready to fly up to Aberdeen any time after Thursday."

JEANNIE HAD STARTED DROPPING hints earlier in the week, implying to the carpenters that the glaziers were pulling ahead of schedule. She'd let the welders know the glaziers were poised to beat their next deadline, and she'd casually mentioned to the masons that the carpenters might soon run out of work if the other trades lost any ground.

A tacit competition had begun, and the week had ended with everybody either on schedule or ahead. She should have been pleased with herself.

"Will you stand up with me?" Dinty asked. "Assuming wee Henry doesn't mind sitting out for a reel or two?"

The Friday night ceilidh was just getting under way, meaning the dance floor wasn't crowded, and the noise wasn't yet deafening. Hugh and Fergus were having a good-natured argument over football teams—no fists thrown yet—and Mrs. Hamilton and her mum were getting out the cards.

Another week happily concluded. So why did Jeannie feel like yelling bad words and stomping out the door instead of turning down the room?

"Are you sober enough to stand up yourself, Dinty?"

"Never been drunk a day in my life," he replied, which was probably true. Dinty was a connoisseur of the Scottish single malt, and the best whiskies were for sipping rather than guzzling. "What's he doing here?"

Max Maitland walked in, looking delectable and relaxed in jeans and an unbuttoned Black Watch plaid flannel shirt. A black T-shirt hugged his ribs, and scuffed cowboy boots completed the picture.

"Tennent's for you, Mr. Maitland?" Fern called.

"Tennent's will suit me fine."

"I thought he was flying back to the States this weekend," Dinty said. "Some people will go to great lengths rather than face me on a shinty pitch, you know."

"Here," Jeannie said, passing him the baby. "Whisper all your secrets to my son. Henry has a great sense of humor."

Dinty cuddled Henry to his chest. "Come with me, young man. I'll show you how to build a perfect pint for them such as yonder Yank who lack the refinement to appreciate our national drink."

Henry walloped him one in the sternum, and Dinty kissed his head. "The lad will be a goalie, or my name's not Dinsmore MacTavish MacFergus Dundee."

Jeannie let Henry be taken on a tour behind the bar, leaving her free to admire Max's backside while Fern was building his pint. When he sauntered over to Jeannie's perch on the raised hearth, she admired the front view just as much.

"You're supposed to be at thirty-seven thousand feet, heading west at about five hundred miles an hour."

He took the place beside her. "Bumped myself to an evening flight tomorrow."

"Won't Maura be upset with you?"

"Should Henry be behind the bar?"

"This is a ceilidh, not a hard-hat area tidied up for inspection." And yet, Max had on his best, guarded poker face.

They'd avoided each other for the past three days, since the Kiss in the Kitchen. Henry had saved Jeannie from making a fool of herself—a worse fool of herself—by hurling Bear-Bear at her head. Max had caught the stuffed animal just short of landing in the mousse, then made a hasty exit from the kitchen with a muttered promise to do the dishes "later."

Jeannie had done the dishes, tormented all the while by thoughts of creative uses for chocolate mousse.

"Morgan stopped by the Baron's Hall to make sure I knew I was welcome here tonight."

A bit bold, even for Morgan. "Everybody is welcome at a ceilidh, though sometimes it's best to leave the team jerseys at home."

Max passed Jeannie his beer. She took a sip and passed it back. Dinty might have done the same with a dram of the Speyside, or Hugh with his ale.

Except they never had.

"Morgan's cottage is booked this weekend," Max said, drinking from the same place Jeannie had, though he probably didn't realize it. "A Mr. Pete Smith, whose credit card tracks to one Peter Sutherland, Baltimore address. Morgan thought it an odd coincidence that two Americans from Maryland should both end up in this corner of Royal Deeside at the same time."

"Is it an odd coincidence?" Was it a coincidence that Max was having this discussion with Jeannie in public rather than over another shared meal, or when they passed in the Hall's corridors?

"She smelled a rat," Max said, sharing his beer again. "Sutherland is my twitchiest investor. He pulls this crap. Thinks he's doing discreet reconnaissance, gathering intelligence by skulking around in the weeds with all the subtlety of a drunken rhinoceros. Is Dinty giving that baby a taste of beer?"

"Oh, probably. Sutherland worries you."

"Worries me enough that I put my flight off for a day, but I can't cancel the trip. Maura would not take that well when she's already struggling."

His posture was relaxed, his voice quiet, his tone casual. His gaze remained on Dinty and Henry, which was why Jeannie loved him. Henry would always be safe with Max on hand, the castle would be safe, while Jeannie would be in big trouble.

Though at the moment, Jeannie was also feeling peevish toward the object of her fond regard. "The fiddlers promised to open the next set with a waltz. Will you dance with me, Max?"

"Fergus warned me about Scottish women." He set his beer on the mantel and held out a hand.

More couples shuffled onto the dance floor while Fergus and Hugh—drinks in hand—scooted toward the restrooms, or toward the back exit at the end of the same hallway.

"Cowards," Jeannie muttered. "They're afraid Mrs. Hamilton's mum will get hold of them."

Max wrapped a hand around Jeannie's middle. "I don't think that's the issue. Do you have plans for this weekend?"

Missing you. Except that's what a pathetic, lovesick teenager would say, and Jeannie had never been one of those.

"I'm supposed to take Henry to see Millicent. Should I vacate my apartment in Perth, Max?"

The first fiddler began the introduction, then the concertina drifted in. If Max said yes, she should leave Perth behind, then Jeannie's future with him had been sacrificed for the good of the castle. If he said no, then her position on the project was temporary and, presumably, her future with him less temporary.

She could think of compelling arguments in favor of both options, though neither was ideal.

"Do you want to vacate your apartment?"

He remained standing with her at the edge of the dance floor, in waltz position, but not moving as other couples moved off to the music. His gaze was on her—nowhere else—and the look in his eyes said he wasn't fencing, wasn't being a lawyer. Her wishes mattered to him.

Jeannie was sorting through possible replies when an odd ripple went through the room. She heard the words *Morgan's holiday cottage* and felt Max not tense so much as focus.

"Sutherland is making an entrance."

An older man who might once have been handsome stood near the door. He took off a woolen newsboy cap—Harris Tweed would be Jeannie's guess—revealing thinning brassy blond hair. His coat was tawny corduroy with suede elbow patches, and about his neck was a bright red Royal Stewart plaid scarf—in high summer.

"Is he trying to look like a local?" Jeannie asked. For certain, Mr. Sutherland was trying to look as if that extra twenty pounds wasn't doing battle with his belt buckle. He nodded to the musicians, though Jeannie would bet Bear-Bear that they'd never seen him before in their lives.

Then his gaze lit on Max, who was still holding her.

"He'll try to dance with you," Max said, sounding none too pleased.

"Then let's not give him that opportunity."

"You never did answer my question, Jeannie."

"I'm considering my options. You know—the tram, the covered walkway, the escalator. I don't like any of the ones you've proposed."

Max smiled, which Jeannie guessed was a mistake, because Sutherland saw that smile and started moving toward them.

"Come on." Jeannie got a good grip on Max's hand. "We'll show him some Highland hospitality he won't soon forget."

SUTHERLAND WAS BEAMING HIS HARMLESS, good-old boy smile around at Max's employees, their families, and the village merchants. From Henry right up to Mrs. Hamilton's mum, Max didn't think a single person in the room considered that smile trustworthy.

Max certainly didn't.

Sutherland's gaze lit on Fern, who was building pints with one hand and holding Henry in the other arm.

Keep your filthy hands off of her begged to be shouted across the dance floor, but that sentiment presumed Fern wasn't capable of speaking for herself, which, of course, she was.

"Max," Jeannie said beneath the soft shuffle and thump of feet and the lilt of the violin. "You're not alone here. We'll deal with him."

She was looking forward to dealing with a man who had little conscience and fewer scruples. On previous jobs, Max would have considered Pete's dodgy morality merely a site hazard, but since coming to Scotland...

"People here don't cheat," he said. "They don't regard making a profit as an excuse to abandon morals."

"Some people here do cheat," Jeannie replied patiently. "They just haven't cheated you."

Sutherland nodded to Max and struck out—right across the damned dance floor—for the bar. That display of cluelessness helped settle Max's battle instincts. Sutherland didn't own this bar, though he did own Max's future and Maura's security.

"We'll stand our guest to a pint, Fern," Jeannie said when she'd all but dragged Max to the bar. "Mr. Maitland, some introductions are in order."

Remind me to listen to Fergus when he's holding forth on the subject of Scottish women.

"Pete, good to see you." Max stuck out a hand.

Henry, who had been deposited back in Dinty's arms, blew a raspberry.

Sutherland's grip was the same as always—cool, soft, manicured. "Max, didn't expect to find you cavorting among the locals or taking time to admire the lovely scenery."

His comment was accompanied by a particular smirk in Jeannie's direction. Fern set his beer on the bar in a manner that assured Max the proprietress had heard Sutherland's opening remarks and was not impressed.

"I can make some introductions, if you like," Max said. "Jeannie Cromarty is our project controller. Jeannie, Pete Sutherland, one of the investors in the Brodie Castle venture, though he might be here simply to take in some fishing."

Or to fire me. The thought flew on the wings of instinct rather than evidence, which meant Max couldn't afford to act on it—or to ignore it.

Sutherland grabbed Jeannie's hand and kissed it, a move Max hadn't seen him pull previously, outside of black-tie charity fundraisers.

"Miss Cromarty, a pleasure. I hope you like working for us. From what I've seen of the project, we need all the talent we can get."

Jeannie withdrew her hand. "Then you must be very pleased to have Mr. Maitland in charge. We are on schedule and within budget, despite the previous earl's tendency to hire first and plan later. Your beer."

She shoved the mug at Sutherland, which would keep at least one of his hands busy. Scottish women...

Sutherland did not consume beer in public. He'd clearly ordered something from the taps in an effort to be less conspicuous. Not drinking good beer only made him more conspicuous.

"I don't think I'm exaggerating when I say the Brodie Castle

project can't possibly stay on budget, much less on schedule," Sutherland said. "Max neglected to factor in a very significant aspect of the
build-out, and we could well end up with two halves of a site rather
than one functioning venue."

Fern and Dinty had both heard that. Hell, based on the baby's
scowl, Henry had heard that.

"You'll excuse us," Max said. "Mr. Sutherland and I need some
fresh air."

Jeannie kept hold of Max's hand, when he would have waded
into this confrontation alone.

Sutherland set down his beer untasted. "We can have this discussion right here, Max. I'm simply stating the obvious."

Jeannie patted Sutherland's arm, much as Mrs. Hamilton's mum
might have patted an unruly child.

"You're stating your fears in front of your project controller, half
your crews and their spouses and parents, though as far as I know,
you've never laid eyes on the site you're so worried about. Your
project foreman and head carpenter were on hand until five minutes
ago, and they are a pair of stout fellows who do not take kindly to
business being discussed at a social gathering. Come along, Mr.
Sutherland."

Dinty gently waved Henry's left hand in the bye-bye motion.
Henry waved the right on his own initiative.

Jeannie settled the matter by hauling Max toward the door,
leaving Sutherland no choice but to follow. Fern dumped his beer as
the waltz ended, and Max added that to his list of grievances against
Sutherland:

He'd interrupted a social occasion Max had been prepared
to enjoy.

He'd started exactly the kind of gossip the project didn't need.

He'd insulted the locals and offended Fern.

But all of that was just Sutherland being Sutherland.

He'd also cost Max a waltz with Jeannie, which was not a trans-
gression Max was prepared to overlook.

THE LANDLADY at Pete's rental cottage was pretty enough and friendly enough, as were a few of the other local attractions—Maitland's little friend was another fine female specimen—but how in the flaming, whisky-soaked hell was a first-class international business venue going to emerge in the midst of this bunch of stomping, half-drunk, skirt-wearing barbarians?

Max Maitland was in more trouble than he knew.

"What is it you have to say, Pete?"

The parking lot was much quieter than the bar, but people loitered on the front porch with their drinks, and a group of teenagers stood in a circle closer to the road.

"I thought you wanted privacy, Max."

The blonde spoke up. "If we're to have a business discussion outside of work hours and on Fern's property, this is as private as it gets. What questions do you have about the schedule, estimates to complete, or incurred costs, Mr. Sutherland?"

"My questions are for Max. He's the project manager." *For now.*

Max looked bored. "As manager, I rely on a crew of talented professionals, among whom Ms. Cromarty numbers."

"She's your—"

Maitland's posture changed, one foot sliding back over the gravel. He twitched the tail of Pete's scarf to lie flat against Pete's chest. The project controller smiled as if invading a man's personal space was something other than rank insubordination.

People thought they were being so subtle, but to a man who'd honed his perceptions over decades at the negotiating table, certain clues were impossible to hide.

Maitland had lost his grip on the project in favor of a grip on the perky little controller. Pathetic.

"Ms. Cromarty's position is project controller for Brodie Castle Corporation," Maitland said. "In that capacity, she has brought order to the chaos Zebedee Brodie left here, supported enforcement of safety standards, improved our relations with the local merchants, and acted as a cultural liaison between me and employees who are rightfully proud of the castle's heritage. As a blood relative of Elias Brodie, Ms. Cromarty has a status here that you and I will never hold."

Tribal politics never did a project any good and always ended up costing money. The reasons to cut Max Maitland loose kept multiplying.

Though Pete didn't intend to be cruel about it. "I'm here without preconceived notions, just kicking tires, getting the lay of the land, showing the flag. No need to get your hackles up. We both know the site has serious, expensive, schedule-busting problems. For me to discuss them in greater detail would be egregiously inappropriate in this setting."

Maitland took a gander around the parking lot. An older couple—holding hands—were shuffling up the walkway with a Scotty dog trotting before them, no leash in sight. Considering the evening hour, the sky was an odd blend of dark and light that annoyed Pete's already unhappy body clock.

To think he'd married a woman from this peculiar place, and now she wanted to buy a house here. Was ready to drag Pete to the closing, in fact.

Maitland's gaze swung to Pete. "If you're referring to the fact that we have primarily a residential property in the Hall and an event venue in the castle, then that's been obvious from the first presentation and is one of Brodie Castle's strengths. Every architect who looked at the prospectus pointed out the challenges of joining the two major buildings in a manner that's efficient, affordable, and aesthetically compatible with the existing structures. What's your point?"

The question was politely annoyed. The project controller looked only mildly curious, but on the hill high above the village, the castle loomed black against the indigo sky. Pete expected the ghost of Braveheart to come galloping from the trees, torch in hand.

No wonder the locals stayed indoors and half-drunk.

"I'll be honest," Pete said. "The other investors didn't read the plans very closely, much less the fine print at the bottom of your financial projections. They're not happy, Max. They feel as if you've tried to put one over on them. You have a job for the next year, they have money wrapped up in a harebrained scheme, and when you've enjoyed the, uh, fishing here long enough, you'll go jaunting on your way. Some of the guys have said as much."

"Then some of the guys need to be set straight. I've never walked out on a project. If I walked out on this one, I'd be leaving behind incentive bonuses I fought hard to get into my contract. I'd also be trashing a reputation in the industry that goes back to my high school summer jobs. You can't boot me off this site except for cause, and that you do not have."

Maitland was both an attorney and an engineer, which made him a special kind of stupid.

"Max, you are a first-rate project manager for any housing development ever planned for the Maryland countryside. You're a hard worker and a stand-up guy, but you're out of your depth here. Maguire said as much, and he knows this type of job much better than I do. I'm giving you an opportunity to get your résumé together and make a dignified exit. Any other response from you under these circumstances would be egregiously inappropriate."

Dignity would mean a lot to Max, though he was looking more amused than affronted.

"Very kind of you, Pete, but I owe the project my loyalty. Getting my résumé together isn't high on my list of priorities."

Fine, then, they'd do it the hard way. "I'll want a complete tour of the premises tomorrow, also the latest weekly reports, down to the penny, with all of the supporting documents."

Those reasonable requests had Maitland looking irritated. "I'm supposed to be in the States this weekend. That's in my contract. Are you demanding that I stay here and play tour guide now when you've had weeks to look this place over?"

The little Scotty dog came over and sniffed at Pete's loafer, then trotted into the building alongside its elderly owners. For damned sure, Pete would not allow animals on the castle premises.

"Mrs. Sutherland is trying to choose between three different houses," Pete said, "each of which is more expensive than the next. I desert her at my peril. The weekend is the perfect time to do a site inspection, because the crews are off and no deliveries will interrupt us. Business is business, Max. You can socialize with whoever you're missing so terribly in Maryland some other time."

And too bad if the idea that Max had a woman waiting for him back home offended his project controller.

"I don't understand something, Mr. Sutherland," the little blonde said. "Your mates commit money without educating themselves regarding the risks, you don't intend to honor the terms of Mr. Maitland's contract regarding visits back home, and you think that by publicly announcing your insecurities mere weeks after project launch, you are somehow enhancing the probability of project success. Why should Mr. Maitland—why should anybody who's hired on—stay around if that's your version of how business is conducted?"

The teenagers had moved closer, as if they sensed a discussion growing contentious. "This whole conversation is none of your business, ma'am, meaning no disrespect."

Maitland's gaze was on the castle, behind which a big, pale moon was rising. "For the last time, Pete, Ms. Cromarty is our project controller. Any element of risk to the project, including your attempts to sabotage me, fall within the purview of her responsibilities. I've already put off my flight once, because I got wind you were doing your usual sneak attack. If you are requiring me to cancel the trip home, then you are materially breaching the terms of the deal."

Damn all lawyers to... to Scotland.

"I'm not telling you what to do, Max. If you're not around tomorrow, I'm sure Ms. Cromarty, or any of the locals you're so fond of, can show me the site. I'll be up at the castle by noon, and I'll expect a complete set of financials by email no later than ten a.m. You simply need to decide where your loyalties lie. As somebody who means you only the best, I'm telling you that it might be time to cut your losses while you still can."

Pete strode off, not too quickly, not too slowly. If Maitland wanted an example of a dignified exit, Pete would provide it. State your piece, have the last word, be on your way. Surely somewhere among the heathen thumping and whirling inside the bar was a female who'd enjoy a little sophisticated company, and the bartenders even in this backwater should have the makings for a decent Bloody Mary.

Pete left Max and his loyal minion outside, where they could enjoy the moonrise over their castle, like the condemned enjoying a last meal.

CHAPTER FIFTEEN

"Glad that's all sorted out, then," Jeannie said, marching down the row of cars. "What a nervy bastard you have for an investor, Max. When he's not spouting clichés, he's leering at the nearest female, and how many of his chins does he think that wool scarf is hiding?"

Max fell in step beside her. "Where are we going?"

"Up to the project office. You heard him. He wants all the reports with backup information by ten a.m. tomorrow. What a toad, making you work on a Saturday. Making you miss your trip home."

What a relief to have somebody angry on Max's behalf. "We can't go up to the project office just yet."

Jeannie whirled around. "Henry! Dear God, I was so cheesed off, I almost forgot my only begotten son. Dinty has doubtless turned him into a sot, and Hugh will turn him into a flirt."

"Jeannie." Max caught her by the biceps before she could barrel back into the Earl's Pint. "Could you have a word with Dinty while you're inside?"

"Of course. What sort of word? You're not leaving us, are you?"

The castle sat above the village, a refuge hewn in granite and loyalty—to family and to the land, but also to a set of values Max shared. Hard work, integrity, honesty.

"I'm not leaving Brodie Castle." *Or you.* "Sutherland pulls this malarkey on almost every project, and half the time his co-investors aren't backing him nearly so enthusiastically as he wants to think. We'll tour the site with him, bury him in paper, and send him on his way."

Jeannie stepped closer, turning what Max had intended as a gentle halt into an embrace.

"Can he fire you, Max?"

"Yes." Pete could fire Jeannie, Dinty, anybody. The contract read that Max had the authority to run the job without "undue interference" from the investors, but that he'd heed the reasonable guidance of the board on all matters of substance.

What a lot of blather.

"Wait for me," Jeannie said. "I'll collect Henry and be right back."

"When you collect Henry, please quietly ask Dinty to introduce good old Pete to the wonders of well-aged single malt whisky. Introduce him thoroughly. If Morgan is willing to help, so much the better. Tomorrow morning, I want Sutherland reeling on the end of a mule kick the likes of which he's never encountered before."

Jeannie kissed Max on the mouth, which surprised him so thoroughly he didn't object—or take advantage of her initiative.

"That's diabolical, Max. Fern has some wretched novelty whiskies she keeps around mostly for display, aged in fish barrels and worse. Sutherland will wish he'd stayed in Maryland."

Would that he had. "Don't be long."

Max retreated into the deep shadows of the trees lining the parking lot. The night was beautiful in a way uniquely Scottish, with the starry sky a deep blue rather than black. Violins in close harmony drifted through open windows, the last strains of the waltz Max should have shared with Jeannie.

Maura would love it here, and but for her, Max would not be

returning to Maryland. That realization was a gut punch. The surprise wasn't that he'd stick around a job site, but that he didn't have any reason besides Maura to return to the place where he'd spent the first thirty-five years of his life.

He'd developed thousands of acres of real estate in Maryland, everything from gentrified cul-de-sacs near the DC line to sprawling mixed-use residential neighborhoods along the main commuting corridors. Good work, all of it, and he was proud of his contribution, but not... not attached.

Jeannie came down the steps, Henry in her arms, the diaper bag over her shoulder. "Dinty and Morgan are on a mission, and Fern's recruiting Mrs. Hamilton's mum to assist. Knows her whisky, does Granny MacPhee. I suspect half the village will take an interest in Mr. Sutherland's education."

She'd spoken quietly, the glee of a determined conspirator lacing her words.

Max took the diaper bag from her and looped it over his shoulder. "Then let's be off, because it's going to be—"

A sound caught his ear, footsteps, soft laughter—a guy—or two guys?

Fergus and Hugh emerged from the trees, their smiles gleaming in the shadows. Fergus's sporran was hanging off his hip, and Hugh's hand was firmly tucked in Fergus's grip.

Well. This explained a few things. "Gentlemen."

They nodded and spoke in unison. "Maitland." Fergus took a step closer to Hugh, the gesture clearly protective—and maybe a little possessive.

"If you two are done enjoying the moonlight, I need some help."

Hugh's sporran was off center as well. "What sort of help could you need at this time of night?"

Henry yawned and offered a sleepy, "Bah-boo."

"Did you happen to overhear any of our conversation with Sutherland?" Max asked.

"Hard not to," Fergus said, dropping Hugh's hand to straighten his own sporran. "I know he's your countryman and your investor, Maitland, but he's a donkey's backside, meaning no disrespect to the jackass. Any damned fool who sank money into this project without realizing the Hall and the castle lie at different elevations doesn't deserve to make a profit."

"He's also pompous," Hugh said. "Never did have a use for pomposity. Henry's up past his bedtime."

Henry waved at Hugh sleepily.

"He'll be up later still," Jeannie said. "Max and I are off to the project office to deal with the reports Sutherland is demanding."

"I hate reports," Fergus muttered. "I hate even more strutting windbags who come around mucking up my project. I can help."

"That leaves me to watch the wee man," Hugh said, "and fetch a tray of sandwiches. What else do we need?"

"I wasn't going to ask you to help with the reports," Max said.

Fergus stepped within chest-bumping range. "You don't trust me, is that it? Because I got a little bit behind and made a few simple mistakes, you think—"

Hugh touched Fergus's arm. "You asked for our help, Maitland. Explain yourself."

"Sutherland is touring the facilities tomorrow, because he thinks the place will be deserted. He can sermonize at me by the hour, find fault with everything, and pretend to take notes on all the mistakes I've made."

"That's bollocks," Fergus said. "You run that site like a surgical operating theater, with everything in its place. We even have a roster for who's supposed to sweep up in the great hall at the end of every day."

"Tomorrow, I want noise. I want hammers pounding so relentlessly the castle shakes. I want jackhammers, blow torches, constant yelling, anything loud. Get our Welsh glaziers going with their rugby songs, and don't let up."

"You're repelling a siege," Jeannie said. "I like that."

"The less time I have to waste with Sutherland, the more likely I am to make my flight, and the less time he'll have to get into mischief."

Hugh drew a finger down Henry's cheek. "Your investor is up to no good, then?"

"No good at all, but then, Jeannie asked Dinty to introduce Sutherland to the worst single malt ever to leak out of a rotten barrel. Granny MacPhee will likely help, and my hardworking crews will all be on hand tomorrow when Sutherland thinks the castle will be silent."

"Dinty isn't the merciful sort when he's riled," Fergus said. "I've always admired that about him. Shall we meet you at the project office?"

Max had hoped for Jeannie's support. He hadn't expected loyalty from anybody else.

"I'd appreciate the assistance. Tell those who can show up tomorrow that they get next Friday off, provided I'm still around to sign off on time sheets."

"You'll be around," Fergus said. "I'm not about to break in another Yank when I have this one almost trained. Come along, Hugh, my lad. We have sandwiches to order."

Hugh threw an arm around Fergus's shoulders and broke into a lovely baritone rendition of *Parcel o' Rogues.*

"I am that surprised," Jeannie said, shifting a sleeping Henry to the other hip. "I had no idea they were besotted."

Good word. "There were some clues."

"Such as?"

A certain desperate gleam in Fergus's eye that Max saw every morning in the mirror. Hugh haunting the solar more effectively than any ghost could.

"They bickered constantly, but if I so much as hinted that Fergus wasn't the best site manager in Scotland, Hugh was glaring daggers at me. If I asked where Hugh had got off to, Fergus was in my face about how a man's entitled to take a break every so often and carpentry being harder work than most people realize."

The diaper bag was digging into Max's shoulder, which was good, because standing in the moonlight with Jeannie conjured impossible wishes.

"You noticed they were growing attached. You regard workplace romances as inappropriate, and yet, you said nothing to either of them. Interesting." She sashayed off in the direction of the Hall.

"Hugh doesn't report to Fergus."

"But I do. Not to you, to Fergus. No prohibition against a work-place romance exists under law or in any of the corporate documents I pawed through. You're simply gun-shy, expecting me to treat you the way your fiancée did."

"She was never my fiancée." A source of relief, now that Max thought about it. "Are we having an argument?"

They turned down the lane that led to the Hall. "We're having a discussion. When you've had a chance to think about what a fool you're being, then we might have a small disagreement."

"Jeannie, I'm getting on a plane tomorrow. I will keep getting on planes until this project is over, and then I'll get on one more plane."

"Is that what you want to do? Leave here and never come back?"

The lane wound between tree-lined pastures, and the moonlight wasn't enough to illuminate Jeannie's expression. Her question held pain, though, and bewilderment.

"No, I don't want to leave. The temperature's dropping. Let me fish you out a blanket to wrap around Henry."

They stopped walking and got Henry swaddled. Jeannie stayed where she was, while Max hefted the diaper bag onto his other shoulder.

"I love you," Jeannie said. "Because you think of Henry, because you noticed our Fergus was falling in love with Hugh. I love you because you have a vision for Brodie Castle that Elias could never have brought to fruition. I love you, because you are trying to protect me from that idiot Sutherland, who will fire me in the same breath he fires you."

I love you.

I love you.

I love you.

"He will, Jeannie, and he'll leverage your job security against me any way he can. Same goes for Fergus, Hugh, Dinty... To spite me, Sutherland will sabotage this whole job. I'll go down fighting, if I go down at all, but you've seen what he is."

I love you too. God, do I love you too.

Jeannie braced herself on Max's shoulder and leaned in, not to kiss him, but to rest her forehead against his chest.

"You'll fight for the castle, for the crews, for the potential you see in this project. You'll fight for a paycheck I badly need and a job I was born to do, but will you fight for *us*, Maxwell Maitland? Will you even try to fight for us?"

She slipped away and was lost in the moon shadows before Max could scrounge up an answer less fraught than, *All I know is that I love you too.*

FRIDAY NIGHTS WERE SUPPOSED to be fun, because the next day was Saturday. No chores, no church, no work, no school—a day completely off.

Maura had plans for her Saturday, plans she'd kept to herself.

Max was not on an airplane. He was not on his way home to Maryland. He said he'd come on Sunday, but Maura knew better. On Sunday, he'd say the planes weren't flying, or he'd caught a cold—you weren't supposed to fly if you were sick—or he had a report to do.

Max did *a lot* of reports.

On Sunday, Maura would be on her way to Scotland. She had her money card, and because she worked in the office in the winter and with the grounds crew in summer, that card was worth a lot. She also had $77.47 in real money. Between her card and her cash, she had enough to get her to Scotland.

"Maura, are you going to eat that fruit-and-nut bar or stare at it all night?" Alex's shift had just started. He hadn't even set up his laptop on the kitchen table.

Maura didn't want to answer him, because his question was nosy and dumb. "You stare at your computer for hours. Why can't I stare at my fruit-and-nut bar for a few minutes?"

He got a power cord out of his backpack. "Valid point. How was school today?"

Change the subject. Staff did that when they'd said something they shouldn't have. Changing the subject was called *redirection*.

"It's summer, Alex, and I'm too old for school. I work." Enough to earn a lot of money.

"Then how was work?"

Maura hoped they had gardens in Scotland, because flowers never said the wrong thing. They never asked stupid questions. They never expected you to wait until next week or next month or forever before they'd smell good or look pretty. Tomatoes got ripe whether there was a report to do or a plane to catch.

"I weeded. I like to weed. You yank out the weeds and say nice things to the flowers and vegetables. Then you take a break in the shade, and you can tell where you pulled out the weeds and where you still have more work to do."

The laptop came out next. "Watch that you don't get a sunburn. Too much sun can be a problem."

Alex really wasn't very bright. Spending time with him was more work than pulling out weeds or shredding paper all morning.

"Alex, the sun is where we get vitamin D, and I wear sunscreen and a hat. I spray my hat with bug spray, and I always, always, always keep an eye out for poison ivy."

He hooked up this and that, powered up, and sat down. "You live an adventurous life, Maura Maitland. Looks like we'll have a pretty sunset."

Oh, that was subtle. *Go outside and watch the sunset, Maura. Don't bother me, Maura.* Even Max had found something else to do besides spend time with his sister.

"I'll be on the back porch."

"M'kay."

He was tapping away at his keyboard before Maura had left the kitchen. She stashed her fruit-and-nut bar in her backpack along with the six others she'd collected. Her backpack also held her phone charger, clean undies, a windbreaker, and a folding umbrella with cats on it. For emergencies, she'd bought a jar of peanut butter and some crackers at the convenience store and two bottles of water.

She could go to the bathroom at any Starbucks or McDonald's, but some clean socks might also come in handy.

She did not live an adventurous life, but that was about to change.

THE REPORTS SPARKLED, Fergus and Hugh sparkled, albeit tiredly to Jeannie's eyes. While Fergus, Max, and Jeannie had completed a marathon data-entry session, Hugh had taught Henry how to crawl through a tunnel of steepled couch pillows.

Henry now slept soundly in the portable playpen in the break room next door.

"I've a mind to see the valley by moonlight from the parapets," Hugh said, tossing the last of the sandwich rubbish in the trash. "Once Maitland is through with this place, that view will cost a pretty penny to see."

Max pulled off his glasses—wire-framed, professorial, and somehow sexy—and rubbed his eyes.

"Nah. We'll put a gift shop up there, so people will have a way to see it for free, and that view will make them want to hold their weddings here, their class reunions, their directors' meetings. Besides, the first earl and his countess like to canoodle on the parapets, and I don't think they'd appreciate me putting a price tag on their lovers' walk."

Max was learning, for which Jeannie also loved him. She loved him for the way he'd casually passed Henry over to Hugh then tucked the blanket around the baby while Hugh nuzzled Henry's cheek.

"Come along, Fergus," Hugh said. "We'll be up and about early tomorrow, hammers swinging."

"My idea of fun," Fergus said, luxuriating in a yawn and a stretch. "We'll leave you two to plot more strategy—or something."

He winked at Jeannie. Hugh kissed her cheek.

"Enjoy the view," Max said. "Or something."

Fergus's smile was bashful, Hugh's naughty, and then, but for a sleeping baby in the next room, Jeannie was alone in the middle of the night with Max Maitland.

No place was more silent than an ancient stone building at two a.m. in high summer. The scent of lavender wafted in through the open windows, and some daft bird was already anticipating the dawn two hours away.

"I can get the car if you don't want to walk down the hill in the dark with Henry," Max said.

He had a leased car now, which Jeannie resented with an irrational passion. "You still plan to fly out tomorrow night?"

"Then back again about twelve hours later. It's the best I can do."

And Max Maitland would always do his best.

"I don't think you should give Sutherland the reports tomorrow. Give him the latest summaries, but fob him off with some excuse about my being off duty, and the reports being my responsibility, and Scottish pride."

Max led her to the couch—an extravagance, to have a new couch in the project office, but so comfortable Jeannie had stolen more than one nap on it. She suspected Max had approved the purchase with her sleep schedule in mind.

"I agree with you," he said, "which makes me doubly worried. Sutherland thinks of himself as bold, decisive, smarter than his buddies. He's greedier for sure and just convincing enough that he often gets his way. I haven't figured out his game yet, and withholding information seems like a good way to slow down his agenda."

Even sitting beside Max felt good. He was warm, slightly rumpled, and up close he still bore his signature scent—more spice than woods at this hour.

"I could simply forget to send him the supporting data," Jeannie suggested. "I trust you've been sending him weekly summaries all along."

Max ranged an arm along the back of the sofa. "I learned not to do that. I send a narrative report: The carpenters are at 17 percent complete, while their budget has been 16 percent expended. The glaziers experienced a weather delay, using up 5 percent of their allotted weather-delay days. Masons are hiring two more laborers to fill vacancies created by two resignations—that sort of thing. I don't provide backup unless requested, because I don't want to be micromanaged."

Smart. "But they're entitled to it upon request?"

Max's arm settled around Jeannie's shoulders, and she rested her head against his chest.

"They are entitled to my soul, according to them. I won't blame your faulty memory for me withholding information. Sutherland will use that against you. I'll come up with another idea."

Jeannie's body was coming up with other ideas. She bundled closer, and Max's other arm made an embrace out of a snuggle.

"Jeannie..." Misgiving, regret, longing, a little amusement. Never had her name held so much emotional cargo or so much tenderness.

"You are getting on a plane tomorrow, Sutherland could fire the lot of us on Monday, and Henry's for once sound asleep. Make love with me."

Max's embrace changed, becoming fierce, though no less cherishing. "I've thought about what you said."

"I say a lot."

"All I want for Fergus and Hugh is their happiness. They're professionals. Their relationship won't intrude on the project, unless it's to improve morale. I'm not horse's ass enough to lecture them about the obvious. Two of the Welsh glaziers are married to each other. I caught a pair of the mason's apprentices enjoying the view from the parapets while naked from the waist down last Tuesday night."

"The castle has a romantic past, and there's a legend—" Jeannie kissed him. Bother the legend. "What were you trying to say?"

"I don't know. I had a little speech, about how I'm the project manager, fiduciary something or other, and your job security. If Sutherland succeeds in getting rid of me, it won't matter a bucket of mud how we spend the next hour. He'll wreak havoc as he pleases. Hold still so I can kiss—"

Jeannie did not hold still. She straddled Max's lap, scooting back far enough to unbuckle his belt.

"You wore a dress." His tone was pleased and a little befuddled, as if his engineer's mind had just now realized the possibilities when a lady wore a dress.

"For dancing, a woman often does. I also wore underclothes." Though not too many. Jeannie hopped off Max's lap long enough to toss her panties onto the desk.

Then she settled in for some kissing.

Max was a thorough kisser—a thorough lover. He pressed his mouth to Jeannie's throat, then worked his way to her ear, her temple, her brows. Her closed eyes—one, then the other—down her nose, and finally, finally to her lips.

She was mad for him. Had spent the past two weeks craving who and what she could not have, and yet, Max was all tender restraint.

"Dammit, Max."

He smiled against her mouth. "Not in front of the baby."

Henry was in the other room, dreaming his baby dreams, the door cracked only a few inches. "This dress has to go, your shirt has to go. Now."

He peeled his T-shirt off—the flannel shirt had been an early casualty—and Jeannie took a moment simply to behold him bare-chested. He was a fortress of a man, roped in muscle, built for strength and endurance both. His proportions were those of a warrior who'd taken good care of the gifts bestowed on him—long bones, strong geometries, a keen mind.

"The dress," he murmured, sliding his hands past Jeannie's knees. "You said the dress..."

"Do that again." His warm palms caressed her knees—her *knees*—and desire leaped from a simmer to a boil. "Keep doing that."

Jeannie got the dress over her head, then arched forward so Max could undo her bra. His breath against her chest was another torment, and then his mouth... oh, his mouth.

Jeannie hung on as he used his lips on her breasts, and his fingers went exploring between her legs. He put his opposable thumb to the use that probably accounted for its evolution, and Jeannie went off like fireworks over the parapets.

"Not enough," she said when she could speak again. "A mere appetizer before I devour you."

"I wish, I pray, and I long for you to devour me, but Jeannie Cromarty, I don't have a condom with me."

His chagrin was as palpable as his frustration. The man with a plan for everything, he who spouted contingent arrangements and safety precautions, had been caught with his pants down and nowhere to go.

"You don't have a condom?" Jeannie said, caressing his arousal. "You're sure you don't have a condom?"

"Jeannie Cromarty." Her name came out half an octave lower than the last time he'd spoken it. "I can't... You shouldn't... Don't stop."

She leaned close enough to whisper in his ear. "You don't have a condom, but I do. What will you give me for the use of it?"

～

A VOICE in the back of Max's mind whispered warnings: *You*

should not be doing this. Don't send mixed messages. What in tarnation is Sutherland up to this time? Jeannie needs her sleep.

He mentally tossed those unhelpful admonitions down the trash chute, because other warnings were more urgent: *Don't blow this. If you lose Jeannie Cromarty, there will never be anyone else for you. This could be the last time...*

Max would have savored and lingered over the silky soft texture of her breasts, over the particular fragrance that gathered at the base of her throat.

Jeannie was having none of that. She unrolled the condom and resumed straddling Max's lap.

"Don't let me yell," she said, taking Max in her hand. "Don't let me wake that baby, or Sutherland will be the least of your troubles."

Henry was exhausted from tunneling though Hugh's pillow-sided A-frames, touring the laundry with Hugh, Fergus, and Max by turns, stargazing, and gnawing crackers.

"Kiss me," Max said. "You're less likely to yell that way, and so am I."

Good God in a plaid nightgown, she could kiss. Her mouth was diabolical, plundering his wits and his almighty determination to make this last. She sank onto him one relentless slide, teasing him with her tongue all the way down.

Then she started to move, and Max could only hang on and try to think of a formula to express the effect of the adiabatic lapse rate between the elevation of the Hall and the elevation of the castle parapets.

Air cooled as elevation increased, but Max was growing hotter by the second. "Jeannie, slow down."

She sped up.

"I won't last... God, that feels... sublime."

She'd shifted the angle and groaned against his shoulder. Something stumbled through Max's too pleasure-drunk mind to qualify as a thought:

Her breasts. Fine notion, and when he applied a hint of pressure,

Jeannie's groan drifted into a sigh. She did not yell—she didn't need to yell for Max to know she'd found satisfaction yet again. As much as he wanted to spend the next twenty years with her on the ever-so-comfy couch, he didn't dare.

Her breath fanned past his ear. "Maxwell Maitland, you are so..." She kissed his cheek and stroked his hair.

"I am so not done with you. Hold on."

He shifted them, still joined, so Jeannie was on her back. The couch was the perfect length for him to brace his feet against the armrest, and *bliss* was too tame a word for the pleasure of making love with Jeannie.

Max kept it sweet and slow for a while, giving Jeannie a chance to catch her breath.

"I have two more condoms," Jeannie whispered. "Don't hold back on my account."

While Max had a plane to catch. The sheer, howling frustration of that put an end to his lazy loving. Jeannie hooked her ankles at his back, and Max got serious.

"This is too..." Whatever thought Jeannie had intended to express got lost in a deep, wet kiss. "Max, I'm going to..."

"No yelling," he managed just before his restraint broke, and any pretenses of finesse shattered with it. He gathered Jeannie close and gave himself up to transcendent satisfaction. She clung to him with a gratifying desperation, and when Max drifted down from an intimacy beyond description, she pulled his discarded flannel shirt from a corner of the couch and draped it over his back.

"I did not precisely yell," Jeannie said some minutes later. "It was a very near thing."

Max left off nibbling her earlobe. "Same here." He held her, trying to hang on to the glow, the peace, the sense of a world put right, but they were on a couch in the project office, the baby asleep in the next room, and trouble awaited them in the morning.

"You have to get up first," Jeannie said, stroking his backside. "I will look fondly upon this couch all the rest of my days."

Max wallowed for the duration of three more caresses to his butt, then shifted off of her. By the glow of the desk lamp, they tidied up and dressed, though with each restored article of clothing, Max felt the weight of reality settling more heavily.

"We should probably pack up the playpen," he said, stashing Jeannie's underpants in his pocket.

"So Sutherland won't make a fuss. Right. Are you going to keep my unders?"

"Yes, if you don't mind."

"I don't mind. What did you do with the—?"

"Flushed it." Bad for the old pipes, but Max was damned if he'd leave that evidence in the trash for Sutherland to come upon.

"Henry will soon be ready for his middle-of-the-night bottle," Jeannie said. "What will you do about the reports?"

The solution to that problem popped into Max's head all of a piece, which was one of the benefits of taking a break from any challenge. He fired up the laptop and took the chair behind Jeannie's desk.

"You give Henry his bottle, and I'll upload the reports to the secure storage box."

Jeannie fished a half-size baby bottle out of the diaper bag. "What good will that do?"

"Funny thing about the storage box," Max said, logging in. "If you're not using the server it initially associated with your computer's address, it will ask for two-factor ID and a password reset."

"I recall reading that, but what's the—?" Henry made a noise louder than a sigh, not quite a whimper. "That child..."

She went into the next room and emerged with a sleepy baby in her arms. "Your pillow-fort friends are gone for now, my boy, but they'll be back tomorrow."

Henry beamed at Max and waved a fist, and Max spared a moment to resent the hell out of Sutherland's tantrums when a happy baby deserved cuddling and nuzzling.

"Same to you, little dude. Just give me a minute while you down a pint." Max clicked a few more keys, typed in a few commands, and watched half a menu fade into unavailability. "Technology is our friend."

"Sutherland is locked out of the files?"

"When he tries to reset his password, he will be, though he'll probably waste a lot of time figuring that out, and I can't override his lockout for forty-eight hours. He'll lock the whole online storage box if he tries to log in more than three times. Pete's a great fan of cyber-security."

While Jeannie gave Henry his bottle, Max folded up the playpen and shoved it between a pair of modular dividers.

When Henry had graced the night air with a manly burp, Max shouldered the diaper bag and escorted Jeannie down the paths to the Hall. The going was slow, though the moon hadn't set, and through the darkened wood and across the lawn to the Hall's kitchen entrance, Max was plagued by two questions.

First, how to link the two buildings. That issue beat like an osti-nato in his head, and like most engineering problems, it wanted time and imagination to solve. Max had the imagination, but the time was running out.

Which raised the second question: Why in the name of all that was profitable was Sutherland up to no good *now*? He wasn't stupid, and he was greedy. Max planned to make all of the investors a lot of money with the Brodie Castle project. Sutherland was jeopardizing that profit, playing fast and loose with contract language, and beyond doubt compromising sound business ethics to get a competent and legally educated manager off the project.

And Max had no idea why. Until that riddle was solved, he'd be fighting with one hand tied behind his back.

CHAPTER SIXTEEN

"Why in the hell are all these men here?" And a few women. Pete still hadn't grown accustomed to seeing women in hard hats, wielding jackhammers, power saws, and other tools. Every work site had a few, but the ladies seemed disproportionately well represented on the Brodie Castle crews.

"They work here," Max Maitland replied. "Are you ready to tour the cellars and dungeons?"

A power saw started up that felt like it was cutting through Pete's last nerve. Again.

"Tell these damned crews to go home."

"Cannae do that, Mr. Sutherland," the site foreman said. He was a big lummox in a dusty black kilt that went well with his unshaven cheeks and dark hair. "We've a shinty tournament next weekend and traded next Friday for this Saturday. The men take their shinty matches seriously."

"What's shinty?"

"You should try it," Maitland said. "I'm sure the men can find you some equipment. It's a sort of toned-down version of field hockey. Very genteel, takes a lot of finesse."

The site manager was seized with a fit of coughing, though this was not a dusty site.

"Perhaps I will. I played ice hockey as a kid in New York, and you don't forget the moves." Most of which these yokels were likely to have seen only on their TVs.

"The main entrance to the lower floors is over here," Maitland said, leading the way to yet another staircase of spiraling stone.

The jackhammer, which had been mercifully silent for the past ten minutes, started up in addition to the power saw. On a floor above, at least three hammers were pounding in no discernible rhythm.

And then—as if the roiling in Pete's gut, the cesspit in his mouth, and the throbbing in his temples weren't enough—a pair of some-bodies began to sing in ragged harmony.

"I don't need to see the damned cellars. They will reek of mildew and dirt, and we aren't putting any guests down there anyway."

The site manager crossed muscular arms and widened his stance. "The wine cellar is a work of art, the pantries show a genius for orga-nization, and Countess Brenna herself oversaw the modernizing of the kitchens. Countess Eulie expanded them during the reign of Edward, and during the First World War, no less than six hundred wounded soldiers passed through the infirmary that Countess Mary made from the Hall's servant's quarters."

Maitland paused at the top of the steps. "During the Second World War," he said, "Countess Lindsey set up the infirmary again, and the Hall still has the remains of an operating theater below the family wing. The number of wounded to pass through the Hall in its hospital days was in the thousands."

He said this as if ancient history had a bearing on the present project. "All very interesting, but I've seen cellars and basements before, and they are not a source of significant concern. We'll build them out into functional spaces—storage, kitchens, laundry, whatever —and the public will never see them."

Maitland and the site foreman were exchanging an unreadable

look. The foreman had an odd name—MacFleagle, Flannery, something with an F—but then, Pete had spent the evening drinking with some guy named Dinty and a woman named Morgan.

Quaint as hell, while the hangover Pete had woken up with was serious pain.

"Have ye seen enough, then?" the foreman asked. "We have ghosts too, you know. The first earl and his lady are often seen on the parapets under a quarter moon, and others say they've seen the pair of them fishing along the Dee. As a boy, I once—"

Pete marched off toward the main doors, great wooden monstrosities that doubtless went back to the Crusades.

"I don't give a royal fart about some long-dead countess, no matter how exquisitely she folded the linen or how many drunken shepherd boys think they've seen her flying around the castle towers on her broom—"

A woman called something from up above—gardyloo?—and a hammer sailed down to land an inch from Pete's loafer.

The power saw paused—"Sorry! M' foot slipped!" the female voice called—and then resumed.

"Maitland, this is not a safe work site if hammers can land on an investor's head."

"It's a safe work site," the site manager replied. "But we insist on hard hats and escorts for a reason, Mr. Sutherland. You ought to be wearing boots as well, but you've been to enough work sites that you know that."

And Mr. Highland Fling ought to be wearing something other than a skirt.

Pete kicked the hammer aside. "I've seen enough here. I suppose now we hike down to the Hall?" Where, please God, no hammers, jackhammers, power saws, or operatic hopefuls were to be found. "Maybe we should invest in a mule train, channel a little Grand Canyon charm to go with our flying countesses and fishing earls."

"You're funny," the site manager said. "Mr. Maitland, shall I have a wee wander down to the Hall with you, or stay up here where I can get some work done?"

The question, while good-humored and deferential, held some vague insult.

"Pete, do you have any questions for Fergus?" Maitland asked.

Pete tried to get the damned door open—it had a huge, carved handle, but not a doorknob. The matching door didn't budge either.

"Over here," the site foreman said, holding open a smaller door cut into the main doors.

Pete had to duck through it, and the sunshine was murderous even with dark glasses, but at least the noise wasn't as bad outside.

Maitland and Fergus joined him on the front portico.

"I don't have any questions for Fergus," Pete said, "but I do want whoever dropped that hammer fired. That was a lawsuit right there, if I'd been any other visitor. I expect better from your site management, Max."

Maitland plucked a sprig of some silvery-green plant growing out of a stone pot. "One of the advantages of doing business here is that nobody's personal-injury-suit happy. There are no medical bills to speak of, and even you had to sign a release before we let you set foot in this castle this morning. *Volenti non fit injuria.*"

"To one consenting," Fergus said, "no wrong can be done."

Was he translating or sucking up to the boss? "In any case, I want that woman fired."

"Can't do that, Mr. Sutherland," Fergus said. "Enjoy your tour of the Hall, and do join us for a shinty scrimmage next time you're in the neighborhood."

He disappeared through the little door, which for a guy with all his bulk should have been ungainly, but Fergus was nimble, and his departure would make the rest of the morning easier to manage.

"Why can't he fire somebody who throws tools around and nearly gets me killed?" Pete asked. "Is it some damned union thing?"

Maitland started walking toward the project office, a pretty little French farmhouse sort of building in a corner of the courtyard.

"No women are assigned to the carpentry crew this morning, and nobody's scheduled to work on that balcony for at least a month."

"So you don't know who's responsible for the accident?"

"That castle has belonged to the lords and ladies of Strathdee for centuries—we're merely leasing it—and you had just insulted Countess Brenna herself. You're in a haunted Scottish castle. You figure it out."

A scent filled the air, fresh, floral, bracing, like expensive soap. Pete wasn't sure if he liked it or not, though he for damned certain didn't like being told a ghost had almost dropped a hammer on his foot.

The tour of the Hall was eerily quiet, and the place was so damned big, and so full of staircases, ramps, and creaky elevators, Pete felt as if he'd been trapped in the labyrinth of Hangover Hell. The last stop on the tour was the earl's apartment, which according to the contract would remain available to Elias Brodie and his family members or descendants throughout the lease period.

The project controller lady was in residence—how convenient for Maitland. And whaddya know, she had a kid, a chubby little infant at the squally, squirmy stage, who appealed to Pete about as much as another glass of single malt would.

"Did you get the reports?" the lady asked, kid on her hip. The baby was fussing, trying to get sticky little fingers wrapped around his mom's hair.

"No, as a matter of fact, I'll need a hard copy. Something wrong with the internet at my rental cottage."

"We have internet here," Maitland said, giving the kid a finger to grab. "Feel free to download. The internet password is Michaeland-Brenna, all one word."

"We can set you up in the main kitchen and make you something to eat," the woman added. "Lunchtime has come and gone, and few of us work well on an empty stomach."

For the love of God, *not food*. "The problem might be with the online storage box. Damned websites are always updating and getting out of sync."

Maitland got out his phone, punched a few keys. "You've locked the storage box, Pete. Did you forget your password?"

"No, I did not forget my password. The site didn't recognize my addy, or something. Just print me out a hard copy of the reports, and I'll take tomorrow to study them." Because somewhere in those reports was bound to be a data-entry error, a bad formula, something Pete could use for further leverage to get Maitland off the project.

Pete would send the reports to Shayla, who could spot a mistake on a spreadsheet from forty yards out. She'd been the one to tell him to ask for the supporting data, though Pete still wasn't sure what had been behind her request.

"When did you lock the storage box?" Maitland asked, putting the phone away.

"The storage box locked me out this morning."

"Then none of us can get into it for forty-eight hours, cybersecurity being what it is. You'll need me and at least one other board member to override your lockout, but even we can't do that until Monday morning."

"Then print out the original files that you generated prior to uploading."

"I don't keep them on my laptop," the woman said. "They all go to secure storage, per project protocol. You don't look well, Mr. Sutherland. Is the jet lag catching up with you?"

Pete did not feel well. He felt like blowing up this whole damned project, though Shayla wouldn't be happy if he did that, and as of yesterday, Mrs. Sutherland had expressed an interest in the castle as well.

"I have so many international frequent-flier miles I could practically buy the castle with them," Pete said. An exaggeration, and most of those miles were Mrs. Sutherland's trips to this godforsaken backward corner of civilization.

The kid began to fuss, and Pete's headache joined his bellyache, along with a thousand other locations of bodily misery. A wet sound emanated from the baby's backside, and a stink worse than swamp gas hit Pete's nose.

"Somebody must have given him some cheese last night," Maitland said. "Ye gods, little dude. We should hire you out for crowd control."

This amused Maitland, while Pete's empty belly began to heave. "Maitland, let's step outside, now."

"Nice to see you again," the woman said. Cromer? Connaught? "Max, you should be leaving for the airport soon."

Pete got the hell out of Dodge before the stink, the good cheer, the damned storage box screw-up, and a surfeit of whisky overcame him. Maitland met him on the front terrace, where despite a pair of Tom Ford sunglasses, the Scottish sunshine bore holes in Pete's skull.

"This place is a nightmare," Pete said. "Falling hammers, dirty diapers, old women dancing until midnight. I had to have been crazy to let you talk me into this project."

Maitland took a seat on the stone balustrade. "I've sent you weekly summaries as required, without fail. They show we are within budget and on schedule, if not ahead. The site meets every occupational safety and health standard applicable here, and I'm meeting with a landscaper next week to see if we can get going early on that phase before winter sets in. You should be doing backflips because this project is off to a great start. Who is pulling your strings, Pete? Does Maguire have somebody else in mind for the job?"

Mag—? Right, Maguire. Interesting angle. "He might. I can't tell where the discontent started, Max, but it's real and it's not going away. You're trying your best—I say that honestly, and I'll see if I can get you some severance—but nothing I've seen today tells me you've figured out how to make a profitable, unified venue out of two white elephants."

Something was different about Maitland, something besides the fact that he was in jeans and a button-down instead of a three-piece suit. The old Max would have come off that balustrade citing

contract chapter and verse, case law, and material facts, all in anticipation of a rousing negotiation. They'd have come up with a dollar
figure that was high enough to soothe Max's pride, low enough that
Pete could sell it to other investors, and conclude with a handshake.

This Max remained right where he was. "I am owed much more
than severance, Pete, and when I find out what has caused this
protracted exercise in stupidity on your part, we'll see if I'm owed
additional damages as well. How's the missus?"

"She's threatening to stop by and see the castle. Said she once
attended a house party at the Hall. First, she's going to get me in hock
up to my retirement assets buying some damned castle of her own."

"Is she the problem?"

Dear Mrs. Sutherland was increasingly a problem. Vague refer-
ences to the prenuptial agreement, along with shopping trips that
now lasted weeks instead of days... No wonder a guy developed a
wandering eye when his own wife wasn't interested in being a wife.

Maybe Shayla... but no. Divorce was a mighty expensive proposition, even with an airtight prenup—sometimes, *especially* with a
prenup—and for the most part, Pete liked his wife.

"You are the problem," Pete said. "You got us into a project that's
going to cost a bundle rather than make a bundle. I'm calling an
emergency meeting of the board, Max. I have no choice."

Maitland rose, though he stayed by the railing, gaze on the castle
gleaming against the sky atop the tree-covered hill.

"We all have choices, Pete, and you are making a mistake. I don't
have time to argue you around, because I have a plane to catch."

"I'll have to bring that up with the board too, Max. You have a
project on the brink of disaster, and you're nipping back home for
reasons I cannot fathom. Your job is here."

Maitland shaded his eyes to watch a pair of birds glide above the
treetops. Pete was no ornithologist, but they were big damned birds,
probably raptors.

"My contract says otherwise," Maitland replied. "My contract
says I get trips home, regularly, and I've already cut this one short to

humor your nonsense. You've shut down the storage box with further ineptitude and insulted my site manager with your cultural insensitivity. If that's not undue interference, I don't know what is. Call your board meeting, and we'll see what the other investors have to say."

Well, that was more like it—a little posturing, but with a lot less fire than Pete had anticipated from Maitland. Maybe Max was considering the severance, or he had a job interview in Maryland. That would make sense. Bit off more than he could chew and needed a little time to get his options together.

"The board will have a virtual meeting tomorrow, then. I'll let you know if you still have a job on Monday."

Maitland ceased his birdwatching. "No, you won't. The by-laws say you can't get rid of me except through a meeting of the full board, and all full board meetings, even the emergency meetings, must be held during regular business hours, as those hours apply to both Scotland and the US Eastern Time zone. You have a three-hour window on Monday afternoon to hold your meeting, and I'll be back by then to attend in my ex officio capacity. Enjoy your walk to Morgan's cottage. My regards to your missus."

He left Pete standing alone in the brutal sunshine, belly roiling, head pounding, and bones aching. For that alone, Pete would make sure Max Maitland lost his job—and got not one dime of severance or payout.

THE TRAIN from Perth to the Edinburgh Airport took a little over an hour, and the journey was through pretty country. Max would be making this trip often, taking advantage of the direct flights between Edinburgh and Newark or Edinburgh and Dulles. Another train trip would get him down to Baltimore, and from there, a rental car would take him to Maura's doorstep. The whole thing could be done in less than twelve clock hours, because five time zones worked in Max's favor flying west.

Flying east in time to make Pete's board meeting would mean a red-eye from Dulles into Heathrow, a connecting flight from London up to Edinburgh, another train trip, and then a drive through the Scottish countryside.

All on very little sleep.

Max's last email to Maura had gone unanswered, but then, she was pissed at him for getting a late start to this visit. He was pissed at Pete Sutherland.

The question of who was pulling Pete's strings had nagged at Max's mind all the way to the airport. As he'd shuffled through security—no bags to check—and made his way to the gate, he'd dragged along many theories, but no answers.

Maybe Pete was encountering a health problem.

Maybe early-onset dementia was playing a role.

Or gambling losses.

Maybe Mrs. Sutherland wanted to manage the job. By reputation, she was a shrewd Scotswoman who'd kept Pete's philandering in check better than her predecessors had.

Maybe land prices in Deeside were due to spike because of some other development Pete had learned of through the clubhouse gossip vine.

Max settled onto a seat near his gate and sent another email to Maura: *At the airport, looking forward to seeing my favorite baby sister tomorrow.* No matter how long he stared at his phone, she didn't reply. Max might have continued to stare at his phone, except a particular rhythm of high heels on a hard surface pierced his brain fog. He knew that walk, knew that exact tempo and force behind a feminine footfall.

Shayla Walters was deplaning at the gate across the concourse. She pulled a smart black overnight case on rollers, and her ensemble was weekend chic. Long legs encased in jeans with a knife-edge crease, the denim just worn enough to look relaxed. White silk blouse; floral scarf in purples, white, and green, draped and knotted just so; deconstructed navy blazer that nevertheless emphasized a great figure. Her dark hair was caught back in a bun, though when released, it would likely hang in silky shimmers to at least midback length.

Without any closer examination, Max knew her earrings, bracelet, wallet, phone case, and shoes would all complete the picture of a woman winning at the game of life and playing every inning by her own rules.

Shayla made an impact, though her impact on Max was mostly a detached appreciation for how passionately she played the role. Other men were discreetly admiring her, women likely were too, while for Max...

A question had been answered. Shayla had set her sights on Brodie Castle, or perhaps on Pete Sutherland. Elias had said that Pete's prospective project manager was a Canadian, an easy mistake to make, because Shayla had been working in Edmonton in recent years. She was all American, though, and probably tired of winters on the lone prairie.

She spotted Max, and guilt flashed through her eyes before her megawatt smile beamed forth and she was crossing the concourse, free hand extended.

"Max Maitland, what a small world. My goodness, it's lovely to see you. What has it been? Two years?" She took his hand and leaned in, not quite a kiss, but enough of an embrace to justify her left foot coming up behind her in a move she probably practiced.

He hadn't seen her up close in nearly four years, and in all that time, Shayla hadn't stopped wearing the same rosy perfume. *Joy*, most likely. Venerable and expensive.

"Shayla, you're looking well." And nervous. He knew her body, knew her mind. Knew the self-conscious smile from the fake-self-conscious smile from the oh-shit-oh-shit smile. "Come to Scotland for a bit of sightseeing?"

With only an overnight bag.

"As a matter of fact, I have. Maybe some fishing, if the schedule works out."

Not from my river, you won't. The temptation to fence with her was balanced by the odd notion that Max felt sorry for her. Relying on Pete Sutherland's loyalty was a set up for disappointment.

"Sutherland is already up at Brodie Castle," Max said, "pissing off everybody from the locals to the ghosts. Now I know why."

She dropped the Welcome Wagon routine. "Max, I have no idea what you're referring to, and as a project manager, you know that discussing proprietary information in a busy airport is egregiously inappropriate."

Egregiously inappropriate. Any doubt Max had harbored went taxiing down the runway. Sutherland had used the same phrase, in the same tone, one of Shayla's signature hyperboles.

"Shay, if Sutherland will backstab me to put you in charge of that site, he'll backstab you. If he'll cheat on his wife, he'll cheat on you." *You deserve better.* Max kept that observation to himself, because Shayla was nothing if not proud.

"Thank you for that advice, though it's somewhat lacking in originality. How's Laura?"

"Maura." Whom Shayla had regarded as the other woman, though Max hadn't figured that out until long after the dust had settled. "She's expecting a visit from me tomorrow and doing well." Max hoped that was so. Maura had been in good health for the past few years, or he'd never have chanced a job overseas. She was not, however, in good spirits.

"You miss her, don't you?" Shayla looked concerned, but then, she could turn up convincingly warm-hearted when it was in her interest to do so.

"Not as much as I thought I would, but it's only been three weeks. What does Maguire think of you stepping into my shoes at Brodie Castle when you've never handled a renovation like that?"

"Maguire? He's the last-minute investor? I haven't met him."

Not a protestation of innocence, though her failure to check every last trap was some comfort. "He flips manor houses and estates like Brodie Castle all over Europe. If Sutherland thinks your credentials exceed my own, then you can bet Sutherland is falsifying your credentials."

Clearly, that hadn't occurred to her.

She readjusted her silk scarf so another inch of cleavage showed. "Then I'll have to convince Mr. Maguire that I'm the better man, as usual. I also bring oil-and-gas connections to the job that you don't have, Max, and oil and gas are holding up a lot of the Scottish economy."

Not like they used to. He didn't bother tossing out that riposte. Sparring with Shayla had been fun once upon a time. Maybe the Canadian winters had taken a toll on her, or maybe Max had learned to see past the regalia, because she looked tired to him—tired and too thin.

"What's your plan for connecting the Hall and the castle?" Max asked. "If that's the pretext on which Sutherland is basing my firing, then Maguire will expect you to have a solution."

Her smile was pure bravado. "My solution is to blame you and point out six other areas where I can either bump revenue or cut costs to make up for the honking disaster you've bequeathed to me. Edmonton gets bloody cold in the winter, and the winters last too bloody long. Business is business, Max."

CHAPTER SEVENTEEN

A year ago, even a few months ago, Max might have offered the same moral dodge Shayla had used: All's fair in profit and piracy. Except... it wasn't. Fergus and Hugh, Dinty and Fern, Granny MacPhee and Morgan... their fates were tied up with what happened to the castle and the Hall. Shayla wouldn't get that, and hammers would start falling like rain.

"That budget isn't extravagant, Shay, and Sutherland had no business sharing it with you unless he had the permission of the other investors."

She took the barrette from her bun and let the shiny mass of her hair cascade down her back. This maneuver was yet another distraction, and half the men in the concourse stopped to appreciate it. Five years ago, Max would have felt some pride that such a magnificent woman had given him her heart.

Now, Shayla struck him as not magnificent, but rather, as a competent impostor whose performance was showing a little wear.

Jeannie, cheerfully offering a badly hungover Sutherland lunch was magnificent.

Jeannie, making love with Max on the project couch—three condoms at the ready—was spectacular.

Jeannie, spinning chaos into order with the project records, while looking after Henry, keeping an eye on morale, and saving Max from a dozen cultural blunders, was the stuff dreams were made of.

Max's dreams, in any case.

"I never said I saw your project budget," Shayla countered. "But I know you. You build in contingencies and weather delays and planning days. There's fat in that budget, and I'll find it, and if I'm lucky, it will be enough to offset the cost of blasting a damn elevator into the side of that hill."

"You can't blast anywhere near the castle, Shay. The ratios involved in the main arch over the great hall are too delicate, the engineering too ancient."

She shifted the grip on her suitcase. "You mean you truly don't have a solution for how to connect those two buildings?"

She'd been counting on him to solve the problem and hand her the solution along with his livelihood, his professional reputation, and Maura's security.

"There is a solution," Max said. He could feel it soaring just out of reach in his imagination, feel the brush of its wings against his dreams.

"So you're being a hard-ass, as only you can be." She took half a step closer, bringing her rose garden scent with her. "Max, this is not your fault, and I know your sister is a drain on your finances. I can get you decent severance, praise the groundwork you've laid, make nice-nice like you never could. As somebody who used to be a friend, I'm telling you, just take the money and run. Pete's wife is determined to move to Scotland, and putting me in charge of the castle is his little rebellion against domestic tyranny. You're not going to win this one. I'm sorry."

She kissed his cheek and sashayed off, a study in success—to appearances.

A near miss, in fact.

The announcement warning that the boarding process was soon to begin came over the loudspeaker. People shuffled themselves into the appropriate lines, parents took children for a last trip to the restroom, while Max resumed his seat.

One dad was playing the walk-me game with an infant, holding the baby's hands while the child tottered step by step in the mother's direction. The baby took the last few steps alone, half falling into the mom's waiting hands, everybody smiling hugely.

If I don't get on that plane, Maura will be furious and disappointed.

The early boarders breezed down the jetway.

If I do get on that plane, I will never see Henry's first steps. I will betray the trust Jeannie, Fergus, Hugh... all of them have placed in me. I will lose the ability to protect their jobs. I will fail the promise I made to Elias Brodie.

First class and the frequent-flier crowd came next.

I will never learn the dances that Jeannie has known since girlhood. Never even watch a shinty match, much less get my ass righteously handed to me in one.

One by one, the seating groups lined up and scanned their boarding passes, and still Max remained in his seat.

I will never get to use Jeannie's remaining two condoms, or not use them, if Jeannie's inclined to present Henry with a sibling someday.

Now there was a thought to give a lonely man pause. The final boarding call came, and Max was on his feet, his boarding pass in hand. Maura had nobody else, but life included many weekends, and her disappointment in Max was part of growing up—for them both.

Max slapped his boarding pass on the podium. "I won't be flying tonight. If you can give the extra seat to the family with the baby, I'd be grateful."

The attendant looked at his boarding pass. "You're sure?"

SCOTLAND TO THE MAX

"Positive." The woman Max had once proposed to was going after his job, the woman he'd loved for her whole life would be furious with him, and the woman he'd fallen in love with deserved a lot more from him than "take the money and run."

The attendant was babbling something about a possible refund or voucher when Max's phone rang.

"I don't need a refund. I'll just keep the miles." God, the ghosts of Brodie Castle, and good luck willing, he'd need them. He moved off to an empty corner of the gate lounge and got out his phone—not a number he recognized. "This is Maitland."

"Connor Maguire here. Why the hell can't I get into the damned cyber-storage box?"

The hour was growing late, it was Saturday night, and Max was not tech support for cranky investors.

"That's a long story, but essentially, Pete Sutherland screwed it up in his attempts to sabotage my role as project manager at Brodie Castle."

"I was told you don't pull any punches. If Sutherland ruins this project, I will set so many lawyers on his ass there won't be a court-room left for him to hide in. What the hell is going on?"

"It's complicated." And Max needed to get back to Jeannie and to the castle. "There will be an emergency board meeting on Monday afternoon, and I'm sure Pete will have all manner of poison-pen emails in the works tomorrow. Now, if you'll excuse me, I have a train—"

"Maitland, I am one of your investors. If you're facing a palace coup, now is not the time to give me the bum's rush." An Irish brogue could make a man sound charming even when he was delivering a threat.

"My apologies, Maguire, but I've had three hours' sleep out of the past thirty-six, thanks to Sutherland's meddling. My crews are nervous, the locals have been given to understand the project is doomed, and my successor as project manager has already been shown the site plans, budgets, and schedules. She has no idea how to solve the riddle of connecting the castle and Hall, but that hasn't stopped her from showing up in Scotland, ready to meet *my investors* the day after tomorrow."

"*She* has no idea?" Maguire asked.

"Shayla Walters, a professional engineer who's as pretty as she is smart, and she's very smart. MBA, summa cum laude." Smart some ways. More than that, Max wouldn't say, even when his future hung in the balance. Shayla's ambition was based in an upbringing that few would connect with the woman she'd become.

Maguire was eating, his chomping coming through the connection clearly. "Ms. Walters is finishing up a job in Edmonton, a regional headquarters for one of the major oil companies. Not much to it once you figure out where the cable and conduit go."

"You know her?"

More munching. "You have trouble, I have connections, also plans for Brodie Castle. I am acquainted with Pete Sutherland's wife, who is in a position to cause a lot of inconvenience for everybody who invested in this project."

Inconvenience, as in court orders, subpoenas, depositions, and witness summonses. Hell hath no fury like a woman scorned—and Mrs. Sutherland was a Scotswoman.

"What do you want to know, Maguire?"

"Find somewhere comfortable and reasonably private, because I want to know everything."

"Give me a few minutes. There has to be at least one bar still open in this airport."

Max ended the call and considered loyalties, confidentiality requirements, and his flagging energy level. He found a quiet corner of a quiet eatery, ordered some sustenance, and dialed a number.

"This is Elias."

"Maitland here. Your castle is being invaded by barbarians, and Connor Maguire is pretending I'm his new best friend. If you know anything, now would be a good time to share."

"I know Connor Maguire well enough. He's smart, filthy rich, and mostly trustworthy."

Mostly trustworthy? "Come to Scotland, you said. The project will put you on the international map, you said. Now you're telling me my wealthiest investor is only *mostly* trustworthy?"

"He's trustworthy as long as you don't play polo against him. He'd never hurt a horse, but put him on one, and he'll find a way to score. What the hell is going on?"

Max wasn't entirely sure himself. "Pete Sutherland wants to replace me as project manager with somebody who's leading him around by his shorts. Somebody I proposed to five years ago. She's a first-rate project manager, but not always so shrewd in other regards and has never done a renovation like Brodie Castle. Mrs. Sutherland is likely ready to start divorce proceedings, which could tie up progress at the castle if the litigation gets ugly."

Elias's silence spoke volumes. Then, "Shite. Bollocks, bastard, bloody, shitting shite. A divorce will stop the engines, Max. Sutherland's money will be tied up, the other investors will get cold feet, and my castle is all but ruined. It's harder to resume a failed renovation than it is to start one from scratch."

At least Elias grasped the scope of the problem—for the castle.

Max's food arrived, a fruit and cheese plate, along with a pot of decaf tea. He plowed through the offerings while briefing Elias. Another call came through, doubtless Maguire, expecting Max to pull plaid bunnies out of Harris Tweed hats.

"I gotta go," Max said. "I called to ask you a favor." He didn't like saying those words, didn't like *needing* to say those words, but he also didn't like vegetables, particularly, and consumed them regularly.

Henry and Jeannie were counting on him.

"Asking for a favor takes balls, considering you've let the Visigoths camp at my castle gates."

"I will save your castle, Elias, but you have to do something for me first."

~

JEANNIE HAD KISSED Max good-bye and pretended good cheer for Henry's sake. She'd fooled her son through the evening meal, and thank every angel who guarded the sanity of single parents, Henry had gone to sleep a little later than usual, but without a fuss.

Jeannie had just settled into bed with the *Toughest Cowboy in Texas* when her phone rang. Her heart leaped in happy anticipation —Max, calling to say his flight was delayed until tomorrow and he was coming home?—but, no.

No, indeed. "Hello, Millicent."

"Jeannie, I hope it's not too late."

And if it had been? If the call had woken Henry? Had woken Jeannie? "Henry's fast asleep. I have a few minutes to chat. How are you?"

"I'm missing my grandson. When are you coming back to Perth?"

A pleasant reply, one that turned Millicent's rudeness into a joke, died aborning. "I wish Harry missed his son enough to ask after him even weekly, but I haven't heard from Harry since the first of the month." Since assuring him that she had a job.

Ah, silence. Jeannie envisioned Millicent swiveling her cannon to take aim in a fresh direction.

"In Harry's absence, you should be all the more appreciative of the interest I take in my grandson."

Because a father's love was that small of a loss? No wonder Harry stayed out of range, if his mother was so lacking in compassion for half-orphaned boys.

"Henry is fine, Millicent. No sniffles, no signs of allergies. He hasn't taken his first steps yet, but it's still a little early for that." *In case you were wondering.*

"That's good to hear. When can I see him?" Not *may I see him.*

"I'm staying at Brodie Castle for the present. I have weekends off, and you're welcome to visit any time, provided you give me a little notice."

Millicent made a sniffy sound. "I heard an American is in charge of the renovations. If you talk to Elias, tell him that was not well done of him."

Americans apparently figured next to leaky septic tanks in Millicent's social hierarchy.

"It's American money funding the renovation, Millicent, and American money keeping me gainfully employed on a job that makes terrific use of my skills and abilities. I'm also involved in the renovation of my family's castle, which will someday be Henry's family castle." *Bad of me, to be so ungracious.* Even Millicent's fancy pedigree didn't include a castle.

"Deeside is a long way to drive," Millicent said.

"Ninety minutes, if the roads are dry. Was there something else you wanted, Millicent?" The conversation was supposed to end with Jeannie making arrangements to drive those ninety minutes, both ways, Henry in tow, at the time most convenient for Millicent.

"Why don't you drive down tomorrow?" Millicent said. "The weather's supposed to be lovely, summer days are long, and I haven't seen Henry for weeks. Babies grow so quickly. We could go shopping for a few new outfits, and maybe find something for you to wear to interviews too."

This was bait. *Do as I say and I'll spend money on you and Henry.*

"Millicent, I have a job. I just said as much. It pays well, I can spend a lot of time with Henry, and like everybody else on-site, I'm welcome to work in my jeans. If you'd care to visit next weekend, let me know and I'll adjust Henry's nap time accordingly."

The silence on the other end was intended to be indignant, though Jeannie suspected *desperate* would have been a better description.

"Is this what comes of working for an *American*, Jeannie?"

The question was ridiculous. The answer was not. "This is what comes from having a good job, working for decent people, on a project that matters to me. Let me know when you'd like to visit."

And this was what came from spending time with a decent, honorable, lovely man who wasn't afraid of a child's vulnerability.

"Harry will hear about this, Jeannie. If you're relocating without his permission, he will certainly hear about this."

The poor woman... "I let Harry know as soon as I got the job. He spared me a seven-word reply: 'Glad to hear it, best of luck.' I suspect he's found somebody new, and I wish him the best of luck as well. I am free to move wherever I please, and Harry—not you, Harry—will have to drag me to court to prove that moving Henry less than two hours from Perth matters, when for all we know, Harry is working in the middle of the Indian Ocean and won't set foot back in Scotland for months. Good night."

Jeannie ended the call and waited for guilt to rise up and swamp her relief.

But... nothing. Not guilt, not remorse, not regret, unless it was the regret of not putting Millicent in her place sooner. Not reading the court orders word-for-word sooner. Not realizing that a typical heels-and-silk-blouses office job wouldn't be right.

Not fighting for the respect any parent was due.

"Though I certainly expected Max to fight," she murmured—quietly. Henry could be a devilishly light sleeper.

She put aside the *Toughest Cowboy*, sat in the middle of the enormous bed—a bed she'd shared with Max—and considered what she'd asked of him.

Save the castle, find us a future, solve your sister's situation, solve the problems with the site. Settle down unruly investors, protect your job, love my son as if he were your own... While I fuss about with spreadsheets and keep track of Bear-Bear?

But how else could she help Max best those challenges?

That question prompted her to pore over every document she could get her hands on that related to Brodie Castle's renovation. Max had sent her a copy of his employment contract, a seventeen-page quagmire of *heretofores* and *provided thats* which most project controllers would have filed under "Too Long, Didn't Read." She read it. She also read the articles of incorporation and the by-laws, the minutes of the directors' meetings, and the project mission statement.

She read them all again and dozed off on the couch in the living room. The directors could turf Max out by a unanimous vote, even in the absence of good cause. He'd get his buyout money, but to be pitched off a job mere weeks after arriving would make finding another job nearly impossible.

In the guest room, Henry stirred. Too early for his bottle, but then, his schedule had been at sixes and sevens for the past few days.

"I'm coming," Jeannie murmured, straightening legs stiff from being curled under her. She turned down the lamps, lest Henry develop ambitions of a post-midnight play session, and fetched his bottle from the kitchen.

Henry took the bottle enthusiastically and drifted back to sleep before he'd even burped. Jeannie laid him in his crib and prepared for a night of dreams in the earl's bed.

The earl... the earl owned the castle. The renovation project was undertaken by virtue of a ninety-nine-year lease. Under the lease, the earl retained certain privileges—such as the use of the apartment, without notice, at any time. He retained the right to collect rent from the properties in the village and the right to open any Highland Games held on the castle, Hall, or village grounds... Among other rights.

The present earl was Elias, and he was five time zones behind than Scotland. Jeannie dialed him up—this was too urgent for emails—and got him on the second ring.

"Jeannie, aren't you up past your bedtime?"

"Don't mess with me, Elias. I've already faced down a half dozen stinky diapers today, put the man I love on a plane bound for America, and delivered a long overdue spanking to my former mother-in-law. Your castle is about to fall into the hands of the infidels. I need a favor."

"I seem to be in the business of giving them out this evening. What do you need?"

"I need a claymore, Elias. One sharp enough to chop off the head of a serpent in the castle courtyard."

CHAPTER EIGHTEEN

The trains in Scotland ran on time for the most part. They did not run overnight, at least not between Edinburgh and Perth past the hour when Max had finished Connor Maguire's briefing. Maguire had asked good questions and lots of them.

Why did Max want to stick with this job when the investors were either meddlesome or easily swayed by a meddler?

That one was easy: Every project hit snags, impasses, and quagmires. Walking out didn't get the problems solved, and Max's job was to solve problems.

Was there a price for which Max *would* walk? The answer to that question had surprised even Max: There was no price for which he'd cave to Sutherland's games. Not only no, but hell no.

He'd committed to seeing the project to completion. Resigning for the convenience of a bunch of squabbling good old boys wasn't going to happen. Not even for the sake of Maura's special-needs trust, which Max would continue to add to as best he could. And yeah, that conclusion had a lot to do with Jeannie Cromarty—and Henry—and also with the castle itself and the community it had held together for centuries.

"Perhaps the Scottish air has addled my wits," Max murmured, hefting his backpack from the passenger's side of the car. Even the wrong-sided cars and backward roads felt normal now, as did the golden morning light and brilliant blue sky over the Baron's Hall.

Max climbed the porch stairs, fatigue and frustration dogging his steps. If he went inside now, he'd lie down, and if he lay down, he'd sleep for hours. The key to clipping Sutherland's wings lay in finding a plan that joined the castle and the Hall without breaking the budget or wrecking the schedule. Blasting wasn't an option. Trams were expensive, and building them required highly specialized crews.

Sometimes, what a problem wanted was a view from a new angle —literally.

Max set down his backpack and descended the stairs, striking out across a meadow devoid of either sheep or cattle. A pair of workmen were repairing the wall, rearranging stones, pausing to talk, then shifting a few more stones. As Max neared them, he realized the shorter, more slender workman, whom he'd taken for an apprentice, was in fact a tallish woman wearing a long duster that might have once belonged to her partner.

The castle sat atop its hill, surrounded by a sea of trees. This was the postern view of the curtain wall, more substantial and less fairy tale than the front view.

"Good morning," Max said, meaning to continue his circuit of the whole hill.

"Mr. Maitland." The man rose from kneeling before the wall and stuck out a callused hand. "Fine day for a wee daunder."

His accent was nigh unintelligible, the breadth of his shoulders putting Max in mind of the curtain wall protecting the bailey.

Max shook hands, and having been taught that a man never presumed to take a lady's hand unless she offered it, he nodded to the woman. "Ma'am."

"Mr. Maitland, good day." The lady's accent was easier to under-stand. "Michael, stop thinking you'll wedge that round rock into the bottom row. A surface that flat belongs at the top of the wall."

"Aye, lovey." He set aside the offending rock like a boy parting with his soccer ball on a sunny school day afternoon.

Max did not recall signing a purchase order to retain the services of a diker and apprentice, but he'd come across the drystone wall tradesmen on other jobs. Many were international vagabonds, traveling from specialty job to specialty job, conducting serial love affairs with the geology and topography of one region after another. Perhaps Jeannie had seen an opportunity and brought these two to the castle in anticipation of a contract.

"I hope you're not working on Sunday morning because of any deadline I might have imposed," Max said. "The day's too pretty for deadlines."

The lady sent her partner an I-told-you-so look. "Mending wall in summer is hardly work, Mr. Maitland, but you should see our spring mornings here in Deeside. The glory of heaven barely exceeds spring at Brodie Castle."

"You'll get her going." The man's grousing was belied by a kiss to the woman's cheek. "Though as always, my wife has an excellent point."

He was big, blond, and bristling with muscle, while the lady was a willowy redhead. They weren't young, but neither did Max detect anything of age about their movements or appearance. Granny McPhee would probably deem them "good stock," and their ages might be anything from thirty-five to fiftyish.

And they were clearly in love.

"Will you be here come spring?" The lady's tone held something of inquisition, though the question was polite.

"I dearly hope to be," Max said. "Isn't there a song about losing your heart to the Highlands?"

"Many songs," the man said, unbuilding an arrangement of stones he'd just stacked. "They all have the ring of truth, but I hear America is quite posh, quite fancy."

"This one," the wife said, using her foot to nudge a chunk of granite. "Start with that one. Have you family in America, Mr. Maitland?"

The exercise of arranging stones into a solid wall was pulling at Max's focus, drawing him into a puzzle that was both mental and physical.

"One sister, and she is entirely dependent on me and likely always will be. That's not for publication."

Michael lifted his wife's chosen rock easily. "No need to fret, Maitland. We'll take your secrets with us to the grave."

His wife smacked him in the ribs. "For shame, Michael. Mr. Maitland faces a dilemma. He's needed both places."

Michael positioned the rock at the base of a gap in the wall. "I wouldn't know anything about that problem, but seems to me that when you canna be two places at once, a loyal minion or two might come in handy. Hand me that hammer, lovey mine."

She handed him a mason's hammer and chisel. With one blow, he whacked off a protruding corner of the large rock, creating a surface he could wedge flat against the standing portion of the wall.

"What do you hear from our Elias?" the woman asked. "One doesn't like to be nosy, but Brodie menfolk are not conscientious correspondents."

This was some sort of criticism of her husband, who grinned sheepishly and pitched aside the broken-off piece of granite.

"Elias is obnoxiously happy with his Violet in Maryland. He's counting on me to defend his castle." Why Max could confide that to these two strangers, he did not know. They would likely be gone next week, but for now, they were a tired man's sounding board.

"That's the trouble with castles," Michael said, scowling at the rocks scattered about the gap in the wall. "Damned things need defending. Lovey, where did I put my skin?"

She passed him what looked like a goatskin bag of the sort shepherds used to carry water, and Michael squirted a stream of liquid into his mouth, then held the skin out to Max.

"Have a nip, Maitland. Nothing like good Deeside water to

refresh a working man's energies. At least that hasn't changed. What manner of enemy threatens our castle?"

The castle belonged to the people, the people belonged to the castle. The concept would strike Americans oddly, but in Scotland, the notion had long created permanence in a dangerous world.

Hence, *our* castle.

"Nothing I can't handle," Max said. "My current challenge is to figure out a way to connect the castle and Hall without using dynamite."

Michael kicked a sizable rock. "You'd use blasting powder on the castle?" He might as well have said *blasphemy* powder.

"No, I will not. No sane engineer would, but I need to get the two buildings functioning as one, or the choice to stay in Scotland will be taken from me."

The couple exchanged another look, one that held volumes of marital information and brought them to some shared conclusion.

The lady took the goatskin bag from Max and jammed a cork in the top. "I refuse to squirt myself in the face with water as well, Mr. Maitland. Michael spent time in the Pyrenees and fancies himself quite the Continental swell."

Max was still learning the local turns of phrase, though the lady's word choices struck him as old-fashioned.

Michael blew his wife a kiss. "I'm your Continental swell, lovey. Always will be. You say Elias is happy with his new lady? They had a grand wedding up in the main hall. Had the place looking festive."

"You are not using that wee pebble to balance yon boulder," the lady said, snatching a modest chunk of rock from her husband's hand. "You are daft, Michael. Too much time on the Spanish plains. Ask Elias about the time he got lost in the wine cellars, Mr. Maitland. Poor lad had just buried his parents, and a more pathetic sight you never saw. He loves that castle, though. He must place a great deal of trust in you if you've been chosen to defend it."

"You heard the man," Michael said, rearranging his rocks. "Elias is in love. Brodie men fall hard and permanently. Do ask his lordship about his adventure in the wine cellar. Gave us all a fright. I must say, whoever built this wall did a fine job."

"So modest," his wife scoffed, though as far as Max knew, the walls in this valley had been built centuries ago, back when farming was a communal venture and stone was the only available building material.

"Consider this," the lady went on. "In former times, having a lot of servants scurrying about in plain sight was not considered the done thing, and yet, the Hall was built to be a family wing for the castle, in a manner of speaking."

"The first earl and his lady had seven children," Max murmured, studying the castle and the Hall. From this angle, one sat directly below the other. If the Hall had been built a few stories higher, or situated higher up the hill, then a skyway to the bailey might have been possible... Though hard to design aesthetically.

Still, a skyway was possible. The Hall would need a tower, the bailey wall an opening. It could work.

"Seven children," Michael said, wedging a bread-loaf-size piece of granite into the gap. "A fine, loud lot of Brodies, whom their mother doted upon, but didn't necessarily want underfoot as they matured and started their own families. Nonetheless, a mama wolf would worry about her cubs."

British country manor houses had hidden stairways, priest holes, and secret passages—were famous for them, in fact.

"I'll leave you to your work," Max said. "If I'm talking to Elias, whom shall I say was asking after him?"

"Auld Michael and his lady," the woman said.

"I'm no' so verra auld," the man grumbled. "But do give Elias our regards, and good luck defending the castle. 'Tis a sorry day when a man's alone with that task. Dearling, where's my flask? All this mending wall has my throat parched."

Max left them to their bickering and rock-wrestling and resumed his hike around the base of the hill. The castle and the Hall *were* connected, by history, by family, by proximity. The hour was still too early in the States for Max to call Elias, but as Max completed his circuit—past hairy red cows chewing their cuds, sheep munching on summer grass—he felt a sense of hope.

He should have questioned Michael and his wife more closely, asked them for any local lore or legend that related to the castle bowels or the building of the Hall. He made the full circuit of the hill and returned to his backpack on the porch steps only to find the diker and his lady assistant were nowhere to be seen.

And the wall undulated across the pasture in a perfect, unbroken line.

JEANNIE BASKED in the lovely weight of sunlight on her closed eyelids. Was any sensation more benevolent than the warmth of sunshine gaining strength on a Scottish summer morning?

She should get out of bed, of course. More to the point, she should wake Henry up. The wee pest had awakened shortly after Jeannie had finished her conversation with Elias, and the rest of the night had been a succession of catnaps, lullabies, and half-finished baby bottles.

Henry had fallen asleep well after sunrise, and Jeannie had sought refuge in the earl's bed what felt like five minutes ago.

The mattress dipped, and the instant before Jeannie would have screamed, Max's scent came to her. Woodsy, clean, freshly showered.

"You're not in America."

His hair was damp, his eyes tired. His smile was pure mischief. "I am in your bed. If that's not okay..."

Jeannie kissed him. "I want to hear why you aren't in America, but later, Max." Two condoms later, at least.

He climbed into bed with her, not a stitch on him. "I've been thinking."

"I've been dreaming."

Max got himself situated between her legs, and the lovely man was already aroused. "I've been doing some of that too."

About damned time.

Max was intent on that lazy, leisurely, stealthy lovemaking that made Jeannie frantic. She wanted no parts of that—this time. "We're going to need a condom, Max."

He nuzzled her throat. "Soon."

"Now, before the scourge of Deeside wakes up. That baby had me on my feet half the night, which is why you catch me abed at this disgraceful hour. He'll sense that you're here and make a fuss, and—"

Max kissed her on the mouth. "Right. Did you know that Scotland is a first world nation where all manner of conveniences are for sale?" He climbed off the bed, fished around in the pockets of the jeans draped over a chair, and held up a small box done in red plaid. "Whisky-flavored, no less."

"Max, if you are not back in this bed immediately..." Her threat evaporated as he unrolled the condom. He stood halfway across the room, out of tackling range, though the rug burns would have been worth the reward.

"I still don't know how to connect the castle and the Hall," he said, prowling toward the bed. "But for damn sure I want to connect me to you."

As he crouched over her and Jeannie wrapped herself around him, she wondered if Max had referred to a connection in the temporary, erotic sense, or if his presence in her bed meant something more.

He surged over her and into her, a masculine force of nature as cherishing as he was relentless. Jeannie mapped his body with her hands, caressed contours and textures into her memory, and met Max thrust for thrust and kiss for kiss.

This loving was different. Max was present in a way he hadn't been on earlier occasions. He was *with* Jeannie, as an urge to cry battled against growing arousal.

"Don't leave me," Jeannie whispered, though she hadn't meant to speak the words. She'd meant to communicate that plea with her touch, with her passion.

"I'm here to stay," Max said, gathering her close. "With you."

The big bed rocked in slow rhythm with them, a galleon on waves of unspoken emotion, and everything—sunlight, hope, desire, pleasure—converged inside Jeannie with all the fears and angers she'd been taking to bed for too long.

She keened, she wept, she shook, and she clung, the force of her cataclysm wringing her out as sunlight scatters the evidence of a storm. She tucked her face against Max's throat as his hand stroked gently over her hair.

"You okay?" He sounded concerned, but calm. A mere bout of erotic hysteria wouldn't scare him off.

"I hated to think of you so far away." Not what she wanted to say.

Max kissed her temple. "You were afraid I wouldn't come back."

"Yes."

He would soon slip from her body. Jeannie stole a few more moments of absolute bliss in her lover's arms, then patted his butt.

"Up you go. I missed you."

He kissed her nose. "I missed you too." Then he was off the bed and strolling into the bathroom. "Is Henry teething?"

"Probably." *What a delectable backside.* "We have to get you into a kilt one of these days."

"Maitlands are Lowlanders," he said from the bathroom. "The tartan is green, black, blue, yellow, and red. The next time I'm in Edinburgh, I'll stop by one of those fancy kilt shops and get measured."

Jeannie's heart beat a slow tattoo against her ribs. "A fancy dress kilt will cost you a fortune." A fortune Max ought not to spend, unless he meant to stay—truly stay—in Scotland.

"No more than a tux. I wear mine about three times a year."

A conversation held across the bedroom as morning sun poured through the windows and afterglow sang through Jeannie's body should have been a mundane pleasure. One of the small gifts any couple could enjoy while the baby slept.

Jeannine nonetheless felt a sense of portents, of her life shifting on its axis, a heavy portcullis lifting.

"What do you think of connecting the Hall and the castle through a skyway?" Max asked, climbing back onto the bed. "Add a couple floors to the Hall, punch a hole through the curtain wall? If the skyway angled straight back from the Hall, the current profile of the two buildings and their arrangement on the hill wouldn't change from most perspectives."

I think I'm in love with you. She knew that for a truth beyond fact. "A skyway is like a bridge over dry ground?"

Max lay back and looped an arm under Jeannie's neck. "It's a possibility. I took a hike around the entire hill and for the first time considered the Hall from the fields that ran along the main drive. The roof of the Hall sits about thirty feet below the foundation of the curtain wall. The buildings seem farther apart when viewed from the parapets, because the top of the castle walls sits another thirty or fifty feet above the bailey."

He fell silent, and Jeannie could feel him thinking. No sound came from across the hallway, suggesting Henry had got his days and nights truly confused.

"This is how I am," Max said. "I get stuck on a problem and it consumes me. Just smack me if I'm being oblivious."

He spoke as if he were offering advice for the long-term, and the thumping of Jeannie's heart quickened.

"You're here to fight for the castle. That's why you're not in America, isn't it?"

"I'm here to fight for the castle," Max said, "and for my job, but mostly, Jeannie Cromarty, I'm here to fight for us."

The words washed through her, brighter than sunshine. "Explain yourself, Mr. Maitland."

He wrestled her over him, so they were face to face. "I can get another job if the wheels come off this one. I can keep adding to my sister's trust fund, some years more than others. I can explain to those who need to know why Sutherland is being such a horse's backend, but if I fail here..."

Jeannie sifted her fingers through his hair. "It won't be your fault. They can call their board meeting, Max. You can't stop them. I studied all the by-laws and articles and whatnot last night."

"They can hold their board meeting, but Maguire is unhappy, and he'll be here tomorrow. I don't want to have to be the guy who explains to Henry why the family castle sits in ruins, or worse, why the build-out turned it into a horror instead of a living monument to his family's history."

"Elias would never forgive you if that happened."

"Elias chose the lady over the castle," Max said. "I don't have that luxury, because you would never forgive me if the castle fell into the wrong hands. I'd never forgive myself."

Jeannie folded down onto his chest, and his arms came around her. "I won't forgive myself if the castle deal falls apart either. You'd have a hard time staying in Scotland for very long without a job that requires you to be here."

"This occurred to me as I was waiting to board my flight."

"So you're truly not fighting only for the castle."

He started a pattern of slow caresses on her back. "I'm fighting for the castle, for my professional reputation, for the crews who depend on me to keep the whole thing from going off the rails, for Henry's legacy, and for the people in the village whose livelihoods will improve if the castle thrives. Mostly, though, I'm fighting for us. I want a future with you, Jeannie, and the best way to keep that possibility alive is to prevent Sutherland from banishing me back to Maryland."

Yes. Yes, yes, yes. "So what's your strategy?"

"Right now," Max said, "I want to make love to the scourge of Deeside's mother. Then we strategize."

Jeannie had just kissed her assent to that plan when the scourge himself began to fuss in his crib across the hall.

SUNDAY GOT AWAY FROM MAX.

Henry was fussy, Jeannie was tired, and Max's brain would not wrap itself around the concept of a skywalk between the Hall and the castle.

"A skywalk is certainly novel," Jeannie said as she made her tenth circuit around the kitchen with a grumpy Henry in her arms.

"You mean it doesn't fit the medieval castle *or* the baronial hall." Max replied, staring at the sketch he'd made. "I also haven't figured out how to poke a hole in the curtain wall that won't ruin the profile of the summit from most perspectives. Give me that baby."

"Gladly."

She passed him Henry and took a seat at the table. "You could build a covered walkway from the top of the skywalk around to the postern gate."

To Max's way of thinking, covered walkways were an acceptable compromise between the eras he was trying to connect. The Georgians and Victorians had glassed-in conservatories, greenhouses, follies, and other structures. A walkway with that feel—a space between natural and man-made—could work.

"Maybe."

Henry swatted him on the chin. "Mah."

"Are you saying Max, little dude, or Mama? Do you mind if I take Henry out for a walk?"

"Am I welcome to join you?"

Jeannie's question illuminated another aspect of the day making Max unhappy. In bed, he'd offered Jeannie the closest thing to a stirring declaration he could muster—he wanted a future with her—but she hadn't replied with the same assurances in Max's direction. She'd been pleased, she'd been passionate, but had Max spoken too soon? Too honestly?

She'd said she loved him, but she was an affectionate woman. What did *I love you* mean when people came from different sides of an ocean? The odd disjunction in their conversations throughout the day suggested Max had been *too* something, though Henry's crankiness wasn't helping.

"You are certainly welcome to join us," Max said, "or to grab forty-five minutes of well-deserved rest. A hot soak, or a cup of tea. I kept you busy yesterday, and this will be your only day off this week."

Unless, of course, Sutherland fired her along with Max at tomorrow's board meeting. Maguire could probably protect Jeannie's job, at least temporarily, but Max hadn't asked it of him.

Yet.

Max wrestled Henry into a jacket, a process complicated by Henry's ability to sprout six extra arms, each one more wiggly than the last. Jeannie produced a wool cap that Henry knocked off as soon as she'd got it on his head.

"So much contrariness in such a wee man," Jeannie said. "This is why people have only children."

How many times had Max's mother wished aloud that she'd had only one child? "What time is it?" Max asked as he coaxed Henry into the infant carrier.

"Going on five. I can start dinner while you're hillwalking. What did Maura say about rescheduling your visit?"

Henry escalated from making faces to *ba-hoo, ba-hoo*'ing. Max jammed the hat back on his little head, and that Didn't Help.

"Maura has not returned my calls or my emails."

"Ah."

"What is that supposed to mean?"

Jeannie got a teething biscuit from the breadbox and passed it to Henry. He took one look at it and would have flung it across the kitchen, except Max caught his fist and stopped him.

"No. You either gum that thing, or wave it around like your light sword, but you're not throwing it against the wall and making one more mess for your loyal minions to clean up."

Henry broke into affronted wailing. Jeannie gave Max a dirty look, and Max almost pitched the biscuit himself.

"You're worried about her," Jeannie said, lifting Henry from the infant carrier. "She'll be angry with you, is that it?"

"She'll be worse than angry. Maura doesn't have a lot of friends, doesn't have much of a social life, but she has a serious temper. I asked Elias and Violet to take her out to lunch, though they'll have to drive halfway to Baltimore to do it. For all I know, Maura refused to talk to them."

Jeannie peeled Henry out of his jacket and cap, which seemed to make him less unhappy. "Call Elias or Violet, then."

Max took a bite of the teething biscuit. "If they did go to lunch, I'd be interrupting their get-acquainted time. These things aren't bad."

"Try dunking them in banana pudding for a real delicacy. Does Henry feel hot to you?"

Max laid the back of his hand against Henry's forehead. "He feels fussy-warm, not sick-hot. I could text Elias."

"You have the uh-oh feeling, don't you?" Jeannie asked, beginning another lap around the kitchen with Henry.

"Something like it. Maura is unhappy with me, and the staff reports haven't been reassuring. She's shutting them out, spending more time in her room, less time in the garden. She loves to make things grow."

"Then she and Violet should have a lot to discuss."

True, because Violet Brodie was a farmer whose agricultural know-how was growing into a thriving e-commerce business.

"I'll give it another thirty minutes." Though Max had asked Elias to call him, to let him know how Maura had taken to a meal shared with strangers. She could be shy, but she liked most people, and most people liked her.

Or pretended to. Whatever her shortcomings, Maura could tell the difference more accurately than Max could.

If Elias blows this...

"Henry's asleep," Jeannie said, leaning against Max. "Wake us in forty-five minutes, please. If I let him have more than that, we'll be up all night again."

She kissed Max's cheek and left the kitchen, Henry in her arms.

The uh-oh feeling, as she'd called it, stayed with Max. He got out his phone and scrolled to Elias the Earl in his contacts.

The phone rang as Max was pressing his finger to Elias's number. His lordship calling. "Maitland, I know you'll want a report."

Elias's tone was annoyed, but then, Elias was usually annoyed with Max, and that sentiment was mutual.

"First, I'd like to hear about that time little Elias got lost in the wine cellar. Sounds like a terrific version of My First Hangover, and don't think to hold out on me because Granny MacPhee will tell me anything now that we've shared a wee dram of the Islay."

"Why in God's name....?" He broke off to say something to some-body on the other end. Max couldn't make out the words, but the tone was worried. "I wasn't lost in the wine cellars," Elias went on. "I was lost in the tunnel between the wine cellars. Somebody came along and shut the cellar door, cut out all the light, and there I was, in complete dark-ness for hours. Amazing how easy it is to get disoriented when you're virtually blind in a strange place, but that's a tale for another time."

An odd sensation prickled over Max's nape. "What tunnel?"

"The tunnel between the wine cellars," Elias said slowly, as if speaking to a simpleton. "A proper Victorian dinner party could go through a hundred bottles of wine, and having the help scampering all over the hillside at all hours wasn't the done thing. The wine cellars for the Hall and the castle connect, as do their root cellars, though they use separate tunnels, not that any of this matters now."

Tunnels. "Where are these damned tunnels?"

"We can discuss the damned tunnels later, Maitland."

"Right. How's Maura?" A slight pause on Elias's end had Max forgetting all about tunnels. "Elias?"

"This is what I've been trying to tell you. Maura has either gone for a walk without telling anybody or she's missing. The staff doesn't know whether she left last night or this morning. In any case, it's too soon to file a missing-persons report, though a public alert might be in the works. I'm sorry, Max. The staff has been desperately hoping she'd turn up, and they aren't required to notify you until she's been gone for twenty-four hours. Violet and I got here fifteen minutes ago, and I've spent fourteen-and-a-half of those minutes yelling."

CHAPTER NINETEEN

The night had been long and hellish.

Max had spent hours poking around in the Hall's cellars and basements, more hours exploring the castle's dungeons. Every thirty minutes, Elias or Violet had texted an update on the search for Maura, though most of those updates had degenerated into "nothing to report."

A housemate had revealed that Maura was intent on traveling to Scotland. The authorities at Baltimore-Washington International Airport, Reagan National, Dulles International Airport, and Newark Liberty International Airport had all been alerted, all to no avail. Maura's ATM card hadn't been used since Friday morning, she hadn't left a note, nobody had seen her leave the property.

And Zebedee Brodie, the previous earl, hadn't left any clues about where the tunnel entrances had been.

Max sat on the front steps of the Hall, morning sun warming his face. Fergus, Hugh, and Dinty had been briefed as soon as they'd reported for work, and half the crews were loose in the bowels of the castle, tapping walls and telling each other to shut up.

Hours ago, Jeannie had set a plate of bacon, eggs, and toast before Max, kissed his cheek, and told him to get some rest.

He couldn't rest, not while Maura was missing, not while Sutherland was plotting the ruin of a great project—and destroying Max's future with Jeannie.

Sutherland had sent out an email alerting the other investors to a possible board meeting at two p.m., the earliest possible time to hold such a meeting. Maguire had kindly forwarded that email to Max, along with a terse direction to "plan accordingly."

Max had several theories regarding Maguire's agenda. The Irishman hadn't promised to thwart Sutherland, but neither had he asked Max to resign. Max did not for one instant consider Maguire an ally. At best, Maguire was "my enemy's enemy."

Please, God, let Maura be safe.

The eagles were enjoying the midday air, cruising thermals and gliding over the treetops. In the pastures, shaggy red cattle and wooly sheep munched grass, and closer to the village, a tributary to the Dee sparkled silver in the summer sunshine.

"I will be damned if I'll let Sutherland wreck this."

Max was too keyed up to sleep, too worried to relax, and too frustrated to sit still. His feet were taking him into the village before he'd made the decision to leave the porch. The Earl's Pint was open—Sutherland's meeting was in less than two hours—and Max's body needed fuel.

He did not need to see Shayla Walters coming out of the Pint. She looked well rested, her hair was in a tidy bun, and her blue jeans and blazer were her normal construction-site attire. She wore some sort of hiking boots that looked both chic and safe, and her signature rose perfume wafted on the air along with the scent of fish and chips coming from the white paper bag in her hand.

"Max. Hello." Not a hint of sheepishness.

"Shayla. I gather you've been invited to Sutherland's meeting?"

"I'm available if Pete needs an engineering perspective on any unresolved issues."

Oh, right. "Maguire said he might attend as well."

"We'll patch everybody in for a video con, if it comes to that. You can still resign."

Which *we* was she using? Certainly not the Scottish we, not the castle's we, not any we Max wanted to be a part of.

"I won't be resigning. If you and Sutherland want to take that castle, you'll have to fight for it with everything you've got, and you'll still fail." He walked past her before he said anything less civil. *Maura is missing, Sutherland is a flaming jerk, and this is not a game.*

"Max, it doesn't have to be like this. Business is business."

He let the door to the Pint swing closed and stayed on the porch. "When did business become an excuse to act without a conscience? When did business become synonymous with 'three for me and none for anybody else'? When did business become permission to carry on like a hypoglycemic three-year-old overdue for a nap? Engineers build the future, Shay. That's business. We solve problems. That's *our* business. We fix what isn't working, we improve what is. That's what we do. The rest is noise, greed, and distraction. When did you forget that?"

She stared at him as if some snappy comeback had disappeared from the tip of her tongue, and Max left her on the steps, trying to get her designer sunglasses disentangled from her hair.

"Mr. Maitland," Fern called from behind the bar. "Will it be fish and chips?"

Over in the corner, Granny MacPhee and her partner in crime were playing cards with the solemn focus of chess masters. A white terrier was curled at the feet of an old guy with a half-dozen fishing lures pinned to his deerstalker hat.

In the kitchen, somebody was singing *Ae Fond Kiss.*

"Fish and chips, with lemon if you have any."

"Ma—another fish and chips," Fern bellowed. "Granny stole the garnish tray, if it's lemon you're after. Approach with caution."

Max saluted with two fingers and made his way to the gin tournament. "Sorry to interrupt, ladies."

"That's gin!" Granny crowed, laying down her cards. "You're my good-luck charm, Mr. Maitland. Save me a dance on Friday."

"That would be my pleasure." *If I'm still here.* "Are you ladies done with the garnishes?"

Somebody had left a single green olive on a plastic sword toothpick.

"Could do with a bit more lemon for my tea," the loser said. "Do you play cards, Mr. Maitland?"

She was some relation to Dinty, a great-aunt or second cousin. Mrs. MacIntyre?

"I played hearts some in law school."

"'Tis a fine game, in its way," Granny said, stealing the last olive. "In my grandmama's day, they had grand card parties up at the Hall. The men would play poker for days, and the ladies always had a table or two of their own. Scandalous stakes, my gran said, and scandalous goings-on too, sometimes."

"Your grandmother attended those parties?"

"Ach, of course not, Mr. Maitland. The MacPhees are humble folk. My grandma was an inside maid for Countess Mary, helped her set up the first infirmary during the Great War. When I was a girl, Gran took me all around the kitchens and pantries, showed me the little trolley that ran from the distillery to the cellars, and let me have a wee ride in it."

Mrs. MacIntyre began collecting the cards. "Dinty says the tracks are still there in the old brewery. Ready for another round, Augusta?"

Max took an unoccupied chair because his knees had abruptly gone unreliable. "You toured the kitchens when you were a girl?"

Granny patted his hand. "Decades ago, laddie. Nothing to see there now but a lot of dust and cobwebs."

"Do you recall where the tunnels were that connected the castle and the Hall?"

"Which tunnel are you asking about? One runs from the Hall's butler's pantry to the castle's brewery—the old brewery, which Countess Eulie turned into a still room, and another runs from the castle's old wine cellar—the one that was a dungeon—to the Hall's laundry."

"That's the porcelain room now," Mrs. MacIntyre said. "Mrs. Hamilton can show you if she hasn't already. The Hall has a fortune in china and silver. Zebedee would lend it out for weddings and wakes. Are we playing another round, Augusta?"

"Could I ask you ladies to draw me a diagram of the tunnels?"

"If you fetch me some more olives, I'll be happy to."

Max set a clean napkin and pen on the table and switched out a full garnish tray for the one Granny had plundered.

"There's your diagram," Granny said. "Zebedee didn't want anybody using the tunnels after Elias got lost that time, but those tunnels date back to Roman times and are part of the reason nobody could besiege the castle. We always had a back door that was easy to defend."

There it was in black and white, and when presented as a schematic, the location of the tunnels made perfect sense. The Hall and the castle nearly touched footprints, and the tunnels traversed the short distance between them.

"Ladies, I can't tell you how useful this information is. You've saved the castle." He kissed them each on the cheek, collected his lunch from Fern at the bar, and left the Pint at a fast jog.

"WHERE'S MAITLAND?" Fergus asked.

"I don't know." Jeannie kept her voice down, because Pete Sutherland and an obnoxiously trim brunette were poring over site maps at the conference table across the room. The lady had signed in on the visitor's log as Shay Walters, PE. She'd slapped on a hard hat and stuck her nose into nearly every corner of the castle, though Fergus had promised not to let her out of his sight.

Was Shay short for *Shayla*? What were the chances...?

"Do we have time to tour the Hall?" Ms. Walters asked.

"If there's one thing I do not respect in a woman," Fergus muttered, "it's using her kitten voice in a professional setting."

"If there's one thing I do not respect in a man," Jeannie retorted, "it's judging a woman for doing what she must to get her ideas across in a male-dominated workplace. Who's this?"

A tall, auburn-haired man was striding across the bailey, peering about at the walls as if deciding where a trebuchet would be best positioned for hurling boiling oil.

"Another bloody investor, would be my guess," Fergus said. "Time I put on my 'I'm just the poor dumb site manager' hat. Phone Maitland and tell him the vultures are converging."

"You phone him. They can't start their meeting until two p.m."

"It's after one," Fergus said. "Maitland better get his arse in gear if he's going to stop this invasion."

Henry was being blessedly quiet after the weekend's uproar, and neither Mr. Sutherland nor Ms. Walters had said anything about the oddity of having a playpen in the project office.

The auburn-haired man let himself into the office. "Hullo. I'm looking for Max Maitland."

Aren't we all? "I'm sure he's on-site somewhere, sir. Is there something I can help you with?"

"You're Jeannie Cromarty. I know your cousin Elias. My name's Connor Maguire."

Shay Walters emerged from the other room. "Mr. Maguire. This is an unexpected pleasure. I'm Shayla Walters."

Shayla was also working a smile and a walk that frankly impressed Jeannie. Just the right blend of welcome and confidence, with a hint of territorial prowl.

Maguire didn't shake her hand; he merely held it, Continental style. Point to the gentleman, because that gesture caused Ms. Walters to blush. "A pleasure, Ms. Walters. Is that Sutherland's voice I hear?"

"Pete is wrapping up a residential purchase," Ms. Walters replied. "The closing was yesterday, and he had to courier the documents to some lawyer's office in Aberdeen. Have you seen the castle?"

It's not your castle to show him. Rather than add that helpful fact to the conversation, Jeannie texted Max: *Maguire flirting with Ms. Walters. Score is tied. Where the feck are you?*

As if her text had conjured him, Max strolled into the project office, looking like Dinty on the losing end of a shinty tournament. His jeans were dusty, his Oxford shirt was streaked with dirt, and the knuckles of his left hand were scraped.

"Greetings, Maguire. Ms. Walters." Max didn't offer anybody a handshake. "Has the firing squad assembled?"

Maguire's smile showed a lot of teeth. "I'm not sure why we have the pleasure of Ms. Walters's company, but I'm here because Sutherland might call a board meeting in a very few minutes. Then too, I like to see where my money's going. You must be Max Maitland."

"Connor Maguire," Pete Sutherland said, jamming a phone in his pocket with one hand and sticking out the other as he emerged from the conference room. "I thought I heard your voice. Glad you could make it. Welcome to Brodie Castle."

It's not your castle to welcome him to.

"You've interrupted my fishing, Sutherland," Maguire said, "and my impatience with poorly run meetings is deservedly legendary. What are we doing here?"

"I can answer that," Max said. "But perhaps we can conduct this discussion in the conference room, rather than in Ms. Cromarty's office."

"Fine idea." Sutherland's tone was overly hearty. "The conference room it is."

"Ms. Cromarty will join us," Max said.

"Why?" The question came from Shayla Walters, who had no business asking anybody anything.

"Because I'm the project controller," Jeannie replied. "To the extent that any decisions made rely on schedules, budgets, incurred costs, or labor hours, I'm the expert." A simple fact, not even a threat.

Ms. Walters turned a simper on Jeannie. "While you're being so expert, who will watch the, um, baby?" She waggled a thumb in the direction of Henry's playpen.

"He's fast asleep. If we leave the door cracked, I'll hear him when he wakes."

"Half of Deeside will hear him," Max said, "and this should be a very short meeting." He led the way into the conference room. Jeannie brought up the rear, and she left the door wide open.

In case anybody was inclined to toss Ms. Walters out on her rubbishing ear.

TO HAVE to conduct this meeting while Maura was missing was a handy summation of everything wrong about working for Pete Sutherland and his usual gang of greedy idiots. Elias had sent along some silver linings: Maura hadn't been spotted at any bus terminals, airports, or train stations, most of which had excellent security. The weather in Maryland had been mild and dry all weekend. No significant withdrawals had been made from her bank account.

She was either safe or...

Max cut off that thought, because it was too awful to allow. He'd not informed Maura of his second change of plans until midmorning Sunday her time. She'd been discovered missing less than two hours later. With any luck, she was camping in some field near her cottage, having a good mad, and missing indoor plumbing.

And the instant Sutherland adjourned his witch hunt, Max was heading straight back to the airport.

"We don't need to do this the hard way," Sutherland said.

"We don't need to do this at all," Max retorted. "The project is ahead of schedule, under budget, at 95 percent of full staffing, and in compliance with all applicable regulations. No one has brought to my attention any significant issues that would reflect poorly on me as the manager."

Sutherland sighed gustily and shook his head. "Max, you force me to state the obvious: You're in over your head, you've sold us a pig in a poke, and you failed to conduct anything approaching due diligence before you talked us into this project."

Repeat a lie often enough, sincerely enough, and it began to sound like the truth. Max had taken enough basic psychology classes to know that tactic when he saw it.

Maguire took a seat. "Maitland, the site can be running like a top, and from what I've seen, it's clearly well organized, but if you've lost the support of a major investor, aren't you tempted to walk out? I'm certain I can reason the other investors into honoring the terms of your buyout."

This was posturing on Maguire's part and had Sutherland looking gratifyingly uneasy.

"I. Will. Not. Walk." Max remained on his feet. "If I'm replaced for anything other than good cause, you owe me bank, Sutherland. What's your cause?"

More sighing and head shaking, while Shayla took the seat halfway down one side, supposedly the most powerful position at an oblong table.

"Max, we have two white elephants," Sutherland began in long-suffering tones, "a medieval castle and a Victorian something. A country house? They might have once been owned by the same family, but that doesn't mean they will make a cohesive unit if we're to turn this project into an international venue. The best we can hope for is some aesthetically disastrous escalator or a tacky fleet of golf carts. Do they make golf carts with snow tires?"

Max didn't castigate Sutherland for arrogance—inherited wealth always brought with it the risk of arrogance—and Sutherland couldn't help that he was stupid. No amount of money guaranteed brains.

But Sutherland was being cruel. Being snide because he could be, because his little games were all he could see.

"Had you bothered to tour the castle from top to bottom when I gave you that opportunity," Max said, "I would have shown you the tunnels."

Maguire went still.

Shayla crossed her arms. "Pete, you never mentioned tunnels."

Jeannie purely beamed at him, all the benevolence of the Scottish summer sun in her eyes.

"I never mentioned tunnels," Sutherland said, "because Maitland concealed a material fact about the site. If there are tunnels, they don't appear on any schematics that I've seen, and some coal chute or glorified storm drain doesn't change anything. My trust in Max Maitland has been obliterated by his untruthfulness, if not his incompetence."

A pivot and raising of the stakes. Max was about to say as much when Jeannie stepped forward.

"How dare you?" she said, voice low. "How dare you disrespect the man who has been working dawn to dusk for weeks to put this project on solid footing—for you. To win over the locals—for your profit. To earn the trust of the most stubborn, backward, independent pack of tradesmen ever to put hammer to stone. You lie, you strut, you connive, you cheat, and then you betray the trust of all who do business with you, and for what? So you can betray your wife as well? I'm not having it."

A snarling lioness exuded a greater sense of menace—barely.

Shayla's mouth was open. Sutherland looked like he was about to wet his pants.

"Listen to Ms. Cromarty," Max said. "She speaks for the whole project team and as a member of the family who owns this castle. Boot me off this job, and you'll see slowdowns. Deliveries will go astray, and hammers will drop from empty towers. The materials will come up short. This castle has been a home, a family seat, a fortress, and a refuge, and I won't abandon it for your convenience. Call your meeting to order."

"You're threatening to sabotage this project?" Sutherland asked.

"If you fire our project manager," Jeannie said, "he'll go back to

Maryland, and your project, which is on schedule, under budget, and in compliance now, will go straight into the diaper pail as a result of your bungling, Mr. Sutherland."

Beautiful word—*bungling*—when spoken in that vigorous, articulate Scottish burr.

"You have to remove me for cause," Max said, "at a full meeting of the board, on the record. I'll settle for a recorded video-conference, but you'll do it by the book or not at all."

Maguire's expression, or lack of one, would have done credit to a high-stakes blackjack dealer.

"Call your meeting, Sutherland," Max said. "Call it now, or not at all. I have a castle to renovate, and you are *wasting my time*."

Shayla was glowering at Sutherland, who was glaring pure venom at Max.

"Not at all," Jeannie snapped.

Sutherland turned his sneer on her. "I think it's time you went back to your desk, missy."

"I'm happy to return to my desk," Jeannie said in the same tones she addressed a cranky baby. "But then you can't hold your board meeting. Your agreement with Elias Brodie and your corporate by-laws state that a family representative chosen by the earl will have a voting seat on the board at all times. Elias has given me that honor, and I can assure you, no matter how many meetings you call, I will never vote in favor of letting Max Maitland go."

The words rang with quiet conviction, because genius did not need to announce itself. The smile Jeannie sent Max said that she'd chosen her words carefully, and that yes, they meant what he thought they meant.

"I suppose that settles the matter," Maguire said. "Sutherland, you've been outfought, outsmarted, and outmaneuvered. Now be a good lad and let me buy you and your golf buddies out, or I'll raise sticky questions about why you chose to share financial details of this very sensitive matter with somebody outside the board and the corporation."

Shayla rose. "Pete, you said this was a done deal. I gave notice. I'm living out of a suitcase. What am I supposed to do now?"

"Ask Maguire," Sutherland said, heading for the door. "Ask Maitland, ask his Highland secret weapon. Nobody said anything to me about tunnels. This could all have been avoided if I'd been kept informed."

Maguire followed them from the room as Shayla got off a volley about reasonably and foreseeably relying, to her substantial economic detriment on Pete's representations that employment would be forthcoming...

Voices rose as Maguire tried to referee, while in the conference room, for one blessed, perfect moment, Max took Jeannie in his arms.

"You were magnificent," he murmured.

"So were you. We defended our castle."

"And our future."

Then Henry started bellowing.

"HE'S PROBABLY unhappy with the raised voices and the strangers," Max said.

Jeannie stepped back, because Max was right. That was not a change-my-diaper-now bellow. "I'll see to him."

"You really were magnificent, Jeannie. When did Elias appoint you to the board?"

Ms. Walters sounded very upset with Mr. Sutherland. Jeannie almost felt a little sorry for her. "Elias and I had a wee chat very late Saturday night. I didn't want you to think I doubted your abilities, so I asked Elias to keep my request quiet. You've worked with Pete Sutherland for the last time, Max."

"Yes, ma'am."

Jeannie crossed into the front office and scooped Henry from his playpen. He quieted, though Mr. Sutherland and Ms. Walters did not.

"They woke the baby," Max said to Maguire. "Get them out of here."

"That's another thing," Sutherland said, rounding on Max. "Why in the hell is that damned infant here?"

"Not in front of the baby." Max and Maguire had both spoken with Jeannie. Their expressions would have wilted an entire team of half-drunken shinty players.

"Take it down to the village," Max said, pointing toward the door. "Take your petty dramas and get off this property, Sutherland, and don't think to darken our castle door again. If Maguire offers to buy you and your friends out, take the deal, because I have a lawsuit coming your way for breach of your fiduciary obligations to me as a fellow shareholder."

"Splendid notion," Maguire said. "Before you file, let's have a chat, Maitland."

"I'm not too happy with your little games either, Maguire. Finish your discussions with Sutherland down at the Earl's Pint, and do not put your bill on the castle's tab."

Maguire grinned and chivied a still-fuming Ms. Walters and a grumbling Mr. Sutherland out the door. "Bye for now. I'll be in touch."

"Bye-bye," Henry said, waving a chubby arm.

Jeannie stared at her brilliant baby, who was still waving at the closed door. "Max, he said a word. He said bye-bye. Henry said his first word, and he's not even a year old."

"Bye-bye," Henry said again. "Bye-bye-bye."

"Our baby is a genius," Jeannie said, kissing Henry's cheek.

Max should have agreed with that statement, but instead he was staring at his phone, blinking rapidly. "They found her. Thank God and all the angels, they found her."

"Maura?"

"Safe and sound. She spent the night in a pup tent in somebody's backyard three doors down, then enjoyed a morning picking blueberries at the farm across the road. I will give that young lady such a talking-to, such a... Hold me, please. Please, just hold me."

"Can you still make tonight's flight?"

Max was wrapped around her and Henry, his embrace so snug Jeannie at first thought he hadn't heard her.

"Elias says she's embarrassed. She didn't realize Scotland is both a country and a town in Pennsylvania. She thought I'd made up that part about the ocean and doesn't want me to know she tried to visit me."

Jeannie stroked Max's hair, loving him with all her heart. "I can drive you down to Perth if you want to catch that flight."

Max stepped back and lifted Henry into his arms. "Elias is asking if Maura can stay out at the farm for a few days with him and Violet. The ladies are already talking chickens and tomatoes."

He brushed a kiss to Henry's crown, and Jeannie understood why he'd needed to hold the baby.

"How does that idea sit with you?"

"Let's go sit in the sunshine," Max said.

They found a bench along the lavender border, the worn wood warmed by the sun. Jeannie waited, while Max tickled Henry's chin with a sprig of lavender.

"Elias is asking me if Maura can visit out in Damson Valley," Max said. "That decision is not up to me."

"Are you relieved or terrified?"

Max started a game of trot-little-horsey with Henry. "Both. My baby sister is growing up. I wasn't sure that would ever happen, but what if I was the one clinging to her, instead of the other way around?"

Jeannie slipped an arm around his waist. "She will always be your baby sister, and if we can get the project a little more ahead of schedule, I'd fancy a trip to Maryland."

They stayed on the bench for a long time, talking, playing with Henry, and dreaming. Perhaps Maura could work for Violet and

Elias in their greenhouses. Perhaps she might enjoy winters in Scotland at the castle.

"We must have her at the wedding," Jeannie said. "I'll need a bridesmaid or two and haven't any sisters to call upon."

"The wedding?"

"Yes, Max. You didn't think my grand speech about voting to keep you was simply boardroom posturing, did you?"

The slight pause suggested Max had been hoping, but not certain. Then he smiled, enough quiet joy in his eyes to make Jeannie believe in magic and happily ever afters.

"Jeannie Cromarty, will you marry me?"

"Aye. Henry says yes too."

"Then it's unanimous."

Max kissed her, and Jeannie kissed him back, for once not in any hurry *at all*.

Two eagles made lazy circles over the pastures below the castle wall, Henry munched on lavender flowers, and from the parapets above, hooting and stomping started up that turned into applause, and a lot of sweaty, nosy tradesmen and laborers grinning down at them.

"I guess this means you're staying?" Hugh yelled.

"And you're all invited to the wedding," Jeannie yelled back.

"Well done, Yank!" Fergus called, amid more cheering, stomping, and clapping. "Everybody down to the Pint. Drinks are on Maitland!"

"You'll miss your flight," Jeannie said.

"I'm where I'm supposed to be," Max replied, rising. "Maura is making new friends, the castle is safe, and Henry's a genius, just like his mama. I think even Auld Michael and Lady Brenna would agree that I belong here."

Ah, he'd probably seen the ghosts then, a sure sign he was worthy to join the family.

Jeannie sauntered down the hill hand in hand with Max, while

Hugh, Fergus, and Dinty took turns tickling the baby and placing bets on how soon Henry would have a younger sibling. The celebration at the Pint lasted nearly until dawn, though by the last light of the quarter moon, Hugh and Fergus saw two figures kissing on the parapets.

As did Dinty and Fern.

And Morgan and Maguire, though that's a tale for another time.

EPILOGUE

"Max Maitland looks damned fine in a kilt, Jeannie Cromarty—or are you Jeannie Maitland now?" Fern held Henry on her hip and swayed gently to the music of the fiddles.

"I'm Jeannie Cromarty, also Mrs. Max Maitland, hopefully forever more."

Max was dancing with Morgan, while Connor Maguire tried to look affable and unconcerned over by the great hall's enormous fireplace. He succeeded mostly in looking besotted and fierce, no matter how many servings of ale Dinty shoved at him.

"Good of Mr. Maguire to let you use the hall for your wedding reception," Fern said. "He does justice to a kilt as well."

Maguire's permission had been sought out of courtesy—he was the sole backer of the Brodie Castle project now that Pete Sutherland was up to his ears in a messy divorce. Maguire's permission had also been sought out of pragmatism. He found excuses to visit the site regularly, and always stayed at Morgan's guest cottage. Not inviting him to the wedding would have been rude, therefore, his permission had been asked.

For Hugh and Fergus's reception, no such courtesies had applied. Max had called an "all hands meeting" at 3 pm on a Friday, the service had taken less than thirty minutes, and the dancing had gone on all night.

"I like that our wedding was the first official function of the Brodie Castle venue," Jeannie said. "Seems fitting, that somebody with ties to the family should start the old place off on its next adventure."

The project was ahead of schedule, though winter was fast approaching. Jeannie looked forward to the nippy days—and the long nights. The first frost had come a week ago, and Henry had added Bun-Bun, Max, Mama, and Bear to his vocabulary.

"Who sent the roses?" Fern asked.

The bouquet—mostly yellow roses with some peach-colored blooms for accents—sat off to the left on the dessert table.

"Harry," Jeannie said. "He's met somebody."

Fern untangled Henry's fist from her hair. "He's always meeting somebody."

"I honestly wish he'd meet the right one, Fern. He'll be back for a visit around the holidays."

The dance came to an end, and Maguire pushed away from the fireplace.

"Does that worry you? That Harry might come around causing trouble in paradise?"

"We'll start adoption proceedings, to which Harry has already consented. He'll always be welcome in Henry's life, but Harry said it himself: A father is as a father does, and a man chasing the next rig is not much of a father."

"Millicent won't like it."

Jeannie extricated Henry from Fern's arms. "Harry for once did not consult his mum before making a decision. I'm encouraged by that. It's Morgan's turn to hold Henry."

"Because if Maguire can compete with a wee laddie, then maybe he's the right one for Morgan?"

"Something like that, and because I want to dance with my husband."

To say the words—my husband—felt different than when Jeannie had said them about Harry. In Harry's case, the words had been a way to describe a legal relationship. With Max they were an admission of intimate connection.

"If it isn't my favorite two people in the whole world," Max said, kissing Jeannie's cheek. "The fiddlers are getting tipsy. I think that means it's time for a slow dance. Maguire!"

Maguire looked up from a conversation with Morgan.

"Your turn to hold the baby," Max said, "though Henry is hardly a baby any more. Babies bring good luck to a wedding." He settled Henry in Maguire's arms, which coaxed a smile from Morgan.

"I dance with Jeannie next," Maguire said. "It's good luck for the castle owner to dance with the bride."

Max took Jeannie's hand. "You do not own this castle and you never will. It's a family property, which is why you will ask Jeannie and me to manage it for you just as soon as the buildout is done."

"*Manage it for me?*"

Henry smacked Maguire on the chest.

"Of course," Jeannie said, kissing Max on the mouth, for she hadn't seen this gift coming. "Brodie Castle is a family enterprise, as Max said. Morgan, why don't you take Mr. Maguire to enjoy the view from the Countess's walk? There's a quarter moon tonight. You never know who you might meet up there."

"Come along," Morgan said, "and mind that baby. He's getting to the mischievous stage."

Maguire fell in step beside her. "But if we bring this dratted imp, then we can't—"

Henry walloped him on the nose.

"The boy's a genius," Max said. "Takes after his mother. Shall we dance?"

Max was a good dancer, much in demand at the weekly ceilidh. Jeannie fell in love with him a little more each time he stood up with

Mrs. Hamilton or sat out with Granny MacPhee. When Hugh and Fergus had gone on their honeymoon, Max had driven them to the airport.

"You are quiet, Mrs. Maitland," Max said, as the fiddlers started up in three-quarter time. "Thinking married thoughts, I hope?"

"Not only married thoughts," Jeannie said. "Family thoughts." Over by the buffet, Niall and Liam were arguing about whisky with Elias. The wives, Violet, Louise, Julie and Megan, were sitting in a circle at the foot of the stairs, while Dinty was in a rapt discussion with Cousin Declan about—from what Jeannie had overheard— hanging flower baskets.

Maura, who'd flown over with Elias and Violet, was sitting next to Hugh, getting a lesson on the rudiments of a bodhran. The current plan was for Maura to spend her winters in Scotland, and then return to Maryland to help Violet and Elias in their greenhouses.

"My people have become your people too," Jeannie said.

"Your son has become my son."

"Do you think Morgan and Maguire will see the ghosts?" Jeannie asked, snuggling closer.

"I think they have eyes only for each other. I know what that feels like."

So did Jeannie. "I hope they see the ghosts, Max, and I hope they see them soon."

"Not too soon." Max sneaked a kiss to Jeannie's temple. "As long as Morgan's keeping Maguire pre-occupied, we can restore our castle in peace. I think we should advertise this place as the Highland Happily Ever After destination. What do you think?"

Elias would have fits to see his castle with that name. "We have time to work on it."

"Years," Max said, gathering her closer. "The rest of our lives, and possibly even beyond."

Jeannie loved the sound of that, and loved the look in Max's eyes when he said it. "The rest of our lives, and even beyond, but the Highland Happily Ever After destination has a nice ring to it."

The fiddles lilted along, Morgan and Maguire strolled the parapets, Maura declared Hugh and Fergus her honorary cousins, and thus did Brodie Castle acquire a name of which even its famously romantic ghosts approved, (though Maguire took some convincing).

Greetings, readin' buddies!

I hope you enjoyed Max and Jeannie's happily ever after, because I certainly had fun writing and researching it. If you missed the earlier books in the series, we started off with *Tartan Two-Step* (my first romance set in Montana), followed by *Elias In Love* (a return to Damson Valley, of **Sweetest Kisses** fame).

If you're wondering who all these other cousins are (Liam, Niall, Declan, Dunstan), I can suggest the **Highland Holidays** novella quartet, which is available as an ebook bundle from my graceburrowes.com website store (or as duets from the major platforms in both ebook and print). I've included a little excerpt from **Kiss and Tell**, the first story in that group, below.

As much as I adore all things Scottish, I know my readers also love a good historical romance. My next Regency will be *A Truly Perfect Gentleman*, book six in the True Gentleman series. Excerpt below.

The big news on my writing horizon, though, is the launch of my new Rogues to Riches series, which begins with *My One and Only Duke*, coming out in November (on Election Day, as it happens).

So many titles, so many happily ever afters! If you'd like to get word of the new releases, pre-orders, and deals, then I suggest following me on **Bookbub.** In my **newsletter**, I go into more detail about what's coming up, what's just come out, and any special events on my calendar.

Happy reading!
Grace Burrowes

Kiss and Tell (from **Highland Holidays** ebook bundle, also paired with **Dunroamin' Holiday** in Two Wee Drams of Love)

Attorney Dunstan Cromarty's back has gone out on him when the only person who can help is the very attorney opposing him in a nasty

Damson Valley divorce. Jane Deluca drives him home, and drives him a bit barmy... or more than bit.

Please, Almighty Merciful God, Dunstan thought, *do not let Wallace be playing turd hockey on the kitchen floor when I hobble in the door with Jane DeLuca at my side.*

"You haven't passed out on me, have you?" Jane asked as she shut the truck off. "Your eyes are closed."

"I'm gathering my strength." For any number of ordeals.

"Don't you move until I've rappelled down the cliff side," she said, scrambling out of the driver's seat.

She was so petite, she had to more or less jump out of the truck, while Dunstan... He moved one leg, then the other. He paused to let the agony bounce around in his body, then used the handles to haul himself sideways, and so it went, one indignity, one torment at a time.

Jane shouldered their various bags, while Dunstan caught sight of Wallace sitting in the living room window, a marmalade ball of gloating feline.

"Oh, you have a kitty! What's his name?"

"Fat Bastard. The door's nae locked."

She opened the door and stood back so Dunstan could totter past her, then she hauled their bags in and closed the door. "Is an unlocked door prudent? You're fairly isolated here."

"I'm hoping somebody will come by and steal the cat." Who, in an unprecedented display of survival instinct, had neither recently used the litter box, nor undertaken any hockey games that Dunstan could see.

It being a hallmark of Wallace's hockey seasons that cat litter was sprinkled from one end of the downstairs to the other.

"I love these old farm houses," Jane said, shrugging out of her coat. "They have charm."

Dunstan stretched out a casual hand and braced himself against the nearest wall, a compromise between his tattered dignity and the urge to crumple in a screaming fetal heap three steps inside the door.

"These old farm houses have heating bills. If you'd like to take my truck back to town, I can have one of the Knightleys give me a lift tomorrow."

He didn't attempt a smile, neither did he try to get to the sofa, a good five yards, three cursing fits, and four prayers off across the living room. Carpeted yards, though, which would make crawling ever so much more comfy.

"I'm not going anywhere," Jane said, and damn the woman, she spoke with the patient amusement of a small female with a perfectly functional sacroiliac. "The first order of business should be to get you into a hot shower, if your bad back is anything like my grandpa's. Is your bedroom upstairs?"

"I'll be adorning the sofa for a wee bit before attempting anything so ambitious as a shower." Though a shower...His muscles stopped pounding on his tailbone long enough to beg for that hot shower even before he opened his last bottle of twenty-five-year-old Glenmorangie single malt.

"So you can't make it up the stairs. Does this level have a bathroom?"

He didn't like this line of questioning one bit. "Aye."

"Then what are you waiting for?"

Disaster for Scotland, to put the situation mildly. "I'm waiting for the floor to open up and swallow me whole. I'll not allow you to undress me, Jane DeLuca."

Not like this, please God. Not like this.

"So we'll put you in the shower with your clothes on. Would you leave me to suffer when my back hurt so badly I couldn't stand the thought of sneezing again?"

He crossed himself with the hand that wasn't anchored to the wall. "You're a cruel woman to mention such a thing. There'll be no sneezing of any kind for the foreseeable future."

And not to put too fine a point on it, his diet would be rich in fiber, once he could stand in the kitchen long enough to pour milk on cereal. Wallace chose then to strop himself across Dunstan's legs.

"He knows I canna kick him."

Jane inserted herself under Dunstan's outstretched arm, which was about three seconds away from shaking. "Lean on me. Anybody who names a cat Fat Bastard has already abused the animal. I assume the facilities are down the hall?"

Miles away, of course. Why didn't old farm houses have bathrooms in the foyer?

"Second door on the left."

He tried not to lean on her—and failed. Jane was surprisingly sturdy, though, and they covered the distance to the bathroom with only a bit more swearing. Then she abandoned him—abandoned him —with an admonition to get off as much of his clothing as he could while she retrieved sweats from his bedroom upstairs.

Sometimes, when his back went out, within twenty minutes, he could tell he was due for only a light penance. A dose of painkiller, time lying prone, a movie or two, and all could be forgiven, provided he took no chances for several days.

This was shaping up to be a less accommodating episode.

Dunstan undressed in the bathroom, his clothes piled into a heap at his feet, for he could not bend down to hang them up and couldn't balance on one foot long enough to hook them with his toes—he knew all the tricks. He could manage to brush his teeth and tend to other standing rituals, and by the time he heard a tap on the door, he was sporting only a towel about his hips.

"It's nae locked."

"Good," Jane said, pushing the door closed behind her. "I found sweats, but wouldn't a kilt be easier? You don't have to step into it."

She brandished a black work kilt Dunstan wore when waging his endless war with the yard.

"That's a fetching ensemble you're wearing yourself, Ms. DeLuca." For she'd changed into gray sweats and a green T-shirt that said *If it takes three years to get there, it had better be one helluva bar.*

"I always have gym clothes with me," she said, turning on the bathtub taps and holding her hand under the gushing stream.

Maybe she frequently found herself sleeping in places other than her own bed? Not a cheering thought.

She fiddled with the taps, and soon, water streamed from the shower head in steamy abundance. The difficulty before Dunstan daunted him: He had to raise each foot high enough to step into the shower and shift his weight without falling.

"In you go," Jane said, showing no indication of absenting herself. "If you think I'll let you risk a slip-and-fall now, you're dumber than I thought." She stepped closer and put her arms around Dunstan's bare torso. "Lean on me, and no heroic measures, because I'll probably topple with you, and I will sue you if I injure anything other than my pride."

He leaned, he tottered, he leaned some more, and finally, finally, found his way to the soothing, hot spray. Jane whisked his towel off and flipped the Royal Stewart plaid shower curtain closed in the same nanosecond, but the bliss of the hot water was so great, Dunstan almost didn't care what she saw, or what she thought of what she saw.

Almost.

From **Kiss and Tell** in the **Highland Holidays** novella collection, available in e-book from the graceburrowes.com website store, as or novella duets (**Two Wee Drams of Love**, **Must Love Scotland**) in print and e-book from all major retail platforms.

Read on for an excerpt from my upcoming Regency, *A Truly Perfect Gentleman* (Sept. 25 2018)

Beatitude, Lady Canmore, has no intention of marrying again. Grey Birch Dorning, Earl of Casriel, must marry well and soon. Alas the course of true love sometimes does stumbling down a woodland path to end up with unlikely declarations from unsuitable parties...

The sun shone at the same angle as it had a moment ago, the water on the lake rippled beneath the same breeze, and yet, Grey's world had endured a seismic shock.

"You would like to have an affair with me," he said slowly. Then, to make sure he hadn't indulged in wishful hearing, "An intimate affair?"

Lady Canmore glowered up at him. "Is there another kind?"

"I would not know."

She stalked along at his side. "You've *never* enjoyed the company of a woman outside the bounds of wedlock?"

"By London standards, I am retiring when it comes to those sorts of amusements. I have reason to be."

Lady Canmore took him by the hand and dragged him down a barely visible side trail. For a small woman, she was strong.

"The hermit's folly is this way," she said. "What do you mean, you have reason to be? To be a monk? I have been a monk for the past several years. Monkdom loses its charms. If you think that makes me fast or vulgar or unladylike, then I think such an opinion makes you a hypocrite. There's not a man in Mayfair who doesn't indulge his appetites to the limit of his means, and a few beyond their means. Roger told me swiving is all many men think about."

"I most assuredly think about it." That admission was not polite. Not gentlemanly. Not... what Grey had intended to say.

Her ladyship came to an abrupt halt in the middle of the trail. "You do? You think about it with *me?*"

Oh, how that smile became her, how that light of mischief transformed her gaze. "You have broached this topic, my lady, but are you certain you want to pursue it in present company?" A gentleman had to ask, for the discussion would soon pass the point where her overture could be dismissed as a jest or flirtation.

"You haunt me," Lady Canmore replied, clearly not a disclosure that pleased her. "Men I've been dancing with for the past eight years now strike me as lacking stature, though I myself am short. When I arrive at a gathering, I look for you, even though all the way to the venue, I tell myself I must not do that. You and I are engaged in a semblance of a friendship, I remind myself, only a friendship. Which reminds me. Are there any new bets?"

She resumed walking. Grey fell in step beside her.

"Your strategy has been successful," he said. "No new wagers, save for one that involves my brother Sycamore. His notoriety has made him Peacock in Residence at my town house, and he wasn't a pattern card of humility to begin with."

Lady Canmore took a turn off the path that Grey would have missed. She knew where she was going, while he was increasingly lost.

"I don't want to be your mistress," she said. "I want to be your lover."

Grey almost sagged against the nearest oak. "Do you frequently make such announcements in the same tone of voice most people reserve for discussing the Corsican, long may he rot in memory?"

The way ahead opened into a clearing that held a small three-sided stone edifice on a slight rise. The surrounding woods had been carefully manicured to give the folly three views. One looked out over the lake, another toward Brantmore House. The third faced the woods sloping away to the east.

A circular portico framed the interior of the folly, where benches provided a private place to rest.

"I am not happy with myself for becoming interested in you," Lady Canmore said. "But there it is. You are kind, gentlemanly, and a fine male specimen. Your flirtation is original without being prurient or presumptuous. You dance well. You humor Aunt Freddy. You love your siblings. You are not afraid of hard, physical work. In fact, I think you need it to thrive."

She paced before the folly, listing attributes that made Grey's heart ache. She *saw* him, saw him clearly, and appreciated who and what she saw.

"You are the comfort of your aunt's declining years," Grey said, "a ferociously loyal friend, a minister's daughter who has learned how to manage polite society without being seen to do more than smile and chat. If I had to choose one word to describe you, that word would be courageous. I can't help but watch you, even when you dance with others, because you have such inherent grace. I see you walking away, and I know I have nothing to offer you, but I want to call you back, every damned time."

She came to a halt before him. "My lord, what are we to do?"

"My name is Grey, and as for what to do... I would like to kiss you."

Order your copy of **A Truly Perfect Gentleman**!

Made in the USA
Middletown, DE
15 November 2018